Into the Fairy Hill

Perspectives in Celtic History, Culture and Myth

Celtic Myth and Religion: A Study of Traditional Belief, with Newly Translated Prayers, Poems and Songs. Sharon Paice MacLeod. 2012

Celtic Cosmology and the Otherworld: Mythic Origins, Sovereignty and Liminality. Sharon Paice MacLeod. 2018

Into the Fairy Hill: Classic Folktales of the Scottish Highlands. Michael S. Newton. 2022

Into the Fairy Hill

Classic Folktales of the Scottish Highlands

MICHAEL S. NEWTON

Ro-ràdh le / Foreword by
Ruairidh MacIlleathain / Roddy Maclean

PERSPECTIVES IN CELTIC HISTORY, CULTURE AND MYTH

Series Editor Sharon Paice MacLeod

McFarland & Company, Inc., Publishers
Jefferson, North Carolina

ISBN (print) 978-1-4766-9002-5
ISBN (ebook) 978-1-4766-4767-8

Library of Congress and British Library
cataloguing data are available

Library of Congress Control Number 2022030346

On the cover: Astro image of Dunure Castle with part of the Milky Way on display © Jim Scott/Shutterstock

Printed in the United States of America

McFarland & Company, Inc., Publishers
Box 611, Jefferson, North Carolina 28640
www.mcfarlandpub.com

Do na gaisgich a ghléidh na sgeulachdan,
is do na curaidhean a chumas beò iad.

Table of Contents

Acknowledgments

I wish to express my appreciation to Am Comunn Gàidhealach for permission to reprint Gaelic texts from their school readers *An Ceathramh Leabhar Leughaidh* and *Leabhraichean Leughaidh: Leabhar 1.*

Mary Rose Laureys at St. Frances Xavier University kindly provided a scan of the tale "Teicheadh ro'n Bhràth" from the microfilm records of *The Casket.* Ulrike Hogg of the National Library of Scotland kindly provided me with a copy of the folktale "An t-Adhbhar mu'n Abairear Iasg Rìgh ris an Dallaig" from the John F. Campbell archives and I acknowledge the ownership of the National Library of Scotland of this tale in manuscript.

The introduction and epilogue were greatly enhanced through the comments and collaboration of my friend Dr. Alastair McIntosh. Dr. Natasha Sumner kindly provided me with a copy of the tale "Seanchan Mór an Éirinn 's Gobha nan Sgeul an Albainn," information about Fenian tales, and extended discussions about Gaelic sources.

I am particularly indebted to Ruairidh MacIlleathain for reading a draft of the manuscript, offering copious corrections and feedback, and writing the foreword. Thanks are due to Críostór Piondargás for producing the maps for this book.

I greatly appreciate the patience of Stephanie Johnston and my daughter Róisín as I spent extended periods away in the *sìdhean* working on this book and their support when I asked for their thoughts and comments.

Ro-ràdh / Foreword

Ruairidh MacIlleathain / Roddy Maclean

Tha cuimhne agam air còmhradh a bh' agam le neach-turais o chionn bhliadhnaichean, agus e a' gearan 'nach robh mòran ri fhaicinn air a' Ghàidhealtachd.' Cha robh eaglaisean drùidhteach no lùchairtean gleansach a b' fhiach againn, bha a' chuid a bu mhotha de ar caistealan meanbh agus nan tobhtaichean, cha robh taighean mòra spaideil againn mar a bh' aig uachdarain Shasainn. Bha e mar gun robh sinn air a bhith a' fuireach fon talamh gu socair, sàmhach agus a' cumail am falach, fhad 's a bha slòigh na bu chumhachdaiche a' togail agus a' smachdachadh mar bu dual dhaibh.

Nam bithinn na bu sgiobalta le m' inntinn is mo theangaidh, bha mi air a ràdh ris nach ann fon talamh a bha na Gàidheil fad nan ceudan ach anns an t-sìthean! Bha iad ag ionnsachadh agus ag èisteachd agus ag innse nan sgeulachdan a tha, chun an latha an-diugh, gan comharrachadh mar shluagh (a bharrachd air am beatha a chur seachad gu dripeil air muir is monadh, baile is àirigh!). Nam biodh an leabhar seo air a bhith nam làmhan aig a' mhionaid sin, bha mi air a thoirt seachad do mo charaid mar dhearbhadh gun robh beartas dha-rìridh againn—ach seòrsa a bhuineas do dhualchas nach gabh làimhseachadh.

Mo bheannachd air Mìcheal Newton airson an cruinneachadh air leth seo ullachadh, agus airson dualchas ar sgeulachdan a thaisbeanadh ann an leabhar—rudeigin a ghabhas làimhseachadh agus math dh'fhaodte a bheireadh dùbhlan dhan neach-turais agam! Tha na duilleagan a leanas làn neamhnaidean a bhuineas dhuinn mar shluagh agus a tha a' dearbhadh cho blàth, buadhach, beartach 's a bha, agus a tha, saoghal nan Gàidheal. Coma leinn togalaichean spaideil a tha a' soilleireachadh a' chaolais eadar beartach is bochd, nuair as urrainn dhuinn sgeulachdan innse a bhuineas dhuinn uile agus a tha a' toirt gach mac is nighean màthar anns a' choimhearsnachd cruinn còmhla. Thug sinn am facal seanchaidh (*shennachie*) do shaoghal na Beurla agus nach eil sin fhèin ag innse sgeul?!

* * *

The epilogue to this wonderful book is entitled "Reclaiming Our Voices," and perhaps no three words more definitively represent the position of the storyteller and the practice of storytelling in the communities that are loyal to the culture, heritage and traditions of Gaelic Scotland. For me, as a modern Scottish Gael, the Voices within this collection are indeed those of my own people, speaking to us with confidence and clarity down through the ages. They are Our Voices, and Michael Newton has given them a newly constructed platform with superb acoustics and effulgent stage lighting. "My blessing on him," as we say in our own language!

The Highlanders of Scotland—those who remained true to the Celtic traditions of their ancestors within an increasingly anglicized polity—once had a loud Voice. Indeed, it was so resounding that the English language adopted the Gaelic sluagh-ghairm, a reference to the cries of clan warriors at time of conflict, and turned it into "slogan." There is a large vocabulary in Gaelic relating to sounds, including those generated by humans, but the tragedy of the last few centuries is that we allowed the Voices of our people to diminish from a beucaich to a blabhd to a borbhan, and finally to a twentieth century bìogail. I don't think I need to translate those terms. Suffice to say that, in the face of an anti-Gaelic establishment, most notably following the passing of the Education Act in 1872 which relegated our language to a grossly inferior status and marked it as unsuitable for inclusion within state-organized learning, we largely lost Our Voices.

There is a Gaelic proverb which in translation makes the observation that "the thing the ear does not hear will not move the heart." Our inaudibility as Gaels within modern Scotland led us to being marginalized—arguably ultra-marginalized—within our own country. We moved precious few Scottish hearts. Those with power and influence largely ignored us. In response, our self-confidence became further attenuated and Our Voices became almost inaudible squeaks. If we are to survive as a people, and to influence positively the country we founded many centuries ago, as it seeks to find a new place in a challenging world, we need to find Our Voices. Indeed, we must seek to Reclaim them, and allow people to hear them so that their hearts might in turn be moved.

Michael Newton has presented for us in the pages that follow an eloquent act of Reclamation. In selecting a representative sample of old Gaelic tales and making them available to a global audience in English translation and in modern idiom, he presents an important part of the heritage of Highland Scotland to a populace that is often seeking connectivity to place, environment and history. Not only does *Into the Fairy Hill* Reclaim Voices of Gaeldom, so that they may be once more be heard among the hills and hearths of the Highlands, but it also reminds many within the globalized anglophone world of the twenty-first century that, not so long ago, their own ancestors, whether Gaels or not, told tales and myths of the magic and "supernatural," of the fantastical origins of landscapes, of talking birds and trusty heroes, of goodness and treachery, generosity and revenge. These journeys of imagination, just like human nature itself, are universal and bear a fundamental appeal to all ages. When it comes to stories, we are all children—and indeed we are clann nan daoine on tàinig sinn, the children of the people from whom we sprang. As a Gaelic saying exhorts us, we should remember those people. Stories help us to do just that.

In human reflection of the natural world, this universality bears enormous richness in the diversity and particularity of its expression at the local level. Just as evolution has granted the Earth a phenomenal array of plant and animal life, so has the evolution of societies produced a profusion of cultures. Within the universalities of narrative themes there is a locality of expression which connects people to their particular part of the planet, a place where their relationship to the environment can be measured in depth as well as breadth. The current writer's own connection to Highland Scotland through the Gaelic story heritage is a source of inspiration, pleasure and fulfilment on almost a daily basis. Our stories, like a cave among the hills or a remote anchorage in a Highland sea-loch, provide sanctuaries to which we can retreat for peace and rejuvenation when daily life throws up awkward difficulties and stormy challenges. Stories are good for our health!

Into the Fairy Hill is a rich resource for scholars of language, folklore and ethnography, and Dr. Newton's analyses of the categories and origins of the tales, and their iconography, characters, allusions and language are accurate, articulate and informative. But, most of all, the stories stand in their own right as celebrations of the language and heritage that made the Gaels of Scotland who they are today.

As the book's author writes in his erudite epilogue, the glories of Gaeldom lie not in the construction of edifice or the creation of empire, but in the fashioning and transmission of stories, poems and songs. For long, this "intangible" heritage was disregarded at best, and vilified at worst, by those in power. Thankfully, UNESCO, an arm of the United Nations, now officially recognizes that the world's intangible heritage is "an important factor in maintaining cultural diversity in the face of growing globalization" and accepts that "an understanding of the intangible cultural heritage of different communities helps with intercultural dialogue and encourages mutual respect for other ways of life." Dìreach sin, as the old Gaelic seanchaidh (tradition bearer) might have said.

Not only has Michael Newton made this collection of tales available in English, but he has also presented to us the original form of the vernacular narratives, thus giving modern Gaels and Gaelic learners a tremendous resource to see, and perhaps even hear, how the seanchaidhean of old would enthrall an audience with their use of language. In this he presents a welcome challenge to future publishers of Gaelic stories to avoid presenting our tales solely in translated form, as if our language had become a fusty, dusty museum-piece. Gaelic has endured as a living tongue—and a wonderful vehicle for storytelling—to this day.

I am confident that this publication will not only encourage an interest in Gaelic folklore but will help to foster a revitalization of the telling of tales in our own language. Whichever language we prefer, many of us will undoubtedly take our own eventful journey *Into the Fairy Hill*, our path therein illuminated by Michael Newton's scholarship and endeavors, in order to explore its nooks and recesses and to locate its treasures. And just as in the tales of old, when we finally emerge from that special world into the bright light of a "normal" day, we might discover that our lives have undergone an irrevocable change!

Ruairidh MacIlleathain / Roddy Maclean is a Gaelic broadcaster, writer, educator and storyteller.

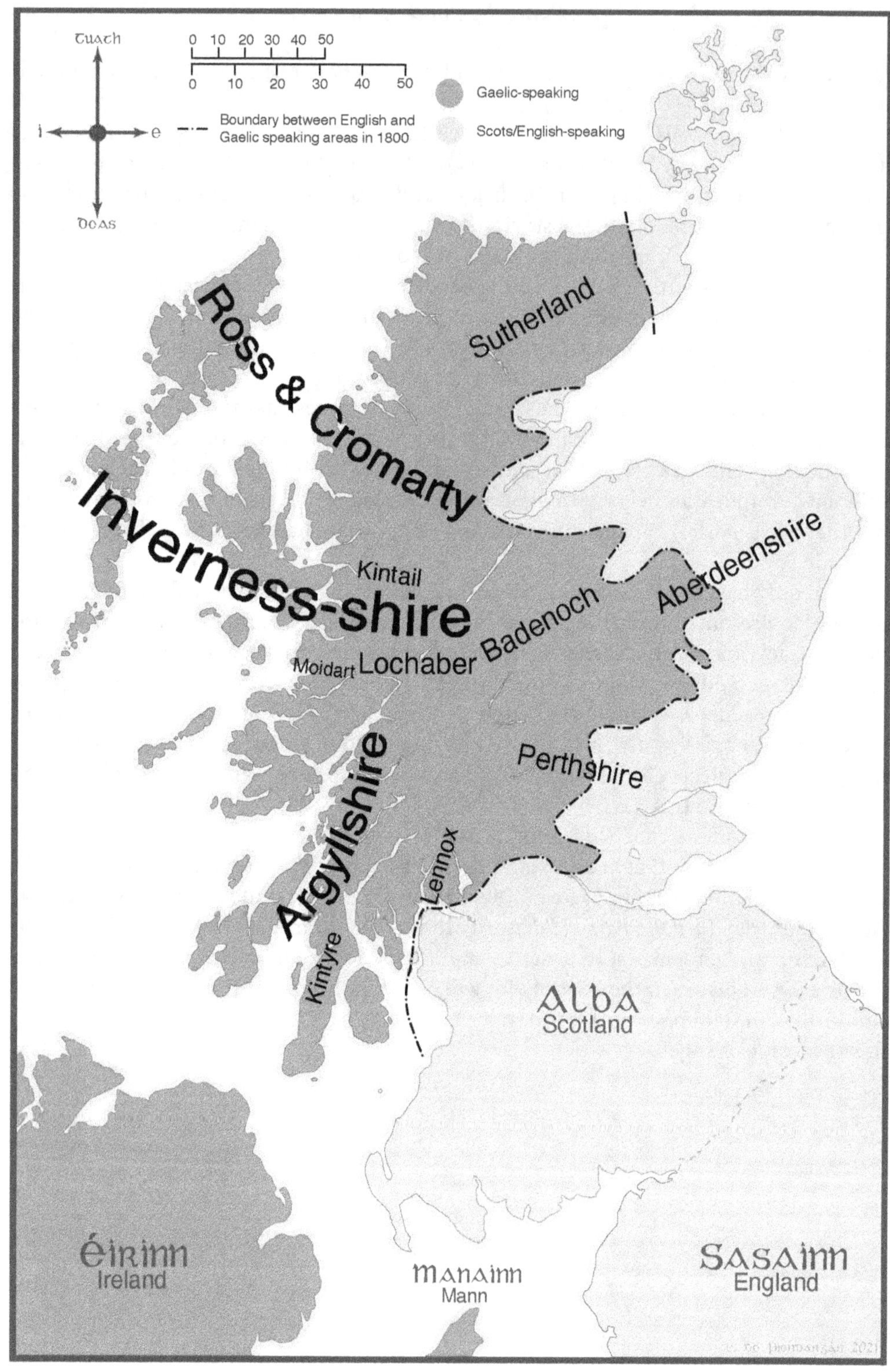

A map of the Highland/Lowland boundary and regions in Scotland (map by Críostóir Piondargás).

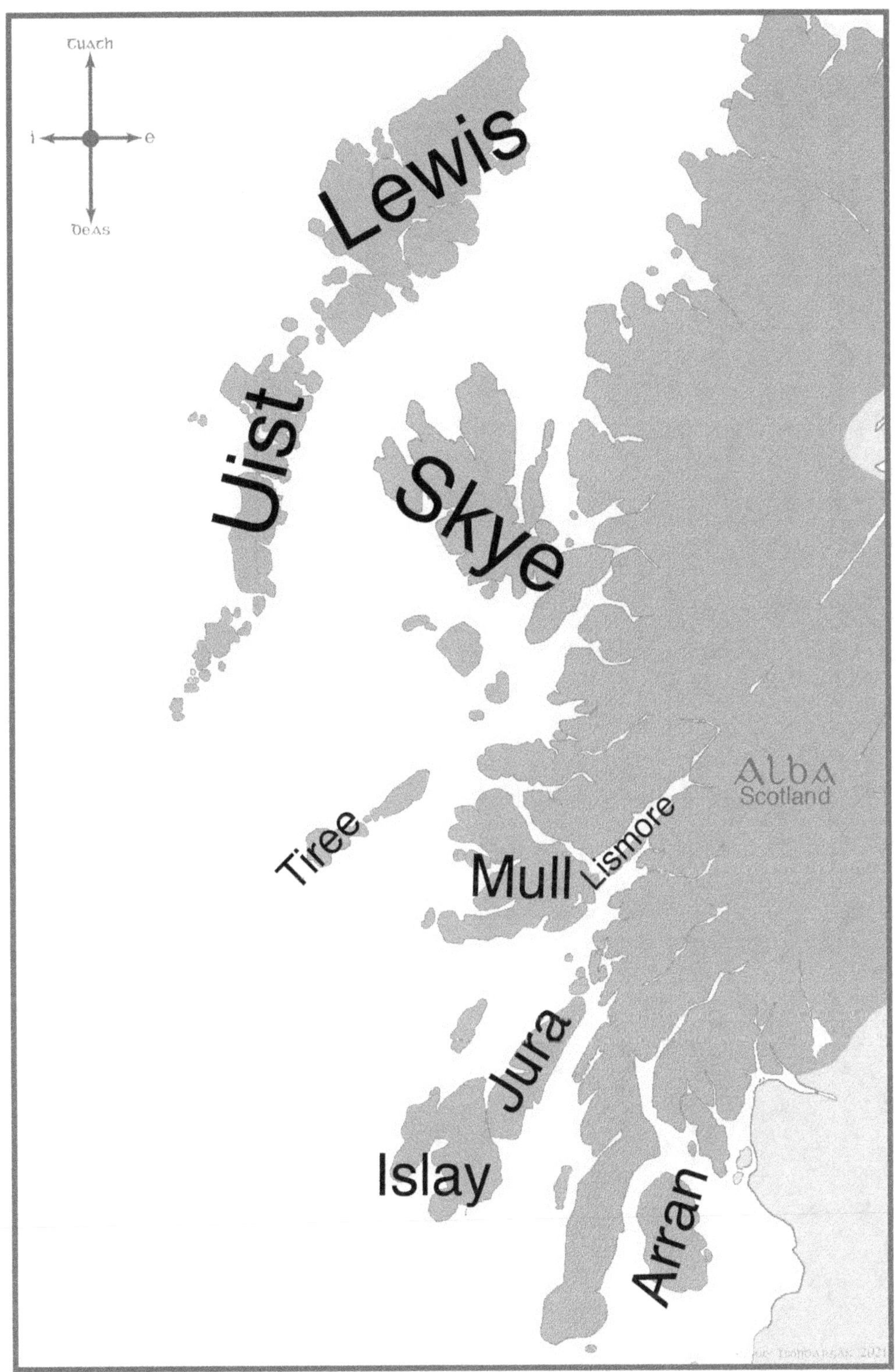

A map of the Western Isles of Scotland (map by Críostóir Piondargás).

Introduction

The Power of Stories

"Once upon a time…." When we hear words such as these, we prepare ourselves to be transported to far-away lands and eras through the power of the imagination. Winter nights are not just cold in the Scottish Highlands: their location so far north means that they can be very long and dark as well. Neighbors gathered together around the peat-fire to find warmth and companionship, and used the opportunity to share their traditions and sharpen their minds. While some of the stories told on these occasions were short and simple anecdotes, others were long and elaborate epics that took several nights to tell in full. The storytelling tradition cultivated capacious memories and long attention spans.

A good storyteller can hold us spellbound for hours as we follow the adventures of heroes and heroines, their friends and enemies, and their encounters with creatures uncanny and unearthly. The fairies are particularly popular figures in the tales of the Scottish Highlands. They live in hills, knolls, and mounds all around the landscape but can show up anywhere and cause the plot of the story to go veering off to unexpected and exciting places. Here is one of many examples:

A long time ago, two men were walking home across the moors after getting the whisky they needed to celebrate Hogmanay. They had to travel far to get the drink. The cask tied to the back of one of them was heavy, so they were walking more slowly than they expected. They were still far from home when night fell.

They sat down for a moment to catch their breath, and one of the men noticed a light shining in the distance where they didn't expect it, as there were no homes or villages in the area. He insisted that they walk over to find out what it was. As they drew closer, they heard the sounds of music and merriment. What did they find but an open door on a fairy hill through which they could see finely-dressed people dancing to beautiful music, having the time of their lives.

"Let's go in!" said the man with the cask on his back.

"Go ahead if you want to," said the other, "but I'm not going in there."

The man with the cask jumped through the doorway and joined in the dancing. His companion watched for a good while, but the man inside paid no heed to anything but the music and the dancers. The man outside finally gave up on him and returned home. He told the other village folk what had happened, but no one would believe him.

The next year on Halloween night he was out spear-fishing salmon with the men from his village. They followed the river to the same area where he had lost his companion in the fairy hill. He looked in the direction of where they had been, and once again he saw a light in the distance.

"Come on and see for yourselves," he urged the men.

They followed the light to the fairy hill and the doorway was once again open. The same finely-dressed crowd was inside, dancing away to the same beautiful music. One of them was the man with the cask on his back.

The other man took the iron spear in his hand and thrust it into the doorway of the fairy hill. He then stepped through it and grabbed his companion by the neck.

"Just wait until this dance is over," said the man with the cask. "I've barely been here a minute."

"I've suffered enough for leaving you before," said the other man. "You're coming out with me now."

He dragged his companion out of the fairy hill, and pulled his spear out of the doorway. He turned to the other men and said, "You see now that I was telling you the truth!"

This is a very common folktale in the Highlands and there are many ways of thinking about its meaning. We could interpret the fairy hill as representing the subterranean depths of the psyche to which we retreat when we are engaged in the arts: music, dance, poetry, storytelling, or any kind of creative activity. Our minds are so focused that time seems to stand still, our senses are heightened, we feel fully alive, we don't want to leave it. We are in the flow.

Reflecting on the multifaceted and multilayered symbolism of the Otherworld in Scottish Gaelic tradition, scholar and ethnographer John MacInnes observed:

> we could take the fairy knoll as a metaphor of the imagination, perhaps as an equivalent of the modern concept of the Unconscious. From this shadowy realm comes the creative power of mankind. An old friend of mine used to say, when he produced songs or legends that I did not realise he knew: "*Bha mi 's a' Chnoc o chunnaic mi thu*" ("I was in the [fairy] Hill since I saw you"). And others had similar vivid expressions.[1]

Stories and beliefs about the fairies, and other paranormal phenomena such as Second Sight, are but aspects of a hugely rich, intricate, and sophisticated cultural ecosystem serving many different purposes for people in different ways in the Scottish Highlands, as elsewhere. The monopoly of science to determine what is natural and what is supernatural, what is rational and what is superstitious, does not hold in Gaelic cosmology. Instead, what modernity labels as "supernatural" and "superstitious" are ordinary aspects of the Gaelic worldview and experience, ways of thinking about the natural environment, human psyche, social boundaries, and the mysteries of the universe.

This volume is a collection of tales originally told in the Scottish Gaelic language in the Highlands of Scotland, stories that were learned by heart and experienced orally. They were written down by fieldworkers between the late eighteenth century and the early twentieth century. Although both the Scottish Gaelic language and the practice of storytelling were already under attack by that time, research among the remaining practitioners revealed a highly developed art form.

Gaelic oral tradition has seldom been given the attention and respect it deserves. Folktales clash with modern literary tastes and conventions, and contemporary readers used to mainstream anglophone fiction may find stories from the oral tradition of the Scottish Highlands to be alien and difficult to decode. Despite this, if we learn how to read them on their own terms, and suspend our disbelief and expectations, they have much to offer. They can provide unique doorways into the mindsets and experiences of the people of the Highlands, contradict common stereotypes, and exhibit keen insight into the human condition.

Scottish Highlands: People and Place

The Highlands and Western Isles are distinct from other parts of Scotland not just in terms of geography but also in terms of language, culture, and identity. The Highland-Lowland divide began to emerge in the thirteenth century, as the incomers who settled in the Lowlands over the previous several generations came to dominate the region. They were different from the "Old Scots"—the Scottish Gaels—who remained in the mountainous areas and the islands of the west.

The original tongue of the Scots was Gaelic. It is a strange irony of history that this language was later rebranded with names like "Erse" or "Irish" that do not reflect its foundational role in the kingdom of Scotland, and that the incomers assumed the name "Scots" in the fifteenth century for their own language, which is essentially an offshoot of Middle English that absorbed a range of other influences.

In the Gaelic language itself, the word *Gàidheal* means both "Gael" and "Highlander." Until the early twentieth century any native of the Scottish Highlands would be expected to speak the Gaelic language. It should be also noted that the term "Highlands" conventionally includes the Western Isles along with the rest of the uplands on the mainland of Scotland to the north-west of the Highland line.

This brief summary must serve as a short-cut for complex processes and interactions that created a fundamental divide across Scotland in the medieval period, one reflected by and in the storytelling tradition. Anne MacVicar Grant (1755–1838) of Laggan, for example, vividly depicts stereotypes and mutual antagonisms on either side of the Highland-Lowland boundary in the late eighteenth century:

> No two nations ever were more distinct, or differed more completely from each other, than the highlanders and lowlanders; and the sentiments with which they regarded each other, was at best a kind of smothered animosity.
>
> The lowlander considered the highlander as a fierce and savage depredator, speaking a barbarous language, and inhabiting a gloomy and barren region, which fear and prudence forbid all strangers to explore. The attractions of his social habits, strong attachments, and courteous manners, were confined to his glens and to his kindred. All the pathetic and sublime charms of his poetry, and all the wild wonders of his records, were concealed in a language difficult to acquire, and utterly despised as the jargon of barbarians by their southern neighbours. If such were the light in which the cultivators of the soil regarded the hunters, graziers, and warriors of the mountains, their contempt was amply repaid by their high spirited neighbours.
>
> They again regarded the lowlanders as a very inferior mongrel race of intruders; sons of little men, without heroism, ancestry, or genius. Mechanical drudges, who could neither sleep upon the snow, compose extempore songs, recite long tales of wonder or of woe, or live without bread and without shelter, for weeks together, following the chase. Whatever was mean or effeminate, whatever was dull, slow, mechanical, or torpid, was in the highlands

> imputed to the lowlanders, and exemplified by allusions to them; while in the low country, every thing ferocious or unprincipled—every species of aukwardness or ignorance—of pride or of insolence, was imputed to the highlanders.
>
> No two communities, generally speaking, could hate each other more cordially, or despise each other more heartily.[2]

It is noteworthy that even at this time Highlanders considered their engagement in storytelling to be something that distinguished them from the people of the Lowlands, who they thought of as "mechanical drudges who could not recite long tales of wonder or of woe."

The modern study of the folktales of Scotland confirms this cultural imbalance to a large degree: three-quarters of the tales in the archives of the School of Scottish Studies are in Gaelic, encompassing 274 different tale-types, in comparison to the 121 tale-types to be found in the stories collected in Lowland Scots or English. In addition, the repertoire of Lowland and Highland storytelling traditions share less than half of possible tale-types. Highland tales are more closely related to those of their Irish-speaking relations in Ireland than they are to those of the Lowlands.[3]

The long-standing connections between the Highlands and Ireland are particularly important for understanding the nature of the Gaelic literary tradition. Professional poets and scholars survived in Gaelic Scotland into the eighteenth century and their sophisticated cultural practices greatly enriched Scottish Gaelic oral tradition among the non-literate classes, including their repertoire of folktales. Kenneth Jackson has valuable notes about these topics in his 1952 article "The Folktale in Gaelic Scotland" in which he highlights the importance of Gaelic folktales in the context of the study of European folk tradition:

> In fact, Scottish and Irish folklore is practically unique in the world in several respects. One is its extraordinary richness and its very high quality, particularly as compared with that of the rest of Western Europe. Another is its relatively large literary content. The medieval literature of the Gaelic people was the property of an educated professional class of men, one of whose functions was to entertain the chieftain and retainers in his hall
>
> I want to emphasise this, as it is impossible fully to understand the language, literature, history, or folklore of the Highlands without understanding also that of Ireland. The relevance of that fact tonight is this: Borrowing a term from botany, folklorists speak of *ecotypes*, meaning by that local variations of an international folktale which develop in a homogenous cultural area; so that a tale will have Spanish ecotypes, and Balkan ecotypes, and so forth. In the same way they have Gaelic ecotypes, developed during the Common Gaelic period and now found to be identical in Ireland and Scotland.[4]

Nevertheless, there were borrowings between storytellers in the Highlands and the Lowlands of Scotland. Scotland is particularly interesting as a crossroads of Celtic and Germanic peoples, with some later input from the Norse, as well as the influence of formal literary traditions.

One important and fascinating exception to the partition between Highland and Lowland communities is the "traveling folk," also known as "cairds" and less kindly as "tinkers." For centuries, these families roamed across the rural countryside from village to village, offering their services to the settled communities while they camped nearby. They offered their skills in repairing metal items, laboring in the fields, doing odd jobs, and selling goods. Neither geographical boundaries nor language restricted their movement. They brought stories with them when they traveled, serving as a bridge between Highlands and Lowlands, and they kept storytelling alive in their camps long after it died out in the settled communities.[5]

John F. Campbell wrote a colorful passage about John MacDonald, a member of a family of traveling folk who recited Gaelic folktales for Hector Urquhart:

> John himself is a character; he is about fifty years of age; his father, an old soldier, is alive and about eighty; and there are numerous younger branches; and they were all encamped under the root of a tree in a quarry close to Inverary, at Easter 1859.
>
> The father tells many stories, but his memory is failing. The son told me several, and I have a good many of them written down. They both recite; they do not simply tell the story, but act it with changing voice and gesture, as if they took an interest in it, and entered into the spirit and fun of the tale. They belong to the race of "Cairds," and are as much nomads as the gipsies are. The father, to use the son's expression, "never saw a school."[6]

Both the folktales themselves and the sketches of the storytellers collected in the nineteenth century preserve a great deal of information that would have otherwise been lost in the Scottish Highlands due to cumulative catastrophes since the mid-eighteenth century: the widespread dispossession of the native population, angloconformist education, the pressures of migration, and other forms of marginalization and assimilation. Given the damage done in earlier generations and the silencing of oral tradition, it is not surprising that people today are prone to underestimate the once ubiquitous presence of Gaelic and the vitality of its many forms of cultural expression across the Highlands.

The folklore of each Highland district resembles a shard of a shattered hologram, retaining small local idiosyncrasies while also reflecting the larger themes and patterns that resonate across the Gaelic-speaking world. Indeed, oral tradition in a common language across social networks of kinship helped to propagate and reinforce a shared culture that found expression in stories, songs, communal customs, and more. Not only are many folktale plots shared between Highland communities from Kintyre to Sutherland, from Glenshee to the Hebrides, but many of the same characters, motifs, symbols, and beliefs recur in them. It can be astonishing to discover a narrative recorded in Braemar that closely matches one in Tiree, for example, and yet there are ample examples of such distant twins. To borrow a phrase from the late John MacInnes, this is the art of a nation.

There are parts of the Highlands where the Gaelic language was given a fatal blow in the nineteenth century or the population was largely removed, and what has survived for us today is largely due to the work of a solitary champion of local tradition gleaning it at the last minute.

Loch Lomond-side, on the southern border of the Highlands and just outside the greater Glasgow area, is a case in point. If it weren't for the labors of John Dewar, we would have precious little evidence remaining of the folktales told by the native Gaels of the area.[7] Dewar was born in 1802 in a cottage in a glen that connects to Glen Douglas, well south of Arrochar. Both his mother and father were local to the area, and Catrìona MacFarlane, a servant maid from Glen Falloch, was an additional member of his household. Dewar described hearing storytellers when visiting his grandfather near Tarbet.

> I remember, in the winter nights, when a few old people would be together, they would pass the time telling each other stories, which they had by tradition. I used to listen attentively,

A portrait of John Francis Campbell made in 1848 (Campbell, *Records of Argyll* [1885]. Frontispiece).

> and hear them telling about the *ceatharnaich*, or free-booters, which used to come to plunder the country, and take away cattle, and how their ancestors would gather themselves together to fight for their property....
>
> I was also sometimes amused, listening to some people telling Gaelic romances, which we called *sgeulachds*. It was customary for a few youngsters to gather into one house, and whither idle or at some work, such as kniting stockings or spinning, they would amuse each other with some innocent diversion, or telling *sgeulachds*. Us that was children was very fond of listening to them, and the servant maid that was in my father's house would often tell us a *sgeulachd* to keep us quiet.[8]

Not only did Dewar write down the many folktales that he heard in his youth from these sources, he spent years collecting them from the natives of parishes close to the Lowland border where Gaelic has long since gone silent. And a cohort of other Gaelic devotees committed themselves to the same cause.

How Highlanders Experienced Folktales

The term "folktale" refers to a story that is told from memory and experienced by an audience aurally. Folktales belong to a community's shared wells of tradition rather than being the compositions of individual authors. It is commonly claimed that until recently Scottish Highlanders had nothing but oral folktales because they were illiterate and had no form of written literature, but this is a misinformed fallacy.

Written Gaelic literature has a venerable pedigree: the literary tradition shared by Scotland and Ireland is the oldest in Western Europe. It was cultivated by a professionally-trained class of scholars who worked for churches and secular rulers. They created sophisticated forms of verbal artistry that had a political role in the Gaelic world and the association with the élite of society gave the literary tradition prestige and made its influence pervasive.[9]

On the other hand, like the rest of Europe, few people were able to read and write texts in Gaelic, or even had a need to do so, until fairly recently. Oral tradition served the needs of the vast majority of people.

It would also be misleading to draw too sharp a line between orality and literacy. Gaelic oral tradition was influenced by the literary conventions of the élite because of the high social status and ubiquitous presence of literary and musical professionals in Highland life. Many of the tales that were written in manuscripts were read aloud at social gatherings and people present at them sometimes repeated them for others. These stories then entered oral tradition, freed from the constraints of the pen and paper to be reshaped in new forms. The professional literati in turn borrowed motifs, characters, and plots from popular tales in oral tradition.

In a song-poem composed by Mary MacLeod describing an ideal evening in the hall of the MacLeods in the seventeenth century, the entertainment culminated with storytelling:

> *Gur h-e b' eachdraidh 'na dhéidh sin,*
> *Greis air uirsgeul na Féinne*
> *Is air chuideachda chéirghil nan cròc.*[10]
>
> Epic adventure tales came after that,
> And some time for the stories about the Fianna
> And the white-buttocked, antlered deer herd.

Folktales, like other genres of oral tradition, could be shared and learned at a number of times and places, but the most important context for them in Gaelic tradition for the majority of the population was the *céilidh*, a gathering at a home in the community. This was a particularly important social ritual during the evenings in the dark half of the year (between Halloween and Beltane). The *céilidh* typically began with general conversation, followed eventually by storytelling. Each story could provoke discussion and commentary after it had concluded.[11]

While all sorts of materials—stories, song, dance, music, riddles, etc.—could generally be shared at a *céilidh*, in large and active communities certain houses specialized in particular genres or were dominated by the presence of celebrated performers.[12] A classic account of the *céilidh* given by Hector Urquhart in 1860 describes how tailors and cobblers, some of the few widely-traveled members of the Gaelic peasantry, transmitted stories between communities:

> In my native place, Pool-Ewe, Ross-shire, when I was a boy, it was the custom for the young to assemble together on the long winter nights to hear the old people recite the tales, or *sgeulachd*, which they had learned from their fathers before them. In these days tailors and shoemakers went from house to house, making our clothes and shoes. When one of them came to the village we were greatly delighted, whilst getting new kilts at the same time. I knew an old tailor who used to tell a new tale every night during his stay.... It was also the custom when an *aoigh*, or stranger, celebrated for his store of tales, came on a visit to the village, for us, young and old, to make a rush to the house where he passed the night, and choose our seats, some on beds, some on forms, and others on three-legged stools, etc., and listen in silence to new tales.[13]

Adults often did manual labor while they listened, such as twisting heather into rope, spinning wool or carving wood. The young men and women might flirt by choice of the songs they sang and the lyrics in them.

As the *céilidh* was a local institution, based in a community, run by and for the members of that community, it could be tailored to their needs, concerns, and resources. People told stories regarding their ancestors, sang songs about events significant in their own communities, created proverbial lore relevant to their own flora, fauna, and sense of place, and engendered an ethos of self-reliance. The *céilidh* was a crucial cornerstone for native education as well as their social cohesion as a community. While Highland society remained intact, oral tradition was capable of transmitting and regenerating vernacular Gaelic culture across countless generations.

One of the foremost living scholars of Scottish Gaelic literature and oral tradition, Ronald Black, contrasts the virtues of the *céilidh* with the common misconceptions that Highlanders were backward people whose intellectual life was destitute before formal schools were imported into their region:

> It is conventional to say that until the Society in Scotland for the Propagation of Christian Knowledge was set up in 1709 there were virtually no schools in the Highlands. Technically that is true. What is overlooked however is that the céilidh-house was an educational institution. Like the schools of its time, it operated on a seasonal basis (during the winter months, when children could be spared from domestic and agricultural labour), but in other respects it had much in common with the educational values of today. Children were not whipped or humiliated for speaking Gaelic or failing to remember their lessons. Children and adults learned together. Girls and boys learned as equals. And the quality of learning did not have to depend on the strengths and weaknesses of individuals, for the visitor to the township—the stranger who told his "tale until dawn"—was eagerly listened to.[14]

This positive assessment of the pedagogic function of the *céilidh*-house was shared by the Rev. Alexander MacLean Sinclair, arguably the best scholar to emerge from the Gaelic immigrant communities of the Canadian Maritimes, in an article he wrote in the Cape Breton newspaper *Mac-Talla* in 1893:

> *Their cuid nach robh móran fiosrachaidh aig na seann Ghàidheil. Chan urrainn mise sin a ràdh. Na seann daoine air an robh mi eòlach cha bu daoine gun fhiosrachadh iad. Gheibhteadh eachdraidh, is sgeulachdan, is òrain 'nam measg. Thug iad uile greis mhór anns an sgoil-oidhche. Sgoil-oidhche! An robh sgoil-oidhche aig na bodaich a thàinig am mach ás an t-seann dùthaich? 'S ann aca fhéin a bha an sgoil-oidhche. Gu dé a bha 's a' chéilidh ach sgoil-oidhche? Agus bu sgoil mhath i. Bha i math gus an inntinn a gheurachadh, gus a chuimhne a neartachadh, agus gu eòlas a thoirt do'n òigridh mu'n t-sluagh bho'n dàinig iad, mu'n dùthaich do'm buineadh iad, agus mu euchdan Wallais, Bhruis, agus ghaisgeach eile.*
>
> Some will claim that the Gaels of old didn't know much. I can't say that. The old people that I have known were certainly not uninformed. They knew history, songs and stories. They were all of long time attendance in night school. Night school! Did the old-timers coming from Scotland have a night school? Indeed they did. What was the *céilidh* but a night school and a good one. It was conducive to sharpening and strengthening the mind and memory and to educate the youth about their forefathers, the country from which they came and the deeds of Wallace and Bruce and other heroes.[15]

The storytelling tradition met with the disapproval of the church because it diverted people from what it considered to be a higher priority: their spiritual salvation. Bishop John Carswell, in his introduction to the Gaelic translation of the *Book of Common Order* of the Church of Scotland published in 1567, denounced these popular secular pastimes:

> And great is the blindness and darkness of sin and ignorance and of the mind among composers and writers and patrons of Gaelic, in that they prefer and are accustomed to maintain and improve vain, hurtful, lying, worldly tales composed about the Tuatha Dé Danann, and about the sons of Milesius, and about the heroes and Fionn mac Cumhaill with his warriors....[16]

The power of the church to influence and reshape the lives and habits of people in the Highlands was very limited until the eighteenth century. The British government saw assimilation to anglophone norms as a priority of its empire-building mission and was particularly alarmed by the political threat posed by the Jacobite movement. The military, church, and schools were used, particularly after the Battle of Culloden (1746), in a concerted and sustained effort to alienate Highlanders from their old customs and allegiances. By the late eighteenth century, observers noted the damage done to Gaelic oral tradition as well as cultural self-confidence in general, as reflected in these remarks of antiquarian John Ramsay of Ochtertyre:

> The Highland muses are said to have dropped their wings more since the last rebellion than at any preceding period.... The Highlanders were also passionately fond of *sgeulachds*, or romances, which were mostly in prose, though in a figurative and animated style. They are full of giants, necromancers, fairies, dragons, &c.... One cannot forbear a wish that some of the best and most striking ones were collected and faithfully translated before they are irrecoverably lost. By this means many curious interesting anecdotes relative to the ancient Gaelic Scots might be rescued from oblivion. Less than half a century ago, when reading was little in request, these tales were listened to with the utmost avidity by persons of all ranks; and of later years they have been one of the chief entertainments of the common people. These customs, however, are at present very much on the wane.[17]

By the time that folktale collection began in earnest in the late 1850s, the anti–Gaelic institutions that came to dominate Highland life had effectively driven the storytelling tradition to the margins. Hector Urquhart noted about returning home to Ross-shire to track down the tradition-bearers of his youth:

> The minister came to the village in 1830, and the schoolmaster soon followed, who put a stop in our village to such gatherings; and in their place we were supplied with heavier tasks than listening to the old shoemaker's fairy tales. From that period till I collected the few in this collection, I have not heard a tale recited. On going to visit my friends last summer I expected that I would get some old tales among them, but I found that the most of the old men who used to relate them in my young days had died, and the few who were then alive of them were so old that they had lost their memories, so that I only got but a trifle to what I expected.[18]

And yet, storytelling continued in some communities and in some contexts, despite the disapproval of the authorities. John F. Campbell and his team of folklore collectors found seasoned storytellers still practicing their craft in the communities least affected by anglicizing processes, especially in the Western Isles. Campbell's description of Donald MacPhie of South Uist, seventy-nine years old in 1860, shows a man with remarkable self-confidence in himself as a tradition-bearer and loyalty to that tradition. This is also a fascinating commentary about the workings of the minds of oral storytellers and how their memory functioned.

> He told me nine stories, and like all the others, declared that there was no man in the islands who knew them so well. "He could not say how many he knew"; he seemed to know versions of nearly everything I had got; and he told me plainly that my versions were good for nothing. "Huch! Thou hast not got them right at all." "They came into his mind," he said, "sometimes at night when he could not sleep,—old tales that he had not heard for threescore years."
>
> He had the manner of a practised narrator, and it is quite evident that he is one; he chuckled at the interesting parts, and laid his withered finger on my knee as he gave out the terrible bits with due solemnity....
>
> I found them to be men with clear heads and wonderful memories, generally very poor and old, living in remote corners of remote islands, and speaking only Gaelic; in short, those who have lived most at home, furthest from the world, and who have no source of mental relaxation beyond themselves and their neighbours.[19]

A long description from 1887 describes a *céilidh*—anglicized here as "cailey" with the participants called "cailiers"—in vivid detail. It describes the social role it played in Highland communities and its popularity among young and old, but it also explicitly acknowledges that educational authorities were generally harsh critics of Gaelic storytelling and were turning the minds of the youth against oral tradition and the authority of the elders.

> In some parts of the Highlands story-telling has not yet been superseded by story-reading. On winter evenings the people still keep up the old custom of going to "cailey." This corresponds to making a call, though not on friends generally, at their homes, but at some acknowledged resort in the neighbourhood, where you will be almost certain to meet them. "Caileying" is, therefore, regarded as a social duty, in spite of the hard things which have been said against it by gloomy Presbyterian ministers. These gentlemen used to have a horror of recreation of any kind, which is not quite the case now. Indeed, "caileying" is not only harmless, but, as a means of intercourse, highly beneficial. Without something of this kind life would be almost intolerable in outlying Highland districts. It lends itself to good-fellowship, being simply an informal social gathering, where everybody is expected to be as entertaining as possible.

If the "cailiers" have the choice of a "black" house that is, a house with the fire on the middle of the floor—they prefer it to any other. Such a house, and especially if it be owned by an old couple, is certain to be in favour as a meeting place. For one thing, there is plenty of accommodation around the fire for a large company; and the old folks take a delight in keeping up the old customs. The good wife, who busies herself with carding or spinning, gives a kind word to everybody that arrives. Having unmarried daughters, perhaps it is only natural that she should show some slight favour in the case of this young man or that. However, the circumstances are understood, so no one feels aggrieved. Each and all of her guests are perfectly at ease. Seated around the blazing peatfire in a circle, it would be difficult to match such a homely, happy scene. Picturesque, too, is that humble interior, with its blaze of focused light illuminating the various features of the "cailiers," its deep shadows, and its outer darkness. The lamp, which the old woman monopolises for her own work, merely casts a gleam across the narrow chamber, while its length is lost in obscurity. Everything is quaint—often at the sacrifice of comfort: the table that folds against the wall, and looks like a notice-board; the chairs in which the natural angles of the wood are turned to such good account, and where there was a deficiency of wood, the bark still adhering to make up the difference; pigeon-holes ranging over the walls, handy receptacles for all kinds of odds-and-ends; the roof as black as ebony, dimly seen through a cloud of smoke that fortunately only invades the lower regions when the wind blows from a certain direction; the chain on which the pots are hung, suspended over the fire, from the roof; and the spinning-wheel, which keeps up an industrious whirr.

The floor is so uneven that every chair is more or less a rocking chair. Consequently, in taking a seat a person has to shift the chair about before he can obtain anything like a solid foundation. After all are seated comfortably, and more peats are heaped on the fire, there is an ominous silence that reminds one of a Quaker meeting. Then somebody moves his or her chair uneasily, generally some old person, who only wants a word of encouragement to discourse of matters appropriate to the occasion, which means something superlatively supernatural. Highland people, like the Psychical Research Society, cannot obtain enough information relating to ghosts and kindred uncanny studies. The old woman stops her wheel long enough to accentuate the silence, and fixes her gaze on the occupant of the restless chair, Willie Murray. She observes in Gaelic that they are very quiet tonight. Willie moves his chair again, and looks doubtfully at the younger members of the company. It is well known that he can never go abroad after dark without seeing fairies and other unsubstantial revellers of which School Boards take no account.

The School Board emissaries nudge each other, and encourage Willie to relate some of his supernatural experiences. This he does at last, and with such earnestness and minute description that the beings that sometimes torment him make their presence felt, so that for the time their influence surpasses that of the School Board. The flickering light of the fire dances through the smoky vault, casting weird shadows across the floor, and vainly endeavors to penetrate the terrible gloom that is "but" in the byre. There is neither wall nor partition of any kind to define where the kitchen ends and the byre begins, and the sounds that come from the animal's quarters from time to time, the clank of chains or a smothered cough, along with the other surroundings, would frighten a nervous person without Willie's story.

And, judging from appearances, Willie is making an impression. The old woman ceases to spin, and with an anxious face leans forward that she may be the better able to drink in every word. Young women slip closer to their male friends, forgetful that they live in a century that has all but exploded the existence of ghosts and fairies. Even the young men, although they think Willie a silly old fellow, are carried away by his wonderfully-circumstantial account. However, when he has finished, they lecture him on his superstition. The old woman immediately reproves them, saying that young people now-a-days are too presumptuous, for she remembers the time when all good people were bothered like Willie; but the world is now so wicked that supernatural agencies have ceased to interfere in human concerns. After this explanation, somebody volunteers to entertain the company with a more rational story. It deals with adventure, and therefore meets the approval of everybody. Then another rises equal to the occasion, story and anecdote following each other in quick succession afterwards until a reasonable hour, when the "cailiers" betake themselves to their own homes, feeling their spirits considerably revived by the night's proceedings.

"Cailiers" have a curious custom of saying "Peace be here!" when they enter a house, the usual reply given by the master or mistress being, "So be it."[20]

Despite the ubiquitous presence of the *céilidh* and its rituals across the Highlands, I do not know of any attempt to articulate the implicit rules of etiquette and conduct until the late twentieth century, when John Macarthur of Bayble, Lewis, drew up this list of seven laws[21]:

1. *Is rìgh fear an taighe* ("The man of the house is king").
2. *Chan eil claon air a' mhodh* ("There can be no deviation from the rules").
3. *Is móide nì 'aithris* ("A tale gains in the telling").
4. *Seanfhacal bho chùil na mònach* ("A proverb from the back of the peat store"): children delegated to supply peat for the fire were encouraged to share proverbs; and *Toimhseachan bho'n t-slige chrùisgean* ("A riddle from the oil lamp"): the person responsible for the oil lamp shared riddles.
5. *Mìn-innse air uirsgeulan gu meadhan-oidhche, garbh-innse gu gairm coilich* ("Detailed narration of tales until midnight, general narration until cock-crow")
6. *Sgeul air sgeul, òran air òran, is deiseil air gach nì* ("Tale follows tale, song follows song, always moving in a clockwise direction").
7. *A' cheud sgeul air fear an taighe agus sgeul gu latha air an aoigh* ("The host tells the first tale and the guest tells tales until dawn").

Stories might be told at any social gathering. Donald MacPhee, a miller in Skye, acquired many tales from people who came with their grain for his services and he, in turn, passed them on to others who listened while the milling was done.[22] John G. Campbell related the anecdote of one of his informants who described how a crew, coming together to build a stone wall, would ask for a tale of the Fianna to be told before beginning their labors:

> The whole party then sat round the storyteller, and listened to his marvellous account. By the time that he was done the sun was drawing westward and some one would then say it was hardly worth while beginning that day, and he might tell some other story suggested by the previous narrative. When the second story was finished the sun was well-nigh setting, and the parties separated after agreeing to meet next day, as nothing had been done that day.[23]

Such was the enchantment of storytelling in the old Gaelic world and the resulting ordering of priorities in Highland life. Little wonder that an anglocentric British empire saw Gaelic culture as incompatible with its own world order and considered it as something that needed to be conquered, reformed, and relegated to the past.

Gaelic Folktale Scholarship in Scotland

The professional literati of the Gaelic world were creating stories that pertained to the interests of the native élite and committing them to manuscript from the early medieval period on, but we only catch occasional glimpses of what kinds of stories the commoners were telling.

It is largely due to the controversy that erupted in the 1760s over whether or not the books published by James Macpherson (1736–96) were authentic translations of the bard Ossian that literate Gaelic-speakers began to document the songs and stories of the Highland peasantry. That debate began to open a window on a much wider range of society and their literary activities.

Macpherson, a young Highlander from Badenoch, published *Fragments of Ancient Poetry, Collected in the Highlands of Scotland, and translated from the Galic or Erse Language*, anonymously in 1760. He took certain elements from the Gaelic ballads of the Fenian cycle of literature—characters, themes, plot-lines—but reworked them considerably in new forms to meet the aesthetic expectations of his contemporary anglophone audience. Rather than own up to his own hand in these creative adaptations, however, he claimed that the epic poetry in this and several further volumes was a literal translation of the work of the third-century Gaelic poet he called "Ossian."

A portrait of John Francis Campbell made in 1868 (MacInnes, *Folk and Hero Tales* [1890]. Frontispiece).

Macpherson quickly became a literary superstar. Napoleon carried a copy of Macpherson's volume *The Works of Ossian* in his breast pocket and commissioned Jean Auguste Dominique Ingres to paint a colossal scene from the epic in his palace. Thomas Jefferson was such a devotee of the "bard of the North" that he wished to learn Gaelic in order to read it in its original form. Poets from Wordsworth and Blake to Goethe and Tennyson were inspired and influenced by the texts attributed to *Ossian*. Highlanders were glad to be the objects of admiration for a change, even if those familiar with Macpherson's "translations" had misgivings about his claims.

There were plenty of skeptics, however, many of whom asserted that Highlanders were too primitive and barbaric a people to have a literary tradition, let alone express the kinds of noble and lofty sentiments to be found in Macpherson's books. Samuel Johnson, one of the most prominent literary critics of his time, undertook a virtual crusade to discredit Macpherson and his work, and described the Gaelic language (called by him "Earse") and literary tradition in starkly negative terms. Given his cultural status, Johnson's views remain influential in modern literary studies, despite the rigorous work done by Gaelic scholars in the generations since to dispel the fallacies he propagated:

> It is the rude speech of a barbarous people, who had few thoughts to express, and were content, as they conceived grossly, to be grossly understood. After what has been lately talked of Highland Bards, and Highland genius, many will startle when they are told, that the Earse was never a written language; that there is not in the world an Earse manuscript a hundred years old.[24]

A portrait of the Rev. John G. Campbell (Campbell, *Clan Traditions and Popular Tales* [1895]. Frontispiece).

Many Highlanders were rightly outraged at Johnson's insults and read them as a rallying cry. Literate Gaels, many of them church ministers, began to transcribe the songs and stories from oral tradition related to Fionn mac Cumhaill (called "Fingal" by Macpherson), Oisean (called "Ossian" by Macpherson), and other characters of the Fianna (also known in English as "Fenians") so that the work of Macpherson could be more accurately

A portrait of the Rev. James MacDougall (MacDougall, *Folk Tales and Fairy Lore* [1910]. Frontispiece).

A portrait of Alexander Carmichael (Carmichael, *Carmina Gadelica*, vol. 1 [1900]. Frontispiece; also appears in *Celtic Review* 8 [1913]: 116).

assessed. Gaelic elders were interviewed. Gaelic manuscripts, some of them already centuries old, were identified and collected.

Into the early nineteenth century, Highland antiquarians and literary critics were largely focused on texts loosely fitting the "epic" category: the praise of great heroes and warriors among the aristocratic classes. The gradual increase in literacy among Highlanders created a demand for reading materials, and in the 1830s, newspapers and magazines written in Gaelic began to appear, largely under the direction of Gaelic minister, journalist, and reformer Rev. Norman MacLeod ("Caraid nan Gàidheal," 1783–1862). Folktales from oral tradition appeared sporadically in these early periodicals, most of them describing clan conflicts and celebrated Highland historical figures.

The formal collection of Gaelic folktales, and the study of folklore as an academic discipline, got underway in Scotland in 1859 due to the initiative of John Francis Campbell of Islay (1822–85). Unlike most of the Highland gentry of his era, Campbell had been raised as a Gaelic speaker among the native population. He was familiar with Gaelic oral tradition but was also educated at Eton and Edinburgh University.

The Rev. Norman MacLeod encouraged Campbell to collect Gaelic folktales, but it was his friendship with George Webbe Dasent that finally spurred Campbell into action. In 1859 Dasent published *Popular Tales from the Norse*, and as Campbell read it, he recognized versions of tales he had heard in Gaelic as a boy. The volume reflected the state of the art of folklore studies at the time and Dasent personally provided Campbell with further guidance about how oral traditions should be collected. Campbell utilized his far-reaching social networks to coordinate a team of fieldworkers across the Highlands who quickly harvested a large corpus of materials. Campbell published four volumes of materials between 1859 and 1862, but left many more materials in manuscript form that have been much slower to come into print.[25] John G. MacKay (1869–1942) edited and translated many more of them for periodicals and books, but others in Campbell's archives still await proper attention.

Campbell inspired others to take similar actions to rescue what was still lurking in the memories of the elders in the Highlands. One of Campbell's young collectors was Alexander Carmichael (1832–1912), a native of Lismore who spent the rest of his life recovering Gaelic oral traditions. Although he continued to transcribe stories and songs, he was also the first fieldworker to focus on much more esoteric folklore such as charms, spells, prayers, and spiritual practices. Another of Campbell's collectors, John Dewar (1802–72), continued for years to collect historical legends and clan sagas in parts of the Highlands that received scant attention before or since.[26]

Campbell's example inspired a host of others, including Catholic priests and Protestant ministers: the Rev. James MacDougall (1833–1906), a native of Craignish who became minister of Duror, Argyllshire, in 1871; the Rev. John Gregorson Campbell (1836–91), a native of Kingairloch who became minister of Tiree in 1860; Father (Rev. Dr.) Allan McDonald (1859–1905), a native of Lochaber who became parish priest in South Uist in 1884 and Eriskay in 1894; the Rev. Dr. Kenneth Macleod (1871–1955), a native of Eigg who was minister in Colonsay and Gigha.

Some Gaels experienced a renewal of self-confidence in the second half of the nineteenth century and realized that it was necessary to create an organized response to policies of anglicization in order to defend the Gaelic language and culture. This became an urgent matter after the Education Act of 1872, which effectively put an end to the use of Gaelic in the schools in the Highlands. Organizations were formed in cities with immigrant Gaelic communities that held public events, campaigned for Gaelic causes, and engaged in activities that fostered and celebrated the language and culture.

The most important of these, in terms of preserving traditional folktales, is the Gaelic Society of Inverness, founded in 1871. It immediately initiated a series of talks about Gaelic issues and published the texts of most of them in its journal *Transactions of the Gaelic Society of Inverness*. In 1877, the Rev. William Watson delivered a talk to the organization entitled "The Collecting of Highland Legends and the Necessity for Collecting Them Now" in which he stated:

> it is manifest that all the legends which are still floating in the language of our people should be gathered as soon as possible. We know not what havoc the decay of our language may be making among our legends. It is probable that, at this very hour, there are legends trembling on the confines of the land of oblivion. Let us capture them ere they vanish into the undiscovered country from whose bourn no traveller returns.[27]

Many more stories and traditions from local lore were printed by them that would have been lost otherwise. Similar organizations were formed in Dundee and Glasgow. There were Scottish newspapers and journals in the late ninteenth and twentieth centuries that included Gaelic columns that featured folktales from oral tradition. *Mac-Talla* was an all–Gaelic newspaper in Cape Breton, Canada, from 1892 to 1904 that printed traditional materials contributed by its global readership.

After the tremendous output of the nineteenth century, many assumed that the work of collecting folktales in Gaelic Scotland was complete. The absence of folklore scholars in academic institutions in Scotland prevented any diagnosis of the situation. Independent scholars John Lorne Campbell (1906–96) and K.C. Craig did fieldwork in the Highlands in the 1930s and 1940s and the troves of traditions they harvested demonstrated that much could still be done.

The Irish Folklore Commission took an interest in the Gaelic traditions to be found in Scotland, so closely related to those of Ireland and in clear need of attention. They employed Séamus Ennis, John Lorne Campbell, and Calum Maclean in the 1940s to collect materials on paper and wax cylinder.[28]

It was not until 1951 that the study of folktales and folklore was given the institutional support it needed in Scotland. The School of Scottish Studies was established at the University of Edinburgh, modeled on centers for folklore scholarship in Ireland and Scandinavia. Calum Maclean was its first fieldworker. Many fieldworkers have contributed to the archives in the decades since, and scholars have continued to research and interpret the reams of folklore in its stewardship.

How Folktales Work

Oral folktales are different from written literature: they have to be. When you read text on a page, you can go through it at your own pace. You can rely on visual memory as well as language to help you remember details, such as the names of characters, and you can always go back to review the text if you forget something or need to refresh your memory.

When you listen to a story being told orally, on the other hand, you must grasp it as soon as you hear it, visualizing the places, characters, and actions instantaneously. You also have to keep track of these essential elements in your head as the narrative progresses. You cannot slow down or rewind the storyteller. This is one of the reasons why oral folktales tend to be very concise and stripped of excessive and unnecessary detail. The mental limitations of listeners dictate, to a large degree, the style and structure of oral folktales.

Storytellers tend to use language that differs from the casual, everyday vernacular. The use of archaic words, musical cadences, or dramatic inflections marks the storytelling performance as an elevated, lofty, sublime, or special experience, and it the signals the transformation of the speaker's persona. Traditional Gaelic folktales sometimes intersperse poetic couplets or even songs in the prose to increase the emotional or aesthetic impact.

The most elaborate linguistic ornamentation in Gaelic folktales is the *run*, a formulaic passage which embellishes the story's details at certain dramatic or transitional moments. Runs consist of alliterative, onomatopoeic, and archaistic words, especially adjectives, meant to impress the listener, echoing the features of poetry. They can also aid the storyteller to prepare mentally for the next episode of the narrative.

> They were much valued by the story-teller, partly because they contain words unintelligible to the audience which were evidence of his learning. They were recited in a kind of rapid nasal chant, which indicates that they were felt to be poetry.[29]

There are recurring runs for episodes in folktales such as the arming of the warrior, the clash between warriors, the launching of a ship, the sailing of the ship, the feasts in the chieftain's hall, and the imposition of taboos. Here is an example of a run about feasting; alliteration is marked with underlining and rhyme with bold face:

Thog iad ceòl is leag iad am bròn;
Bha deochan mìne misgeach
Is deochan garbha gachanach
Ceòl leis an caidleadh fir leòinte
Daoine a' sìor ghabhail a' chiùil sin
'S na dorsan 'gan dùnadh
Air eagal 's gun teicheadh an ceòl.

They raised up music and they let go of their sorrow;
There were smooth, stiff drinks,
And rough, strong drinks;
Music that would cause wounded men to sleep,
Musicians playing those melodies without stopping,
The doors being shut
To stop the music from escaping.

It is virtually impossible to recreate these poetic features in translation, so runs lose much of their magic when rendered in English.

Another basic feature of storytelling is what folklorists call *metacommunication*: the verbal or non-verbal clues that the storyteller uses to indicate how the audience should interpret what he says and how it relates to the tale itself. When a storyteller says, "Once upon a time," for example, you know that you should interpret it to mean "That person is starting to tell a story now." When the storyteller says, "and they lived happily ever after," you are given a signal that you understand to mean "The story is now over." Gaelic has its own set of metacommunication signals that work similarly.

Danish folklorist Axel Olrik (1864–1917) proposed a set of universal laws of oral literature in an article published in 1909, based on a systematic analysis of the folktales of many countries.[30] Some of the most important of these are:

- The Law of Repetition: Sequences of action or dialog are repeated in the narrative; repetition builds dramatic tension and fills out the body of the story.

- The Law of Three: People and actions repeat in sets of three in the story.
- The Law of Two to a Scene: Only two characters occupy "the stage" of the narrative at a time, minimizing possible confusion about the cast involved in dialog and action.
- The Law of Contrasts: People and things are defined in stark contrast to one another (young/old, large/small, light/dark, male/female, pretty/ugly, etc), making it easier to distinguish between elements of the story and remember them.
- The Law of Importance of Initial and Final Position: In a sequence of people or things, the last is that with which the audience is supposed to identify or empathize.
- The Law of Action: The characteristics of people and things are expressed primarily through action and dialog rather than providing detailed descriptions or explanations of internal feelings or thoughts.

Olrik also noted that the plot is usually made of a single linear thread rather than multiple simultaneous branches, as is often the case in written literature. In a written text, a reader can review the text and reconstruct the narrative when they get lost, but in oral performance, the plot must be easy to follow and not require keeping track of multiple "theaters" where events are playing out.

Folklorists have noted that Olrik's laws are not universal to all cultures and genres and they underestimate the creativity of individual performers, who do not always stick to convention. Folklorists also observe that the expectations of audiences can change how a story is told. Regardless of these exceptions, Olrik's list provides useful guideliness for analyzing the structure of folktales, including those in Gaelic tradition.

Motifs are the basic building blocks of oral folktales. Folklorist Stith Thompson defined a motif as "the smallest element in a tale having the power to persist in tradition [that] may be centered on a certain type of character in a tale, sometimes on an action, sometimes on attendant circumstances of the action."[31] Motifs can serve to create conflict, flesh out characters, resolve predicaments, and develop the plot in many ways. The jealous stepmother, the assignment of impossible tasks, and the article of clothing that can uniquely identify someone (like Cinderella's shoe) are common motifs which can be found in folktales around the world.

Oral tradition is fluid and dynamic by definition. Stories can become more or less elaborate, gain details or lose them, as they pass from community to community, from person to person. There is no single definitive version of a folktale: it is instead always found in variation. Folklore has a natural predisposition toward diversity and variety.

About the Texts in This Volume

My goal in the selection of folktales for this volume is to represent the wide range and diversity of materials that exist in Gaelic tradition. Some of these tales have never been translated into English before; others were translated in the nineteenth century in a style that was deliberately old-fashioned or attempted to mimic idioms of Highland English, often derived from Gaelic, with which few people are familiar today. My translations are meant to render the folktales into standard contemporary English without taking too many liberties.

My translations occasionally expand on short phrases or unstated assumptions. Many stories are not as intact as they used to be. Many storytellers were out of practice when they were re-discovered and they left out parts of the tales. Transcribers were racing to keep up with oral performances and did not always capture all of the text verbatim. In addition, audiences would generally hear the same or related folktales many times and could extrapolate meaning from just a few words that audiences would now find truncated and cryptic.

I have prioritized texts in Scottish Gaelic, but I have used English versions of tales if they are particularly relevant and no Gaelic text is available. Gaelic names, words, phrases, couplets or verses were sometimes interspersed in the texts by the original writer. I have tried to make the tales consistent in terms of the presentation of language.

I have attempted to include material that represents the geographical spread of Gaelic oral tradition, including Kintyre, Perthshire, Aberdeenshire, Ross-shire, and Sutherland, as well as the Western Highlands and Western Isles. In fact, I have highlighted material from the parts of the Gàidhealtachd that have been under-represented in recent decades. I have also attempted to include diverse genres and themes of Gaelic folktales, and to the degree to which it is possible, offer a modicum of gender balance in terms of the subjects of tales and the tradition-bearers from whom they were collected.

Folklorists have created genre categories for oral folktales such as wonder tales, myths, legends, romantic tales, animal tales, and so on. I have not followed these classifications rigorously in dividing the Gaelic stories into chapters but have grouped them in a way that I think would be natural for Gaelic-speaking storytellers and audiences.[32] The introduction to each chapter explains the types of tales included and any cultural background or folklore terminology needed to understand the tales and analysis of them.

I have prefaced every tale with information about the storyteller and the fieldworker who collected it, whenever those details are available. I have attempted to explain aspects of Gaelic culture or history that are mentioned in tales the first time they appear in the volume. I also offer some of my own interpretations and observations on some of these folktales in order to try to decode their meaning and value from a Gaelic point of view. This is not to imply that there is only one, single, correct interpretation of the tales or set of tools to interpret them: they are rich in their symbolism and offer many potential readings and meanings.

Most of the Gaelic texts have never been edited to modern standards. I have attempted to update the orthography to make them accessible to contemporary readers, but I have used a more conservative orthography than the GOC standard dominant in Scotland at the present. I have left some words and spellings as they were, based on my intuition of the dialect in play, although it is not usually clear whether the idiosyncracies are that of the storyteller or the transcriber. Some transcribers were at pains to represent the oral performance on paper, abbreviating words (due to elision) and thus making them harder to find in a dictionary. I have generally restored them to fuller forms for the sake of clarity.

Names present some of the most difficult challenges in both Gaelic and English. I have attempted to update spellings in the Gaelic text if the current understanding of a place name provides an improvement over the form in the contemporary source. When there is a place or personal name with a well-established English equivalent, I have tended to use that in the translation. This is the case for all surnames and many personal names.

Even this, however, does not solve the complexities of names because the Highland naming system works according to very different principles than that in English.[33] Personal names in the tales are sometimes given as lines of descent, sometimes as first name and clan surname, and other times as a nickname. I have tended to translate the adjective used to create personal nicknames, such as *Fionnlagh Dubh* "Black-haired Finlay." Sometimes what appears to be a personal name is actually the honorary title of a clan chieftain: *Mac Iain*, for example, is the style of the chieftain of the MacDonalds of Glencoe, while *Mac 'ic Ailein* is the style of the chieftain of Clanranald.

There are occasionally illegible gaps and errors in the original texts that I have used for the sources of the tales. Whenever I have had to reconstruct or extrapolate text, I have marked it in angle brackets < >.

This volume presents just a tiny sliver of the many Scottish Gaelic folktales in existence waiting to be edited, translated, analyzed, and, most importantly, enjoyed as a lasting testimony to the literary prowess and cultural creativity of the Gaels.

Chapter One

Tales of Wonder

This chapter offers a small sampling of the kind of stories that most modern readers associate with the word "folktale": tales of wonder and imagination, associated nowadays with children's books and films by Disney and Pixar. They are generally understood to be works of the imagination and were enjoyed by Highlanders of all ages, not just children.

This type of tale is classified by folklorists as the International Wonder Tale, also known as the Wonder Tale, Magic Tale, Fairy Tale, or *Marchën*. These tales are meant primarily for entertainment, even though they may impart useful information or implicit life strategies as incidental aspects of the story.

International Wonder Tales have many common characteristics, regardless of the part of the world in which they are told. They generally depict an ordinary human's encounter with the supernatural world, which usually causes him or her to be endowed with extraordinary qualities, like magic or great strength. They may be set in the real world or some supernatural world, or some combination. The narrative usually exudes the atmosphere of the feudal age, with kings, queens, and knights, but no specific chronology. The International Wonder Tale contains layers of prehistoric totemism, medieval feudalism, and material from the local context in which the tale has been creatively adapted to suit the expectations of the audience.[1]

International Wonder Tales told in Highland communities tend to acquire Gaelic features: there is a preference for characters of aristocratic origin, especially with some connection to Ireland; famous heroes from established literary cycles, such as Cù Chulainn or Fionn mac Cumhaill, can get drawn into the cast of characters; dialog between characters may take the form of song or poetry for dramatic effect; formulaic passages told with poetic features (alliteration and rhyme) add to the linguistic artistry of the storyteller.[2]

Even if understood to be imaginary, Wonder Tales draw on the dramatic scenarios and conflicts of real life to add to their appeal and to give movement and tension to their plots: there are jealousies between family members, bitter rivalries between factions, tragic losses and accidents, likable heroes and despicable foes, acts of kindness and ill-will, and so on.

The psychoanalytical school of folktale analysis points to the ability of International Wonder Tales to represent personality traits and to symbolize aspects of human development or social conflicts. This has been an enduring approach to interpreting the meaning of folktales and arguing for their value to children. By using imaginary people and places as the backdrop for tales, difficult situations and events can be explored that might cause a defensive or guarded reaction if a person were confronted with them in literal terms. Social norms require that humans restrict their behavior and repress thoughts and emotions deemed to be unacceptable, but folktales can allow for the release of such repressed feelings in an encoded form as well as for the vicarious enjoyment of wishes and fantasies that cannot be fulfilled in real life.

Some folklorists have criticized the psychoanalytical approach for claiming a singular and oversimplified meaning for folktales that does not take into consideration what individual storytellers or specific cultures understood their meaning to be.

Regardless of how useful psychological interpretations of individual tales may be, John F. Campbell contended that storytelling contributed to the resilience and ebullience of Gaelic youth:

> There on winter nights, children with wondering eyes and mouths agape, sit in the ruddy light of the peat-fire, under the grey canopy of smoke, and listen breathless to these weird old myths. They cease to be ragged, bare-legged lads and lasses, with shock heads of dark or flaxen fair, unkempt and unshorn; they hear how the bold bard fought the dragon, and won the princess and the kingdom, and their spirits are up and doing like him. Potatoes and milk, wooden noggins and good horn-spoons cease to exist; while the golden basin and the giant's stores are spread before them by the eloquent voice and gesture of some grey wrinkled old man.
>
> And when the story ends, and the fire burns low, and they coil themselves up to rest in their cribs, lads and lasses dream on, and so they dream till they grow up, and grow old, and the old tale becomes a part of their quiet lives. The child's dream of romance is the bright spot in a dull round of hardship and toil, and the man never forgets it while he lives.[3]

From the beginning of the formal study of folktales in the early nineteenth century, scholars noticed that the same plots and sequences of motifs could be found in many different places far apart from one another. They began to catalog folktales and summarize their plot structures so that variations of the same stories could be recognized. Scholars began to ask how the stories had traveled—through the migration of people or of words from mouth to mouth?—and where stories might have originated.

John F. Campbell recognized the migratory nature of the texts he collected in the mid-nineteenth century, and in a characteristically colorful passage in the introduction to his pioneering volume *Popular Tales of the West Highlands*, he compared debris floating on ocean currents from the Americas to the shores of the Highlands to folktales passing from mouth to mouth until they finally reached the local *céilidhs*:

> As it is with drift-wood in the Highlands, so, as I imagine, it has been with popular tales everywhere. They are as old as the races who tell them, but the original ideas, like the trees from which logs, masts, and ships are made, have been broken up, cut, carved, and ornamented lost and found—wrecked, destroyed, broken, and put together again; and, though the original shape is hard to find, the fragments may be recognized in books, and wherever else they may now be found.[4]

Whole narrative plots as well as individual motifs can travel from community to community, across languages and continents. The first catalog of folktale types was published by the Finnish folklorist Antii Aarne in 1910 and American folklorist Stith Thompson revised it in 1961. The Aarne-Thompson index remains the standard means of classifying folktales, especially those of Eurasian origin. The German folklorist Hans-Jörg Uther further refined the catalog in 2004, so more recent folklore scholarship assigns tales an ATU number. The story of Cinderella, for example is indexed as ATU-510A.

It might easily be assumed that the borrowing of a tale into a community indicates a lack of creativity or a dependency on external sources for new ideas. We can instead recognize the fluidity of tradition and the creativity of storytellers to adapt tales to the tastes and expectations of their audiences. In other words, we can ask why certain plots, characters, and motifs appeal to a community and others do not, or how storytellers modify and ornament the tales they know to suit the preferences and conventions of a particular society.

The concept of the *ecotype* was briefly mentioned in the Introduction. This term refers to a specific restructuring of a tale within a particular cultural zone that tends to stay cohesive and consistent. International Wonder Tales that were borrowed into Gaelic tradition tend to have been adapted to reflect the natural environment, social norms, and cultural touchstones of the Gaelic world.

You do not have to subject folktales to any kind of academic scrutiny or classification scheme to enjoy them, however. You must simply suspend your disbelief and allow yourself to be led to a world long ago and far away.

The Frog Prince

John F. Campbell printed this story in *Popular Tales of the West Highlands* under the title "The Queen Who Wanted Pure Water from a Certain Well." Mrs. MacTavish of Port Ellen on Islay, one of the few women who collected Gaelic folklore in the nineteenth century, sent the tale to Campbell. Campbell tells us that she was one of his oldest friends, that she was brought up in a large family, and that she had an excellent memory that allowed her to learn many stories.

This is a variant of a tale type commonly known to folklorists as "The Frog Prince" after the title given to it by the Brothers Grimm in their 1812 collection of German folktales. They started their volume with that tale, considering it to be one of the "oldest and most beautiful in German-speaking regions." It appears elsewhere in Europe as well as in the Far East and is classified as ATU-440.

This Gaelic variant is shorter and more fragmentary than versions from the Scottish Lowlands or Germany but it has also accumulated other motifs. As in many folktales, it is not the older and more headstrong siblings who fulfill the responsibilities asked of them but the youngest and most humble. This text suggests that unexpected beauties or benefits may be hiding behind something that appears to be frightening or repulsive at a surface level. The repeated refrain of the frog in the original Gaelic was voiced so as to imitate the croaking of a frog.

Once upon a time there was a queen who was ill and she had three daughters. She said to the eldest daughter, "Go to the well of pure water and bring to me a drink to heal me."

The daughter went and arrived at the well. A frog appeared from down below and asked her if she would marry him if she got a drink for her mother.

"There is no way that I will marry you, you wretched creature!"

"Well, then," he said, "you won't get the water."

She went home and her mother sent the second daughter to get a drink of the water from the well. She arrived at the well and the frog appeared from down below and asked her if she would marry him if she got a drink for her mother.

"There is no way that I will marry you, you wretched creature!"

"Well, then," he said, "you won't get the water."

She returned home and the youngest daughter went to get the water from the well.

When she arrived at the well, the frog appeared from down below as usual and asked her if she would marry him if she got the water for her mother.

"If there is no other way for me to get a remedy for mother, I will marry you," she said. She got the water and she returned home.

They had just gone to rest that night when the frog came to the door saying, "O dear one, o dear one, do you remember the little promise that you made to me at the well? O darling, o darling."

He kept repeating this until the girl came to the door and let him inside. She put him in back of the door and went to lie down. She hadn't been lying down long when he began saying again, "O dear one, o dear one, do you remember the little promise that you made to me at the well? O darling, o darling."

He kept repeating this until she got up and put him under a wooden cup. That kept him quiet for a little while. She hadn't been lying down long when he began saying again, "O dear one, o dear one, do you remember the little promise that you made to me at the well? O darling, o darling."

She got up again and prepared a little bed for him at the side of the fire. But this did not satisfy him. As soon as she got back into her bed, he began saying again, "O dear one, o dear one, do you remember the little promise that you made to me at the well? O darling, o darling."

She got up then and made him a little bed right next to her own bed, but he was still restless, saying, "O dear one, o dear one, do you remember the little promise that you made to me at the well? O darling, o darling."

She paid no attention to his complaint until he told her, "There is an old, rusty sword behind your bed; it is better that you use it to take off my head than keep me in this state of agony."

She took the sword and she cut off his head. As soon as the steel touched him, he turned into a handsome youth, and he expressed his sincere gratitude to the maiden who was the means by which this enchantment, which he had endured for a long, long time, was removed from him.

He then got his kingdom—for he was a king—and he married the princess, and they lived for a long time together in happiness.[5]

Silver-Tree and Gold-Tree

The tale commonly called "Snow White" (ATU-709) is one of the best-known folktales in the world, with variants across the Eurasian landmass. Most of us know it today in the form in which it was adapted by Walt Disney as a film in 1937, but the name of the tale and the cast of characters differ greatly according to culture.

The following version was collected by the Rev. Kenneth Macleod, a native of the Isle of Eigg, from his home island in the third quarter of the nineteenth century. He gave it the title "Craobh-Airgid agus Craobh-Òir" ("Silver-Tree and Gold-Tree"). Two other variants of Snow White were collected in the Highlands in the nineteenth century, and folklore collectors have transcribed several others in Ireland.

The female characters in this Gaelic variant initiate most of the action and directly control most of the plot of this tale; the male characters are secondary. Rather than the familiar "jealous stepmother," the nemesis character is the birth mother of the vulnerable heroine who is in competition for the love of the husband/father. Some folklorists believe that this is the older and more authentic psychological dynamic of the tale.[6]

This text has received some characteristically Gaelic embellishments. In most of the variants collected in Scotland and Ireland, the queen's informant is a trout in a well rather than a talking mirror, which relates to ancient Gaelic ideas about poetic inspiration as well as more recent folk practices.[7] In Scottish Gaelic praise poetry, a person's qualifications as a leader can be asserted by depicting them at the helm of a ship,[8] which the queen does twice in this tale.

Once upon a time there was a king who had a wife, whose name was Silver-Tree, and a daughter, whose name was Gold-Tree. On a certain day of days, Gold-Tree and Silver-Tree went to a glen where there was a well, in which there was a trout.

Said Silver-Tree, "O little trout, o handsome little fellow, am not I the most beautiful queen in the world?"

"Oh! indeed, you are not."

"Who is then?"

"Gold-Tree, your daughter."

Silver-Tree went home and was blind with rage. She lay down on the bed, and she would never be well, until she would get the heart and the liver of Gold-Tree, her daughter, to eat.

At night-fall the king came home, and it was told to him that Silver-Tree, his wife, was very sick. He went where she was, and asked her what was wrong with her.

"Oh, only a thing which you may heal, if it be your will."

"Oh, indeed, there is nothing at all which I could do for you that I would not do."

"If I can get the heart and the liver of Gold-Tree, my daughter, to eat, I shall be well."

The king went and sent his lads to the hunting-hill for a male goat, and he gave its heart and its liver to his wife to eat; and she rose well and healthy.

What happened about this time was that the son of a great king came from overseas to ask to marry Gold-Tree. The king agreed to this, and they went overseas.

A year after this Silver-Tree went to the glen, where there was a well in which there was the trout.

"O little trout, o handsome little fellow," said she, "am not I the most beautiful queen in the world?"

"Oh, indeed, you are not."

"Who is, then?"

"Gold-Tree, your daughter."

"Oh, well, she has not lived for a long time. It is a year since I ate her heart and liver."

"Indeed, she is not dead. She is married to a great prince overseas."

Silver-Tree went home, and made the king put his sailing ship in order, so that she could go to see her dear Gold-Tree, since she had not seen her for a long time. The sailing ship was put in order, and they sailed away. It was Silver-Tree herself that was at the helm, and she steered the ship so well that they were not long at all before they arrived.

The prince was out in the hunting-hill. Gold-Tree knew the sailing ship of her father coming. "Oh!" said she to the servants, "my mother is coming, and she will kill me."

"She will not kill you at all; we will lock you in a room where she will not get near you."

That is what they did; and when Silver-Tree came ashore, and she began to cry out, "Come to meet your own mother, since she has come to see you."

Gold-Tree said that she could not, that she was locked in the room, and that she could not get out of it.

"Will you not put out," said Silver-Tree, "your little finger through the key-hole, so that your own mother may give a kiss to it?"

She put out her little-finger, and Silver-Tree went and stabbed it with poison, and Gold-Tree fell dead.

When the prince came home, and found Gold-Tree dead, he fell into a great sadness, and she was so beautiful that he did not bury her at all, but locked her in a room where nobody would get near her.

In the space of time he married again, and the whole house was under the control of this wife except for one room, and he himself kept the key to that room. On a certain day of days he forgot to bring the key with him, and the second wife got into the room. What did she see there but the most beautiful woman that she had ever seen.

She began to turn her and examine her, and she noticed the poisoned barb in her finger. She took the barb out, and Gold-Tree returned to life, as beautiful as she was ever.

At the fall of night the prince came home from the hunting-hill, looking very downcast.

"What would you bet me," said his wife, "that I could make you laugh?"

"Oh! indeed, nothing would make me laugh, except if Gold-Tree came back to life."

"Well, she is alive down there in the room."

When the prince saw Gold-Tree alive he rejoiced, and he began to kiss her, and kiss her, and kiss her. Said the second wife, "Since she is the first one you had, it is better for you to stick with her, and I will go away."

"Indeed, you will not go away, but I shall have both of you."

At the end of the year Silver-Tree went to the glen, where there was the well, in which there was the trout. "O little trout, o handsome little fellow," said she, "am not I the most beautiful queen in the world?"

"Indeed, you are not."

"Who is, then?"

"Gold-Tree, your daughter."

"She is not alive. It is a year since I stabbed her finger with poison."

"Indeed, she is not dead; she certainly is not."

Silver-Tree went home, and made the king put his sailing ship in order, so that she could go to see her dear Gold-Tree, since she had not seen her for a long time. The sailing ship was put in order, and they sailed away. It was Silver-Tree herself that was at the helm, and she steered the ship so well that they were not long at all before they arrived.

The prince was out in the hunting-hill. Gold-Tree recognized her father's sailing ship coming.

"Oh," said she, "my mother is coming and she will kill me."

"Not at all," said the second wife, "we will go down to meet her."

Silver-Tree came ashore. "Come down, Gold-Tree, my love," said she, "since your own mother has come to you with a precious drink."

"It is a custom in this country," said the second wife, "that the person who offers a drink take a swallow out of it first."

Silver-Tree put her mouth to it, and the second wife went and knocked it down her throat, and she fell dead. They had only to carry home the dead corpse and bury her.

The prince and his two wives were long alive after this, happy and peaceful. I left them there.[9]

The Grazing of Cruachan

The Rev. Duncan MacInnes transcribed the following tale between 1881 and 1882 from Archibald MacTavish, a shoemaker in Oban. This is a variant of the tale known to folklorists as "Ogre's Heart in the Egg" (ATU-302), which can be found all across Eurasia.

This is a perfect exemplar of an International Wonder Tale: the plot is easy to follow; it has lots of repetition, often in threes; the characters are clearly distinguished from one another; it has animal helpers and magical objects. Readers of the *Harry Potter* series will recognize the origin of the idea of the "horcrux" in the motif of the hidden life-force.

Typically Gaelic elements have been added to the story. The heroes play shinty, for example. The imaginary kingdom *Sorcha*, translated here as "Lightland," features in many medieval Gaelic romances.

The Gaelic placename "Cruachan" can be found in both Scotland and Ireland and describes a large, conical mountain. What is at stake for the hero in the tale is the right to continue to hold the land centered at Cruachan where he grazes his cattle. The title "herdsman" in English is too humble and mundane for what would have been a high social rank in a pastoral economy. The storyteller breaks with the title "herdsman" once and calls him "the son of the King of Cruachan," alluding to a more elevated social position.

The herdsman of Cruachan had three sons. He became sick with a fatal disease and sent for his eldest son to come to speak to him. The son came and his father said to him, "My son, the reason why I have sent for you is that I am not likely to be long in this world, and I wish you to take the grazing of Cruachan."

His son said to him, "I will not take it nor thank you for the offer of it."

And his father said, "Ask your middle brother to come here to speak to me."

The middle son came and said, "Father, what do you want with me?"

His father said, "I wish to know if you will take the grazing of Cruachan?"

His son said, "I will not nor thank you for the offer of it."

His father said to him, "Ask your young brother come here."

His young son came and said to his father, "What do you want with me today, father?"

And his father said to him, "It looks as though I am near to death."

The son said, "I will take the grazing of Cruachan."

His father then said, "When I die and you have buried me, you will in a day or two set out to go around Cruachan, and you will go round it once and go round it twice, and you will sit on a pleasant, green-sided hillock on which the sun rises early and sets late. And there will come to you a young, curly-locked, brown-haired nobleman[10] with a gold ball and silver shinty stick who will say to you, 'You must play with me today, young son. You have lost Cruachan.' You will then say to him, 'Who would say that I must not?' And you will play together on that day. And he will say to you, 'Choose your reward for winning,' And you will say, 'My reward for winning is the best woman on your estate.' He will then bring you to his estate and show you women as beautiful as you ever saw, but you will take none of them. You will see a small, untidy, swarthy woman cleaning the byre, and you shall say to the nobleman, 'That is the woman that I will have.' And he will give her to you and you will marry her and bring her home. And she will tell you everything that you should do. Farewell now! And may Cruachan bring you prosperity."

His father then died and was buried. And the first day that he set off to go around Cruachan, he went round it once and went around it twice, and he sat on a pleasant, green-sided hillock on which the sun rises early and sets late. And the young, curly-locked, brown-haired nobleman came where he was with a gold ball and a silver shinty stick and said to him, "Must you play with me today, young son? You have lost Cruachan."

The young herdsman said, "Who would say that I must not?"

They played that day hotly and keenly. The son of the King of Cruachan won and the nobleman said, "Choose your reward for winning."

And the herdsman said, "My reward for winning is the best woman on your estate."

The nobleman then brought him to women as beautiful as could be seen. And he saw a small, untidy, swarthy woman cleaning the byre and said, "That is the woman that I will have."

He then brought her home and married her.

The next day he set off to go around Cruachan again. And he went around it once and went round it twice, and he sat on a pleasant, green-sided hillock on which the sun rises early and sets late. And the young, curly-locked, brown-haired nobleman came where he was with a gold ball and silver shinty stick and said to him, "Must you go to play with me today, young son? You have lost Cruachan."

The young herdsman said, "Who would say that I must not?"

They played that day hotly and keenly. The son of the King of Cruachan won and the nobleman said to him, "Choose your reward for winning."

And he said, "My reward for winning is the best filly on your estate."

The nobleman then took him to fillies as beautiful as could be seen. And he saw a pale, shaggy filly, and said, "That is the filly that I will have." He took the filly with him and went home.

His wife said to him, "How did you fare today?"

"Well," said he, "I have won the day."

The next morning he set off to go around Cruachan. And he went around it once and went around it twice, and he sat on a pleasant, green-sided hillock on which the sun rises early and sets late. And the young, curly-locked, brown-haired nobleman came where he was and said to him, "Must you go to play with me today? You have lost Cruachan."

The herdsman said, "Who would say that I must not?"

They played that day hotly and keenly. The herdsman of Cruachan lost the day, and said to the nobleman, "Choose your reward for winning."

"The reward for my winning is," said the nobleman, "that you get for me the White Sword of Light that the King of Lightland has."

The herdsman went home that evening and when he reached his house neither his wife nor the shaggy dun filly was to be found. The big giant, the King of Lightland, came, and stole away his wife and the pale, shaggy filly. He passed that night in his own house and went to bed. When morning came he made breakfast for himself, and set off in search of his wife and the filly. He baked a bannock to take with him, and departed.

He traveled for a long time, until at last his soles were blackened and his cheeks were sunken, the yellow-headed birds were going to rest at the roots of the bushes and the tops of the thickets, and the dark clouds of night were coming and the clouds of day were departing. And he saw a house far from him, and although it was far from him, he did not take long to reach it. He went in, and sat in the upper end of the house. And there was no one indoors. And the fire was newly kindled, the house newly swept, and the bed newly made.

And who came in but the hawk of Glencuaich and it said to him, "Are you here, o young son of Cruachan?"

"I am," he said.

The hawk said to him, "Do you know who was here last night?"

"I do not," he said.

"The big giant, the King of Lightland, your wife, and the pale, shaggy filly were here," it said. "And the giant was threatening horrifically that if he could get hold of you, he would cut off your head."

"I well believe it," he said.

It then gave him food and drink and sent him to bed. It rose in the morning, made breakfast for him, and baked a bannock for him that he would have on his journey. And he went away. In the evening he saw a house far from him, and although it was far from him, he did not take long to reach it. He went in, and sat in the upper end of the house. And the fire was newly kindled, the house newly swept, and the bed newly made. The green-headed duck came in, and said to him, "Are you here, o herdsman of Cruachan?"

"I am," he said.

"Do you know," it said, "who was here last night?"

"I do not," said he.

"The big giant, the King of Lightland, your wife, and the pale, shaggy filly were here," it said. "And the giant was threatening that if he had you, he would cut off your head."

"I thoroughly believe you," he said.

It prepared food and drink for him, and sent him to bed. It arose next morning and made breakfast for him, and baked a bannock, which it sent with him for the journey. He then set off and went on his way. He was walking on all day long, and in the evening he saw a little house far from him, and although it was far from him, he did not take long to reach it. He went in, and sat in the upper end of the house. And the fire was newly kindled, the house newly swept, and the bed newly made. The fox of the scrubwood then came in and said to him, "Are you here, o herdsman of Cruachan?"

"I am," he said.

"Do you know who was here last night?" said the fox.

"I do not," he said.

"The big giant, the King of Lightland, your wife, and the pale, shaggy filly were here," said the fox. "And the giant was threatening horrifically that if you were here, he would cut your head off."

"I do believe it," said the herdsman of Cruachan.

It gave him food and drink, and sent him to bed. The fox arose in the morning, and baked a bannock, which it sent with him for his journey. He then set off, and went on his way. In the evening he saw a house far from him, and although it was far from him, he did not take long to reach it. He went in, and sat in the upper end of the house. The fire was newly kindled, the house was newly swept, and the bed was newly made. And the brown otter of the stream came in and said to him, "Are you here, o herdsman of Cruachan?"

"I am," he said.

"Do you know," said the brown otter of the stream, "who was here last night?"

"I do not," said the herdsman.

"The big giant, the King of Lightland, your wife, and the pale, shaggy filly were here," said the brown otter. "And the giant was threatening that if he had you here, he would cut your head off."

"I do believe it," said the herdsman of Cruachan.

It gave him food and drink, and sent him to bed. And when he first awakened in the morning, he saw the hawk of Glencuaich, the green-headed duck, the fox of the scrubwood, and the brown otter of the stream dancing together on the floor. They then prepared breakfast, and had it together, and said to him, "Should you be at any time in urgent need, think of us and we will help you."

After that he bade them farewell, and went away.

On the evening of that day he arrived at the cave where the big giant, the King of Lightland, was living. And who was in before him but his own wife. The big giant was away from home, hunting. She gave her husband food, and hid him in the upper end of the cave, and put clothes over him to keep him hidden.

The big giant came home and said, "Ee! Oh! Hohageech! The smell of a stranger is in the cave."

"No, my love," said she, "it is only a little bird of the air that I have roasted that you smell."

"Oh! If that is the case, then I don't care," he said.

She then said to him, "I wish that you would tell me where your life-force is kept, so that I may take good care of it."

"It is in a grey stone over there," he said.

When he went away next day, she brought in the grey stone, and dressed it well, and placed it in the upper end of the cave.

When the giant came home in the evening he said to her, "What is that there that you have dressed?"

"Your life-force," she said, "and we must be careful with it."

"I notice that you are very fond of me, but that is not where it is," said he.

"Where is it ?" she said.

"It is in a grey sheep on yonder hillside," he said.

When he went away the next morning, she got hold of the grey sheep, took it in, dressed it well, and placed it in the upper end of the cave.

When he came home in the evening he said to her, "What is it that you have dressed there?"

She said, "Your own life-force, my love."

And he said, "That is not where it is."

"Well!" she said. "You are putting me to great trouble taking care of it, and you have not told me the truth these two times."

He then said, "I think that I may tell it to you now. My life-force is below the feet of the big horse in the stable. There is a place down there in which there is a small lake. Over the lake are seven grey hides, and over the hides are seven sods from the heath, and under all these are seven oak planks. There is a trout in the lake, and a duck in the belly of the trout, an egg in the belly of the duck, and a thorn of blackthorn inside of the egg. And until that thorn is chewed into a small splinter I cannot be killed. Whenever the seven grey hides, the seven sods from the heath, and the seven oak planks are touched, I can feel it wherever I am. I have an axe above the door and unless all those are cut through with one blow of it, the lake cannot be reached. And when it will be reached I will feel it."

When he went off next day to the hunting hill, his wife said to the herdsman, "Shouldn't we try to cut through the hides, sods, and planks with the axe?"

"Yes, we had better," said he.

They then went out to the stable and the herdsman took hold of the axe in order to strike the spot with it, when the big dappled horse said, "You hold the axe and I will strike it."

The herdsman of Cruachan held the axe on the top of the seven grey hides, the seven sods, and the seven oak planks and the big dappled horse rose on his fore-legs, and drove the axe through them until it reached the lake. The trout then sprang out of the lake into a flowing river and they could not catch it.

"Ah!" said the herdsman. "If I had the brown otter of the stream it would not take long to catch the trout."

The brown otter of the stream came and said, "What do you wish, young son? You have lost Cruachan."

"I wish that you would get the trout that has leaped into the river for me," said the herdsman.

Out into the river went the brown otter and he found the trout and gave it to the herdsman of Cruachan. The herdsman of Cruachan opened the trout and a duck sprang out of its belly and flew into the air and he could not get it and he said, "If I had the hawk of Glencuaich, it would not take long to catch the duck."

The hawk came and said to him, "What do you wish, o herdsman of Cruachan?"

"I wish that you would catch the duck that is flying away there."

The hawk went after the duck and caught it. The herdsman opened the belly of the duck and an egg sprang out of it into the air. He then said, "If I had the green-headed duck, it would not take long to find the egg for me."

The duck came and said to him, "What do you wish, o herdsman of Cruachan?"

He said, "Go as fast as you can and get the egg that has sprung into the air. The big giant is coming here."

The green-headed duck went and got the egg and he broke it and the thorn sprang out of it and went into a thorn-bush that was near him. And he could not distinguish it from any other thorn when he began to search for it. The giant was coming, and drawing near him and he said, "Ah! If I had the fox of the green-wood, he would not take long to find the thorn for me."

The fox came and said to him, "What do you wish, o herdsman of Cruachan?"

He said to the fox, "Go as fast as you ever went and find for me the thorn that has sprung out of the egg. It is in that thorn-bush."

The fox went and got the thorn and gave it to the herdsman of Cruachan. And he chewed it and the giant, who was within twenty yards of him, fell down there cold and dead. The herdsman and his wife spent that night in the cave. And they took away with them all the gold and silver that the giant had, his White Sword of Light, the big dappled horse, and the pale, shaggy filly. She rode the filly and he rode the horse home to Cruachan.

They were to go around Cruachan the next day and he took with him the White Sword of Light. When he was setting off, his wife said to him, "The young nobleman will come to meet you and you shall hand him the sword. And he will say to you, 'Is there a sword like mine anywhere in the whole wide world?' and you will say to him, 'There is none anywhere, except for one small flaw that it has,' and he will say to you, 'Show me the flaw.' As he intends to cut your head off, you will catch the sword to show him the flaw and then you shall draw it and cut his head off and say, 'That is the flaw that it has.'" He set off this day and went around Cruachan once and went around it twice and he sat on a pleasant, green-sided hillock on which the sun rises early and sets late, and he saw the curly-locked, brown-haired nobleman coming.

"Have you come, o herdsman of Cruachan?" said the nobleman.

"I have, once again," said the herdsman.

"Have you got the White Sword of Light for me?" said the nobleman.

"I have," said he, and he handed it to him.

The nobleman said to him, "Is there a sword like mine anywhere in the whole wide world?"

"There is none anywhere," said the herdsman, "except for one small flaw that it has."

"Show me the flaw," said the nobleman.

"Put the sword in my hand," said the herdsman, "and I will show you the flaw."

The herdsman then drew the sword and swept the nobleman's head off and said, "That is the flaw."

He left him dead there and he returned home. And he enjoyed the grazing of Cruachan for as long as he lived.[11]

The Language of Birds

The Islay schoolmaster Hector MacLean transcribed this tale in 1860 from Janet Currie of South Uist, a descendant of the famous MacMhuirich Gaelic literary dynasty who served the Clan Donald for many centuries. She told MacLean that the tale could ultimately be traced back to Niall MacMhuirich (c. 1637–1726), the last fully functioning official poet of Clanranald. This gives the tale added significance and suggests that it reflects something about the interests of the native learned classes.

This tale, classified as ATU-671 ("The Three Languages"), includes many common motifs: a prophecy of changed fortunes alienates parents from their son; a parent commands someone to kill his child but he takes mercy on the child and feigns its death;

an unrecognizable hero displays a ring given in the past that reveals his identity. This Gaelic tale is situated on the continent of Europe in its entirety and features aristocrats from France, Spain, and Greece.

Axel Koehler has recently traced the remarkable origins of this tale to a tract often called "The Seven Sages" in English. This cycle of stories reached Europe in about the twelfth century through contact with the Islamic world. It is likely that a manuscript of these tales was brought into the Gaelic world by the Anglo-Normans no later than the fifteenth century and some of the texts were translated into Scottish Gaelic in the seventeenth century by a professional poet likely associated with the MacMhuirich dynasty. Despite the popularity of "The Seven Sages" in continental Europe and anglophone Britain, however, it made relatively minor impact on the Gaelic world. The two tales that did enter Gaelic oral tradition must have done so because they appealed to Gaelic sensibilities and subject matters.[12]

There is a great deal of Gaelic lore about the language of birds, such as the imitation of bird song. From at least the mid-eighteenth century there were Gaelic poets who declaimed that they were the metaphorical mavis of their clan. This association with bird song, and the pretensions of occult knowledge and powers claimed by the poets, may have drawn the Gaelic literati to this tale. Like the protagonist Alastair, they were very conscious that language is a form of power that can make or break kings.

One of the main themes in the tale is the contrast between the bonds of biology and those of fosterage and affection: the biological father rejects the son, who is later adopted by the mariner; the flock of birds that afflicts the king is in a quarrel about whether the biological mother or the father who took over the responsibility of incubating the egg should have custody over the chick; the King and Queen of Spain are so attached to Alastair that they sacrifice their own children for his sake. This theme would have appealed to professional poets whose long and arduous apprenticeship in their youth was likened to adoption by a master-poet and who, upon completion of their education, could be grafted onto the family structure of the clan who hired them. Conflicts of identity and allegiance were inevitable, but the idea that the male bird who incubated the egg has a greater claim to it than the biological mother is consistent with the Gaelic ideals of fosterage.

There was once an old French knight and he had an only son. The knight did not know how he could give him a better education than others had. His son's name was Alastair.

After giving him all sorts of education, he decided to send him to the Island of Birds, to learn the language of birds. He was therefore sent to the island with enough provisions for a year and a day to learn the language of birds.

After a year and a day, he was taken from the island, and his father said to him, "What have I gained after a year by having you in the Island of Birds?"

The boy said, "I can see something."

"Did I gain nothing else?" said the father.

"No," said the son.

"I'm sending you back for another year," said the father.

So he sent him back for another year. After that year was over, he came back, and the father said, "What have I gained after a year by having you in the Island of Birds?"

The boy said, "I can see something and I can hear something."

"Did I gain nothing else?" said the father.

"No," said the son.

"I'm sending you back for a third year," said the father.

So he sent him back for a third year. After that year was over, he came back, and the knight said, "What have I gained by having you there for a third year?"

"I can see something, I can hear something, and I can understand something," said the son.

The next morning, a finch leapt up to the window tweeting. The knight said to his son, "What is he saying?"

"It doesn't matter what he's saying," answered the son.

"I will not ignore that and your effort is in vain," said the knight to him. "That is the first puzzle I've given you and you must solve it."

"Well, then," said the son, "if I must answer that, the finch was saying that you will untie the laces of my shoe with your teeth and that my mother will hold the washing basin for me with a towel in her hand."

"If that is the case, that I am to become as debased in my life as that," said his father, "you will not survive to give me that offense."

The next morning, the knight sent word to his four foster-brothers to drown the boy. It was difficult for those foster-brothers to do this, but to fulfill his request, each one of them dressed the boy with a part of their own clothing and his clothes were sent to his father to make it look like he had died. They sent him back to the Island of Birds where he had been before and he stayed for another three years.

When the birds recognized him, they gathered around him, and he killed and ate them, so that he could get whatever he lacked of the language of birds in another three years.

After another three years had passed, his hair and fingernails and toenails had become overgrown. He saw a boat passing by and began to shout at the people onboard, but he was so hideous that they were afraid of him and they would not take him with them at all. One of them said that even though he was hideous that he seemed to be human and so he went to retrieve him.

He asked, once he had him on board, "What crime did you commit?"

"I didn't do anything," said the lad. "I was on another boat, and I went ashore here, and the boat left me here."

"Well, I never had any children," said the captain. "If you will agree to be my son, I will be your father."

They came to land in Paris, France, where the king lived. The captain took the lad to his house and he said to his wife, "I had a son out of wedlock. I have never brought him home until now."

His wife made a big fuss when she saw the lad. She told her husband that there was some important news in the kingdom, that there were three short-tailed, black ravens that had been causing problems for the king's palace for three years. They would fly away every day, and they would come back every night, screeching and shrieking into the chimney of the room in which the king slept. The king made a pronouncement that if he could find any man who could put a stop to the ravens, that that man could marry his daughter and have half of his kingdom.

"Well, then," said the lad, "given those conditions, I would put a stop to the ravens."

"Well," said the captain, "If you do, I will be happy forever and will be able to retire from sailing."

The captain went to the king and he said to him, "Given those conditions, I have a son who will put a stop to the ravens."

The king told him to fetch the lad. He went back then to the house and he brought the lad to the king and he got the conditions written on a contract from the king. This is what the lad said to the king:

"You had a famine three years ago and it caused famine among birds as well as people. There was a female raven and a male raven living together and the female raven laid three eggs. After she had sat warming the eggs with only a week before they would hatch, she said that she would depart and leave them because she had to keep herself alive. 'Oh dear,' said the male raven, 'I'll return myself to see if I can hatch the chicks.' So the male raven returned and hatched out one of the chicks but one of the others died. When the famine was over, the female raven returned and began to hatch out the third raven but it died on her, and now she had neither egg nor chick. She began to assert her claim to the first egg, saying that it was her own, since she had laid the egg. 'Well,' said the male raven, 'if I had left it as you did, it would have died like the others, and so you have no claim over it.' And so, until you bring justice to the matter, o king, of who the egg belongs to, they will continue to come to you."

"And which of them," said the king, "has the right to the chick?"

"You are the one who must do justice," said the lad.

"I myself think," said the king, "that it is the male raven who has the right to the chick, since he is the one who stayed and hatched it."

"Then all you have to do," said the lad, "is to say, when the ravens come tonight, 'O male raven, the chick is yours; the female has no part of it.'"

That very night, when the ravens came, the king did justice for them and he used Alastair's words.

The male raven and the chick left then, and they circled clockwise around the palace but the female raven circled counter-clockwise around the palace.

As the birds left, the contract now had to be fulfilled. When the king saw after time had passed that the ravens no longer came to harass him, he stated that the lad had to be rewarded according to the contract. Indeed, as per the contract, he and the king's daughter were married, and he got half of the kingdom.

It wasn't long after that that the king died and the lad was crowned king of France. After he was married, since no one knew who he was, he was not allowed near his wife. He was sent for a year to a king who taught manners to the children of kings. There were two other royal children there: Ludovic, the son of the King of Spain, and David, the son of the King of Greece.

The King of Manners had a beautiful daughter and Ludovic, the son of the King of Spain, was courting her. If her father were to find out that they were sweethearts, he would give them a thrashing.

When Alastair came, Ludovic, the son of the King of Spain, made fast friends with him, and he parted company with the son of the King of Greece, because he knew that Alastair was married and that he didn't have to suspect him of courting any woman.

Alastair began to woo the daughter on behalf of the other man. He acted as intermediary between them all that year. When the year was over, Alastair went home.

The son of the King of Greece let it be known that the daughter and the son of the

King of Spain had been courting. When her father heard this, he sent for them to fight each other, believing that the liar would lose.

The daughter said to the son of the King of Spain, "It's a pity that Alastair isn't here. I'm afraid that you will lose."

So he left, and he reached France, and he went to where Alastair was, and when Alastair saw him, he asked him what was wrong, and he told him. Alastair took off the clothes that he was wearing, and said to the other, "Go on, and take my place until I return."

Alastair left and arrived at the house of the King of Manners. He struck the son of the King of Greece and he wounded him, and he said to the King, "Is that enough?"

The King said that it was and that the only thing left was to drive off the man who had lied back home to Greece. Alastair returned to France, and spent two nights on the road. He returned home. He went to lie down with his wife for two nights. Then the third night came. He went to lie down that night with his wife, and she said to him, "Why aren't you doing tonight what you did last night and the night before that?"

"What was that?" he asked.

"You put a naked sword between me and you last night and the night before."

"That will no longer be here," he said. "That was just a little vow I made to my mother, to stay away from a woman for that length of time but the sword will not be here any longer."

Malicious people began to say that no-one knew who his father or grandfather was—that he was only a man who was found on an island in the ocean. They were trying to convince her of this. They finally persuaded her to make poison and to give it to him, until his hair fell out.

He was driven out of the kingdom and she married another king.

He wandered for four years until he found out where the son of the King of Spain was, who was now the king himself. Alastair reached the kitchen of the King of Spain was but he was not allowed to stay there.

"Before I leave," he said, "tell the female servant to come over to me."

The female servant went over to him and he asked her, in the name of God, to take him where the King of Spain was.

"Anything," she said, "that you ask of me in the name of God, I will do it."

The female servant went to the queen and she asked her to bring him to her. He had become quite hideous and ghastly, from all that happened to him. He went inside where she was and she had a glass in her hand. She filled up the glass for him and he drank it, and after he drank it, he let the ring drop into the bottom of it. When she noticed the ring, she took it out, and saw that her name was on it.

"Who gave this to you?" she asked.

"You did," he said.

"That's to say," she said, "that you are Alastair."

"Yes, that's me," he said.

People all overheard what the French had done to him. They ordered for him to be cleaned and they clothed him in the clothes of the king, and gave him a room.

When the King of Spain came home, the queen said to him, "What man would find it most difficult to be a hairless, mangy servant in the kingdom?"

"Oh dear," he said, "That would be Alastair."

"Yes," she said, "and he is in a pitiful state."

They both went over to where he was and the three of them wept sorely. Despite how hideous he had become, they insisted that he go with them to eat their mid-day meal. They sent him to rest again.

The King of Spain also went to sleep. What did the king hear in his sleep but a voice saying to him, "If the blood of your children were to be drawn from their three breasts and he were bathed in it, he would become as handsome as he was before."

The king arose early and he slit the throats of the children and he bathed Alastair with their blood, and he became as handsome as he had been before. The king then went to his wife, and he said to her, "What would you sacrifice in order for Alastair to be as handsome as he was the day that he struck the son of the King of Greece on my behalf?"

"I've never seen anything," she said, "that I would not sacrifice for him, but you yourself."

"Would you sacrifice your three children?" asked the king.

"I would," she answered.

They went to where Alastair was and the three of them went to lament the children where they were lying. There were three necklaces on the children and they were playing in bed. They realized that it was a miracle from God and they gave thanks to God and they were happy and joyful together.

The King of Spain was away from home the next morning, and the day after that, and the day after that, and no one knew what he was doing while he was away the three days. After the third day, he said to Alastair, "Go and tidy yourself up. I have raised an army in order to win your kingdom for you."

"I will not go," answered Alastair. "I will never part from you."

Nothing would satisfy the king but to set off with the army himself. They came upon France unawares, and they inflicted ruin upon every man, and he killed the king in front of the queen. She asked for mercy for herself, and she said that there was never a day that she did not regret parting from Alastair.

Alastair was crowned the King of France as he had been before. He would go to the hunting-hill every day and he started to inquire whether his father, the old knight, who had been in a corner of France, was still alive. He found out that he was alive but that he had become so poor that he was in need of charity.

Alastair left and he wrote to the knight telling him that the King of France was coming for a night's lodging with him. The old knight sent a message in return that he was so poor that he could not offer him a night's lodging, that there was a time that he was able to do so, but now he could not offer it even to someone below him in rank.

The king took off for the knight's house. The knight was inside and was obligated to accept him when he arrived.

"If you were knight of this place," said the king, "you certainly have fallen on hard times!"

"Indeed, I have!" said the knight.

"Did you ever have any children?" asked the king, "who could keep up your affairs better than this?"

"No," answered the knight, "except for an only son, and he left and is no longer living. It's no wonder that I'm poor!"

In any case, the king took a bed that night and slept. When he arose in the morning, the old knight tried to loosen up the king's shoes and there was a tight knot on the laces, so he put his teeth on them to loosen them. The knight's wife came over with a towel and basin of water.

"Oh, mother!" said the king. "Set that down on the floor and let go of the towel. The finch's words have been fulfilled."

She fell into a swoon.

"If that's true," said the knight, "I deserve to be killed."

"There's no way to know," said the king, "if I would have been king unless these things had happened. But you will never have to beg again."

And then I parted with them.[13]

Great Seanchan and the Smith of the Tales

Monsignor Patrick J. Nicholson (1887–1965) recorded this tale from Peter Currie (1868–1944) of MacAdam's Lake, Cape Breton, in 1938 and contributed it to the Gaelic column in *The Casket* that he edited in Nova Scotia, as well as to a fledgling Celtic Studies periodical at Columbia University that same year.

Nicholson says that he heard this tale several times in his boyhood in Beaver Cove, Cape Breton, a community that consisted mostly of immigrants from the islands of South Uist and Barra. Inspired by the work that Scottish folklorist John L. Campbell had done in Cape Breton, Nicholson returned to the island himself and recorded several folktales from Peter Currie.[14] This text provides us with more evidence of the rich inheritance of the MacMhuirich literary dynasty that extended even into the North American diaspora.

This tale is littered with allusions to literary characters, motifs, and phrases connected to the erudite learning of the Gaelic poetic order and the aura of magic they cultivated. Seanchan is the name of a famous character in medieval Gaelic literature who was supposed to have retrieved the epic tale *Táin Bó Cuailgne* from the memory of the dead. He was also understood to be the founder of poetic bands who roamed Scotland and Ireland, engaging in poetic duels with people who were forced to provide them with hospitality or be insulted with satires.[15]

This tale reflects the rivalries that often flared up between the professional poets who flourished into the seventeenth century. In this case, the children of Seanchan are able to trick the Smith into divulging arcane lore to them so that they can enhance their father's intellectual predominance. Iain is able to procure knowledge of a cosmological nature, while Young Donald learns about the most appropriate etiquette for storytelling at *céilidhs*.

The feigned dispute between the brothers at the tree, meant to confuse and deflect the Smith, draws on learned symbolism of the literary order. Poets were said to have had branches of Otherworld trees as emblems of their office, and the ogham alphabet was named and described using the names of trees. The terms *cam* ("crooked") and *dìreach* ("straight") were used of the different types of verse composed by the poets.[16]

The final episode in this composite story is known to folklorists as "The Man Who Had No Story to Tell." It is widespread in Gaelic Scotland and Ireland. The story gives a man who otherwise has nothing to share at a *céilidh* an extraordinary experience in which he changes gender and has a life as a woman, wife, and mother before returning excited to share the tale. This gender-bending narrative can be traced back to the medieval Irish tale of the Abbot of Druiménaig.[17]

There was once a famous Irishman who was so learned that he was given the nickname Great Seanchan. The nobility and scholars would come from all corners to seek his counsel, and seldom was a question posed to him that he could not answer.

But there were three things in particular of which he was ignorant and there was not a living person alive in the world who knew of them, apart from the man who was called the Smith of the Tales, who lived in Scotland.

Great Seanchan had three sons who were responsible and renowned, and it also vexed them that there could be anyone on earth who was wiser than their father.

One day, Young Donald, the youngest son, said, "It is my opinion that we ought to leave our fine home and to go to find employment. It is said that the Smith of the Tales is hiring man-servants, and we are likely to get employment from him, and more."

With the approval and blessing of their father, the three departed. They arrived at their destination at a good time. The Smith of the Tales asked Iain, the oldest son, what work he preferred, and he answered that it was cooking.

Then he asked Donald, the middle son, what he would like to do, and he said it was gardening.

When the same question was asked of Young Donald, he answered, "All I ever did was read and tell my father tales."

"You seem to be very capable, lads," said the Smith of the Tales. "I will hire the three of you and I will set each one to the responsibility he prefers."

At an appropriate time, the new servants were directed to their sleeping quarters and then all those indoors went to rest. When the three brothers were by themselves, Young Donald advised Iain what he ought to do the next day.

Early in the morning, each one was doing his own duty and everything was progressing in an orderly fashion. But at the peak of the afternoon, one of the servants came to the Smith in a frenzy and he said that the cook had lost his mind.

"Come here," he said, "and see what he is doing."

The Smith of the Tales went out and he found Iain a short distance from the house with a roast-spit in his hand. The next moment, he would thrust the spit into the ground as far as that could be done. The next moment, he would pull it out, stand on his tippy-toes, and he would lift it as high as he could.

The Smith asked what the meaning was of this behavior.

"It is just this," said Iain. "My mind was restless because I did not know which goes further, the earth's crust[18] below us or the sky above us."

"Well, lad," said the Smith of the Tales, "whatever was heard about the earth's crust below us, no account was ever heard about the skies above us."

When the house went to rest that night, Young Donald settled what should happen the next day. After getting put into motion in the morning, things progressed well until word came to the man of the house that something had gone wrong with the gardener. The Smith hurried outside and he found Donald had abandoned his work duties and was acting senselessly. He would put on his coat, but no sooner than that he would strip it off, and he would put on his waistcoat. But then he would rip off the waistcoat and he would put on his coat.

"What is the meaning of this behavior?" asked the Smith.

"That is easy to say," said Donald. "I have a coat that I got from my father and a waistcoat that I got from my mother, and I am anxious because I don't know to whom I should give greater deference, my father or my mother."

"Deference to your father," said the Smith of the Tales, "and obedience to your mother."

On the third day, it was Young Donald himself who was doing something odd. He would be at his books for a while and then he would leap out of the doorway. He would return inside, he would sit and he would start to read again, but it wouldn't be long before he would go out again.

After the Smith of the Tales came into the room, he asked what was wrong.

"Please excuse me," said Young Donald. "I am certainly confused. This question has been troubling me and I can hardly be still until I resolve it. Although I had read and studied a great deal of arcane lore, I have never learned who should tell the first tale, the man of the house or the guest."

"The man of the house tells the first tale, and the guest goes from night to morning," said the Smith of the Tales.

When the three lads went to sleep that night, Young Donald said, "Now, we got the three facts that our father lacked! But when the Smith of the Tales goes to lie down and he ruminates on what we have done, he will realize that he has been tricked. We must, then, depart. The Smith has a good horse and there is no way for us to escape except to take the horse and ride it until he collapses. It won't be long until the Smith comes into here and he will strike the bed with his sword. When he sees that we are not in it, he will take off after us. He has hidden another horse that is as fast as the eddy of the stream."

They did as he said, but the three lads had not gone long before the poor animal they were riding fell down with exhaustion. Then they ran off but it wasn't long before Young Donald said, "Listen! The Smith is coming and we cannot escape unless we create a ruse. Let us change our appearance as best we can and let us start a dispute around this tree. When he comes and asks what is wrong, you will answer, Donald, that there is a tree here that your father gave you and that we are taking away from you. When he asks what rights he gave you to it, you will say that he gave all that is crooked and straight of it to you. Then, you will say, Iain, that your rights are just as good, that he gave all that is rotten and healthy of it to you. When I get a chance to speak, I will say that my right is better than all of yours, that he gave all that is below and above ground to me. This will perplex him. He will turn his face toward the elements of the weather and he will spend twenty-four hours meditating. We will be far away before he comes to himself."

This is how it was, the three of them began to quarrel and fight around the tree. The man who was after them arrived and everything happened as Young Donald had said. When the Smith of the Tales turned his face toward the elements of the weather, the lads took off.

After twenty-four hours, the Smith came to himself. He set off for the residence of Great Seanchan in Ireland and although it was far away, it didn't take him long to reach it. He went inside, dressed as a beggar, and when he found no one there but Great Seanchan alone, he asked where the lads were.

"They are not home," answered Seanchan.

"I have come a long way," said the Smith, "and I need some food."

"Well, I have a pot of red-seaweed soup cooking, but the fire is about to go out," said Seanchan. "There is a boat over there on the shore on which I was working, and there is plenty of wood shavings around it. Now, I am unsteady on my feet and it is not easy for me to go to get the shavings. It would be better for you to bring an armfull of them inside and that will expedite the pot."

No sooner than the Smith was out of the door, Seanchan took out his bag of wizardry. When the other man reached the boat, he bent over to pick up the wood shavings and he leaned his chest against the stern for support. But when he lifted his head, the boat was out on the sea. The next thing he saw was that he appeared to be a woman, in woman's clothing. It was not long before the boat reached a land unknown to him, and before him on the shore there was a line of handsome young bachelors, all of them yelling, "Will you marry me?"

She chose one she liked. They married and after a year they had an infant son. The next year, they had another son, and the third year, the third one was born.

The sons were growing to the point of manhood and one day, the entire family went out to get fish. The three sons were in the prow of the boat, and when they arrived at the fishing grounds, the father asked the oldest son to put out the anchor.

He did so, but he fell head first after the anchor.

The next son rushed to save his brother, but then he himself fell in.

The same thing happened to the youngest son and then to the father.

The Smith of the Tales then raised his head and he was holding a bundle of wood shavings. He brought them inside to Great Seanchan. The pot boiled and he had some of the red-seaweed soup.

"Are you pleased with your trip?" asked Great Seanchan.

"Pleased or angered, that's enough from you," answered the Smith of the Tales.

And then I left them.[19]

The Tale of Mànus

Hector MacLean transcribed the following tale from Donald MacPhie of South Uist (see a sketch of the storyteller in the Introduction) in 1860 who in turn learned it from Iain MacDonald before the year 1800.

This tale is classified as a medieval romance tale, as it has a long and convoluted plot composed by professional literati in written form and was meant to be read aloud from a book to élite audiences. Alan Bruford suggested that this tale had been originally composed by a member of the MacMhuirich literary dynasty but survived only by word of mouth until captured by fieldworkers. The Tale of Mànus was considered in local Uist tradition to be a literary masterpiece.[20]

The Gaelic name *Mànus* is derived from the Norse name "Magnus" and this tale attests to many Norse associations that lingered in the Western Isles long after direct contacts with Scandinavia were lost. Nonetheless, the cultural milieu and ethos of the tale is solidly Gaelic, including the practice of fosterage and the playing of shinty by young heroes.

There was a King of Norseland, and he was married, and two sons were born to him. Oireal was the name of one, and Iarlaid of the other. Their father and mother died. An assembly was called to set up a regency for the kingdom, until the children should come of age and could be installed to rule the kingdom themselves.

The sons were sent for; Oireal was a feeble man and Iarlaid was the larger. Oireal said to the assembly that he would not yet have anything to do with the kingdom.

"You shall not have a clod of it," said the assembly, "unless you take it this day."

Iarlaid said to Oireal, "You take one half and I will take the other half."

"Well, then," said Oireal, "I will do it."

A contract for the kingdom was written for the sons. In a few years Iarlaid married the daughter of the King of Greece and Oireal married the daughter of Sgiath Sgial, King of Orkney. Sgiath Sgial gave six maids of honor with his daughter, and the King of Greece gave the same with his own daughter.

Three seasons after that night, the daughter of the King of Greece became pregnant and likewise, the daughter of Sgiath Sgial became pregnant, and sons were born to them, and twelve sons were born to the maids of honor. The son of Oireal was named "Mànus" and the son of Iarlaid was named "Eochaidh." The sons began to mature; Mànus was growing big, but Eochaidh was small. They were sent to school and each one of them had the company of his own foster brothers.

They were playing shinty on the field, coming from school, and Mànus drove the ball against Eochaidh.

"I will have my own father's kingdom," said Mànus.

The daughter of the King of Greece said, "It would be my wish to put an end to Mànus, by murder and ruination and slaughter."

"Well, it would be a great loss to do that to the son of my own brother," said the King.

"If you will not do it, I will do it," said she.

She went inside, and smacked the ear of her own son, and drove him out of the house.

"Be gone," said she, "and wander to ends of the earth, and let me not see you settled on the self-same sod for as long as the world lasts. I will take Mànus and he shall be like a son to me."

She took Mànus in with her, and she set her own son in a beautiful greenhouse on a single pedestal, where he could see everyone but no one could see him. Mànus was inside the house with her, and he couldn't get out to see his mother at all. Then his mother said that she would go where her foster-mother was and that she would take her counsel.

A year later she sent word for Mànus. And in a few years the wife of his father's brother sent word for Mànus.

"What, o Mànus," said the daughter of the King of Greece, "are you thinking of doing today? If you will marry, you will get a third of the kingdom: territory, fertile fields, and wealth."

"Well, I am not of age to marry at all," said he.

"You need not be," said she. "There is one man on my own land who will consent. Go and ask for his daughter, and you shall marry her. He is the Earl of the Forest; you shall marry the daughter of the Earl of the Forest."

She went away, and she brought a retinue with her, and she would be accompanied by five hundred men. She reached the house of the Earl of the Forest, so that Mànus could be given to marry the girl.

The wife of the Earl of the Forest said to her, "My daughter is not of age to marry yet, and Mànus is not of age to marry."

"Well," said the daughter of the King of Greece, "you shall not have house or home upon my land unless you give your daughter to him."

The Earl realized that it was useless for him to refuse her, and so Mànus and the daughter of the Earl of the Forest were married to each other. They went to lay together that night in the house of his father's brother.

"Is it you that is here, o Mànus, o mighty son, o evil man? Do you know what kind of woman it was who dealt it to her own son, Eochaidh? She cast him off like the swift March wind. It was no mortal human wife to whom she married him, so that he might behead you. You and a wife in bed at this time of night! You will be challenged every day, and you will not be able to hold up in battle against him."

"What do you mean?" said Mànus.

He went where she was.

"Leave the kingdom," said the wife of his father's brother to him, "or else you will have nothing but what you will pay for."

"That would be," said he, "the third-part of the kingdom that you promised to me."

"You shall not have a clod here," said she. "Your land is full of stones and rough mountains in Old Bergen."

"Well, since you are sending me away, give me the six foster brothers of Eochaidh, so that I may have twelve."

That is what he got. He departed, and made his way to Old Bergen. When he reached Old Bergen, no man dared to come near his castle. There were sheep in Old Bergen, and they were called "the crimson sheep." People began to dig pits in the earth, the sheep were falling into the pits, and they were catching them and killing them, to get enough meat for themselves. This happened for a year in Old Bergen.

"Woe is me! Woe is me!" said Mànus, "It is a year since I saw my foster mother; I had better go and see her."

"I would not advise you to go there," they said, "but if you are going, you have twelve foster brothers, take them with you."

"It would be a great help for them to be in my company," he said.

He took off. The daughter of the King of Greece was looking out of a window, and she noticed Mànus coming. She went down to where his father's brother was.

"The son of your brother is coming here," said she, "with hasped, multihued belts on his left side, that win the love of young ladies, and the infatuation of maidens." She said that it was her wish to put an end to him, by murder, and ruination, and slaughter.

His father's brother said that it would be a great loss, and that he would not be around to do that to him.

"If you won't do it, I will," she said.

She went out of the house, and she took his twelve foster brothers from him, and she had them give an oath of fealty to her. He went back to Old Bergen by himself, gloomy, tearful, sorrowful, and it was late. What should he see but a man in red raiment.

"Is that you here, o Mànus?" he said.

"It is I," said Mànus.

"I think that if you had weaponry, bad or good, you would be able to be the King of Norseland."

"I do not have such," he said.

"Well," said the Man of the Red Raiment, "if you would give me a promise, I would give you weaponry."

"What is the promise that I shall give to you? I don't have a thing to give you."

"Well, I will not ask much of you. I was the armourer of your grandfather, and your great-grandfather. If you would promise me that I should be your armourer, I would give you weaponry this very night."

"I will give you that, if I am ever to be a king."

They departed and they reached the house. The Man of the Red Raiment took out a key, and he opened a door, and when he had opened it the house was full of weaponry, and nothing in it but weaponry.

"Go ahead and choose arms," said the Man of the Red Raiment.

Mànus grabbed a sword, and he broke it, and he broke every one that he grasped.

"Don't do that, Mànus, don't be breaking the weapons, in case you might yet have need of them. When I was a young man, your grandfather had a war, and I wore an an old helmet and an old mail shirt. Try them on," said the Man of the Red Raiment.

Mànus seized the sword, and he could not break it. He put the helmet and the mail shirt on. What should he see hanging down from the ridge of the house but a cloth.

"What is that cloth good for?" said Mànus.

"It is," he said, "that when you spread it out to seek food and drink, you will get it, according to your effort. It has another power. If an enemy should encounter you, he would give a kiss to the back of your fist."

He gave the cloth to Mànus, who folded the cloth under his arm. What should he see but an iron chain hanging down from the ridge of the house.

"What is that chain good for?" said Mànus.

"There is no creature in the world that would not have the fighting power of a hundred men if it is hung around its neck," said the Man of the Red Raiment.

Mànus took the chain with him. When he was going, what should he see but two lions, and a whelp with them. The lions came in front of him to eat him, and to tear him apart. He spread out the cloth, and the lions came, and they kissed the back of his fist, and they went past him. The lion whelp got in among the folds of the cloth, and he wrapped the cloth about it, and he brought it with him to Old Bergen.

When he reached Old Bergen, the daughter of the Earl of the Forest was indoors. He put the chain around the neck of the lion whelp. The lion whelp went, and it cleared out the castle; it did not leave a creature or a monster alive. He set fire to the castle. He was there a year, and he lacked for nothing.

He went out one day, and he said he would go to see his foster mother.

He took the lion whelp with him, and he went away. She noticed him coming. There was a sword at his side that day. She came out to meet him, and she had a brown pet dog. It set out to meet Mànus with its mouth open, to tear apart Mànus, and to eat him. Away went the lion whelp, and it went in front of Mànus, and it set its paw at the back of the throat of her pet dog and it wrenched out its guts.

"Proceed, Mànus," she said, "but put your whelp inside on the ridge of the lion's house."

He put the lion whelp inside on the ridge of the house, and he put the chain about its neck, and it did not leave a lion under the roof of the house alive, and it laid itself down stretched out for dead along with them.

Mànus went home without a whelp or a man that night. What work did he set his twelve foster brethren to, but to clear out the lion's house. When they were sent out, they found that every lion under the ridge of the house had its throat cut. The lion whelp didn't have a drop of sweat upon it, and the iron chain that Mànus had put on him was still around its neck. One of them said that the lion seemed strange to him, without a drop of sweat upon it, unlike the rest.

"That is the lion whelp of the man dear to me," said one of the company. "The lion whelp of Mànus."

"Well," said one of them, "although we are sworn not to go out of the town, before he rises we could go out, and deliver a message."

"There is no man who leaves this settlement," said the others, "after the coming of night that does not suffer seven years' worth of pain afterwards."

They went over to the window, and when they went over to the window, the lion whelp opened its eyes, and it came alive.

She went where her husband was, and she told him to put the combat vehicle in order, with five hundred men in it.

He said that anyone who should go out after the falling of the night would suffer seven years' worth of pain.

She said that even if there should be seventeen years' worth of pain, they should go to get Mànus's head.

The Deaf Cripple was what they used to call the man who was guarding the kingdom at that time, and he could not hear a thing unless there were nine groups of nine people shouting in his ear. He could kill nine nines behind, and nine nines in front, with his sword. What should awake him but the stormy sound of the combat vehicle coming, and he thought that it was an enemy. He sprung up on the combat vehicle, and he did not leave a single man of the five hundred alive; himself and the lion whelp. The lion whelp and the twelve foster brothers of Mànus went to Old Bergen.

"Never mind," she said. "Even if Mànus did that to me, there is the Red Knight, the son of the King of Greece, and he will carry Mànus's head out of Old Bergen."

Then Mànus's mother left, and she sent a ship to him in Old Bergen to take him away before the Red Knight could behead him. What did his foster mother do but cause the ocean to thicken like jelly, so that Mànus could not get away. His mother sent a pilot in the ship, and what did the ship do but get stuck in the gelatinous ocean.

"Is there a ship in the world that will take us out of this?" said Mànus to the pilot.

"Indeed, there is the speckled ship of MacBalcan the smith," said the pilot.

They were on board, and they could not budge.

At the coming of the night, the lion whelp thrust his head under the arm of Mànus, and he went out of the ship, with Mànus on his back. He went and he reached a skerry. He left Mànus on the skerry, and he himself leaped down the other side of it. Mànus fell asleep, and he would prefer to die along with the rest, rather than be left by himself on a rock. A voice came to him, and it said to him, "Arise." He stood up, and he saw a ship.

What was here but the ship of MacBalcan the smith, with the lion whelp at the helm. And the son of MacBalcan the smith and his twelve sailors were dead on the deck. He reached the ship, and he put his twelve foster brothers and the daughter of the Earl of the Forest in the ship of MacBalcan the smith. He began to sail through the gelatinous ocean.

What should he see but land, and when he saw the land he saw the very finest castle he had ever seen. He went on shore, and he put MacBalcan the smith and his twelve sailors on shore on a headland. He reached the castle, and he went inside, and there was a beautiful woman inside there, and twelve bald ruddy maidens. His twelve foster brothers sat beside the bald, ruddy maidens, and they said that they would never leave until they should get them to marry.

It was not long before the White Knight, son of the King of Lightland, came home with a great, clumsy, red-headed woman, his mother.

"Who is here," he said, "gazing at my twelve bald, ruddy daughters face to face? I never saw a man who looked at them whose head I would not lop off from his neck."

"I have twelve foster brothers, and they have fallen in love with your bald, ruddy daughters, and you must give them to be married," said Mànus.

"Well," said the White Knight, "I would do that on one condition, which I am sure you would not agree to: that is, to ally with me against my father, with whom I have been in conflict for seven years."

"I will do that," said Mànus, "as long as you yourself go with me."

They departed the next day, and they reached the King of Lightland. The King of Lightland came out, and he gave his right hand to his own son, and his left hand to Mànus. The lion whelp went, and he seized him, and he knocked him down.

"Call the monster off of me before he takes my life from me," said the King of Lightland.

"I will do that," said Mànus, "but write with a drop of your blood that your son is your rightful heir."

"Well, I would have done that long ago, if he had come himself to ask."

Then he went and he signed it, and they went away to come home. When they were coming the daughter of the Earl of the Forest was down in a stream.

"Ach," said the White Knight, "I am good as dead."

"What troubles you?" said Mànus.

"There is a stone," he said, "in the stream, and there are three trouts under the stone, and they are in your wife's apron. As long as the trouts should be alive, I would be alive. Your wife has one of them now in the fire."

"Is there anything in the world," said Mànus, "that would be of use to you?"

"The King of the Whole World has a horned, venomous creature, and if I could get his blood, I would be as healthy as I ever was."

They reached the house and the White Knight was dead.

Then Mànus departed, and the speckled ship had been stolen from him, and there was no knowing who in the world had taken it from him. One of his foster brothers said that Brodram, the son of the King of the Whole World, had taken it with him.

He went off to Brodram. He asked him what made him take that ship from him. He said that Mànus had stolen it previously himself, and that Mànus had no right to it. He said that his father had a venomous horned creature, and that as long as the venomous horned creature was alive, that his father would be alive, and that if the venomous horned creature was slain, that he would have the kingdom.

He went with Brodram, and the venomous horned creature was in a field. The lion whelp went into the field, and he put his paw into the hollow of the throat of the venomous horned creature. The venomous horned creature fell dead, and the king fell dead inside.

Brodram was now the King of the Whole World, and Mànus got the blood, and he returned, and used it to bring the White Knight back to life.

"It cannot be the case that you will refuse to go with me now to put me in charge of the kingdom," he said to the White Knight.

The White Knight said that he would go. He reached Brodram, and Brodram said that he would go with him. Balcan and his twelve apprentices were working in the smithy, and he revived his twelve sailors. Mànus asked him to accompany him, and Balcan said that he would.

Balcan departed, and the White Knight, and Brodram, and the Knight of the Tower, the son of the King of Siginn, went with him. They reached Norseland. The Man of the Red Raiment met them. The White Knight and the Red Knight began:

Terribly, hostilely, maniacally,
They produced three destructions each
Shooting shrapnel into the air and the heavens.
There gathered stag hounds, savage hounds,
To revel in the monsters:
They would make the sea dry up,
And the earth burst,
And the stars fall.

The Red Knight was slain, and his head was stuck on a stake. Mànus was crowned King of Norseland, and he did not leave a man alive in Norseland.

Chapter Two

Tales About Life and the World

The tales in this chapter are meant to reflect on or teach about aspects of the real world, whether the topic is human nature or the make-up of the earth and universe. Tales reflecting on human nature and social issues are sometimes portrayed with a cast of animals, drawing upon zoological archetypes and a sense of humor. Some traditional Gaelic folktales that explain why the natural world is the way it is include people from Christian scriptures, such as Jesus or Mary, or important Gaelic cultural heroes, such as Saint Columba. Some of these tales could be classified as *myths* because they explain the origin of things and how they came to be the way they are today.

Science is the product of modernity and it reflects a very different mindset from folklore. If you bring the biases and priorities of science into your expectations when you experience folklore, you are bound to be misled. It is unfair to judge folklore—and even more so those oral traditions that form the basis of indigenous knowledge systems—by the standards of modernity, as they serve very different purposes.

Science empowers humanity so as to dominate and manipulate all other beings and relationships through the power of rationality and technology. Folklore, on the other hand, tends to be concerned with collective culture in ways that reinforce our sense of belonging and our understanding of communal forms of expression. It often represents the natural world in terms of multiple, overlapping communities of different kinds of beings, each with its own history, personality, set of relationships and responsibilties.

Folklore in this sense creates a moral universe that can provide guidance about living in a specific ecosystem that requires balancing mutual relationships and reading cues in the environment. Sean Kane's observations about oral tradition in early cultures helps to elucide the difference in mentalities.

> For those people, who gave us myth, we need a different conception altogether. A starting point for that conception is the activity I call mythtelling. The word calls attention to the oral nature of myth. It means the passing on of stories from generation to generation—forms that exist only in the sensuous moment of their actual performance, and forms that take their inspiration not from texts, temples or other monuments at the center of human effort, but from the life of nature surrounding it. Because a people coevolve with their habitat, because they walk the paths their ancestors walked, mythtelling assumes that the stories already exist in nature, waiting to be overheard by humans who will listen for them. Such stories have a wild existence; they are just barely domesticated and so are free to enact the patterns of the natural world.[1]

We should try to understand the meaning of folklore on its own terms. We should avoid loaded words such as "superstition," "primitive," and "irrational." If you use these words, you are projecting the biases and stereotypes of modernity, and may not have tried hard enough to understand folklore from the perspective of the people to whom it belongs. *Folkloristics*—the study of folklore—provides us with tools to discover why folklore has had such a powerful grip on the human imagination and how it works within its own frame of reference.

Alexander Carmichael relayed the testimony of Duncan Macniven, an itinerant teacher in Argyllshire who was impressed by the traditional lore of the older Gaels in the region and eventually expressed regret about the damage done by his evangelical mission:

> The old people were full of old stories, and of old rhymes, many of them scarcely Christian, but very grand all the same. The stories and poems were about everything—the sun and moon and stars, the beasts and birds and fishes, old feuds and old cattle-raids. I was instructed to unteach these, and to teach the Bible and the Catechism.[2]

This is one reason why so few tales explaining the natural world remain in Gaelic tradition. Those that do survive often took the form of children's tales.

Taken together, folktales such as these reassure the listener that the world is an ordered and knowable place, with a large and diverse range of personalities, features, and qualities. Stories are the glue that transmit this cultural logic from one generation to the next, helping to bind the community together in these shared understandings and reciprocal relationships.

How Scotland Was Formed

This text was written in the early twentieth century by Katherine Whyte Grant (1845–1928), a native of Oban, who tells us that she inherited traditions from her maternal grandmother, who was born in 1774 in Nether Lorn.

There is a great deal of fragmentary oral lore about archaic goddesses in Gaelic tradition who are responsible for creating the landscape or features of it, influencing the weather, safeguarding the creatures of the wilderness, and participating in the renewal of ecological cycles. The most widespread name for this goddess in the Highlands is *A' Chailleach Bheur*, but other figures such as *Cailleach Beinne Bhric* (centered around Lochaber), *Cailleach Bheathrach* (around Braemar), *Cailleach Beinn a' Ghlotha* (in Atholl), and *Cailleach Mhór Chlìbhric* (in Sutherland) are local manifestations of the same cluster of stories and ideas.[3] There is also some overlap with the *Muilgheartach*, a Norse sea-hag who terrorizes the Fianna.

Just as cattle are animals that belong to the domesticated, human realm, the Cailleach has the creatures of the wild as her companions, especially the deer. Unusual and striking features of the landscape are evidence of her activities. The anecdote about how Loch Awe was formed is paralleled in similar stories about the origin of Loch Ness, Loch Tay, and Loch Eck in Cowal.

A very long time ago, there was an enormous hag who came over from Norseland. She had a creel on her back and a magical staff in her hand. There was soil and rocks in the creel in order to create Scotland.

On the way over, some of the soil and rocks fell in the water. That is what made the islands.

This hag was the daughter of Grianan. She had just one dull eye in the middle of her face, but the sight of that eye was as quick as the sea mackerel. Her face was colored shiny black and she had jagged, rusty teeth in her mouth.

She had a kerchief on her head,—as the women did in olden times—but rather than being white, it was speckled and striped and her grizzled locks were like a hoar-frosted aspen tree hanging down around her shoulders.

Sometimes she wore hose, and sometimes she wore grey moccasins, but she was never seen without a tawny plaid cloth around her shoulders.

The hag had herds of deer and many herds of goats and sheep that were as white as the snow. She would travel with them across the tops of the cairns and down the mountains. The Falls of Connel formed the stepping-stones across which the goats would be driven down from Ben Cruachan, although most often she would drive her deer down from Glen Nevis.....

There was a well of pure water on the top of Ben Cruachan where the Cailleach would stay at night with her herds. It was her duty to keep watch over this spring and to place a stone over the mouth of the well when the sun set.

But one night, as she was exhausted from driving the herds, she fell asleep without putting a stone over the mouth of the well. The water ran over until it surged like a mountain torrent through the craigs at the Pass of Brander and it gushed down over the plateau, wreaking destruction in its wake on every person and animal that was living on it. The path is there still where the River Awe flows out of Loch Awe. And that is how Loch Awe was formed.[4]

The Eagle of Loch Tréig

Donald C. Macpherson, a native of Bohuntin, Lochaber, contributed this tale to the periodical *An Gàidheal* in 1872. It was one of the most popular items shared in the *céilidhs* of Brae Lochaber around the turn of the twentieth century.

In order to gain a better understanding of the tale's significance, it is useful to compare it to two other Gaelic variants: a version that Calum Maclean collected from noted tradition-bearer John "the Bard" MacDonald of Highbridge, Lochaber, in 1951, and a version collected in County Mayo, Ireland, for the Irish Folklore Commission in the early twentieth century.[5] These all belong to a Gaelic ecotype based on the tale type AT-221 "The Legend of the Oldest Creature," which was popular in Celtic literature and tradition.[6] What might seem to be a quaint children's tale has incorporated archaic motifs from Gaelic cosmology.

In all three tales, an unusually frigid Beltane morning sends someone on a quest to find out if there has ever been a colder Beltane. In both the Irish variant and that from John MacDonald, the first character to appear is the local manifestation of the chthonic goddess figure (*Cailleach Bhéarrthach* in Mayo and *Cailleach Beinne Bhric* in Lochaber), who helps to begin the quest. Although she has been lost to this variant, her presence in the ecotype indicates its mythic nature.

Beltane marks the end of the dark and cold half of the year, and the beginning of the light and warm half of the year. For a Beltane to be unusually cold suggests that there were unusual climactic conditions that broke the expected norms of the calendar's cycles. Gearóid Ó Crualaoich suggests that this refusal of the winter to yield to the summer may be an ancient memory of the Ice Age.[7] The salmon asserts that even those who survived that extreme event suffered losses.

The place where the salmon is found in the Irish variant of this tale is also significant: Eas Rua (anglicized as "Assaroe"), where Fionn mac Cumhaill ate the salmon of wisdom (see the tale "How Fionn Got His Psychic Powers" in the next chapter). This association underlines the role of the salmon as a keeper and bestower of wisdom, as is befitting for the oldest of elders. The similarity between the name of Eas Rua in Ireland and the river Ruaidh in Lochaber likely helped to relocalize the tale in Scotland.

The name of the bird at Bunroy also requires comment, as there is a pun lost to translation. I have used the term "dipper-bird" in English for what is also called the "water-ouzel," a bird that can dive, swim, and walk in the water. In Gaelic it is called the *gobha dubh*, which literally means "black smith." That is why the eagle is told to find the bird at the smithy.

There was once a great eagle elder dwelling in a peak in the middle of Loch Treig, where her kind often was. She was grey with old age for as long as she could remember. And so, because of that, she expected that she was the oldest creature alive in her era.

But to be sure that she did not have a contemporary who had survived somewhere, she decided, at the first chance she could get, to travel around.

That year there came the very coldest Beltane Eve she had ever felt or seen, and she thought that would give her a good excuse to put her plan into action. And early in the morning of that very Beltane Day, rather than any other day, before other birds had tasted water, she started on her journey's quest.

She asked every living being she met, who appeared to be old, "Did you ever see a Beltane Eve as cold as it was last night?"

But not one had. However, the day had just begun and she kept moving on, without rest, until a kindly wren elder met her.

"Welcome to the wren, on this bright Beltane day," she said. "Did you ever see a Beltane Eve as cold as it was last night?"

Although the form and complexion of the wren was old, he was not aware that he had seen such a night. He did not know of any creature that was older than himself, but he had heard that there was an old dipper-bird a long time ago at Bunroy, and if he were still alive, it was probable that he had seen the likes of it, if it had ever come. And he pointed out the way to her.

She gave thanks to the wren, and she took off for the smithy at Bunroy.

She arrived but there was nothing there but a cold ruin: everyone, high and low, had departed, except the dipper-bird, and he himself had long since become blind with old age, and had made a hole in the anvil cleaning his beak.

She gave a Beltane greeting to the dipper-bird, and she explained the reason for her journey.

"Did you ever see," she said, "a Beltane Eve as cold as it was last night?"

The dipper-bird made a sad shrug, and he said that he had never seen one, and that he never heard of the likes of it, but that there was an elderly stag frequenting Coille Innse and that its bristles had been grey with old age from his earliest memories as a fledgling fluttering through the bushes.

"Many is the time since then," he said, "that he has come to pay me a visit to while away the long winter's evening, and to give me news about the state of the country. But that stopped. The last time that he was here, old age had come so heavily on him that I'm afraid that he cannot move very much. We spent so much time together as neighbors that I take great pleasure, as you will understand, in his aged bellowing, even if it is hoarse, when I hear it at twilight. He is the most elderly creature that survives today as far as I know, and if you speak to him on your way, tell him the reason for your journey and that you saw me. Unless he has declined greatly, he will make you entirely welcome."

He then recounted to her the notable matters that happened during the era of the chieftains he remembered seeing, and the great deeds of his ancestors, and how his children had prospered. As they were sharing the morning together, he urged and exhorted her to visit him the next time that she was going off to Coille Innse.

And she found the stag stooped over in the shelter of an old alder stump with icicles in his nostrils.

She gave him a Beltane greeting, and she explained the reason for her journey: "Did you ever see," she said, "a Beltane Eve as cold as it was last night?"

The stag was so old that he drooped his antler on his shoulder blade but he said very sluggishly that he could not remember that he had ever seen one.

He was warm and welcoming to her, and he asked kindly about the dipper-bird. They then spent a while discussing ancient lore and genealogy, and the eagle was going to assert her rank as the elder of the two. But just as they were parting, the stag said that there was a one-eyed salmon in the little loch of Coire na Ceanainn that he knew when he was a very young calf at his mother's feet traveling over Làirig Leacach from Beinn a' Bhric.

"Even then the dullness of age weighed heavily upon him," he said, "and if you have time, it will be worthwhile for you to see him: he is a great talker."

So it was that she took off again, and she reached the little loch.

She drank a toast of acquaintance to the one-eyed salmon and she explained the reason for her journey: "Did you ever see a Beltane Eve as cold as it was last night?"

The salmon said that he had: there was one other night that it was so cold that, although he was vigorous and at the height of his strength, he had to begin to leap and jolt through the water to keep himself warm.

"And," he said, "on one of the leaps that I took, I jumped out of the water and struck the side of my head against the dark flagstone over there. But the depth of the freeze was so intense that before I could pull myself back, my eye stuck to the flagstone, and that left has me one-eyed to this day."

When the eagle heard that, she gave the rank of age to the salmon. And she returned to the middle peak to tell her tale to her chicks.

They saw many a fair, sunny day after that but for as long as she could flap a wing, not a Beltane Day, whether hot or cold, went by without her going for a while to visit those excellent elders: the dipper-bird, the stag, and the salmon.[8]

Escaping Doomsday

This story appeared in the Gaelic column of *The Casket* in 1928, probably edited and contributed by Monsignor Patrick J. Nicholson from his own childhood memories. The editor said that he did not know of it previously appearing in print even though it was a popular children's tale in Gaelic tradition.

This folktale is clearly related to the well-known story known as "Chicken Little" in English (ATU-20C). As such, it can be read as a cautionary tale about how fear can make us irrational and reckless, and bring about the very disaster that we are trying to avoid. The names of some of the characters in this tale are nonsensical and have transformed a great deal during oral transmission: they may be as much about the whimsical impressions they evoke in their Gaelic forms than any intentional meaning.

In a study of many variants in Scotland and Ireland, John Shaw has argued that the Gaelic ecotype of this folktale has absorbed ancient Celtic beliefs about Doomsday, which was believed to come in the form of a massive flood. Another sign that archaic lore has been incorporated into the text is the appearance of the names of the pre-Christian Gods Crom and Donn, although the names have often mutated in recent tellings of the folktale (as Cromach and Duan, respectively, in this particular version).[9]

Peat-Stack Song went to the beach one day and he heard the scraping of the crabs, and he fled to escape Doomsday.

He hadn't gone far when he happened upon Tubby daughter of Tubby. She asked him, "Where are you going?"

"I'm escaping Doomsday!"

"Who heard it?"

"I'm the one who heard and saw it, and it came up to my very own toes!"

"I am leaving!"

"Whether or not you're leaving, I'm leaving!" and they left.

It wasn't long before Bent-one daughter of Bent-one happened upon them.

"Where are you going?" she said.

"We're escaping Doomsday!"

"Who heard it?"

"I'm the one who heard and saw it, and it came up to my very own toes!" said Song.

"I am leaving!"

"Whether or not you're leaving, we're leaving!" and they left.

Then the Two Sons of Big-Buttocked Boy happened upon them.

"Where are you going?" they said.

"We're escaping Doomsday!" they all replied.

"Who heard it?"

"I'm the one who heard and saw it, and it came up to my very own toes!" said Song.

"We're leaving!"

"Whether or not you're leaving, we're leaving!" and they left.

Who happened upon them then but Desert Behind the Fox.

"Where are you going?" he said.

"We're escaping Doomsday!" they all replied.

"Who heard it?"

"I'm the one who heard and saw it, and it came up to my very own toes!" said Song.

"I'm leaving!"

"Whether or not you're leaving, we're leaving!" and they left.

Who encountered them then but The Grey Man and his son.

"Where are you going?" they said.

"We're escaping Doomsday!"

"Who heard it?"
"I'm the one who heard and saw it, and it came up to my very own toes!" said Song.
"We're leaving!"
"Whether or not you're leaving, we're leaving!" and they left.
Then the Son-in-Law and his Lyre happened upon them.
"Where are you going?" they said.
"We're escaping Doomsday!"
"Who heard it?"
"I'm the one who heard and saw it, and it came up to my very own toes!" said Song.
"We're leaving!"
"Whether or not you're leaving, we're leaving!" and they left.
Priest Smart Lad was the next one that they met.
"Where are you going?" he said.
"We're escaping Doomsday!"
"Who heard it?"
"I'm the one who heard and saw it, and it came up to my very own toes!" said Song.
"I'm leaving!"
"Whether or not you're leaving, we're leaving!" and they left.
Then they arrived at the Two Wives of the Dye.
"Where are you going?" they asked.
"We're escaping Doomsday!"
"Who heard it?"
"I'm the one who heard and saw it, and it came up to my very own toes!" said Song.
"We're leaving!"
"Whether or not you're leaving, we're leaving!" and they left.
Then Fruit Morsel and Cheese Rind happened upon them.
"Where are you going?" they said.
"We're escaping Doomsday!"
"Who heard it?"
"I'm the one who heard and saw it, and it came up to my very own toes!" said Song.
"We're leaving!"
"Whether or not you're leaving, we're leaving!" and they left.
It wasn't long before they met the Speckled Hen and her brood.
"Where are you going?" she said.
"We're escaping Doomsday!"
"Who heard it?"
"I'm the one who heard and saw it, and it came up to my very own toes!" said Song.
"I'm leaving!"
"Whether or not you're leaving, we're leaving!" and they left.
Finally, who came their way but the White, Crippled Horse.
"Where are you going?" he said.
"We're escaping Doomsday!"
"Who heard it?"
"I'm the one who heard and saw it, and it came up to my very own toes!" said Song.
"I'm leaving!"
"Whether or not you're leaving, we're leaving!" and they left.
They were running and leaping about until they reached a river. They had to stop to

confer with one another to figure out how they could get across. They decided that each of one them would get on the horse's back and that he would wade to the other side.

That's what they did, they went riding the White, Crippled Horse: Peat-Stack Song, Tubby daughter of Tubby, Bent-one daughter of Bent-one, the Two Sons of Big-Buttocked Boy, Desert Behind the Fox, The Grey Man and his son, the Son-in-Law and his Lyre, Priest Smart Lad, the Two Wives of the Dye, Fruit Morsel and Cheese Rind, and the Speckled Hen and her brood.

That poor creature tried its very best to get across but when it was in the middle of the river, it broke its back and they all fell into the water, and they were drowned![10]

The Origin of the Milky Way

There is not much remaining lore about the origins or meanings of celestial bodies in Gaelic, but the following excerpt explains the origins of the massive cloud of stars known in English as the "Milky Way." It is called *Sgrìob Chloinn Uisnigh* ("The Furrow of the Children of Uisneach") in Scottish Gaelic. The explanation for its origin occurs in the tragic conclusion of the story of Deirdre as it was told in the Highlands. This variant of the story was written by Hector MacDougall of Coll (1889–1954) in the early twentieth century for a Gaelic school reader.

The tale of Deirdre is one of the most celebrated stories in the pan-Gaelic canon. She was selected by King Conchobhar of Ulster to be his wife when she came of age. She instead fell in love with the young warrior Naois, one of the three sons of Uisneach, and went into hiding in Scotland with him and his two brothers. Conchobhar did not forget his jealousy or forgive the insult, however, and he eventually wreaked his vengence on them.

The three sons of Uisneach were lying dead, breathless, side by side, on the smooth, green, grassy plain and Deirdre was bent down above them, shedding tears.

A grave was dug and the three brothers were stretched out side by side in it. Then Deirdre said, "Move over, o Naois, darling."

When the dead made a space for her, she leaped down into the grave, and she stretched herself in the same grave as Naois. But what happened was that Deirdre was reburied by herself on the other side of the loch.

Over time a pine tree grew there out of each grave, and their branches met, and they formed a knot over the middle of the loch.

Conchobhar cut them both down, but they grew a second time and they formed a knot. The king cut them again, but they did not grow a third time. The pine branches did not grow either. But on that very night, after they had been cut the second time, on a clear, starry night, without as much as a speck of clouds in the sky, at about midnight, at about the time that people would be resting, a magnificent glittering was seen in the constellations of the heavens.

A bright, white streak was ascending from two directions in the sky, corresponding to the two sides on which Deirdre and Naois were lying and they met as warm lights in the height of the firmament over the middle of the loch: The Furrow of the Children of Uisneach! That was its name the first night that it was seen and that is its name tonight.

That is exactly when Conchobhar saw that it was of no use for him to attempt to keep Naois and Deirdre apart from one another and he brought a halt to his evil work.

In Gaelic oral tradition, the beauty and tenderness of Deirdre is still remembered, as well as the strength and heroism of Naois.

Likewise, The Furrow of the Children of Uisneach can be seen every evening like a belt around the earth, and every beam of light that is seen shining in it is like a pulse of love constantly traveling and circulating between their spirits, that cannot be separated at any time.[11]

The Origin of the Will o' Wisp

The Rev. John MacRury (1843–1907) presented the following tale to the Gaelic Society of Inverness in 1894. It is an origin myth for the will o' the wisp, called in Benbecula *An Teine Mór* ("The Big Fire").

Besides explaining how the will o' the wisp came to be, this is a cautionary tale about the fragility of the ecosystem of low-lying sand banks along the northern coasts and islands commonly referred to in English as the "machar." This is a borrowing of the Gaelic term *machair.* A wide variety of flowers and plants grow in these sandy soils, which are the product of many centuries of careful human management as well as environmental conditions.[12]

The Gaels have never been inferior to any other people when it comes to providing an account of why unusual phenomena are to be seen on earth. The theories they have had about the unusual phenomena of the world have generally been no more wise or foolish than those of the other people of the world. It seems as though they themselves were very satisfied with their theories, and for that reason, we will leave the theories of the worthy elders where we found them, and how we found them. Although we think of ourselves as being wise, it may well be that some of our theories are just as foolish as theirs were.

Over two hundred years ago the majority of the population of the Highlands were fed and clothed by the bounty of the land to which they belonged. There were very few merchants at the time, and for that reason, the population had to be content with the items that they could get from the land.

At that time they would dye with the colors of the land. They would make green dye and yellow dye as beautiful as anyone had ever seen from the tops of the heather.

In the wet areas of the peatmoss they would find ground which they called *dubhach.* I remember seeing some of the pits from which they would dig up the *dubhach.*

I often heard about the color mixtures that a particular old woman would make long ago. These were the colors: "The black of the *dubhach*, the duskiness of the berries, and pale green, and deep green."

It is said that the population of the Western Isles is fond of red dyes. When the peddlers traveled the Highlands in the past, they used to sell red dyes such as cochineal and madder.

There was one thing to be found in the land that would make a red dye, and that was *rudh. Rudh* is the root of a grass. It is only found on dry sand banks. Women would go to harvest at night for fear that the factor or one of the officers would find out.

It seems as though the landlord was very much against harvesting the *rudh*, since a great deal of the dry machar would be dug up during harvesting, and a great deal of the dry sand of the banks would drift away throughout the machar when the dry part of the spring would come.

There was a farmer in Benbecula who was commonly called "The Priest's Calum." The Priest's Calum was descended from the MacCormacks. I knew his grandson Iain son of Angus son of The Priest's Calum very well. I never heard why he was given the nickname The Priest's Calum. But if it happened that he was in the employ of a priest, it would be natural for them to call him The Priest's Calum. Then the name would come to be as I heard it.

It seems as though The Priest's Calum was as well-mannered and proper a man as could be found in the entire country. But according to what I heard, he had the worst wife in Uist. She was a she-devil. It has been said that if a she-devil gets her wish, her soul will not find mercy.

It seems as though The Priest's Calum's wife did get her wish at least one time. The Priest's Calum had a daughter who, as has been the case with many women before and since, was keen to get unique dyes to put in her clothing.

She decided that she would go to harvest *rudh* in order to dye yarn or wool. She couldn't go to harvest it during the day, for fear that she would be handed over to the factor, and in order to keep the matter as hidden as possible, she decided that she would go to harvest it on the Monday-Sunday night, that is to say, after midnight on Sunday night.

Her mother was totally against her going out to harvest the *rudh*. But the daughter would neither listen or yield to one word that her mother would say to her. If her mother was a she-devil, it seems as though the daughter was as stubborn as the Devil himself. Since she decided to go to harvest the *rudh*, she would go even if the eastern sea flooded into the western sea.

When her mother saw her going out the door, she said, "You are now leaving with the curse of your mother hanging over you. May the day not come when we see the sight of your feet."

It seems as though her mother got her wish, as the daughter of The Priest's Calum was never found alive or dead, whether at sea or on land. But after all hope had been given up of her returning home, her kin and neighbors went to search for her corpse, and they found some of her clothing on the machar where she was harvesting the *rudh*.

A short while after this happened, a light was seen which is called "The Big Fire." It seems that everyone who heard what happened believed that The Priest's Calum's wife got her wish, and that the daughter of The Priest's Calum became "The Big Fire."[13]

How the Wren Became the King of Birds

Despite being a very small bird, the wren has the reputation of being of being bold and cheeky. The wren was known as the "king of birds" in many European traditions, including in Gaelic Scotland and Ireland. The following tale, which according to John G. Campbell "may be said to be as widely extended over the Highlands as the birds themselves,"[14] explains how this diminutive creature managed to get the upper hand on much larger competitors. This variant of the tale, published in a Gaelic school reader, does not include the widely-known rhyming couplet belonging to the tale:

> *"Càit' am bheil thu nis', a dhreathain dhuinn?"*
> *"Fada, fada os do chinn!"*
>
> "Where now, wren, do you fly?"
> "Up above your head so high!"

A dispute once broke out between the birds about which of them ought to be the king over them. The eagle said that the honor should be given to the bird that could fly highest in the heavens.

A certain day was specified to find out which bird would get the honor. One beautiful summer day, all of the birds of the air gathered together in one spot. They came from the four directions of the sky, big and small, and of every color.

On the same tree there was the thrush, blackbird, sparrow, and the robin, and their music would bring joy to anyone who heard it.

The birds of the moor and hillside came as well, such as the female red grouse and the black grouse, the pheasant and the snipe.

The birds of the sea were there too: the seagull, the tern, the goose and wild duck, the crane and oystercatcher.

The eagle came and it looked haughtily at the little birds. And who finally came but the wren, and when the other birds saw it, they all laughed.

The competition was prepared and all of the birds rose up flying into the air. Most of them did not go very high and after a while they all returned to the earth but the eagle.

Hold on, they did not all return: the wren seized its chance and it leaped onto the back of the eagle and then it crouched between the two mighty wings.

When the eagle thought that it was as high as it could go and was now getting tired, it cried out, "I am the king of birds!"

The wren rose up from the back of the eagle.

"You are not at all," it said. "I am the king of birds. I am here high above you."

The eagle had to descend to the earth and admit that the wren had beat it.

And the wren has been the king of birds from that day to this.[15]

Why the Dog-Fish Is Called "the King's Fish"

Hector MacLean transcribed this tale from Angus MacKinnon of South Uist in 1860. It provides an explanation for a Gaelic nickname of the dog-fish. Most of the Gaelic stories that explain the origins of names and natural beings involve either Biblical characters or saints, such as Columba. This tale is fairly unusual in bringing in Fenian characters to create an account of origins.

The dispute over the rightful owner of the fish, and the details of the argument, are in character with the old Gaelic laws, which were quite elaborate and comprehensive, and show Gaelic society to be a litigious one.

Who came to spend a little time with the King of Ireland but the King of Norseland.

One day the King of Norseland and Fionn went fishing in a little boat of theirs, and there was no one there but them. They spent the greater part of the day fishing and they didn't get a bite.

Then a creature tugged at Fionn and he made a cast such that it took the hook. He brought in the fish and what was it but a dog-fish! The hook of the King of Norseland was in its maw, under Fionn's hook, which was in its outer mouth. The King of Norseland then started to take out the dog-fish, since it was his own hook that was deeper inside of it.

They started to dispute this with each other, and Fionn would not yield one bit to him until they consulted the law.

They then came to land with the boat and they consulted the law and it was judged that the fish should go to Fionn and that the King of Norseland should be fined since he did not notice the fish when it first tugged at him.

The King of Norseland took such offense that he went home to Norseland and he told his foster-mother and his foster-father what had happened. The Muilgheartach was his foster-mother and the Smith of the Song-Poems, who was married to her, was his foster-father.

She said that she was the one who would take vengeance. She then went to Ireland and the King of Norseland and the Smith of the Song-Poems were with her.

The dog-fish was always called "the king-fish" after that.[16]

The Hawk Teaches the Fox a Lesson

The following tale was collected by the Rev. John G. Campbell in Tiree sometime in the later 1800s and published by him in English only. There are many such humorous parables in Gaelic that use animals to teach simple life lessons, usually assuming an audience of children.

A hawk was dozing sleepily by the side of a river when a fox came and caught it in its mouth and was going to devour it.

"Oh, don't, don't!" said the bird, "and I will lay an egg as big as your head."

The bird exclaimed so loudly and insistently that the fox let go of his hold on the bird which flew up to the branch of a tree above it. Here it sat, safe from harm by the fox.

"I will not lay an egg as big as your head," said the bird, "because I am not capable of that, but I will give you three pieces of advice, and if you obey them in the future, it will do you some good."

"First, never believe an unlikely story from an unreliable authority," he said.

"Second, never make a big fuss about a small matter," he added.

"And thirdly—" and because the bird paused and straightened itself up, the fox took special interest to listen carefully, "whatever you get hold of, make your grip very firm."

And with this, the hawk flew away. The fox, having thus realized his mistake, was left humiliated.[17]

Oh, Adam!

Pàruig Mac an Easgair transcribed the following tale from the Gaelic storytelling tradition of eastern Perthshire in the early twentieth century. It is a humorous tale in which a man is shown that his opinion of his own virtues is far too high and his expectations of others are correspondingly unrealistic.

Highland Perthshire was closely situated and connected to the world of the Stewart Kings, and so the appearance of King James V (1512–1542) in the tale, and the casual acquaintence between king and Gaels, is less surprising here than it would be in the western Highlands or Hebrides.

King James V is portrayed in Lowland tradition as something of a trickster figure who enjoyed disguising himself as a beggar and wandering among the unsuspecting peasantry. The song "The Gaberlunzieman" is associated with him and portrays a Scottish king in this very role. This tale is an example of the interaction between Highland and Lowland traditions that sometimes happened, especially along that cultural border.

King James the Fifth enjoyed spending a week now and again at Scone Palace. And when he would be there, he particularly enjoyed clothing himself not as a king but as a beggar-man and to make a visitation upon the Gaels of Strathbraan.

One day when the king was on his way through Glenshee and getting close to Strathbraan, he saw a large and plump old man who belonged to the people of that strath pulling heather. The old man was attending to his business at a very leisurely pace. After every clump of heather that he pulled, he would put his hand on his hip and he would say, "Oh, Adam!"

The king stood and observed him for a good while, and there was no tuft of heather that came out of its root that was not accompanied by "Oh, Adam!" coming out of the old man.

Now, the king spoke plenty of Gaelic, just as his father and grandfather did before him, and therefore the words of the man made him exceedingly curious.

Finally, he asked, "Why are you saying, 'Oh, Adam!'?"

The old man answered boldly and impudently, without realizing who he was speaking to, "I certainly can say, 'Oh, Adam!' If he had not made a fool of himself in the Garden of Eden, I would not be eating my bread by the sweat of my brow today!"

"Do you think, then," said the king, "that you would do any better in that garden than Adam did?"

"Better, indeed!" said the old man. "I could not do worse if I tried to."

"Your complaint about Adam's disobedience," said the king, "is not of use to you or anyone else. But I will tell you something that will be of use. Take a cart-load of that beautiful heather to Scone Palace tomorrow and I give you my promise that you will be well paid for your labor. Inquire there for James Stewart, since I am very well acquainted with him and he will set you right. Do as I ask of you and you will have your reward in your hand tomorrow. Farewell!"

The king set off and he spent the rest of that day and night in the warm kindness of the Gaels who lived along the river Braan of the beautiful trout. The next morning the king and the old man of the heather were on the road to Scone Palace but they were not in each other's company, as the king was taking every shortcut and keeping himself out of the sight of the other man. When the old man arrived with his horse and his cart, the king was waiting for him at the great door of the palace, arrayed in another deceptive outfit so that the poor Braan-man did not recognize that he had ever seen him.

The old man asked, "Does James Stewart live here?"

"Yes," answered the king, "I am that man and I will give you a very good payment for that heather, if you haven't already sold it."

"The very reason for my journey is to sell it to you," said the man, "and I will leave it to you to decide on its price."

The king motioned his hand to the stableboy. He took the horse under his care and he guided the man inside to a great guestroom. There was a beautiful table there on which was set the loveliest dinner that he had ever seen in all of his life.

"Now," said the king, "I have to go out for a bit, but make yourself at home. Help yourself and partake of anything you would like. But by all means, do not touch that silver decanter that is in the very center of the table. No one dares to lay a finger on that decanter except only the king himself."

The king then left the room, shut the door, and put his eye to the keyhole.

"I do not understand," said the old man to himself, "what can be in that silver decanter. Whether or not the king is here, it cannot hurt anything to just look at it."

He arose and he lifted the prized item. No sooner did he do that than a white mouse leaped out of the decanter. And that is when the intense chase started. As fond as the king himself was of hunting, he had never more hotly pursued the "antlered lad" than the Braan-man pursued the mouse. It was running and leaping among the vessels, and the old man with his huge, clumsy paws was turning some of them upside down and breaking them in the heat of the chase. Those accidents, and the fear that the man who went out would come back, sent the man into a panic. But, finally, the mouse leaped into a little, narrow decanter. He then grabbed it and quickly shut it in its own place.

The king nearly lost his strength behind the door laughing at what was going on but when he opened the door, he pretended to be angry, and he said, "You certainly were not so ill-mannered and so shameless as to do anything with the king's silver decanter, did you?"

"Oh, no, not at all," said the old man, "I didn't lay a finger on it."

"O you old sinner," said the king, "you are telling me an absolute lie to my face! You are worse than Adam, since he admitted his guilt but you deny it. Let me not hear 'Oh, Adam' or 'Oh, Eve' coming out of your mouth again. Get out of my sight, you rascal, and go home!"

The poor old man was in such a state of confusion from everything that happened that he did not notice when he was going out of the door that a purse was put in his sack in which he later found five golden coins.

There was no story that the king himself enjoyed telling, when he was in a good mood and among Gaels, more than "Oh, Adam!"[18]

The Clan of the Sixty Blockheads

This tale was printed anonymously in the Nova Scotian journal *Mac-Talla* in 1898. It was probably penned by the editor Jonathan G. MacKinnon, whose parents were from the Isle of Skye. Several different variants of this tale were recorded from the mid-nineteenth century through the early twentieth century, all of them agreeing on the basic facts of this episode in the history of the MacCallums. Some versions give the place of their fatal encounter as *Acha Bheann*, between the parishes of Melfort and Craignish. Two branches of the family survived, one based in Argyll and the other at the north end of Loch Lomond.[19]

This tale seems to have given rise to two proverbial expressions widely known in Argyll and beyond: *gun fhios có bu Chalum*, literally "without knowing who was Calum," but used to mean "who was who"; and the nickname for this clan, used as a taunt, *Sliochd nan Trì Fichead Burraidh* ("The Clan of the Sixty Blockheads").

The anglophone world commonly stereotypes Highland clans as strong-headed, sword-slinging barbarians who think little of shedding blood to defend their honor. This is a cautionary tale from within Gaelic tradition itself against this very behavior, an internal critique of the results of excessive pride and violence.

I don't know if readers have heard the old story that used to be told in some corners of the Highlands about two brothers who took off on the same day, who left their father's house and went out into the world to find out how they would succeed. One of them went one direction and the other went another way.

After they had been away for a long time, and had both made their fortune, it seems that it occurred to both of them at the same time to return to their own homeland again.

They took off with their descendants and their livestock, and according to the account, each one of them had thirty descendants. Whatever good-fortune or ill-fortune was guiding them, the two groups happened on one another in a glen or at the base of a hill which is called, if I am correct, Sliabh an Tuim, in Craignish. The sun was descending and the afternoon was fading in such a way that if the two old men saw each other, the one brother did not recognize the other brother.

The two companies sat down to rest and to have a small meal, the descendants of one man a short distance up the slope and the rest at the bottom of the glen.

It seems that one of the group who was above threw something down on those who were below, whether intentionally or unknowningly, or he gave some foolish reason or other for them to think that they were insulting them and whatever was bothering him, the men arose.

They unsheathed their swords and went after one another, without knowing "which one was Calum." And the conclusion of the conflict was that none of those who had been there were left alive but the two old men. When they saw the devastation that had been done to their children, they thought it was time to bring an end to it.

They sat on a hillock and began to ask about one another's history, when they were most astonished to realize that they were the two brothers who had separated so long ago. If they had had some kind of joy in meeting one another, they had plenty of sorrow to see the utter ruination that their foolishness and reckless rashness that meted out on the sixty youths who were lying lifeless at their feet.

Ever since then, the Highland clan that carries the same name as them has been called "The Clan of the Sixty Blockheads." If I were to say who they are, there is no telling if I would displease the MacCallums![20]

Chapter Three

Tales of Culture Heroes and Ancients

This chapter contains folktales that are closely related to and associated with the professional practice of literature in the shared cultural traditions of Scotland and Ireland. These narratives portray characters who might be loosely labeled as "culture heroes," figures who lived in the distant past who play an important part in the Gaelic canon in a broad sense. They provide social precedents, historical touchstones, legendary ancestors, role models, and cautionary warnings that belong to Highland society at large. Stories about these figures are marked as texts of high prestige in the repertoire of storytellers of many communities and are not limited to specific families, clans, or districts.

Literacy came to the Gaelic world with the Roman Empire and the Christian church in the early medieval period. Church leaders composed literature that legitimated their own positions of authority in Gaelic society. The lives of native Celtic saints were among the first texts to be written by the Gaels of Scotland and Ireland. Christianity was highly influential in the restructuring of society in the early medieval period.

Christianity did not obliterate the memory of all that came before it: indeed, literate Gaelic scholars in Christian monasteries were very fond of their native traditions and were keen to find a way to adapt some version of stories about ancestors and heroes from their pagan past into the literature they were creating. Their approach to their own native literature was inevitably influenced by the Classical and Biblical texts that were integral to their education.

A series of tales about the warriors of the court of Conchobhar mac Nessa at Emain Macha (modern Navan Fort) in Ulster was the first to enjoy popular success. Modern scholars generally call this set of related stories the "Ulster Cycle" and the main hero is Cù Chulainn, who was said to have received his training in Scotland. The central epic of the cycle, *Táin Bó Cuailgne* ("the Cattle Raid of Cooley"), drew in many smaller stories which added to its size over time. Oral versions of the *Táin* were popular among Scottish Gaels and episodes from it were recorded in the twentieth century in both the Highlands and Nova Scotia.

Eventually surpassing the Ulster Cycle was the series of tales centered on Fionn mac Cumhaill and his band of warriors, the Fianna, who defended Ireland and Scotland from invaders. Modern scholars refer to this series of tales as the "Fenian Cycle" or the "Ossianic Cycle." Fionn mac Cumhaill may have originally been a god of the men of Leinster who was given attributes of wisdom and prophecy, but he was represented in later oral and written literature as a model warrior-leader who personified Gaelic ideals and virtues.

The Fenian Cycle was set in the pre-Christian past even though the Norse are the arch-enemies, demonstrating that historical timelines can become quickly blurred in oral tradition and are less important than archetypes and dramatic potential.[1] The heroism of Fenian warriors in defending the Gaelic realm took on particular resonance with the invasion of the Anglo-Normans in Ireland and the conflicts between Highlands and Lowlands in Scotland.

The Fenian Cycle became the dominant literary canon in Gaelic tradition. Even prehistoric ruins in the Highlands were named after Fenian warriors and were understood as proof of their existence. Some of the Fianna were believed to be founders of clans and lineages. Hector MacLean of Islay, one of John F. Campbell's collectors, remarked:

> They speak of the Ossianic heroes with as much feeling, sympathy, and belief in their existence and reality as the readers of the newspapers do of the exploits of the British army in the Crimea or in India; and whatever be the extravagance of the legends they recite respecting them, it is exceedingly remarkable that the same character is always ascribed to the same hero in almost every story and by almost every reciter. Fingal, or rather Fionn, is never called the king of any country or territory, but the king of the Fian, a body of men, who were raised, according to the traditions current in the Long Island and other parts of the Highlands, in Ireland, and in the Highlands, to defend both countries against foreign invaders, more especially against the Scandinavians.[2]

The Rev. John G. Campbell remarked that Fenian tradition was so popular and pervasive in Gaelic Scotland "that it became a saying, that if the Fians were twenty-four hours without anyone mentioning them they would rise again."[3] There are also other ancient heroes about whom epic tales in Gaelic oral tradition were told into the twentieth century, such as Conall Gulbann.

Many of the narratives about Gaelic heroes were used as the basis of song-ballads during the medieval period, performed in the halls of the chieftains. Song-poetry was felt to be the most elegant and eloquent means of relaying stories to an audience. This chapter can only provide a small sample of the prose tales from what is a rich, vibrant, and varied literary tradition.

The Boyhood Deeds of Cù Chulainn

Alexander Carmichael transcribed this tale in Gaelic from Hector MacIsaac of South Uist in 1873, when the reciter was 76 years old. MacIsaac heard it 60 years before that from Ruaraidh Ruadh MacQueen, a native of North Uist who was a traveling catechist and renowned *seanchaidh*.

This is just the beginning of the tale that Carmichael transcribed, which contains a surprising amount of detail that echoes the ancient tales of Cù Chulainn and the Cattle Raid of Cooley. This variant had been given the title *Tòireachd na Tàine* ("The Pursuit of the Cattle Herd"). The many correspondences between this text and those in manuscript suggest that the tale had been read aloud for an audience in North Uist in the eighteenth century, from which it entered oral tradition.[4]

There was a nobleman in Ireland who was called Dubhaltach. He was not of the landed gentry but possessed most of the world and great learning, and was from a respected family, and given that, he had a seat among the nobility.

The only offspring that he had was a single son who was named Cù Chulainn. He and the Earl of Gleann Chuilisg had been in college together and they were close friends and companions.

The daughter of the earl was getting married and the earl sent an invitation to the wedding to Dubhaltach a week beforehand. Dubhaltach and his wife departed for the wedding with their servants and horses. Cù Chulainn wanted to go but he was not allowed. When they left, he left after them. He had a shinty stick and ball and he was playing shinty all day long on the way.

At dawn, as the sun was setting, they arrived at a great bridge that led to the earl's palace. There was a hound on the bridge to safeguard it and it wouldn't let anyone go by without paying. But the boy didn't have any money.

He thought to himself that it would be embarrassing for him to return home and so he placed the shinty ball on a jackdaw and he struck it into one end of the hound and out the other end and he left the hound lifeless on the bridge.

That was Cù Chulainn's first heroic feat.

He went into the settlement and he saw boys playing shinty and he started playing with them.

When the night came, he said to one of the boys with whom he had been playing, "Isn't this," he said, "where the house of the earl is?"

"It is," said the other boy. "What business do you have with him?"

"Isn't there a large wedding?"

"There is."

"I would like you to lead me to it."

"They won't let you in."

"My father and mother are at the wedding and I'll see if they'll let me in."

The castle was illuminated by massive bonfires casting light all around. He went inside and among the company and ran over between his father's knees.

"Is that you, Cù Chulainn?" said his father.

"Yes," said Cù Chulainn.

"How did you get in when the hound was on the bridge?"

"I killed the hound."

What happened but one of the stewards was in the room and he went and he told his master Cù Chulainn's words. The earl leaped down.

"Who is this," he said, "who has killed my hound on the bridge?"

No one said a peep: they were afraid.

Dubhaltach said, "Here he is, and he tells me that he killed your hound."

"I do not believe that, that a wee lad like that could kill my hound."

"Oh, I am indeed the one who killed him and you need not blame anyone but me," said Cù Chulainn.

"Well," said the earl, "You must stay on the bridge for seven years to safeguard it until I raise another hound to take your place, or else you will pay me seven hundred English pounds."

"Well, I will pay that for my son," said Dubhaltach, "but if I do, I won't be worth much myself afterward. But if I could have time, I could pay that and recover to what I was before."

Cù Chulainn stood up and he said, "You will not pay, father, one cent, but I will go to the bridge to safeguard it for him and I will stay for a year, and he must do right by me just as he did the hound."

Cù Chulainn spent a year on the bridge. He was exceedingly keen to get training, and he told every person who came to the bridge, "I will not let you pass unless you teach me some lesson." And when a nobleman came, he would pay him money along with the lesson. He worked so diligently that he gained a great deal of training in this manner. And then he came home.

At this time, there was a college at Dùn Sgàthaich in the Isle of Skye and there was no nobleman worthy of the name in the kingdom of Scotland, or in England or Ireland, who did not send his son there for training. No man was worthy of honor unless he had been trained at Dùn Sgàthaich. There was no training or learning or tactic that could not be found there, and all tactics that were respected were to be found there. Cù Chulainn could not bear it if he could not be sent for training at Dùn Sgàthaich, and so he was allowed to go.

He was there for nine years. There was a Scottish nobleman there by the name of Feardiag son of Daimban at the college at the same time as Cù Chulainn and he was the foremost warrior in the world in his generation.

Feardiag and Cù Chulainn went to bed and arose together throughout those nine years and they were close companions to one another. At the time that they parted, they made a vow to one another that neither would ever cause the other any trouble. There was nothing that one of them learned that the other did not, except for one tactic that Cù Chulainn learned which was called the Belly-Spear (*an Gath-Balg*).[5]

How Cù Chulainn Killed His Only Son

There are many different episodes about the life and exploits of Cù Chulainn that were related in prose and song form, but one of the most popular of these in Scotland was the story of how the Ulster hero killed his only son, Conlaoch. Its popularity is likely both due to the poignancy of the story and its connection to Scotland. Several variants of a medieval ballad about the death of Conlaoch, probably originally composed by a member of the MacMhuirich literary dynasty, were transcibed between the sixteenth and nineteenth centuries across the Highlands.[6]

This text is a short summary of the story written in English by Duncan Kennedy, a schoolmaster in Kilmelford, Argyll, that prefaced a long poem in Scottish Gaelic. Kennedy recorded many heroic ballads from tradition-bearers in Argyll between 1774 and 1783, although he also seems to have composed a few himself based on existing stories. James Macpherson's *Ossian* had a tangible influence on Kennedy and the style of the texts that he produced: Fionn mac Cumhaill is here referred to as "Fingal" (which was Macpherson's name for him) and the established name Conlaoch (meaning "hound-warrior") is re-interpreted through a romantic lens as Ciùinlaoch.

The medieval Gaelic ballad and the later prose accounts based on this story present it as a tragedy about the collateral damage of a warrior culture and a cautionary tale about the excesses of violence.

The following poem is a perfect tragedy. Conlaoch, or rather Ciùinlaoch (signifies a mild hero), was a son of Cù Chulainn, born and brought up by his mother in the Isle of Skye, with whom he mostly resided during his minority.

Cù Chulainn, having held the chief command of Conall's army in Ireland during Conlaoch's minority, prevented his coming to visit his son to Dùn Sgàthaich so often as he wished. Conlaoch was disciplined in hunting, eloquence, music, and the art of war, under the tuition of his mother and her friends in Dùn Sgàthaich during his childhood. Before he became an adult he turned out to be the bravest hero and the most accomplished warrior in the Hebridean Isles.

His mother all this time being surprised that Cù Chulainn took so little notice of his son during his boyhood, although a natural son, indeed her malignity to send him to Ireland in disguise to see his father, sworn not to tell his father or any person whatever who he was or to whom he belonged, but one who could defeat him in a single combat, she not doubting but he would overcome his father, overturn his authority in that nation and supplant himself in his place and become King of Dùn Sgàthaich in Scotland and Dundalk in Ireland.

The brave and beautiful Conlaoch set sail with two hands from Dùn Sgàthaich to Ireland and arrived near the palace of Conall the king, and pitched their tent upon the shore. Fingal and a great many of the nobles of Ireland were feasting in Conall's halls at Conlaoch's arrival.

Conall sent sixteen chosen men to Conlaoch to inquire after his news, and to invite him to his halls, who, upon refusal, encountered him one by one, but were all defeated and bound upon the shore.

Dall, who watched the shore, went to Conall and told him how it had happened to his men at the shore; whereupon Conall set off and addressed himself to Conlaoch surprisingly pretty, requested his news and who he belonged to, which the noble youth durst not discover on account of his oath or promise to his mother.

They at last engaged, and Conall is defeated. A scout arrived from Cù Chulainn, who was stationed at Dundalk, with whom intelligence is conveyed back of Conall's defeat.

Cù Chulainn set off in a tremendous career towards the shore where the mighty Conall lay vanquished. He addressed Conall with the highest encomiums, and likewise the brave and beautiful stranger who he strenuously pressed to disclose his intentions and tell who he was, and what place or people he belonged to, which the brave stranger durst not make known until defeated.

The invincible and intripid Cù Chulainn unwillingly engaged his only son, who tremulously studied only to defend himself and spare his father. Cù Chulainn, finding himself uncapable to overcome him by arms, begun to throw the *Gath Bolg* or arrows, wherewith the valorous Conlaoch fell as being not accustomed to.

This method of fighting is thought to have been executed by warriors who threw their darts and lances at each other upon the water, one standing upon each side at a certain distance. But it is more probable it was shooting arrows, as being always mentioned under the term of *Còmhrag. Gath Bolg* signifies fighting by arrows.

No story can be more tragic than this of Cù Chulainn conversing with his son and reflecting his odious and cruel mother, whose avarice and spirit of revenge rendered herself miserable and Cù Chulainn unhappy by the unfortunate death of their noble, valiant, and beautiful son Conlaoch.[7]

The Origin Story of Fionn and the Fianna

Father Allan MacDonald transcribed a long Gaelic text about the Fianna from Alasdair Ruadh Johnston of Eriskay in the late nineteenth century; this is just a portion of it. Johnston was descended from one of the MacDonalds of Glencoe who fled to the Hebrides after the infamous massacre in 1692.

This style of this text is not particularly ornate and Johnston rambles at first about genealogical matters before getting the story moving fluidly. This text has never been translated before, probably because it is surprisingly racy: there is mention of genitalia, sexual intercourse, and bestiality. The name of the antagonist, Arca, is an obscure slang word meaning the vulva of an animal.

Some of these details are only hinted at in literary versions of the tale. Having them revealed explicitly from an oral source is helpful in unraveling the potential symbolism of the narrative.[8] It certainly speaks to the trust placed by his congregants in him that Fr. MacDonald was able to elicit a tale of this nature from a storyteller.

The Fianna were proliferated by the great-great-grandfather of the King of Ireland over five generations. Every year they found two or three large men and women that were over six feet tall and they married them to one another, and the offspring that came from them were huge, until they finally made an army of them for the Fianna.

When they finally gathered them together, it was for the purpose of making them soldiers and defenders of the kingdom against the Norse. They were originally raised in order to get rid of the Norse.

When they found that they had become so powerful, the Fianna sent a letter to the King of Ireland saying that he shouldn't expect their help whether for life or death. They then made Cumhall their own king. There were originally nine-nines of them, although there were more when they made a king of Cumhall.

I never heard about Cumhall's family origins but Diarmaid, Goll and Oscar were the children of Fionn's sister. When those three left the King of Ireland for the Isle of Skye to keep the deer from the Fianna, except for the worst member of the herd, that was the one that was left for them to kill for themselves.

They only allowed each of the Fianna to have a small meal of meat and a mouthful of stock. They had to put oaken skewers in their stomachs to hold it inside. That's how they were for a long time, until Fionn came to them.

Diarmad, Goll and Oscar were the children of Fionn's sister. They were related to Fionn, although they were not related to the other Fianna. Fionn was the brother of their mother.

When Cumhall was their king, no one dared to oppose them, even though there were plenty of people in the world who were more powerful than they were. King Cumhall made a law that any person who would cause harm, their life would be made difficult. One of their members, what did he do but lie with a cow. They seized the cow and they killed it, and they put the vulva of the cow around his neck, and they attached it to him so that no one could remove it. They banished him from them entirely and they wouldn't call him anything but Black Arca.

He and his wife went to the palace of the King of Ireland. He sent word to the king that he had a small matter of business with him. The king came out and took note of him and asked him who he was.

Arca then said that he was one of the Fianna.

"Have you lost all sense of shame, coming here before me, after my great-great-grandfather brought you all together, and then you later leave me, saying that we should not expect to get any help from you?"

"Well," he said, "since I was the one who was asking them to follow you, they put this around my neck as an insult and they sent me away. I came to you so that you could help me."

"I am not capable of helping such a giant of a man."

"I only ask you to fish on the river, and I will supply you with fish for your breakfast."

"You will get that—and tell me how Cumhall can be killed."

"The only people who Cumhall bothers to look at," said Arca, "are women who are gorgeous."

"Well," said the king, "I just happen to have the most gorgeous daughter in the world. We ought to write him a letter."

The King of Ireland then wrote a letter to Cumhall, for him to come where he was so he could be forgiven for what he did against him.

Cumhall then departed and he went to the palace of the King of Ireland. And when he arrived, dinner was prepared for them. They sat at a table and Cumhall could not keep his eyes off of the daughter of the King of Ireland.

"It seems to me that you have fallen in love with the girl."

"Well," said Cumhall, "I favor her over all others that I have ever seen."

"If so, then you and she should marry."

They married then and on their wedding night, Black Arca was sent to hide in the same room where they were. When Black Arca saw that it was time (that the man was losing a third of his energy while having sexual intercourse), he cut Cumhall's head off with his own sword, Mac an Luin. His wife struck her palms (in the manner of keening).

When (Cumhall's hound) Bran saw that Arca had Mac an Luin, he followed Arca and Mac an Luin. Cumhall's wife became pregnant and the king issued a proclamation, that if she had a daughter, they would be indifferent about it, she would not cause her father to pursue her. But if she had a son, he would be killed as soon as he came into the world.

At the end of three seasons, she delivered a daughter, and the king was so overjoyed, that there was no one around the camp who was not comatose from drunkenness.

She said to the midwife who was closest to her, "Look at what I have now."

"You now have," she said, "a son."

"Arise," she said, "and take him and raise him."

"Indeed," she said, "after I have vowed that if there would be a son that I would give him up to the king, and it is a son."

"Leave and raise him, and as long as I have a bannock, you will have a bannock, or anything else that I have, you will have a share of it, if you raise the boy."

The nursemaid left, and she lifted the infant up and she took off.....

Fionn had no idea what he should do, but the plan he came up with was to follow the river he chanced upon and he saw a giant man fishing on the river and he went to where he was.

"What's your news, wee lad?" said the giant man there.

"Well, I don't have any," said the lad, "but I would like you to give me a salmon from the fish that you have, as I'm at the point of starvation."

"Well," he said, "if you bring enough luck with you that I catch a salmon now, you will get it."

He caught a salmon then and he had never caught one as big as it.

The man said, "You certainly will not get this one. I've never caught the likes of it since I've been here and the king will think that it's really big, to get this kind of fish. But you'll get the next one that I catch," he said.

He then caught one and it was larger than the first one that he caught.

"You certainly won't get this one," he said.

"Tut," said the lad, "you'll keep me here forever without giving me any, promising to give me each one, although you haven't given one to me."

"Well, lad, I promise by the end of my fishing rod that even if it is as big as those two, you'll get it."

He then caught one and it was bigger than any he had caught.

"Well, good lad," he said, "here you go now. You will make a fire on the far side of the river, and you will put the salmon on this side of it. If you let it get burnt or blistered, you won't get a bit of it."

The lad made a fire on the far side of the river, with the salmon on this side. As the fire crackled so much, a spark burst from the fire and struck the side of the salmon. The lad leaped across the river and he put his finger on the blister that puffed up on the salmon and he pushed the blister down on the salmon and he burnt his finger and he put his finger in his mouth and he got psychic knowledge that this was the man who killed his father Cumhall, and that the hound that was with him at the river was his father's hound, and that his father's sword was under this man's bed.

When he had then cooked the salmon, he thanked Black Arca for giving it to him. Then he left and he went to Arca's house and he said to Arca's wife that Arca had sent him to get his sword.

Then she said to him, "I don't think that he has any sword other than the sword that is on his hip."

Then he told her that it was under his bed. They tried under the bed and didn't find it. Then he went outside and he was wondering if it was just something that flitted into his head when he thought of the likes of it.

He put his finger into his mouth again and he found out that it was buried under the post timber of the bed. He returned inside and told her that he was saying that it had been buried under the post of the bed. They lifted the bed, they found Mac an Luin. He grabbed Mac an Luin and went off to where Black Arca was.

"You have returned again, lad," said Arca.

"Yes," said the lad.

"What do you want now?"

"Only that they say that it is you who killed Cumhall."

"Well, it is me," he said. "Are you going to be asking for me to be arrested?"

"No, but I'm sure that you enjoyed what you did."

"Indeed, I did," Black Arca said:

> "He squealed like a pig,
> And he farted like a horse,
> While the end of my shaft was in his backside."

"Well," Fionn said, "you son of a bitch," as he was wielding Mac an Luin, "If that's how you dealt with my father, that's how I will deal with you," and he sent Arca's head down the river.

When Bran then saw Mac an Luin, he quickly arose and he followed Fionn. Fionn was now wondering if he would go home or if he would remain away. But he went to the forest to find out what kind of stuff Mac an Luin was made of. He started on the trees, and he was felling the trees as though they were grain under the blade of the scythe.[9]

How Fionn Got His Psychic Powers

This text is an extract of a transcription made in 1803 by schoolmaster John MacPherson from the recitation of Donald MacLean, born in 1715, who learned folktales from his grandfather, Calum MacPhail, a native of Torosay, Mull. This is a very early example of the collection of Gaelic oral tradition, although this narrative was not far removed from the manuscript literary tradition, almost certainly as practiced in the nearby court of the MacLeans of Duart.[10]

This episode of the roasting of the salmon is the best known scene from the Fenian cycle of tales. In comparison to the story from Alasdair Ruadh Johnston above, this text has a simpler plot even though it uses a more elevated register of the Scottish Gaelic language.

In this text, Fionn's psychic powers are called *Fios an Dà Shaoghail* "the Knowledge of the Two Worlds," a facility similar to what is called "the Second Sight" in English. It seems as though this and similar tales help to authenticate and provide an ancient precedent for this phenomenon, which is well attested in Gaelic society to the present day. The two worlds are the mundane world of "normal reality" and the Otherworld of the fairies and the dead, access to which allows the seer to transcend the usual limitations of space and time (see Chapter Five).

He didn't dare to show his face in any place where his foster-mother was wont to frequent. Fionn went into the unknown, without knowing where he was, and every path was new to him, but he went by a waterfall called Assaroe.

And he saw a man fishing at the falls, and Fionn said to him, "I am," he said, "growing weak, I beseech you to give me a wee creature of those fish that I can eat."

"I will not," said the fisherman.

"If you would be so good as to put out your fishing rod," said Fionn, "for my sake."

The fisherman did so, and he immediately caught a full-grown salmon.

"I won't give you this creature, it is too big and too good. This is a fish for a king."

"If you would be so good as to give me the rod."

"You'll get that," said the fisherman.

After Fionn got the fishing rod, he threw out the hook and he pulled to land a salmon that was even larger than the fisherman's salmon.

"I can't give you that creature," said the fisherman. "I will give you a smaller creature. But you must roast it on the far side of the falls, although the firewood is on this side, and if there is one spot on it that is raw or burnt on it, you will lose your head for it, and," said the fisherman, "I'm going to sleep, and let it be roasted before I wake up."

Although this was difficult, he had to accept it. Fionn started to light the fire and to roast the fish, and the fisherman went to sleep. Fionn was vexed, keeping the fire going and roasting the fish, but at one point, a burning bubble arose on the salmon, and as quickly as he could, he put his finger on it and it was burnt to the bone. He quickly put his finger in his mouth, and he got the Knowledge of the Two Worlds, as they call it. He discovered at that moment that it was the fisherman who had killed his father and that his name was Black Forca and that he had Fionn's father's sword with him in a hidden place.

He arose hurriedly and he got his father's sword and he cut off Black Forca's head and Fionn set off to leave after that. He got away from here, as the salmon was drying up at Assaroe, neither cold nor hot. After decapitating the fisherman, Fionn set off on his trip and did not stop or rest until he reached the house of the smith, his grandfather.[11]

Garaidh and the Women

This tale was printed in 1909 in the periodical *An Sgeulaiche* from the papers of Father Allan MacDonald. No further information was recorded about the source of the text, although the tale is a popular one in the lore of the Fianna in Scotland. Several variants were recorded in the nineteenth century that explain the origin of the place name Kylerhea, but this seems to be the only version that also attempts to explain the nearby place name Kyleakin.

There are interesting aspects of gender in the tale, including rivalry between the sexes. The secret diet of the women is a fascinating insight into the resourcefulness of Gaels who derived their sustenance from the local environment, but the specific ingredients of the female super-foods differ across variants according to the location of the storytellers. In inland communities, the foodstuffs were said to be such items as the leaves of trees, the roots of the heather, and the tops of the hazel.[12] The choice of shellfish and seaweed in this variant suggests that the tale was collected from a seaside community, probably one that had been driven to the shore during the Clearances and had to resort to such fare to supplement their meager diets. The "holdfast" of the seaweed is what attaches it to rocks.

Garaidh's spying on the women was an unwelcome intrusion into their private domain. They humiliate Garaidh by stripping him of his long hair, which was a marker of high social status among men in Gaelic society. The women further intimidate him by seizing his sword, another token of masculine power.

The tale conveys a subtle disapproval of endemic violence and cycles of vengeance. Garaidh's murder of the Fenian women could not go unpunished, but Fionn is cruel to force Garaidh's son Aodh to carry it out. Garaidh's release of doves suggests a desire for peace and Aodh's condition that the beheading of his father be done against Fionn's own flesh reflects the self-destructive nature of this violence. Aodh becomes so deranged with anger and resentment that Fionn sends him to take out his battle frenzy against the rising tide of the ocean, which brings about his own death.

The wives of the Fianna were at the point of falling apart because of being fat and plump. The Fianna were about ready to depart. They didn't know what was causing the women to be so weak and faint.

The Fianna were going to the beach from the first ebbing of the sea to the half-water mark, as long as they could get shellfish.

Garaidh said mischievously, "I will pretend that I am unwell today, and I'll find out what diet the women have that is causing them to be so fat, and leaving us so thin."

The Fianna went to the beach, some of them to the mainland at Glenelg, and others to the land across from that at Kyleakin.

Garaidh was here in bed, unwell. The women gathered together and they went to the beach. There were small shellfish on the beach—we call it blue-rayed limpet—and they filled their aprons with all that was there. They then brought an armful of the seaweed there, and they scraped and cleaned the attach of the seaweed. They boiled the shellfish, they took the meat out of it, and they ground up the seaweed holdfasts. They boiled the seaweed holdfasts and the shellfish together, and they made a dish of it. That was the food that the women had that made them so fat—you have long heard that the knuckle-marrow of the deer is in the holdfasts of the seaweed.

After they ate that, Garaidh then began to bestir himself, and the women immediately piled on top of him. And they said that they would not leave him alive to tell the Fianna about their food, for if they found that out, they would not leave shellfish on any rock at the beach of the seaweed to be harvested, or to be boiled.

They grabbed hold of Garaidh then, and they made nine ropes of braids of hair on his head, and they wove Garaidh's head to the ground with nine oaken stakes. They took his own sword in order to cut off his head. He made a surging leap up but the skin of his head and his hair stuck to the ground, and he took off, and he lit every single bothy of the Fianna in Sleat on fire.

There was fresh snow that night, and the Fianna saw that the bothies were on fire, and Reatha went out and set off for the strait, and he put his spear under his arm, and the spear broke as his own weight was resting on it in the middle of the strait, and ever since that day, that strait has been called *Caol Reatha* ("the strait of Reatha," Kylerhea in English usage).

And Kyleakin: Arca's spear broke under his weight, as he was in the middle of the strait, and he himself was drowned, and ever since that day, *Caol Arcainn* ("the strait of Arcainn") has been its name.

The Fianna came home now, and there was no bothy that they ever had that was not aflame.

"It was," said Fionn, "Black-haired Garaidh who did this."

But they found the tracks of blood that his head had shed on the snow, and they followed the tracks of blood until they led to the mouth of a cave.

Garaidh had gone inside walking backward, and after he had been inside for a while, he turned around facing inward, and what did he do but he grabbed a dove, and walked in a little distance further, and he grabbed two more doves. Then he went to the far end of the cave. And when the Fianna came to the cave, Fionn said to Aodh the son of Garaidh, "Go on and bring your father out of the cave."

Aodh left and when he gazed toward the beach, he returned to Fionn.

"My father's tracks," he said, "are going out of the cave."

"Oh, you go on," said Fionn, "and never mind Black-haired Garaidh's tricks walking in the direction of his buttocks."

Aodh went in, and as he did, his father released a dove, and Aodh returned outside to Fionn, and he said to him, "If my father were in the cave, there wouldn't be a live dove in it."

"You go on," said Fionn, "and never mind Black-haired Garaidh's tricks grabbing live doves in there."

Aodh went in then and after he had been in for a moment, his father released two of them together.

Aodh returned to Fionn and he said to him, "Even if my father grabbed a dove, he couldn't grab three live ones."

"Go on," said Fionn, "and bring your father out."

He left then and he found his father at the far end of the cave.

"Go on now, Aodh!" said Fionn, "and cut off your father's head with Mac an Luin."

"Is there anyone here," said Aodh, "who will cut off my father's head instead of me?"

"No," said Fionn. "You will cut it off, and you will get your wish."

"If I get my wish," said Aodh, "you will put my father's head on your thigh."

The sword Mac an Luin never left anything remaining uncut when it was used. If Fionn were to put Garaidh's head on his thigh, Mac an Luin would go through Fionn's thigh. And Fionn was useless after that.

"Well," said people, "we will dig the length and width of Fionn's shank on the beach. We will put three oak beams on top of Fionn's shank, and we will put Garaidh's head on top of the beams."

That was done, and Aodh son of Garaidh took hold of Mac an Luin, and he drew it, and it cut off the head of his father, and it went through the three beams until the beach met the tip of Mac an Luin. Aodh then went into a battle rage and he asked Fionn, "On whom shall I wage my battle?"

"Wage it," said Fionn, "on that incoming tide."

Aodh started then on the incoming tide from the start of the high tide until the end, and then he fell dead when the tide began to ebb.

Fionn thought that that was the most difficult thing that he ever did: to bring down the best warrior he ever had.[13]

Fionn in the House of Yellow Face

Donald C. Macpherson of Lochaber wrote down this tale in 1870 as he learned it from his grandmother long before.

Several different variants of this tale were recorded in the nineteenth century, all of which can be seen as outgrowths of a narrative subgenre called the *bruidhean* tale in which characters are lured into the dwelling of a supernatural being. That transition from the mundane world into the Otherworld is signaled in this story by the thick mist in which the Fianna get lost, the appearance of the hare that they chase, and the building at the fairy hill into which they enter. The plot borrows prominent motifs from tales in this subgenre, especially those of being immobilized and being freed by a magical liquid.[14] A deadly game played by throwing an apple appears in other Gaelic folktales as well.[15]

Macpherson's version is a very well-crafted oral folktale, containing word play, combat, magic, repetition, and role reversal. In most variants of the tale, however, *Blàr Buidhe* is the name of the place where the house of the giant is located, meaning simply "Yellow Field." In this Lochaber variant, the place name has become reinterpreted as a personal name: "Yellow Face."

One day Fionn mac Cumhaill and the rest of the Fianna were hunting in the mountains and it began to snow heavily. Before they had gathered their quarry together, the evening came upon them. As they were tired and wearied, they descended toward the village.

As they were moving along, heavily and slowly, they came to an empty hut in the top of a glen and they went to rest in it. They made a fire and the lads became rowdy and, while they waited for the bird-stew to be ready, they began to pass around the drinking horns and to discuss the days of old. The memory of the renown of their ancestors gave them the usual excitement, and they all said together that any man or beast that would come to trouble the Fianna or insult Fionn that night would have cause to be pitied.

In the very middle of this conversation, a slender brown hare came in, and without care or fear, it turned around once or twice on the hearth, tossed the ashes up to the rafters, and then ran off.

Even so, that did not discourage them. They made a sudden leap out after her. But they entered a mist that was so thick with the descending darkness that they could not even see each other.

Fionn and his twelve lads followed it carefully across the shoulder of the glen. And they did not lose sight of it until it leaped into the window of a gloomy-looking house that they encountered at the base of a fairy hill. And what house was this, but the House of the Yellow Face, a giant that lived upon venomous boars and human flesh.

They went in, and told their tale, but they found no trace of the hare. The only one inside was a woman who was baking. The Yellow Face had not come home from hunting on the mountain. She gave them food and drink and she said that it would be best for them to leave now, before the Yellow Face would come home.

Fionn said that they had never fled before any man and that they would not begin with the Yellow Face, and they pressed farther into the house.

"Stay until the end," said the wife.

As it happened, they had hardly settled themselves down when they heard clitter-clatter at the door. Who was there but the Yellow Face and his lads with a great toothy venomous boar on his back! He gave himself a great big little shake to take the snow off of him and he made the door post and foundation of the house quake.

"I smell the odor of the stranger before me, o wife! Who do you have here tonight?" said the Face.

The wife told him who the guests were who came to visit her since he had left.

"Bring out your lads, o Fionn, to take this load off of me," said the Face.

Fionn never turned down a request to any man, so he sent six men out to the Face. But they barely went past the threshold when the Face struck them with his magical staff and they became stone pillars. He set them on the north side of the door to stop the wispy wind. He left them there and he and his lads brought in the boar. They only waited until after they gave it a rough scraping before the wife put it in the great kettle, that's how the carcass was!

Before it even reached a boil and a simmer, the Face stuck the meat fork into it and he had it out on the floor. And without any further delay, he and his lads sat around it. They tossed each bone to Fionn and his lads as they picked it. It was poor hospitality, but it couldn't be helped.

Fionn was silent and pensive and no wonder. When the feasting was done, and that was not long, Yellow Face asked his wife to bring out the golden apple so that Fionn might pass the long winter night. She brought out the apple and gave it to him. They went at each other with the apple and before long the Face destroyed all of Fionn's lads.

The Face realized that he could not overcome Fionn with the apple and he said that they had to wrestle. They engaged their backs in the struggle, and although they wrestled on, he could not give Fionn as much as a wobble.

When the Face saw that he had met his match, he asked his wife to put on the griddle so that Fionn's feet could be warmed, for surely he was cold in this frozen-hard night. The griddle was heated until it was blazing red and they all circled Fionn (that was when he said, "A man alone is not a man"), and they forced him on the griddle until his legs were burnt to the hips.

Now he was unable to sit. The Face gave a gruff laugh and he stuck the spit through the back of his buttocks and he could not stand up or sit down. The Face believed that he didn't have a gasp of breath left in him and he threw him aside into a corner.

Fionn had never been in a worse plight than this one, except when he was between refusal and need, but he remembered that he had the war-trumpet of the heroes and that it could be heard in the five provinces of Ireland.

When the house was at rest, he crawled out, in the pitch black silence, to the top of a hill and he blew the war-trumpet three times. Throughout this time, the other members of the Fianna were tearful and sad in search of Fionn. They searched every nook and cranny for him, thinking he was dead.

Finally, when they had given up all hope, Brown-haired Diarmaid, his sister's son, heard the trumpet. And when he did, it did not go unanswered. He knew that Fionn would only blow it when he was in mortal danger. He understood that the situation was dire and he swore by his sword that he would take neither meat nor drink until he came to the aid of his mother's brother.

He stirred himself and his lads, and they took unknown paths over hill and dales. And although they were far from Fionn, it did not take them long to reach him.

They found Fionn in a pathetic state, unable to stand up or sit down, in the shelter of a thicket. Diarmaid asked him what he had experienced.

"Never mind," said Fionn, and he told him everything that happened: how the Yellow Face had slain the lads and the abuse that he had received from him, and he advised him to return home before the same thing should happen to him; that he (Fionn) was already as he was.

Diarmaid vowed that he would not return until justice was done and without saying anything more, he went to the house of the Yellow Face.

There was only a woman inside baking. She gave them meat and drink and listened to their tale. She told them that the Yellow Face was hunting on the mountain and that they had better leave before he came home or that they would suffer the same fate as Fionn.

"Let him do as he wishes," said Diarmaid, "but we will not leave until we see justice done."

And they sat inside.

"Stay until the end, then," she said.

They were not there long when they heard clitter-clatter at the door. Who was there but the Face and his lads, with a great, toothy, venomous boar on his back. He gave himself a great big little shake to take the snow off of him and he made the door post and foundation of the house quake!

He shouted, "I smell the odor of the stranger before me, o wife! Who do you have here tonight?"

She told him it was Diarmaid and his lads.

"Bring out your lads, o Diarmaid, to take this load off of me," said the Face.

Diarmaid himself leaped out and before the Face knew what was happening, he killed half of his lads, and he piled them topsy-turvy at the right side of the door across from Fionn's lads.

"You're a bad guest," said the Face.

"If you don't see worse than that from me before day break, don't complain," said Diarmaid.

And without saying anything else, he brought in the boar. They prepared the boar very well, and he and his lads ate their fill of it. They tossed each bone to the Face and his lads as they stripped it.

"You're a bad guest," said the Face.

"If you don't see worse than that from me before day break, don't complain," said Diarmaid.

And he asked for the apple to be brought out so that the Yellow Face could pass the long winter night. The wife brought out the apple and the game began. At the first hurl that Diarmaid made, he killed two to the right of the Face.

"You're a bad guest," said the Face.

"If you don't see worse than that from me before day break, don't complain," said Diarmaid.

The Face hurled the apple back but he did no harm to Diarmaid's lads. Diarmaid hurled the apple next and he killed two to the left of the Face and so it went until he had killed the last of them.

The Face kept saying, "You're a bad guest."

And Diarmaid answered likewise.

When they were tired of the game of the golden apple, Diarmaid said to the Face that they should wrestle. And the men went to wrestle. The fight did not go on for long before the Face was on the ridge of his back on the bare stones of the floor.

"You're a bad guest," said the Face as he gave a tortured grunt.

"If you don't see worse than that from me before day break, don't complain," said Diarmaid, and he asked the wife to heat the griddle so that the Face's feet could be warmed, for surely he was cold after coming home from hunting on the mountain.

The griddle was made red-hot and Diarmaid gave the Face a lift up and there he was, like an oaf on the griddle.

"Ow, ow, ow," said the Face.

"Take it easy," said Diarmaid, "your yellow bones will suffer if I don't help you."

And he held him on the griddle until his legs burned to the hips. The Face was now unable to sit down, and Diarmaid quickly stuck the spit through the back of his buttocks and then he was without the ability to stand up or to sit down. He threw the Face on his side in the corner.

When he was totally sick and tired of hearing the whimpering of the Face, Diarmaid seized him by his chin-hair and said, "Your death hangs over you, old man! What is your ransom?"

"Ow, ow, ow," said the Face, "I have nothing to give for ransom except a healing chalice that is at the foot of that craig, and it will heal Fionn!"

When Diarmaid heard about the chalice, he didn't wait any longer to bargain for more, given that his mother's brother was in agony in the shelter of the thicket and so he went to the cave.

He put his first hand on the chalice and he struck off with it to Fionn. Diarmaid washed Fionn's wounds with it three times. The first time, his legs grew back to the knees; the second time, they grew to the ankles; and the third time, Fionn was unhurt, unharmed, alive and whole as he ever was.

One palmful of the water of the chalice was enough to break the spells of the lads. Then he went to the Face.

"You pathetic wretch," Diarmaid said to him, "swear that you will never again play your tricks or lay your spells on the Fianna."

The Face swore to that and many other things, and Diarmaid generously gave him and his lads their fill of water from the chalice, and then they took leave of each other.

To make a long story short, the Fianna kept the chalice and I left it with them.[16]

Diarmaid and Gràinne

Hector MacLean recorded this tale from Alexander MacDonald of Barra in 1860. It is one of the many versions of the highly popular story about how Gràinne fell instantly in love with Diarmaid after seeing his love-spot and made him elope with her, despite being newly married to Fionn, bringing about tragic consequences.

This variant of the story was risqué by the standards of nineteenth-century anglophone Britain. At the beginning of the tale, Gràinne threatens to accuse Diarmaid of rape if he will not run away with her. Campbell did not print or translate all of the repartee between Gràinne and Diarmaid where she taunts him as being more timid than the trout that has touched her thigh, in the hopes of daring him into being her sexual partner. Fionn throws this mockery back at Diarmaid at the end of the tale, which seems to shame him into accepting the ill-fated hunt that brings his own doom.

Earlier versions of this tale make it clear that Fionn and Oscar play a board game, something akin to chess. Diarmaid helps Fionn by dropping a rowan berry on the square where Fionn should move his piece.

When the Fianna used to go to hunt, one of them would always stay at home to watch the women. One day, Diarmaid happened to be the one who stayed behind. There was something that they used to call "love juice" in the man's face, and he had a helmet that he wasn't supposed to lift up, for there was not woman who would see the love juice that would not fall in love with him, and Diarmaid knew that he was endowed with this.

On the day that he stayed at home, he thought that no one was watching him, and he lifted up the helmet and Gràinne, the daughter of the King of the Province of Ulster, saw the face of Diarmaid. Her soul would not survive unless she could run away with Diarmaid.

Diarmaid said, "That will not suit me: go away."

"Oh, we will go, or else I will rip my clothing, and I will hand you over to Fionn."

"I have no doubt but that he will believe you, because you are his own faithful wife, indeed."

They went away, and they were together for three days and three nights, but he stayed free of her. They kept going. As they were crossing a river, she lifted up her clothing so it wouldn't get wet, and a little trout came up and bumped up against her thigh.

"You are my hero, you cocky, wee trout! Diarmaid hasn't given me even that much pleasure during the three days and three nights that he has been with me. If you were able to travel on land with me, it seems that the smaller man would be the better."

"Well," he said, "given all of the embarrassment I have endured for the sake of chastity, I will not take any more of it."

[Gràinne's response was left out]

"Fionn has now," he said, "come home, and they will not find us indoors. They will then come after us, and they will find us."

"They will not," she said. "Whether or not they find us, we will try to hide ourselves. This is what we will do, we will go up to the forest up there, and the branches and foliage of that tree will hide us."

They then climbed up the tree, and they went into the core of the tree, and they gathered the branches and foliage of the tree around them.

The Fianna came to the house, and they did not find Diarmaid or Gràinne at the house.

"Here, here, lads," said Fionn, "I am without a wife, and the Fianna is without Diarmaid. We ought to go to find them."

They went in pursuit of them, and they went over the same river.

As they crossed it, Fionn said, "We have been walking for a while, and since we have, we will rest a while at the base of this tree ahead of us."

They took Fionn's advice, and they sat at the foot of the tree.

Fionn said, "We should strike up a game, lads."

"We are willing," they said.

Fionn and Oscar used to be the two team leaders of the game. Diarmaid would always be on Fionn's team. Fionn knew that Diarmaid was gifted at games. Oscar needed someone on his team, and it was usually his own father (Ossian).

They started to play. Every game that they played, Fionn was losing, and Oscar was winning. They played three games.

Fionn said, "I am missing Diarmaid terribly, as I would rarely lose a game when Diarmaid was with me. I'm losing now that we've parted. But I'll play you again."

Diarmaid was listening. He went and he put his hand against his right side like this, and he grabbed of one of the red rowan berries that was on the tree, and he let it fall down the tree, while Fionn's back was against the tree. He noticed something hitting him on the back, and put his hand behind him, and he caught the rowan berry, and he put it into his pouch. They began to play a game, and this time Fionn won.

"I've won one," said Fionn.

"Yes,"said Oscar, "but you have lost two."

"Will you play any more?" said Oscar.

"Yes, yes," said Fionn. "Try again."

Diarmaid dropped the next rowan berry, and Fionn won this time.

"Will you play any more?" he said.

"I will," said Oscar. "Although you have won twice, you have lost once."

Diarmaid dropped the third one, and Fionn won the third one.

"Now we are even," said Oscar. "You have won for all of the times that I won."

"Will you play any more?" said Fionn.

"I will," said Oscar. "We will know of the good or bad this time."

They played again. Diarmaid dropped the fourth one, and Fionn won.

"I was winning for as long as you did not have Diarmaid. However this is happening, Diarmaid's influence is around you today, before you won for the fourth time."

Ossian said, "My father did not win against us fairly at all, o son."

"I did so," said Fionn.

"You did not," said Ossian.

"I did: and as proof that I did, I have four rowan berries in my pouch for every game that I won."

He took out the four rowan berries, and when he did, he said, "Come down from there, o Diarmaid, you and Gràinne, daughter of the King of the Province of Ulster, for you are together."

Diarmaid and Gràinne came down. The men were divided again, and Fionn and Oscar bickered. They started to fight, and to hurt each other, and they were doing a lot of harm to each other. The other faction of the Fianna saw that Oscar was about to win against his grandfather's faction.

Goll son of Morna said, "Even though we had no part in the dispute, we ought to intervene and reconcile the children of Treunmhor."

Conan said, "Let the children of Baoisge tear up each other's corpses."

Then Fionn asked Oscar to put down the weapons, before the children of Morna would outlive them in Scotland.

Fionn took notice of Diarmaid, and he said:

> The bottom of my heart, and my hand, and my eye
> Are willing to do you honor!
> O Diarmaid Ó Duibhne, o brave man,
> Leaving with my partner without my knowledge!

There was a woman who was called *Mala Lìth* ("Splendid Brow"), and she had a herd of swine, and their leader was a venomous boar. Many a good lad who went to hunt him did not return intact from the boar.

Fionn said to Diarmaid, "Go and hunt the boar of Mala Lìth among her swine. Many men went who did not come out of the river over a trout."

Diarmaid went to hunt the boar.[17]

The Hunt for the Venomous Boar in Ross

This tale was collected from Donald MacDonald, presumably a native of Ross-shire, and printed in 1910. Nothing else was recorded about this tradition-bearer. This story relates another well-known episode in the Fenian cycle: the hunting of the deadly boar that causes Diarmaid's death.

There are many variants of this tale that locate the scene of the hunting of the boar and the death of Diarmaid in different parts of the Highlands: near Oban, near Portree in Skye, at Ben Loyal in Sutherland, in Glenshee in Perthshire, in Brae Lochaber, and elsewhere. In the case of this version, local storytellers at some time used these characters and this scenario to provide an explanation for the origin of Strath Bran and Loch Bran, making it an interesting example of Fenian place lore in Scotland. There is little doubt, however, that these places bore the name *Bran* before these stories were used to explain them.

This tale echoes others that portray the Fenian heroes as superhuman giants who created features of the landscape, such as the Giant's Causeway in the north of Ireland. The motif of the warrior who is invincible except for one part of his body, and who is killed by a jealous rival with knowledge of that vulnerability, will be familiar to readers of Homer's *Illiad.*

The Fianna were one day hunting in Càrn na Béiste ("the Cairn of the Beast"), a round, high hill in the Achanalt moor, opposite Allt Dearg, where a wild beast called "the venomous boar" dwelt, and from which the cairn got its name, as well as a little loch, near the cairn, called Loch na Béiste ("the Loch of the Beast").

The Fianna saw the beast in the cairn, and Fionn sent his hound Bran against the beast, but when he came near the boar and saw his horrible, wild appearance, he refused to face him, and fled back with his tail between his legs.

Fionn sent him back a second time, but when he came to face the beast he would not engage him. He returned with fear and shame, skulking through the heather to hide behind his master for his own protection. But Fionn became enraged and he turned on the hound and gave him a kick with his foot for his cowardice.

The hound bolted off, shamed and embarrassed, down the brae until he reached the level ground of the strath near the river bank, where he dug a hole for himself, and quickly disappeared out of sight, ashamed from being struck.

The Fianna followed in pursuit of the dog, but when they reached the hole he was out of sight. They tried to coax him out, but he would not answer. And when they lost patience waiting they began digging for him. But the deeper they dug, the deeper Bran would dig, until finally the water rose upon them, and they had to stop. The hole filled with water, and there is a little loch there till this day called Loch Bran, and the entire strath received the name Strath Bran from that time.

The Fianna then returned back to the cairn in pursuit of the boar, and they themselves set on him with their weapons and he was slain by Diarmaid.

Diarmaid was a very handsome man, with a beauty spot in the middle of his forehead, which caused every woman who saw the beauty spot to fall deeply in love with him.

Fionn was jealous of him because of his own wife, and was seeking some way or other to destroy him without being directly involved in the deed.

There was a mole on Diarmaid's left heel that was very vulnerable, and Fionn was aware of this. For this reason, he commanded him to go and measure the boar precisely along the back against the bristles. The venomous bristle pierced the mole and the venom caused the death of Diarmaid.[18]

Chapter Four

Historical Legends and Clan Sagas

Folklorists use the term *legend* to refer to tales about the past that storytellers believe to represent actual people, places, and events. While these tales may be elaborated with details that may not seem realistic to us today (such as encounters with supernatural beings), or literary flourishes and devices that sound unnatural to us now (such as people communicating in the form of poetry or song), these are, nonetheless, forms of narrative that encode and explain the past in Gaelic tradition that can be accurately classified as legends.[1]

There is a very large body of legends in Gaelic oral tradition which function as the collective memory of clans, communities, kin-groups, and families, often intimately bound up with the land on which they live. They typically feature characters whose deeds were worthy of reflection (whether good or evil), or events that had a significant impact on the community that preserved them. Although John F. Campbell's mission in the mid-nineteenth century was to collect International Wonder Tales in the Highlands, he tells us that he was very aware of the ubiquity of legends in Gaelic oral tradition:

> There is popular history of events which really happened within the last few centuries: of this, I have gathered none, but I heard a great deal in a very short time, and I have heard it all my life. It is a history devoid of dates, but with clear starting points. The event happened at the time of Shamas (James) at the battle of Shirra Muir; at Inverlochy; after Culloden. The battle was between MacNeill and MacLeod. MacLeod came from that castle. They met on that strand. The dead are buried there. Their descendants now live in such a place. He was the last man hanged in Harris.... The history is minute and circumstantial, and might be very interesting if faithfully collected, but it is rather local than national, and is not within the scope of my work. It is by far the most abundant popular lore, and has still a great hold on the people.[2]

Campbell also reflects on the fact that these legends are shaped by literary habits and styles—by the practice of storytelling that conveys personal experience—and thus do not follow the logic of historical reasoning or the standards of documentary evidence such as expected by modern historical scholarship.

> The Highland people who followed chiefs to battle in 1745, and earlier, knew less of politics; but they knew accurately what happened to their own relatives at Culloden, or after it, and their descendants remember and tell stories which have been told over winter fires ever since, on the same spot where the first narrator told his tale fresh from the event. Tradition, so far as I have gone, seems to have no power of preserving history entire. I have never found a trace of Bannockburn. But the popular mind, especially in an old country where people vegetate, has

> an almost unlimited power of retaining fragments of history, which, like fragments of glass in a kaleidoscope, take strange form, and become myths.[3]

The distortions, omissions or fabrication of facts in these tales does not mean that they have no value: it merely means that we must always keep in mind that they are literary expressions rather than historical documents to be read literally.

The oldest legends relate to the early Celtic saints, especially Saint Columba. These sometimes contain actual historical details, but they also reflect foundation myths about local religious establishments, practices or beliefs. After these chronologically come tales relating to conflicts between Gaels and Norse invaders (the ninth through twelfth centuries). There are also a few scattered narratives from the era of the Lords of the Isles (the twelfth through fifteenth centuries), but the period of chaos and instability unleashed by the dissolution of the Clan Donald Lordship at the end of the fifteenth century—known in Gaelic as *Linn nan Creach* ("the Age of Plunder and Chaos")—provides the backdrop and subject matter of a large segment of these tales.[4]

In a seminal article published in 1991 devoted to this topic, John MacInnes drew attention to a subgenre of legends that he labeled "clan sagas," tales that represent events in the history of Highland clans that are sometimes linked together in sequences or cycles due to the focus on particular historical characters or themes.[5] As MacInnes noted, the Gaelic clan sagas are told in a specific, consistent style that suggests connections with both medieval Gaelic literature and Icelandic sagas:

> The style of Gaelic clan sagas is always bare and economical. Dialogue is laconic and acts as a narrative device to further and explain the action. In stories of violent events, dialogue also is frequently sharp and violent—which sometimes leads translators to modify or even omit the crucial words.... Exchange of insult and innuendo is central to the plot in saga after saga; and we may find that otherwise distant variants of a story preserve these crucial exchanges virtually unaltered. Some of the utterances are in more or less rough verse; for example, a couplet linked only by one internal rhyme. But some are in quatrain form. They are often veiled but frequently succeed in conveying a sense of dramatic power.... The controlled detachment of the narrative, the spare descriptive style, and the vivid exchanges of dialogue which we find in these stories make them, to my mind, the most interesting of all Gaelic oral tales.[6]

Clan sagas occasionally appeared in Gaelic periodicals of the 1830s and 1840s, but they only began to be collected from Gaelic oral tradition in a systematic way in the 1860s, especially due to the dedication of John Dewar. The Highland élite sometimes included fragments of clan sagas and episodes from them in the histories that they began to write in the seventeenth century, but these were usually translated into Lowland Scots or English and were generally written with a non-Gaelic audience in mind, and thus lose their literary qualities.[7]

One frequent element in Gaelic historical legends is the explanation of the origin and meaning of place names. Although they commemorate many kinds of events, the death of a person at the spot is probably the most common. A preoccupation with the origin and meaning of place names is one of the oldest and most recurring patterns in Gaelic literature. There was an entire genre of the learned tradition called *dindshenchas* concerned with this subject.[8] Although it was not formalized and canonized in Scotland as it was in Ireland, very similar materials and motifs occur in the vernacular oral tradition of Gaelic Scotland. Digressions into place names both serve to anchor a legend in place and provide proof of its veracity.

One of the surprising but historically accurate details in the clan sagas is the use of bows and arrows for warfare. Until firearms became widely available in the Highlands in the late seventeenth century, warbands depended upon archery for attacking enemies at a distance.[9]

The clan sagas are arguably the genre of tales with the greatest gender imbalance, as they reflect the patriarchal nature of clan society when formal institutions and political power were almost completely dominated by men. Women could and did influence social and political matters in less public and direct ways, often through words of praise or shame, as is evident in several of these tales.[10]

Although these historical legends and clan sagas reflect the cycles of violence and retribution that often ricocheted back and forth between clans, they also show the capacity for empathy and reconcilition.

Columba and Mo Luag in Lismore

The renowned folklore collector Alexander Carmichael recorded this tale about his native island of Lismore in the nineteenth century. Calum Cille (521–597, "Colm Cille" in Irish form), known as Saint Columba in English, was the national saint of Scottish Gaeldom. Other early saints play prominent roles in Gaelic tradition within particular regions. Like Columba, Saint Mo Luag (*c.* 510–592) was born into the native élite of Ulster but spent his life serving the Christian church in Scotland.

This tale of rivalry between Columba and Mo Luag, who were in reality contemporaries but not brothers, reflects the competition between religious circles who were active in northern Britain in the early medieval period, each associated with specific saints and kin-groups.

The tale portrays Columba as a sore loser. Having conceded the island to Mo Luag, he engages his mastery of word magic to try to ruin his rival's winnings. Mo Luag, however, responds with corresponding turns of phrase to protect the virtues of his new home. This tale, then, explains both the religious associations of the island and its physical characteristics as the outcome of this struggle. The motif of someone winning a race to land by cutting off a body part and throwing it ashore appears elsewhere in Gaelic tradition, as in the Red Hand of Ulster.

It is said that Columba and Mo Luag were brothers. Each wished to possess Lismore and to make it the centre of his missionary labors, for there was much emulation among the saints of old, striving who should win most souls to Christ.

The brothers arranged to run a race and that the first to land should possess the island. They left together, each saint with his crew of clerics singing the Psalms of David while they rowed their coracles as the Highland boatmen still sing their *iorraim* ("boat-songs").

When approaching the island, the brethren still straining at their oars and the saints chanting their psalms, Mo Luag lifted his axe and cut off the little finger of his left hand, and throwing it ashore exclaimed, *M' fhianais air Dia agus daoine, m' fhuil is m' fheòil air tìr, a Chaluim chaoimh* ("My witness be to God and man, my flesh and blood are on the land, o beloved Columba").

Upon seeing the devotion of his brother, Columba turned aside the bow of his boat and did not land. It is alleged that he tried to depreciate the island as represented in the following dialog:

Calum Cille: Slios mór mar ainm an eilein.
Mo Luag: Mas e slios mór guma slios tarbhach.
Calum Cille: Slocach, cnocach, creagach.
Mo Luag: Brìghmhor, miamhor, preasach.
Calum Cille: Faobhar a chloich bhos a chionn.
Mo Luag: A goimhe foipe.
Calum Cille: Feàrna mar chonnadh da.
Mo Luag: Gabhail mar a choinneal da.
Columba: May "the great plain" be the name of the island.
Mo Luag: If a plain that is great, may it be a fruitful plain.
Columba: Full of pits, hillocks, and craigs.
Mo Luag: Full of juice, dairy, and fruit-shrub.
Columba: The points of its rocks projecting upward.
Mo Luag: Their harm underneath.
Columba: Green alder for fuel.
Mo Luag: May it burn like the candle.[11]

Columba and His Brother Dòbhran at Iona

This tale was recorded by Father Allan MacDonald, probably from one of his parishoners on the island of Eriskay in the late nineteenth century.

There are many tales about one of Columba's followers being buried as a sacrifice at Iona. The earliest appearance of this tale is in a manuscript of the twelfth century which names him as Odhrán. This particular variant makes him Columba's brother named *Dòbhran*, which is the Gaelic word for "otter." It might be this name for a sea creature that pulled the motif of the mermaid into this tale. This creature is certainly an unlikely messenger for the Christian God!

There are many ways of interpreting this symbolically rich tale and its many variants in Gaelic tradition. The pagan-like sacrifice in the very foundation of Iona might suggest that the establishment of Christian centers was building on top of, and obscuring, earlier holy sites. The desire to silence and bury Dòbhran might also be understood as an anti-authoritian critique of institutional religion among Gaels. In addition to these readings, a scholar of medieval Scotland has recently suggested that it describes the ritual landscape at several religious establishments laid by the Columban church.[12]

Columba began to build Iona. He gathered a large work force. But whatever he built during the day was knocked down at night.

He started to send people to keep watch of Iona at night. Every morning, those people were dead at the base of Iona.

He didn't continue sending people for long, but since he was a holy man, he went and he kept watch over Iona himself, to try to see if he could find out what was going wrong.

He was looking far and wide, and they say that she was on the craig's edge, close to the ocean (I didn't see her myself). He saw a creature coming from the shore and one half of her was fish-like, and the other half in the form of a woman. She was old with scales.

When she shook herself, she caused Iona and the ground to tremble. She made a rattling sound, as though jugs were being shaken.

Columba went down to meet her and he spoke to her and he asked if she knew what was killing the people he was sending to watch over Iona at night.

She said that she knew.

"What is happening to them?" he said.

She said that it was just that they were taking fright at her: when she was coming to land, their hearts were giving out on them.

"Do you know," he said, "what is knocking down Iona, which I am trying to build?"

"I do," she said. "Iona will always fall like that, o holy Columba. I am not the one knocking it down, but regardless, it is being levelled."

"Do you know any way that I can make progress on Iona?"

"I do," she said. "O holy Columba, tomorrow you will ask the question of the people working for you, to see which man will be willing to be buried alive under the earth, and his soul will be secure if he is willing to do that, and they will never see me after that. Iona can progress without any worry." She also told him that the pit needed to be seven measures deep.

The next day, he asked the great crowd if any one of them would be willing to be buried alive on the condition that his soul would be secure in heaven. No one was willing to go into the pit even though it was related that his soul would be secure by God's word.

Poor Dòbhran his brother was at the edge of the crowd. He came over and he stood behind his brother Columba and he said that he was entirely willing to be buried alive under the ground on the condition that Iona could be built for his holy brother Columba, and he put faith in Columba that his soul would be secure under God's word.

Columba said, "Although poor Dòbhran is my only brother, I am pleased that he is willing to go into the pit. And on top of that, the creature will never been seen coming to the shore again."

The pit was made as deep as the height of seven men. When Dòbhran saw the pit, he turned to Columba and he asked him as a favor to put a top on the pit and leave him standing for as long as God wanted him to stay alive.

He got his wish, to be put into the pit alive. He was left there. Columba came and he started again on Iona and he was working for twenty days and Iona was progressing fabulously. He was pleased that the matter was succeeding.

After the twenty days, when it seemed like everything was going well, he said that they ought to see what end came to poor Dòbhran, and to open the pit.

Dòbhran was walking on the bottom of the pit. When Dòbhran saw that the pit had been opened, and he observed the entire world before him, he made a standing leap up to the mouth of the pit and put his two hands on the mouth of it. He suspended himself there on the pit. There was a large, smooth water meadow up from Iona filled with rushes. All of those that Dòbhran saw turned rusty red and the tops of them have remained rusty red every since.

Columba cried while he was over there, "Soil, soil, over Dòbhran's eyes, before he spies the rest of the world and its sins."

They put soil over him and then they returned to their work. And nothing went against Columba again until he finished Iona.[13]

Saints of Kintail

Alexander Carmichael collected this tale from Màiri MacRae of Kintail in 1876 when she was nearly ninety years of age.

According to some traditions, Saint Comhghan was the uncle of Saint Faolan, both of whom had competing cults in the Kintail area. Although Comhghan was venerated elsewhere in Scotland, his following seems to have persisted the longest around Lochalsh. As in other tales depicting conflicts between individual saints, this scenario can be best understood as representing the conflicts between the church networks associated with each saint.

The story portrays the very human weaknesses and concerns of the saints, and seems to serve to explain unusual characteristics of the parishes associated with Saints Comhghan and Faolan as curses exclaimed by them after a bitter dispute about their enraged cattle. There is also an interesting geographical symbolism to the story: just as Loch Duich (named after Saint Dubhthach) lies between the areas associated with each of the two other saints, so too does Saint Dubhthach attempt to insert himself between the sparring partners.

There were three saints in the district of Kintail, three famous, honorable saints: Comhghan was the saint of Lochalsh, Faolan was the saint of Killilan, and Dubhthach was the saint of Kintail, on both sides of Loch Duich.

The three saints were kind and loving friends, as saints usually are. They would meet up and chat, pray and worshop, now and again. The three would deliberate about the mysteries of religion and the harms of sin, about the state of the luminaries in heaven and the ignoble in hell. The men were kind friends in every way that neighbors and devotees ought to be.

But one day, what misfortune arose but that Saint Comhghan's cow encountered Saint Faolan's cow in the narrow footpath of the ravine as the summit ascends. Neither one of them steered clear of the other in the narrow pass and, without a peep from a puss, or a word from a wide mouth, without a profanity, they went at each other! They fought and they clashed there all of the live-long bright summer's day, with strong grip and cheer, just as Gaels are wont to do, cattle and humans.

Finally, in this struggle, Saint Comhghan's cow pushed Saint Faolan's cow backward down the precipitous craig above the pool of the river. The cow was a dead blob: the clods and its four legs were on top of it in a winding pool of the river.

All hell broke loose, my dear, and it is no wonder, and there was no way to avoid it.

The two saints met about the two cows, they met, my dear, and they quarreled, they quarreled sharply, bitterly, grievously, hurtfully, and coarsely, my dear, the two radiant saints were like dark sinners.

Dubhthach was struggling to make peace between the men, but they would not listen to him and they paid no heed to his words. As often happens to those who mediate, he got very little gratitude for entering the melee.

Saint Faolan prayed that Lochalsh would suffer the fate that neither a drop of ocean water nor a fresh-water trout would ever go up the river Nostie. And that has not happened from that day to this: not a drop of the ocean nor a fresh-water trout have gone up the river Nostie.

And Saint Comhghan prayed that Killilan would suffer the fate that neither offspring nor luck nor the gift of fecundity would ever come to a couple who went to the wedding stool in Killilan. And that has not happened from that day to this: neither offspring nor luck nor the gift of fecundity have come to any couple who ever married in the parish of Killilan.

From the day that the two saints quarreled until our own day, when there are two people in Killilan who are going to get married, they come over quietly and meekly to the wedding stool in Lochalsh, or to the minister of Kintail, or the priest of Dornie. They will certainly not get married in Killilan. I remember myself a couple who married in Killilan and they never enjoyed the gift of fecundity, or offspring, or good luck. Indeed, they both died within a year of their wedding.

Quarreling is evil! Quarreling is evil, my dear, whether done by saint or neighbor, by devotee or sinner. Och, by Mary of the graces, quarreling is evil![14]

The Norse Princess's Mock Lament

This tale was written down by John Maclean, in Glasgow, from the recitation of his mother, a native of Tiree, and was published by George Henderson in 1910.

The tale is set during the period when Norse power prevailed in the Western Isles of Scotland. A mixed Norse-Gaelic identity emerged around the mid-ninth century as Norse settlers in and around the Irish Sea began to speak Gaelic and assimilate to Gaelic norms. In 1098, King Edgar of Scotland signed a treaty that formally recognized the Western Isles as Norwegian territories. Although people of this mixed background continued to rule the area, their allegiances and identities were increasingly Gaelicized, and the 1266 Treaty of Perth officially returned these islands to the Scottish Crown. This could have accelerated a pre-existing trend to downplay the Norse connections of the region's hybrid culture.

This tale can be interpreted as a parable about the eclipse of Norse culture and cultural memory in the Irish Sea as the area was reabsorbed into a Gaelic milieu in the later medieval period. These Norse cultural ties are metaphorical children that have been abandoned, with people of the Western Isles instead coming to stress adherence to a Gaelic identity, thus causing sickness and death in symbolic terms. By the early modern period, the Norse were represented only as foreign invaders in Gaelic tradition.

This story shares motifs with a tale recorded in several parts of the Highlands about the fiery Norse princess *Dubh a' Ghiubhais* ("Pine-Soot"), whose father was jealous of the forests of Scotland and sent her to burn them down. As in the tale of *Dubh a' Ghiubhais*, animal mothers and their brood are separated from one another and their loud wailing pulls the heart strings of an otherwise ruthless adversary.

During the time that the Norse controlled Tiree, there was a Norse noblewoman (the islanders say that she was the daughter of the King of Norseland) who lived in the island with her husband and her two children. Although she was noble, for all of that, she was extremely bad-tempered, and the Tiree folk were very afraid of her. And although she had such a violent nature and even the men feared her, she greatly loved her two children, a son and a daughter.

I don't remember now how she ended up coming to Tiree at first, whether she intended it or in the company of her husband and his men seeking shelter from storms

(I think it was for the last reason that she came), but in any case, she fell deeply in love with the place and she made a home there.

She never wanted to leave the island although her husband left her by herself frequently when he departed with his followers, to see where they could take plunder or murder and kill people, until a day came when word suddenly came from Norseland asking her to return home as quickly as she could.

Whether the message came from her father, the King, or her husband, I don't remember now, but she was compelled to leave in such a hurry that she didn't have the chance to take her children with her, and she left them in the care of the people of the island, warning them to take the best care of them they could, and threatening them that if any harm should come to the children that she would wreak her vengence on every one of them for it.

The Tiree folk were very glad to be free of the Norse woman for a while, for they endured a great deal of hardship from her, but they were very willing to take good care of her children, as it seems that they were good youths and the people of the island were very fond of them.

Whatever the reason was that took the Norse woman away from Tiree, it detained her longer than she expected, and more than two years passed before she returned again.

A short while before she returned, the two children died, despite all of the good care that they received from those who were looking after them. The Tiree folk were quite sad about the death of the two youths, but they were even more worried about what could happen to them when their mother returned.

It seems that it was the beginning of summer when the Norse woman returned. Before she arrived at the island, the Tiree folk got word somehow or other that she was close at hand, and they were terrified, for they were sure that if her anger could not be assuaged when she heard about the death of her two children, that she would not leave a home or habitation unruined and unburnt, and not a person or creature living.

Therefore, when it was heard that the Norse woman was coming closer to the island, all of the people of the island met together, to see if they could find a way to avoid the wrath of the Norse woman.

After they heard and rejected many opinions, an old, grey-haired man came forward and he said that it was of no use at all for them to try to defend themselves with military means, that the Norse were far better equipped with weaponry and that they were far more expert in warfare than the Tiree folk, and despite every battle deed that they might achieve, that they would be slaughtered and ruined in the end.

"Dear compatriots," he said, "I think, even though we are terrified because of what could happen to us on account of the death of the two children of the daughter of the King of Norseland, I don't expect that there is one of us who is not lamenting the two children who passed away, because they were good youths, and we all loved them greatly, and every one who is here today knows and is certain that we never denied them a single thing that would have brought them joy as long as we had them, and we never held back anything that would have been of use to them when they were sick, and that our hearts are filled with sadness because they passed away. Now, friends, I think that if we can show to the Norse woman the sorrow that we are feeling in such a way that it is impressed on her heart and mind that we could dispel her wrath and we could be free from the predicament in which we find ourselves. Therefore, what I am advising to you is that we gather to the port at which she will land every cow and calf, and every lamb and ewe, in the land, and we will separate them from one another, with cattle and sheep on one hill and the calves and ewes on the other hill, where they will see each other but cannot get close to one another, and I wager that that wailing will pierce the heart of the Norse woman, even if it is harder than the craig on which this island is built."

The Tiree folk took the advice of the old man, and long before the ship of the Norse woman reached the port, she was filled with surprise and with anxiety about the sorrowful wailing that she was hearing on land. As soon as the ship reached the port, the Norse woman sent word to the elders of the island and she asked them what was the meaning of this wailing that she had heard since she came within sight of land.

One of the elders answered that a great tragedy that befallen the island a short while before, a loss so great and so sorrowful that the animals themselves were in sympathy with the people about it.

This answer surprised the Norse woman even more and when she looked around her and she saw how miserably sad everyone looked, she said kindly that she was sorry for the loss that came upon them, and if she could do anything to lessen their sorrow, that she would be glad to do so.

The elders were encouraged then and in words that were kind and composed, they told her what had happened to the two children that she left behind her, how they fell one after the other in sickness, how every cure that they could get was tried in order to return their health to them, and about the sadness that fell on the people of the island when they died.

Long before the elder concluded his account, the Norse woman was crying and keening as though her heart would break, and rather than carrying out murder and ruination on the Tiree folk, as she had threatened when she departed, she thanked and blessed them for their kindness to her children.[15]

The Sea-People of Arran

This tale was collected by James Craig of Kilpatrick in the late nineteenth century from unnamed local tradition-bearers from the Isle of Arran. This tale fuses elements from several different stories about the relationships between land and sea, including an origin myth tracing a family's roots to the union between a seal woman and a human man. Very similar tales of family origins are also told about the MacCodrums of North Uist and as well as a family also known as *Sliochd an Ròin* ("the Seal Clan") in Sutherland.[16]

In fact, these stories about human-seal unions can be found in Ireland, Iceland, Scandinavia, and much further afield. The motifs about the enchanted island, and the ways in which it could be seen, have close parallels in Irish folklore,[17] which is not surprising given the close proximity of Arran to Ireland. As folklorist Bairbre Ní Fhloinn notes:

> In their own way, the beliefs and stories can be seen to reflect an infinitely more refined and sophisticated understanding of the delicate balance which exists between mankind and the natural environment—and of man's place in the overall scheme of nature—than we find in what would usually be regarded as more advanced systems of belief. As such, the legends and beliefs still have much to offer us.[18]

According to oral tradition, the Island of Eabhra is an enchanted island, lying under the sea near the Iron Rock off the Corriecravie shore. At times it would be so clear that you could see the stacks of grain in the fields, and the women putting out their clothes to dry.

It is now about fifty years since it was last seen. One day a farmer was out looking after his flock and what did he see but the island rising out of the sea close to the shore, and in order to get a better sight of it he ran towards the shore.

For a short time he lost sight of the sea in a hollow through which he had to pass, and on reaching the height from which he could view the sea, the island was nowhere to be seen: it had entirely disappeared.

One time an Arran boat was about to leave the Ayr pier, and just before it sailed away, it is said that a certain man—a stranger—came leading a grey filly by the halter, asking for a sea voyage.

The skipper took them on board, and the boat was put off to sea. When they approached the Iron Rock, the filly began to neigh, and the neighing of other horses was heard from the depths of the sea in response.

Then the stranger asked the crew to throw her over the side, and after that was done, he gave a sudden leap after her and they both disappeared.

A year later, who met the skipper at Ayr market but the same man to whom he gave the passage on his boat.

"I've seen you before," said the skipper.

"If you did," said the man, "you will never see another." In the twinkling of an eye, he struck the skipper on the face with his palm, leaving him totally blind.

It is said that the fishermen would hear, on calm, still nights, as they waited to lift their nets, the crooning of gloomy music and verses of songs coming up from the Island of Eabhra:

> Where have you left the fair men, *Hó ró golaidh u lé*
> We left them on the sea-girt isle, *Hó ró golaidh u lé*
> Back to back with no breath in them, *Hó ró golaidh u lé*

If the story is true, a Kilpatrick farmer one day came upon a mermaid from the Island of Eabhra while she was sound asleep on the shore, with her magic skin by her side.

He snatched the skin and made his way to his house. She had no choice but to go with him. They got along together so well that they got married and she bore him a son and daughter.

Seven years after that he was at church on a certain Sunday, and on returning home, he could not find his wife.

It happened that the children were playing in the barn, and they came across something that amazed them. They quickly ran to their mother, shouting, "Mother, mother! Come and see the beautiful thing that my father has hidden in the threshing-corner."

Their mother understood very well what the "beautiful thing" was, and she said to the children, "Bring it in here and I will give you a tasty butter sandwich."

The children did as they were told, and as she expected, it was indeed the magic skin. She took hold of the skin, and no sooner did she get it into her hands, than she went off to her old home in the sea.

Sometimes she would come to Rudha an Lòin to call on her children, and they would be seen in her company, and she would comb their hair and sing songs to them.

One day the little boy followed his mother to the sea, and never was seen again, but the girl returned home. She grew up to be a beautiful woman. She married, and according to the tale, some of her offspring—known as *Sliochd an Ròin* ("the Seal People")—are alive to the present day.[19]

The Feral MacDonalds of Braemar

John Grant of Glengairn printed this story in his 1861 collection of folktales from Braemar in Aberdeenshire. This area was Gaelic-speaking into the twentieth century. Grant peppers his stories with names, phrases, dialog, and verses in Gaelic, even though most of his text is written in Scots-inflected English. "Ferlie" is a Lowland Scots word meaning "oddity, curiosity" and can also be used in a disparaging way of people.

Two different family lineages in Braemar claim this "feral MacDonald" as their founder figure. One of them is Glen Muick, whose name means "Pig-Glen": hence the association with the wild boar. Both boars and canines have strong associations with warriors in Celtic cultures, as demonstrated by tales about Cù Chulainn. The words for hound and wolf feature in the names of many Gaelic heroes, and king Cormac mac Airt was one of numerous Gaelic figures said to have been suckled by wolves.[20]

Long, long ago, wild and ferocious beasts roamed through the forests of the Braes o' Mar—the wolf, the boar, the wild-cat. They are all away now, like the people with whom they contended for possession, save a few cowed-down and spiritless wild-cats.

The child of a widow MacDonald, crawling about the door—a very naughty imp, no doubt—was snatched away by a wolf or wild-boar in quest of a tender bit for his young, and tossed heedlessly by him among the brood.

Strange to tell, the mother, on arriving, did not discover the intruder, nor chew him down into crowdie for her legitimate offspring as a sensible affectionate mother ought to have done. In a mistake, I will hope, she used him as one of the family, allowed him the due as to suckling, and treated him to all the tit-bits that came in the way, as a rather delicate nursling. He must have astonished the good lady in various ways, and no doubt been considered a prodigy among the race.

What I know is that he came on well with his companions, grew up a hairy monster, joined in all their plundering expeditions, and had dogs at his heels—his proper mother not unfrequently the hounder-on—so often that he was a credit to his teachers. It is not, indeed, known to what a height of glory and power he might have brought his republic, for he was unfortunately taken captive by the people of a farm adjoining the one he was stolen from.

They were not a little astonished by the discovery of this novelty in the fauna of the country, and kept him carefully as a wondrous *ferlie*. He got tamed down a bit, in time picked up some phrases, and thus far civilised, was recognized by his mother, one time she called at the farm, from a certain mark on his face.

He took no offence at his re-establishment among the human race, to which, it was proved, he belonged; but he had a decided objection to return to his mother, choosing rather the society of a young damsel of his captor's family, in a bothy put up on their behoof.

He reproached that mother in after-time thus:

'Bhean ud anns a' bhail' thall,
Chuir coin a' bhaile air mo lorg:
Ged dh'òl mi bainne do chìche
s laigh mi naoidh mìos 'do bholg.

O yon woman in the village over there
Who sent the village dogs on my trail:
Even though I drank the milk of your breast
And I was nine months in your womb.

This union became the cause of a wild but brave race appearing in the country. Both Glen Muick and Glen Cluny claim the legend, with this difference: Glen Muick, true to its name, attributes the taking away of the child to a wild-boar, and furthermore bestows on that child the name of Andrew, deriving from him the MacAndrews in the three united parishes. Glen Cluny stands by the wolf, and holds that the MacDonalds, long called *Sliochd a' Mhadaidh-Allaidh* "The Clan of the Wolf," of whom there are yet three families in Braemar—one at Altchlar, one at Ardearg, Corriemulzie, and the third in Glen Cluny itself—are the descendants of this hero.[21]

The Big Blacksmith of Glen Urquhart

William Mackay, a native of Glen Urquhart, transcribed this clan saga in 1873 from local traditions he gleaned from family and neighbors. It is a fascinating amalgam of elements from Gaelic tradition and motifs from oral folktales, set in the distant past but made to connect to events known from historical documents about the Battle of the North Inch in 1396.

The storyteller also authenticates the tale through the explanations of the names of places and families in Glen Urquhart. The Macmillans are one of the old families of the glen and the tale derives their name from the "Bald Lad" who sought refuge with the blacksmith: Macmillan in Gaelic is *Mac 'ic 'ille Mhaoil* ("the Grandson of the Bald Lad").

Although it is not explicitly stated, we can infer from similarities with other Gaelic stories that the Big Blacksmith's secret formula for the creation of the extraordinary swords was given to him by his fairy lover. The white fairy cattle are another significant marker of his connection with the Otherworld. In addition, his acquisition of the shaggy philly from the fairies gave him an enhanced social status and material prosperity until he broke the taboo he was given—another common motif in supernatural tales.

There was once a particular man in Polmaily who people called "the Big Blacksmith." The Blacksmith had seven sons and he and his sons were as skilled at making weapons as anyone who had ever struck an anvil. They were particularly renowned for the cold-iron swords they made. These swords were made without any fire, only the heat put in the iron with the striking of the hammers.

The Gaels prized them because they brought victory. The Big Blacksmith was not only renowned as a blacksmith, he and his seven sons were famous as warriors.

The Blacksmith had cattle in Polmaily that were especially beautiful, but they very quickly became so sickly that they could barely stand up in the byre. And regardless of what they ate, they didn't seem to improve.

Tornashee ("the Fairy Mound") is a beautiful mound near Polmaily and in the

Blacksmith's day, it was a residence of the fairies. It was said that the Blacksmith had a fairy as a lover even though his wife was still alive.

One day when he and she were in the woods, she told him that the fairies had stolen his beautiful cattle and that fairy-cattle were now in the byre.

The Blacksmith made for the byre, enraged, and he attacked the cattle with an axe. But in the twinkle of an eye, they took their heads out of the halters and they ran out of the byre.

The Blacksmith firmly seized the tail of the last of the cattle and he kept hold of it until they came to Càrn an Ràth ("the Cairn of the Fort") in Beinn a' Gharbhlaich near Achnababan ("the Field of the White Cow"). The cairn opened and the cattle went inside.

And even though they did, the Blacksmith followed them until he came to a beautiful room in which were the most valuable things imaginable. And he was asked to name the thing that he most wanted and that he would get it.

There was a little, shaggy filly in a remote corner of the room about which the Blacksmith had heard his fairy lover speak as the best filly in the kingdom. And he said that he would take the filly.

"May the mouth of your informant lose a tooth," said the fairies, because they recognized that he got good advice. But they gave him the filly, with the command to never attach it to a cart, for as long as he attached it to a plough, there would not be a filly in the land who could pull it as well as it would.

> It could plough Achadh nam Bò ("the Field of the Cattle")
> And Lurgamor from end to end;
> And likewise Gorstan Keppagach
> Before it was unyoked from the plough.

The Big Blacksmith had the shaggy filly for a long while, and it was very useful to him and the entire population of the area. But eventually a cart was attached to it in order to spread manure. And ever after that, it was no stronger than any other filly.

The seven sons of the Blacksmith were sleeping in the barn on a hill which is still called Torran nan Gillean ("The Hillock of the Lads"). The Blacksmith's daughter was married to a man who was named Gille Phàdraig Gow. At that time, he happened to kill a Cameron in Lochaber and he fled to Glen Urqhuart, where he got work in the smithy of the Big Blacksmith.

Cameron of Lochiel heard that the murderer was in Glen Urquhart, and he sent men to capture him.

When the Blacksmith heard that the Lochaber men had come, he convinced the man they were pursuing to cut off his hair and beard. The Lochaber men came into his smithy and they asked for the man, who was at that moment striking the hammer.

"Strike the hammer, o Bald Lad," said the Blacksmith.

The Bald Lad struck the hammer like a true blacksmith and the men didn't recognize him. They returned home and they said that they were not successful. A while after that, Cameron of Lochiel found out that the Bald Lad was actually the man they were after, and he was enraged against the Blacksmith and the people of the Glen. And he resolved to injure them grievously.

He and a large warband came and they seized Urquhart Castle. The countryside was now under his control except for the blacksmith and his sons, and he didn't dare to try to fight them directly. But he thought that there was another way.

He sent word to Gille Phàdraig Gow, the Blacksmith's son-in-law, and he promised him that if he found a way to kill the Blacksmith and his sons, that he would get the Blacksmith's land in Polmaily.

"Choose the most capable men that you have," said Gille Phàdraig Gow, "and let them follow me in the middle of the night tonight."

That's what happened, and the lad and the Lochaber men left the castle at midnight, and they made for the barn where the Blacksmith's sons were, thinking that if they killed them, it would be easy to kill the Blacksmith.

Some of them stood at the barn door and the rest went inside and they assaulted the sons. The sons tried to get out, but as they crossed the threshold of the doorway, the Lochaber men knocked their brains out with a shaft.

As these deeds were happening at the barn, the Blacksmith's wife was having a dream that large, black sow and its litter of piglets was burrowing under the foundation of the house. She had this dream three times and then she woke the Blacksmith, and she made him go to the barn to see how the sons were.

The Blacksmith took his claymore with him, and after he arrived at the barn and saw the Lochaber men, he attacked them. They fled and he followed, killing with every blow. He was working hard to get at his son-in-law, and when that coward saw this, he started to yell, "It's me! It's me!"

"I know that it's you," responded the Blacksmith.

The Blacksmith finally got hold of his son-in-law after he went over a stream which is still called Gille Phàdraig Gow's Stream and he cut his ear off.

"There's a message for you," he said, "to take to Cameron of Lochiel. Tell him that I will be at my morning meal tomorrow with him."

Then he returned to the barn and he found all of his sons dead except for the youngest. The young man's back was broken, and ever after that, he went under the name "the Bent Blacksmith."

The Big Blacksmith was so heartbroken by the death of his sons that he died shortly thereafter. After his death, the Bent Blacksmith loaded his tools on a Highland pack-saddle on a horse, and he left Glen Urquhart, saying that he would stop where the pack-saddle broke. The pack-saddle didn't break until he reached Perth.

In that town he built a smithy, and the people of Glen Urquhart insist that the Bent Blacksmith was in the bloody conflict between the Davidsons and Clan Chattan in the presence of the king, on North Inch, in the year 1396.

To the present day there are people in Glen Urquhart who maintain that they are descended from the Big Blacksmith and that the MacMillans in the Glen are descended from the Bald Lad.[22]

The Camerons' Doomed Raid on the Lennox

John Dewar wrote down this tale in about 1860 and sent it to John F. Campbell. It was probably drawn by Dewar from the traditions of his family and community *céilidhs* around Loch Lochmond-side. Dewar may be alluding to this tale in a letter he wrote to Campbell:

> I remember, in the winter nights, when a few old people would be together, they would pass the time telling each other stories, which they had by tradition. I used to listen attentively,

> and hear them telling about the *ceatharnaich*, or free-booters, which used to come to plunder the country, and take away cattle, and how their ancestors would gather themselves together to fight for their property....[23]

The Gaelic word *ceatharnach*, borrowed into Lowland Scots as "cateran," is what Dewar uses in this tale for men who have come to take away the cattle of another clan. It is rendered into English here as "raider" and "plunderer." This was not considered a crime per se—as private property in the modern sense did not exist—but a customary form of inter-clan aggression. The long distance between Sunart, the home of these Camerons, and the Lennox is a testimony to the physical endurance of cattle raiders and their knowledge of travel routes across the Highlands.

The MacFarlanes controlled the top of the triangular landmass flanked by Loch Lomond, Gareloch, and Loch Long, referred to in Gaelic by the nickname *An t-Eilean Leamhaineach* ("the Island of Lennox"). Given his strategic control of this bottleneck, MacFarlane of Arrochar ran a protection racket whereby the inhabitants of the territory paid him a fee and in return he ensured that their livestock would be safe from hostile intruders. The tale reminds us that this region, so "wild" and empty today, was once full of a Gaelic-speaking population and their livestock.

The name of the warrior who leads the party of MacFarlanes pursuing the Cameron raiders is Calum Garbh MacEóghainn, which could be translated into English as Rough Malcolm MacEwen. As both "Calum" and "Garve" have been borrowed from Gaelic and are fairly common in Scotland, I have brought them over into English without translation.

It used to be a custom in Gaelic Scotland that when any disagreement occurred between two clans, for one of them to go and raid the lands of the other. Pursuers would be sent after them, and many a time did the raiders and pursuers fight a battle against one another.

On one occasion a band of warriors came from Sunart, and made a raid on the "Island of Lennox." At that time it was the Laird of Arrochar who imposed blackmail in the isle, and if any livestock were stolen from the land, he had to pay for them, or else recapture them and return them to the people to whom they belonged.

If any raid was taken from the island, it was the Laird of Arrochar's duty to drive the plunderers back and to recover the raid, or else to replace them with new animals.

The Laird of Arrochar sent a band of his men to recover the plunder and Calum Garve MacEwen was the captain over them.

Calum Garve and his men followed the raiders past Tyndrum, Leac an Dogha in the Brae of Glen Orchy, and Inveroran, and they found the cattle grazing on the side of a mountain, with no one watching over them. The Camerons from Sunart were all asleep.

Calum Garve and his men encircled the cattle and drove them back to take them home. When they had arrived at a place called Leac an Dogha, one of Calum Garve's men looked back, and saw the Camerons coming after them.

The Camerons had been asleep when MacEwen and his men came and took away the cattle. When they woke up, the cattle were not where they had left them.

They looked for them, and they saw MacEwen's men had the cattle, and were in front of them and were now high up the face of Leac an Dogha, at the top of Glen Orchy. The Camerons followed them.

A very battle-hardened man called MacGillony headed the Camerons, and he had heard about Calum Garve MacEwen, and he was greatly pleased to see him and to find out which of them was the greater warrior.

As one of Calum Garve MacEwen's men was looking around in the direction from which he came, he saw MacGillony and his men coming after them, and he said to Calum Garve, "Over there is the banner of the Camerons, coming after us: it is white."

Calum Garve said, "If it is white now, it will be red before it returns."

Calum Garve had heard about MacGillony and was greatly pleased to see him, so that they could find out which of them was the greater warrior.

Calum Garve asked who the capable men would be who would go off with the cattle, while the rest would remain at Leac an Dogha to face the Camerons and hold them back. But not one of them was willing to leave with the cattle, for fear that they would be called cowards.

Calum Garve had a great deal of trouble with his men before he could find any who would stay with the cattle. Calum Garve said at last that the two oldest men of the company should be the ones to drive the cattle on, and then if they were needed, they would be brought back to help those who would fight. But they had to draw straws to decide, and the straws fell on two of the oldest men in the company. They went to drive the cattle off but they stopped at a watchpoint, in sight of the place where the battle was to be fought.

When the Camerons moved forward, the MacFarlanes would not let them pass and the battle began. They fought so fiercely that every man fell on the field except MacGillony himself and he was not wounded. He went back and forth over the battlefield seeking Calum Garve but not one of Calum Garve's men would tell him which one he was.

MacGillony finally came to where Calum Garve himself was lying and MacGillony asked Calum Garve if Calum Garve MacEwen was lying in that battlefield.

Calum Garve replied that he was.

MacGillony said he would like to see him and asked him where he was.

Calum Garve replied that he was very thirsty and if he could get a drink, he would show him where Calum Garve was.

MacGillony said that he had no way to get him a drink, that he didn't have a flask.

Calum Garve was lying down, with his foot cut off, and the foot was still in the shoe. Calum Garve pointed at it with his finger and said, "Take the wooden block out of the shoe, and get me a drink from the stream over there," stretching out his hand in the direction of the stream.

MacGillony took Calum Garve's foot out of the shoe, and he went to the stream with the shoe, and he began to wash the blood out of it in order to get the man a drink of clean water.

While he was doing that, Calum Garve arose on one knee and put an arrow in his bow, and aimed it at MacGillony. He pulled the bow-string, and shot the arrow at MacGillony, hitting him in the small of the back.

When MacGillony noticed the arrow piercing him, he put his hand to his back where the arrow had hit him.

Calum Garve shouted to him, "Ha hó, o friend, look for it on your other side: when Calum Garve shoots an arrow from a bow, it will be found poking out on the far side of the target."

When MacGillony heard this, he drew his sword, and went over to where Calum Garve was. Calum Garve was waiting for him with his sword drawn, whenever he would come.

The two fought each other, and tore each other with the swords, until they both fell, side by side. Then the only two left standing on their feet were the two who had gone away with the cattle.

The only thing those two could do was for one of them to bring the news to their relations, and for the other to look after the wounded until people came to help them.

The dead men were buried there, and the wounded were taken away home. Calum Garve was taken to Stuc na Cloiche beside Loch Lomond, in Arrochar, but I never heard what happened to the Camerons who were wounded on the battle field.[24]

The Outlaw Black-Haired Finlay MacRae

The Celtic Annual published this folktale contribution from Hector MacDougall in 1916. Although a native of the island of Coll, MacDougall was active in Gaelic circles in Glasgow and probably collected this tale from an emigrant from Kintail, where it was popular.

Finlay's weapon of choice is not explicitly stated, but he is known from other tales as a bowman. This tale seems to relate to the circumstances of the sixteenth century, when the MacKenzies of Kintail and the MacDonalds of Glengarry and Sleat were in conflict. The actions of the hero are also attributed to other outlaw archers in clan sagas from elsewhere in the Highlands.[25]

This tale features a motif that is commonplace in clan sagas: while men may carry out heroic or horrific deeds, it is often the words of women who incite, goad or shame them into action. There are plenty of harsh words and hostile repartee between the men in the tale as well, however.

There was a famous hunter who lived in Gairloch in Ross-shire who was named Black-haired Finlay MacRae. Most of his time he spent managing the hunting forests of the chieftain of the MacKenzies, but due to a killing in which he had a part, he left MacKenzie's service and he began to poach on his own because he was as renowned a stalker and man of the forest as ever lived in the Highlands.

I intend, at the moment, to given an account of the grisly murders in which he was involved, although he did many other deeds that are worthy of recounting.

During the time in which Finlay was in MacKenzie's service, there was a poacher who lived in Lochaber who was named Big Donald Kennedy. This man went great distances to hunt the deer. He would often travel even as far as MacKenzie's hunting forest and leave a deer or two stretched out on the heather without Black-haired Finlay knowing it, even though he was quite observant.

After a while, the chieftain's wife, Lady MacKenzie, suspected that the deer were thinning out. And one day she asked Finlay to go and get some venison, "if there was a deer left in the area."

Those words wounded Finlay to the heart and he took off for the hillside. He didn't go far when he came upon a man in a hollow on the side of a mountain who was gutting a deer. He approached closer to him and it was none other than Big Donald Kennedy from Lochaber.

"The hunt belongs to you but the venison belongs to me," said Finlay, with the words of his mistress still ringing in his ears.

"The hunt belongs to me. My feet were quicker to meet it when MacKenzie and his servants had not even arisen yet," said Big Donald, "and the venison belongs to the man who has the best right to it."

Without any further delay, the two stalwarts attacked one another, and whether or not it was an accident, or however it happened, Finlay's dirk stabbed Big Donald to the heart, and he fell lifeless on the ground.

Finlay hid the corpse in the heather and headed off to the castle with Big Donald's deer. But little did he know of the calamity that was to be stirred by that day's work, when he set the deer down in front of the lady.

She was perplexed that Finlay could hunt and kill a deer so quickly. But he told her what had happened and that Big Donald was cold and dead, hidden in the heather.

"Well," she said, "although I was the cause of it, it is as well for you to flee, as Kennedy has left behind in Lochaber those who will seek vengeance."

That is was Finlay did. He took off as far as Strathfarrar, where he built a bothy for himself and his wife, and after that he brought his brother and his brother's son to live with them, and they began to do some farming along with hunting and fishing. For a while, they lacked for nothing.

But one day, when Finlay returned home from across the mountain, he found the house roofless and his brother and nephew cold and dead on the field where they were slaughtered on the spot while they were ploughing. There was no sign of his wife, but after a short while, he saw her, on the verge of losing her senses with fright, returning from across the mountain where she had fled for her life when the fracas began.

She then told Finlay how four large men came, one of them old, as though he were the father of the others, up from the direction of Sgurr nan Lapach, and when they finished with their horrific business, they returned in the same direction.

"Their deeds will not go unavenged," said Finlay as he began to sharpen the dirk, and without any further hesitation—without even burying the corpses that were freezing in their own blood on the field—he took off for Lochaber as he knew very well that that was the quarter from which the people had come.

He arrived and he took a careful scan of the house where he believed that they lived but no one could be seen indoors except for an old woman who kept going in and out as though she was expecting somebody. And he understood from that that the ruffians had not yet returned.

But at about midnight he saw them descending toward the house and going inside. He waited patiently until they had gone to rest. He went inside carefully and silently and they were there stretched out on the floor on beds of straw in deep sleep—a sleep from which they never awoke, as Black-haired Finlay's dirk carved a nest in their bodies.

And he drew the red blood of their hearts to the floor, man after man, and he was close to Strathfarrar before anyone in Lochaber knew about the murder that was carried out in their midst.

But the relations of Big Donald did not stop at that, even though they fared no better. Black-haired Finlay was one day on the way home, descending from the mountain, when he noticed six strangers who were also making for the house. As soon as he saw them, he realized what their intentions were.

But he made for them as though he had no doubt in his mind.

"Do you know," asked the oldest man, who was, apparently, the leader of the rest, "the location of the house of Black-haired Finlay MacRae? It seems to me that he lives in this area."

"Yes, I do," said Finlay, "I was just there."

"So you know the man," said the stranger, looking Finlay over carefully.

"Yes, I do very well," said Finlay, "I have shepherded his flocks for many years now."

They then asked him to direct them to the house. And Finlay made straight for the bothy.

"The man of the house is sick and in bed," he said when they reached the doorway, "but come inside. He will be glad to see you all."

They did so, man after man. Now, the doorway was so low that a person had to stoop down until they were nearly crawling, to go in or out, and as soon as the last of the men was on his hands and knees to enter the house Finlay drew his dirk and slaughtered that man in the doorway.

"The man of the house is here," he then cried, "Who is seeking him?"

In the blink of an eye, his wife tossed the rest of his weapons to him out of a window, and she quickly followed them, and not one of them came out of the house alive.

Their efforts stopped at this, and it was enough. Altogether, twelve men lost their lives on account of one deer and the wounding words of a lady![26]

Donald of the Songs and the Deer

A contributor identified only as "Diarmad" sent this mix of stories and songs to the Gaelic periodical *An Gàidheal* in 1876. The subject of these anecdotes, Donald son of Finlay of the Songs, was a famous hunter and poet who lived in the late sixteenth century.

Donald was the author of one of the oldest and most remarkable song-poems to have survived in Scottish Gaelic oral tradition. It is usually referred to as "Òran na Comhachaig" ("The Song of the Owl"). To quote John MacInnes's remarks about this lengthy epic:

> It celebrates mountains and deer-hunting with hounds. It is also concerned with great men, the passage of time, old age, and with many other topics besides. To use Auden's terms, it is full of Sacred Events; and because that ultimate reach of the imagination has been attained, it is simultaneously mundane, vibrant, unmystical, and limitless. The observation in it is a kind of obsessive regard, which at times finds expression in a curious understatement: what emerges has a powerful, disturbing eloquence.[27]

We can expect that the author of such an exceptional poem would have been equally extraordinary, and oral traditions certainly say as much.

The Fenian cycle has exerted a strong influence both upon the poem composed by Donald and stories about him.[28] The tale of the last stag he felled bears a striking resemblence to a tale about Ossian's last hunt.[29] In any case, this tale about Donald and the song he composed are strong testimonies to the Gaelic sense of place and belonging and love of nature.

According to the traditions of Lochaber folk, he belonged to the people of Glencoe and his father, Finlay, was the standard-bearer of the chieftain of Glencoe. His mother was a Lochaber woman. His mother's father had been the poet and master-hunter of the chieftain of the MacDonalds of Keppoch and he lived at Creag Guanach.

Donald spent the earliest years of his youth with him. And because he did, from the beginning of his life, he was raised with poetry and hunting, as he says himself:

> I was always, since I was born,
> In the company of deer and hinds.

When he came of age and his father died, he went to live in Glencoe. It is not certain how long he spent there. But it can be seen in the poem that he and the chieftain had a falling out. Whatever the reason for the discord, Donald left "the Birds of the Craig House" and he vowed that he would never return, and he never did.

He returned to his familiar haunt at Creag Guanach and he received a warm welcome. It happened that his grandfather had just become old and weak at the time and the chieftain of the MacDonalds of Keppoch then made Donald his bard and master-hunter. He gave him two residences: Creag Guanach and Feàrsaid Riabhach. He spent all summer as though he were at a shieling at Creag Guanach at the upper end of Loch Tréig, and he used Feàrsaid on the other side of the loch as a winter residence.

Once he was settled as he wished to be, he married a woman of the MacDonalds of the Braes of Lochaber, but they enjoyed but a short time together. He remained ever after a bachelor and the one daughter that they had—Mary—remained unmarried to keep house for him. Donald was a well-built man, without being overly tall. He was active and healthy, and he lived a long life.

He had no equal when it came to archery. Until this very day, it is said to a man who is good at the bow that "he aims as well as Donald son of Finlay." He knew an enormous treasure of song-poetry and stories, and he composed many songs. The only one which is named is "The Song of the Owl." The song "The Aged Bard's Wish," which many people fancy, does not come close to it.

There are many tales told about his archery, his hunting misadventures, about himself and the Spectre of Death, about how he allured the ear of the deer, and other things, but it will suffice for me to relate just one or two of them.

During Donald's time, as has often happened since then, there was a renowned stag frequenting Gual an Liath-Ghiubhais, and on this day, he thought that he would take a jaunt over to seek it out. He went over across Uisge Dubh, and as fate would have it, who else was on the hunting hill that day but Black Duncan Campbell of the Cowl, whose servants were on the same path, and before Donald was able to notice him here or there, they had him in their snare.

There was no way around it: he had to accept their capture and leave with them to Finlarig Castle.

Donald's renown had spread far and wide, and there was jealousy of him in the court that incited the servants to want to kill him, but the Knight of Finlarig was a bard himself, and he would not let them lay a hand on him.

As they were traveling, they saw a deer hind lying down at a spring, and they said to him, mocking him, "We will release you if you shoot an arrow through the right eye of that hind over there."

It was not likely that he could do this, given the way that the hind was lying down, and the direction of the wind. But regardless, Donald readied the bow, and he took stock of the wind and the landscape, but he couldn't make a scratch on her. When he failed to attract her attention, he made a sort of meowing whistle and the hind raised her head. He made it again and she turned around so that she faced him.

Then he took his chance, and he aimed the arrow at her eye, and "there was not an inch of the arrow that would not be plunged into the target, from the tip to the notch."

When the Knight of Finlarig saw how well he did, he released him. Not only that, he invited him to come and stay with him for as long as he lived.

Donald thanked him, and he said that even if he granted him Finlarig Castle from its foundations, he could never leave behind the deer and Loch Tréig.

At that time, a great deal of Lochaber was heavily forested, and wolves were sometimes found there. Donald was once traveling in the twilight around Dubh Lochan (the small loch behind Feàrsaid Mhór) and the hairy beast was seen in the stones and logs returning from the mill where he was searching for plunder.

Donald followed him and he killed him and his wife was greatly surprised by the first thing she saw that day in a tree, close to the door.

He killed another one at Lùb a' Choire Chreagaich.

Donald's house was at the same site as the White House of Feàrsaid—owned by foreigners today, tragically.

After he had become old and weak, and could only move between the bed and the fireside, he was once looking out the window at the mountain in the gloaming, and he noticed a huge stag moving furtively to the garden in the back of the house.

Mary was sitting at the fireside, and she heard her father gasping for breath. She arose quickly and asked him what was bothering him.

"Hush," he said. "Get my bow."

She thought that he was becoming deluded by being close to death. The bow had been put up in the rafters for who knows how long, but she brought it down.

"Put the string on it," he said.

"Heavens!" said Mary. "There's not a man in Lochaber today who could put the string on it."

"Give it a try," he said, as he showed her how to do it, giving it his all. The bow was readied.

"Where are the arrows?" he said.

Mary grabbed the quiver and she put it on his knee.

Donald chose an arrow and the deer fell!

"Thanks be to God," he said. "I never expected to do the likes again, but that is the last hunt for me."

He asked to be buried in the hide of that deer, and for his grave to be made at the door of the church with his face toward Cròidhearg, a mountain on the high ground of the Feàrsaid.[30]

The Battle of Tràigh Ghruinneart

This account of the Battle of Tràigh Ghruinneart is the longest of many surviving variants of the event and is one of the most interesting Gaelic clan sagas to have ever been transcribed from oral tradition. John Dewar wrote it from the recitation of Neil MacTaggart, then living in Glasgow, likely in the late 1860s.

Lachlann Mór MacLean instigated the Battle of Tràigh Ghruinneart (in the northwest of Islay) in 1598 in an effort to take the Rinns of Islay out of the hands of his nephew James MacDonald of Dunyveg and the Glens. The account of the battle is dense with tangential details about many people and their interactions in the battle, as well as explanations of the origins of names and traditions. The narrative constantly moves backward and forward in time, anchored primarily by the landscape and the progression of the battle.

The tale contains many archaic elements. This is one of the few narratives in Scottish Gaelic to feature the motif of a taboo imposed upon a hero whose violation eventually leads to his death, which is called a *geas*. These ritual injunctions appear in many medieval Gaelic tales. The tale also reflects the idea that nursemaids and foster-mothers were fierce defenders of their foster-children, even to the point of violence to their own household. The name "Niall Nèonach" is probably a garbled form of *Niall Noígíallach* ("Niall of the Nine Hostages"), an ancient Gaelic hero from the fourth century who founded the O'Neill dynasty. The name of the assassin Dubh Sìth means "Black-haired Fairy" and is the basis of the surname MacPhee. In most versions of this tale, MacPhee uses a bow and arrow rather than a gun.

The tale is used as a framework for explaining the origins of things known in Gaelic tradition in Islay, connecting them to this momentous event, providing the circumstances that led to the creation of bagpipe tunes, proverbial expressions, place names, and the founding of new branches of families.

This legend also unsettles the stereotype of Highlanders as war-mad savages by providing counter-examples of the brutality of warfare, particularly the reconciliation of the MacEachern brothers, the kindness shown to the MacLean survivor of the battle, and the generosity of the people of Mull to MacTaggart in return for the care he gave to the MacLean warrior.

The sister of James MacDonald the younger of Islay was married to Lachann MacLean of Duart and MacLean was to get the Rinns of Islay as dowry with the daughter of MacDonald. The bounds of the Rinns of Islay are as follows: there is a township called the Gearrach in the parish of Cille Chomain, and there is a spring in a garden of the old house of Gearrach, and there is a brook running out of it going southeast and into Loch na Dàlach at Port Sgioba (which is now called Port Charlotte); and there is another brook running out of the same spring going to the northwest and into the sea at Cille Chiarain, and all that lies between those two brooks and the sea is the land which is called The Rinns of Islay.

One of the MacKays was MacDonald's councilor[31] and he held the Rinns of Islay in exchange for his service. MacDonald was going to move MacKay out of the Rinns and give him Kildalton instead, since the Rinns belonged to MacLean of Duart, but MacLean never pressed for possession of the dowry lands of the lady, who was the sister of MacDonald, who was married to him.

When young Lachann MacLean grew up, he went to Islay to see the Rinns of Islay, and he thought it was a shame that there was no port for a boat to come to land. He said to MacDonald, "Your father treated my father poorly, to give him a place where there was no pier where a boat could be landed. You must give me a place where I can land my boat."

MacDonald said, "Bring your boat in at Loch na Dàla, and make landfall at Port Sgioba. There is a very good pier there."

"I will not do that," said MacLean, "but will instead take Port Asgaig—I must have it."

"You want more than you will get," said MacDonald. "You want all that is between Port Asgaig and Loch Na Dàla, but you won't have it."

"That is what I expect, and I will have it too," said MacLean. And they parted like that, without coming to an agreement.

They had a battle at Beinn Bheigeir and the MacDonalds lost. The next battle was at a place which is called Muladradh. All of the MacLeans were killed except for Lachann Mór himself. At another time, Lachann Mór came with his men to the islands of Loch Gorm and they were wiped out.

There was a green, round hillock across from the great house of MacLean of Duart and it was the custom of the chieftain of the MacLeans before going into battle that he would go out in the morning before he tasted his first meal and walk three times clockwise around the hillock.

On the morning before Lachann Mór was going to go the Battle of Tràigh Ghruinneart, a wise-woman came into Lachann's house. She said to him, "Did you follow the customs of your ancestors?"

"What is that?" asked Lachann.

"To go out in the morning before you taste your meal and walk three times clockwise around the hillock—if you don't do that, you won't succeed."

"All right—if it was their custom to go clockwise, I'll go three times in the opposite direction." And that's what he did.

The wise-woman said, "When you reach Islay, don't drop your anchor at Poll Nùstaig, and don't drink out of the well of Niall Neònach and don't plant the pole of your banner on the hillock of Cnoc nan Aighean."

Regardless, Lachann Mór did not take heed.

When Lachann reached Islay, he didn't want to land at Tràigh Ghruinneart for fear that MacDonald would see him and resist him, so he came to land at Poll Nùstaig and dropped the anchor there. He went past Àrd Neamh and when he was on his way, he became very thirsty and he said, "I'm thirsty and would be the better of a drink."

The people searched high and low and one of them saw a well at the base of a small, green hillock there and he said, "The most beautiful well ever seen is right here."

MacLean went and he drank a drink of water from it, and after that he asked, "What is this place called?"

One of the men there was familiar with Islay, and he said, "This is the Well of Niall Neònach."

"And what is the name of the place where we dropped our anchor?"

"That place is called Poll Nùstaig."

Lachann said, "That's two of the wise-woman's taboos that have happened."

They proceeded to a place where there was a beautiful, sandy hill. Lachann said, "Plant the pole of the banner on that hill and unfold the banner."

The pole was thrust into the ground and the banner was unfurled and Lachann asked, "What is the name of this place?"

One of the men said, "The name of this place is Cnoc nan Aighean."

Lachann said, "Now three of the wise-woman's places have been encountered."

MacDonald planted his banner in the low-land of Corsabhal, at a place called Creagan, and after that it became called MacDonald's Rock.

There was a crafty servant who worked as a messenger between the two camps, and he would report to one camp what happened in the other one. The servant wanted to increase the blood-lust between them so that he would see a battle, so when he went with news from MacLean to MacDonald, he did not report the words that MacLean asked him to send to MacDonald, and when MacDonald sent news to MacLean, he did not report the words that MacDonald asked him to send to MacLean. He thus made the blood-lust between them worse than it was before.

The two clans stayed across from each other for three days trying to come to an agreement, but with the deception of the messenger who was going between them, the two clans became angry with each other to the point that they had to go to combat.

MacLean had three times as many men as MacDonald at that time, but MacDonald was expecting Black Ronald from Inishowen in Ireland to come with the men of Inishowen, and he also expected men from Kintyre and men from the island of Arran to come to help him. They did not come forth, however, so MacDonald had to face MacLean with only a third of the men that MacLean had.

There was a very small man who was called Dubh Sìth Shaw. Some people called him Black Shaft. He went to MacLean's camp and asked to speak to MacLean himself. MacLean went over to him and asked him, "What is your business with me?"

Dubh Sìth said, "Weapons and armor to go with you into battle."

MacLean looked at him disparagingly and said, "Even if you brought your own weapons and armor, I wouldn't give you a place among my men."

"Aye, aye," said Dubh Sìth as he left. Dubh Sìth went and reached MacDonald's camp. He asked to speak to MacDonald.

MacDonald went to where he was and he said, "What is your business with me?"

"Weapons and armor, if you give me enought for a man."

MacDonald said, "I will give you a man's place in my army, and I wish that I had five hundred more like you."

Dubh Sìth said, "If you take care of everyone else, I will take care of Lachann Mór."

MacDonald didn't want MacLean to get killed, so he said, "Do what you can with the troops, but spare Lachann himself."

Dubh Sìth said, "The command has been given." He turned away from MacDonald and he left. Dubh Sìth had a gun but there was no other gun at the battle but that one. Dubh Sìth hid himself, seeking a way to kill MacLean from a hiding place.

When MacDonald was commanding his troops to array themselves for battle, he said to his bagpiper, "Play a new tune, o piper, a tune that you have never played before." The bagpiper looked around to see if he could notice anything that would remind him of a song melody and he saw a cattle-maid at Roinniche Ruadh struggling to separate the cattle from the calves after they had banded together. He suddenly remembered the ditty:

O i a thò, the calves suckled,
O i a thò, the young ones suckled,
O i a thò, the calves suckled,
O gentle cattle-maid, the young ones suckled.

And that tune is still called "the Bagpipe tune of Tràigh Ghruinneart."

The two armies moved towards each other around the shore and they met at a place that was named the Bend of the Battle after that. The two armies shot arrows at each other across the mouth of the estuary there.

The morning had been calm until then, but at that moment a strong wind from the west began to blow and with it came a heavy rain. The two armies strove to see which of them could get around the rain first and get the wind at their backs and get the upper hand, so that the wind and rain would be to the detriment of the others. The MacLeans of Mull got there first and the heated battle began at a place called Earasaid, on the boundary of the township of Baile an Àbaidh, and the MacDonalds were repelled.

There was a blacksmith in Islay of the surname MacEachern and MacLean took one of his sons who was named Donald to Mull. Donald was with Lachann Mór at the Battle of Tràigh Ghruinneart. The blacksmith had another son named Niall at the battle. He was very young when his brother Donald went to Mull and Donald could not recognize Niall. The two brothers encountered each other at a bend in the river and they fought each other with battle axes. Finally, Niall thought that he recognized Donald and he said :—

O black-haired man of the red locks,
Your battle-blows were hard and fast:
You broke the stroke of my axe
And even though you did that, I'd prefer you to live.

Donald said, "Would you prefer me to live?"

"Yes," responded Niall.

"Why?" said Donald.

"Aren't you the son of the blacksmith MacEachern in Islay?" asked Niall.

"Yes," said Donald.

"Well, I am Niall, the youngest son." The two brothers then stopped fighting and sat down and caught up with each other, and they cried, and they did not strike another blow in the battle.

There was a bog to the rear of the MacDonalds and many of them went into the bogland and were badly beaten, and the place was later called the Desperate Place of the MacDonalds. Just as the MacDonalds were at the point of surrender, they heard the skirl of the bagpipe coming toward them. MacDonald realised that these were the men of Inishowen who were coming to help him and he shouted to his men, "Take heart, lads, this is Black Ronald who has come from Inishowen in Ireland to help us."

Black Ronald came in the vanguard of the men of Inishowen and the MacLeans had to retreat and the MacDonalds followed them.

The men of Kintyre and Arran were expected and MacLean put men under his command to look out for the men of Kintyre and to keep them at bay. MacLean's men arrived at the brae of Leireabas and they stopped there. In order to keep themselves awake, they began playing rabbits and did not pay careful attention. The men of Kintyre proceeded wearing only their shirts and short kilts, and they reached the top of Boire Chill and they sat down in order to put on their kilt hose and they saw the men of Mull below them as they played rabbits but the Mull men did not see them, they kept on playing. When the men of Kintyre put on their socks, they hurried themselves and charged down the slope where the Mull men were and they reached them without the Mull men knowing it and killed them. The Mull men were buried at that very place and so the place was later called the Mound of the Mull men.

The men of Kintyre could see Tràigh Ghruinneart from where they were and they saw that the MacLeans were retreating, and they went to head them off. They encountered the Mull men close to Camag na Gobhainn and they struggled to gain the hard ground at Bruach an Adhraidh. The men of Kintyre were in front and the men of Arran were behind them coming to Cruadhlach.

When the men of Arran were going to the Battle of Tràigh Ghruinneart, they went with their war-galleys to Port na h-Abhainn, at the mouth of Loch an Dàla. They brought their war-galleys to land. There was a man of the Fergusons who was called Duncan of the Moccasins who lived at the township called Baile nan Càrn on the land of Cladh a' Bhaile and after the Arran men had hidden the little money that they had, they arrived there and they asked, "Where is Tràigh Ghruinneart?"

Duncan said, "It is in the northern part of Islay." He was so old that he couldn't walk but he got his white horse and he went with them so that he could show them the location but none of them ever returned to the boats, and the boats lay there until they rotted.

The Mull men realized that they had to travel through boggy land where there was a quagmire, as their feet sank down in the mud, and they were losing their moccasins, and many of them were killed there, and later the place was called the Desperate Place of the MacLeans.

When Lachann Mór saw the desperate plight that his people were in, he himself went to the frontline of the battle and he cut a path through the MacDonalds with his sword and he kept the path open until his men got through. Then they went from there to the brae of Bruach an Adhraidh. The men of Kintyre were then close to the MacLeans, who were in terrible shape. Lachann Mór himself went to the frontline of his men and once again he cut a path through the MacDonalds and let his people through it.

Dubh Sìth was at that place with his gun, hidden within a dense rowan tree, and when Lachann Mór had cut the path through the MacDonalds, he went through the path until he was on the far side of it. As soon as Dubh Sìth got sight of Lachann, he quickly pointed the barrel of the gun at him and fired the bullet and the bullet hit Lachann.

When Lachann Mór was wounded, he moved forward with his head looking downwards. Although Lachann's servant was wounded by a sword, he kept watch on Lachann and followed about twenty yards behind him. Lachann Mór continued about another two hundred yards and then fell down and his servant couldn't go any further and he lay himself down on the battlefield.

One of the MacDonalds observed Lachann Mór and noticed that he had a ring on his finger. He followed him to get the ring. When he reached Lachann, Lachann was dead. He grabbed Lachann's hand in order to take the ring off of his finger but Lachann's hand had swelled so much from the sword blow that the ring would not come off. The MacDonald put Lachann's hand on a clump of heather that was there and he lifted up his sword in order to cut Lachann's hand off so that he could remove the ring later at his leisure. MacLean's servant was observing him and when the MacDonald raised up his sword in order to strike the blow, MacLean's servant made a sudden move: he put an arrow into his bow and shot it at the MacDonald and killed him.

When Lachann Mór fell, his men scattered in every direction and every man was fighting for his own sake and the place where the battle ended is called the Arable Field of MacLean's Battle. The Mull men fled to Poll Nùstaig, where the boats were, but the boatmen were keeping watch, and when they understood that the MacLeans had been destroyed, they fled from the shore with the boats. When the Mull men saw that it was likely that they were going to be destroyed, they ran inside of the Church of Cille

Naomh, expecting that they would not be killed in the church, but they were deceived. The MacDonalds shut the doors of the church and lit it with a firebrand. The direction of the wind was changing at the time and a strong wind blew from the northeast and it was not long before there was a hole through the thatched roof of the church.

There was one of the Mull men whose surname was Currie. He was strong and fast and he climbed to the top of the wall of the church. He leaped across it and ran off. A part of MacDonalds chased after him. He fled to Caol Naomhaidh but the boats had departed and Currie didn't have a chance to get on one, so he ran to the beach and attempted to swim out to Eilean Naomha. One of the MacDonalds shot an arrow after him. The arrow struck him in the buttock. He didn't attempt to remove the arrow but swam to a large rock out in the ocean which is called Badag which had seaweed on it which swayed with the ocean. Currie stood on Badag and took the arrow out of his buttock. It was high-tide at that time and Currie stayed on Badag until the pursuers thought that he had drowned and left. Then he swam back to land. That man stayed for the rest of his life in Islay. He got married there and had children and they are called the Descendants of Currie of Badag. There was a proverb in Islay which said, "As patient as the bow-man."

All of the other Mull men in the church were burnt to death.

When the MacDonalds thought that they had found that all of the MacLeans who were in the battlefield had been killed, they were scattering apart and each man going his own way home. MacTaggart of Stoiseagh—the brother of MacTaggart of Corsabal—had to go ten miles through moorland. He came to a place and heard a cry there. He made a step off the road in the direction of that cry. There was a wounded man lying there and MacTaggart asked, "What is the reason for your cry, o man?"

The wounded man said, "The cry didn't come from a wound. I was dreaming that a raven came to eat my bowels and that it ripped the guts out of me and couldn't fly away." So MacTaggart lifted MacLean and took him home. MacLean spent nine months in MacTaggart's home.

When MacTaggart was about to go home with MacLean, he went to Corsabal and he asked Niall – the son of his brother—to go with him to Mull, so that he could have someone he trusted with him. Niall came with him, and he brought two of his own sons. He brought the MacLean man to Mull and the Mull-people were very kind to him. He came home again, but he returned to Mull after that, and the MacTaggart family were welcomed into Mull.

Lachann Mór had a nursemaid who lived in the Rinns of Islay. She found out that Lachann Mór had been killed at Tràigh Ghruinneart and she decided that she would bury him. She had a man-servant. He was called Black-footed Duncan because he had black fuzz growing on his feet. She made Black-footed Duncan hitch a sled to one of her horses, and they went to Tràigh Ghruinneart to get the corpse of Lachann Mór to take him to be buried at the graveyard of Cille Chomain.

They left and reached Tràigh Ghruinneart. They didn't have any help in getting the corpse of Lachann Mór or anyone who would assist in putting his corpse on the sled. But they lifted him up and left with him. She had the reins and was maneuvering the horse and Black-footed Duncan was attending to MacLean, keeping him aright on the sled. As they were on their way, one of the legs of the sled fell into a bog-hole and caused MacLean's open mouth to waggle. Duncan laughed.

Lachann's nursemaid went to the servant and she asked him, "What is the cause of your laughter?"

"It's just that Lachann Mór's open mouth waggles when the sled leg goes over bumps and into holes."

She reached her hand into her plaid and took out a dirk and stuck it into the manservant and killed him. The servant was buried right there and later that place was called Duncan's Cairn.

The woman proceeded towards Cille Chomain with the horse and sled, carrying MacLean's corpse, and she got the corpse buried inside of the Church of Cille Chomain. She put a gravestone on top of it and a portrait of Lachann Mór MacLean, with his sword at his side, was engraved on the stone. Lachann Mór's grave was inside of the church until a new church was erected in the era of the Reverend Alex Cameron, close to the year 1840. The grave of Lachann Mór was left outside of the church. Lachann's gravestone can be seen in the north-east corner of the church.[32]

The Glen Quaich Bridge

This tale was contributed to *The Highlander* newspaper in 1877 from an anonymous contributor drawing from local Breadalbane folklore. There is no way to date the incident described by the tale. It is one of many tales that describes how a few plucky heroes trick a much larger group into thinking that they are about to be attacked by a sizeable army.

When a person takes the road from Kenmore to Glen Quaich over the high moor which is called the *Làirig* ("Pass"), a bridge is seen over a stream in a hollow, a little before getting to the summit. The bridge is called the Bridge of the Hollow of the Cowards until the present day because of something that happened many years ago.

At that time, it was a common thing for able-bodied men to raid livestock, or as we say nowadays, to steal cattle and sheep. It was a respectable thing in those days and noblemen often went to raid cattle from their enemies.

It happened that a band of men came in to Glen Quaich about the afternoon on a particular day when all of the men in the area were away, and they made a complete plunder of every four-legged animal in the upland of the glen. There was no one there to stop them but old people, women and children, and it would be a pointless gesture for them to engage with the raiders.

The men went to the Làirig with what they had, but after ascending to the summit, the night became so dark that they couldn't see the steps of the path. They decided to rest in a hollow of the stream until daybreak, as they were entirely certain that there was no fear that they would be pursued.

There was an old man in the glen who was called Big Iain and he decided to make an attempt to get back the plundered livestock.

As soon as the raiders went over the summit and out of sight, Big Iain went after them, but without anyone with him but a plump lad, his grandson, and three or four hounds.

He saw where the men were with the cattle and once he came to a hillock that was close to them, he shouted out loud, "They are here, lads, they are here! Have at them!"

The lad make a shout to answer him on the other side, and then, they set the hounds after the livestock.

The cattle went back on the road from which they came, and the raiders thought that the people of the glen had risen against them. They rushed down the slope without stopping until they were on the other side of Kenmore.

That night, there was sorrow and misery in many houses of that beautiful glen, but before daybreak the sound of the bellowing of cattle coming up the hillside was heard, with Big John in the back of them, sending the hounds on them.

Because of this, the place where the raiders were spending the night was named "the Hollow of the Cowards" and that is its name until the present day.[33]

The Battle of Carinish

The following tale was contributed by "Iain" to the periodical *An Gàidheal* in 1876 from the local oral tradition of North Uist. The story describes a feud between the MacDonalds of Sleat, who also held land in North Uist, and the MacLeods of Dunvegan and Harris, and how that antagonism led to the Battle of Carinish in 1601.

The height of the battle is marked by a run, a somewhat unusual feature for an historical legend. The storyteller also makes use of several proverbial expressions and idioms. This tale can be complemented by a famous song attributed to the foster-mother of Donald son of Iain son of James that describes her coming to tend to his wounds after this battle.[34]

In the year 1601, the MacDonalds of Uist and the MacLeods of Harris fought a bloody fight at Fèith na Fala ("the Marsh of Blood") in Carinish in North Uist. It was a dispute between the MacDonalds of Sleat and the MacLeods of Dunvegan that caused the Battle of Carinish. It is said that the quarrel began like this.

Donald Gorm of Sleat married the daughter of MacLeod of Dunvegan and whatever he had against her, it seems that he and she did not get along very well, and the outcome was that he gave her a letter of divorce, and sent her packing off home to her father's house.

This greatly offended Sir Rory MacLeod and all of his kin, but what particularly infuriated them was the way in which she was sent home.

She had only one eye, and in order to make the matter as insulting as possible, Donald Gorm found an old white one-eyed horse, a one-eyed servant, and a one-eyed dog, and he sent them all off to Dunvegan together and sent her with them. The one-eyed lady was riding on a one-eyed horse, with a one-eyed servant leading it, and a one-eyed dog following them.

When this oddball company arrived at Dunvegan, and when the significance of the news was apparent, there was not a MacLeod on the shores of the Isle of Skye, or in Harris, who was not ready to kill Donald Gorm and his kin everywhere.

There is reason to believe that many a person paid dearly for this shameful deed for many years, even though we do not have a full account of it.

Donald Glas MacLeod was the chief of the MacLeods of Harris. At one time of his life he had been a very sturdy man but by this time he had grown heavy and feeble, and was unable to lead his sturdy warriors, in order to raid cattle or to wage battle.

But his son was a young man, capable and heroic, at the height of his strength, and keen to earn glory and honor for himself and his clan.

He heard about the offence that had been given to his kin in Dunvegan, and he could see nothing more fitting to do than to go to North Uist leading forty sturdy warriors to raid cattle, in order to take vengeance upon the MacDonalds in one way or another. As the proverb says, "If you won't pay for it yourself, your accoutrements will."

The men took off and left, some in the war galley belonging to the son of Donald Glas, and others in ferry-boats.

When they reached Uist, they anchored at Loch nan Cealla, at the mouth of the North Ford.

They moved forward and they carried out the raid in Carinish easily enough, and since they didn't have enough time to bring the cattle to the boats, what they did was they gathered them to the Temple of the Trinity until they would leave the next morning. They took possession of the House of the Hill, because it was in an elevated place with a good view, in the high ground of the township.

They passed the time away with every amusement and diversion possible, fully believing that everything would succeed as they expected.

But it was not fated that they would have their wish in this matter, for before the sun went down on the next day, "Calum's cloth bore a different pattern."

There was a sturdy man in South Uist who was commonly called Donald son of Iain son of James. This man was famous in his era for his great love of truth, honor, and justice. If the tale is true, it is said that he was always striving to put an end to raiding, plundering, and violence, which were so commonly practiced at the time.

When the MacLeods landed in North Uist, the people of the place understood very well what they intended, and, accordingly, they quickly sent word to the son of Iain son of James, to tell him what seemed to be happening.

He was as swift as the message, as usual, and off he went with twelve of the bravest and fiercest warriors that could be found in South Uist. As night was fading, they crossed Fadhail nan Larnan and Fadhail 'ic an Aoidheir, and a little before daybreak they reached Carinish. When they had observed things in the township, and had determined that the raiders had not yet left, they hid themselves in a marsh, in the upland of the township.

When the day began to brighten, they saw that there was a bigger crowd at the "House of the Hill" than there ought to be, and they then realized who was there.

The son of Iain son of James shot an arrow, and wounded one of them. With the next arrow, he took down another man.

This frightened the MacLeods, and one of them said: "I am very greatly deceived if the arrows have not come from the hand of Donald son of Iain of James, and, if so, I greatly fear that it will be a dark day for us."

They were not yet certain what direction the arrows were coming from, so what they did was to turn to each of the four directions, and when the third arrow struck, they realized that the arrows were coming from the north-east.

They rushed down the hill as quickly as they could.

When the son of Iain son of James saw them descending the slope of the hill, he said, "Now, lads, if you have ever done it, do it today, for I think that there are three men for each one of you to knock to the ground."

"Well, then," they said, "it won't take long."

He and his lads were so expert at the bow that that they thinned out the MacLeods before they had descended the slope of the hill.

Once they came close to each other, that was when the combat grew hot and intense:

The champions clashed with each other,
Like the tumult of waves on the crest of the ocean,
Thundering blows came thickly,
With death overcoming strength on the hillside
Like a cloud of rough hailstones
With a hurricane rising up in its wake.

Of the forty men, only two of them escaped. All of the rest, with the exception of their leader—the son of Donald Glas—fell in the battle.

He fled and survived.

The son of Iain son of James gave a strict order not to kill him upon any account, but that, if it were possible, to take him alive.

He went nearly two miles before one of the warriors of the son of Iain son of James caught up with him on the shore, close to Baleshare.

Although both of them had been badly wounded before that, they fought with sword.

The son of Donald Glas would not surrender as long as he lived, but he was pushed backward, and he retreated into the sea until the water reached his midriff.

Although the other man wanted to take him alive according to his master's command, once the salt water began to enter his wounds, he ran out of patience and with one thrust of his sword, he quickly put an end to the other on the spot, and left him dead on the shoal.

The shoal is called the Shoal of the son of Donald Glas until this day.

The bodies of the MacLeods were buried where they fell: on the Slope of the Stricken, as the place has been called ever since the battle was fought. The heads were put in the window of the temple, where some of them can probably still be seen.

We have no account of how many MacDonalds fell in this bloody battle, but, for all that, we can be sure that the majority did fall.

Donald son of Iain son of James himself was wounded many times, even though he won the battle. But he recovered from it afterward.

It is said, although we need not believe it, that the marsh ran with blood, and for that reason, it is called Fèith na Fala ("the Marsh of Blood") until this very day.

Some people may not think that it was possible for twelve men to kill nearly forty, but, as the proverb says, "One (good) man is better than many (lesser) men."

Besides that, when the MacDonalds were hiding themselves in the marsh, and the others were descending the hillside, the MacDonalds had the upper hand on them, and before they could look one way or another, a good number of them had been wounded. In this way, a large part of them completely lost all their courage.

With regard to the MacDonalds, it is reported that they were exceedingly expert with the bow, and likewise that their bows were so stiff that they were the only ones who could pull them.

It is easy to understood that they could shoot arrows a very long way. With these things entirely in their favor, besides being very sturdy men, it is clear that it was no difficult task for them to win the day.

When Donald Gorm heard about the Battle of Carinish, and about the heroic conduct of his kinsman, he was very pleased, and as a token of his gratitude for his bravery, he gave him the land of Gabhaltas na Cuidrich, in the Isle of Skye. He was certainly worthy of that and more.[35]

The MacGregors and the Campbell Bloodhounds

Duncan Campbell (1827–1916), a native of Glenlyon and newspaper editor, sent this tale to the periodical *An Gàidheal* in 1874. Campbell was a keen collector of the local oral traditions of Perthshire. Despite being a Campbell himself, and even sharing the name of the adversary in the story, he seems to be sympathetic to the MacGregors and critical of their notorious persecution by the Campbells. This tale is one of many commemorating the protracted, bloody conflicts between Campbells and MacGregors during the sixteenth amd seventeenth centuries.

Sir Duncan Campbell (1550–1631) has many nicknames in Gaelic that indicate that he was aggressive and greedy. Once the MacGregors were outlawed as a clan, many of them went into hiding and assumed other clan names. There were MacGregors in Fortingall who took the surname MacEwen for themselves.[36] Whatever the factual basis behind this particular anecdote, it reflects the type of guerrilla warfare carried out by the Clan Gregor against a more powerful foe and the aid offered to them by many others in resisting these injustices and the Campbell stranglehold on power.

When the royal decree was made to destroy the Clan Gregor, and not to leave a single one of that bold and high-spirited clan alive, young or old, large or small, none of their blood-thirsty enemies were more keen in their pursuit than the Campbells and Black Duncan, the Laird of Balloch. They didn't think it sufficient to rout the MacGregors and murder them: they had two hounds that would pursue a MacGregor so intensely that they couldn't escape.

The Campbells seized a MacGregor woman and they forced her to nurse these two pups on her breast. And when the hounds grew up, they were so fond of the MacGregors that they could detect the scent of one of them among a hundred men of any other clan.

With this method, many of that poor kindred were captured in their residences by those black bloodhounds and put to death, until a way was finally found to kill the hounds. This is how it happened.

At that same time there was a man named MacEwen who lived on Loch Tayside who had a MacGregor woman as his wife. He was afraid that his wife would be murdered by the hounds and he had warmth in his heart for the Clan Gregor because of his wife.

So he decided to destroy the hounds if he could. He started by saying that the hounds would just catch hold of anyone who came their way, and that everyone was in danger from them.

When a fair was held in Kenmore, MacEwen went to the fair, but before he left his own house, he wetted his hand and his wrist with his wife's blood.

The hounds were loosed among the crowd to see if they could catch one of the MacGregors in the company. MacEwen put himself in their way after he had told everyone around him that the hounds would follow a Campbell as soon as anyone else.

One of the hounds smelled the blood that was on his hand, and in the twinkling of an eye, it leaped upon him. But everybody knew that MacEwen was not a MacGregor.

The crowd grew agitated and one of the hounds was killed then and there, and the other one a day or two afterward.

And that is how the black hounds were destroyed.[37]

The Battle of Sròn a' Chlachain

This tale was submitted to the periodical *An Deò-Ghréine* in 1921 by "Diarmad," probably the pen name of John Macdiarmad of Killin.[38] The battle described by the story occurred in the hills above Killin, Perthshire, and has been dated to 4 June 1646.[39]

Gaelic poets from both MacDonald and Campbell factions allude to the incident in their verse. John Dewar collected a legend in the 1860s that provides a MacDonald perspective on the event. According to this other narrative, a Glencoe man found out that a large wedding celebration was going to take place at Finlarig Castle and, expecting that this would distract the Campbells and make them incapable of retaliation, he convinced the Keppoch MacDonalds that they should coordinate a raid on their Campbell rivals.[40]

About the middle of the seventeenth century, when Sir Robert Campbell was Lord Breadalbane, it happened that there was a large and wonderful wedding at Finlarig Castle near the village of Killin.

The Knight of Balloch was giving his daughter in marriage to James Menzies of Culdares in Glenlyon, a soldier who had earned great renown in the wars of Gustavus Adolphus.

When the wedding feast was at its climax, a messenger came, running with urgency, to report that a band of the MacDonalds of Keppoch and Glencoe had crossed the River Dochart at Baile Chroisg, driving away the cattle that they had plundered from Breadalbane and elsewhere.

The Campbells of Breadalbane were zealous to go after them, but Menzies, who was expert in warfare, cautioned that it would be dangerous to go after them while ascending the upland of Sròn a' Chlachain, because the steep ground, the afternoon sun, and the wind would all give the advantage to the MacDonalds and go against the Campbells. He wanted for them to go around Glenlochay so that they could get to the summit of the high ground, and then they could come at the MacDonalds from the top of Sròn a' Chlachain.

But the youths who were at the wedding were swollen with arrogance, and probably also with wine, and they would not take counsel. Instead of that, they mocked him, saying, "Wimpy Menzies, wimpy Menzies."

"Go on ahead, then," said Menzies, "and we will see who is wimpy before the end of the day comes."

Everything happened just as Menzies expected it would. The MacDonalds were victorious and the Campbells were routed.

Menzies performed many heroic deeds in this bloody, deadly battle. With one blow of his sword, he struck the head off of MacDonald of Glencoe.

This famous soldier had been given the nickname "The Red-Haired Crowner of the Hens." MacDonald of Glencoe was insulting him with this nickname to his face when he approached him in order to fight him, and it is said that when his severed head was rolling down the slope, turn by turn, it was saying, "Hen, hen, hen."

James Menzies was the last man to cross over the river Lochay when they were returning to the castle after they had been routed.

When he looked behind him, he noticed one of the MacDonalds swimming after him, up to his neck in the water. He killed him immediately and he flung the corpse of the dead man on his own back to protect it from the arrows of his pursuers, and when he let it fall down at Finlarig Castle, there were seven arrows stuck in it.

The slaughter of the Campbells was so great that eighteen of their nobility were buried at the castle's chapel the next day.

Angus, the leader of the MacDonalds of Keppoch, was killed at the Battle of Sròn a' Chlachain, as well as MacDonald of Glencoe, and many others besides.

It is said around Killin and throughout Breadalbane, although it is hard to believe, that Menzies and a band of men, a little after this, went after the MacDonalds, caught up with them, and took the raided cattle from them.

There was one person who was wounded in this battle who fled to the shieling of Coire Charmaig in Glenlochay, and he was hidden for a few days by a woman from Lochaber. But when the husband of this woman found out where he was hiding, he killed him.[41]

The Loch Earn Robber

This tale was contributed in 1922 to the periodical *The People's Journal* by James MacDiarmad, a champion of Perthshire Gaelic tradition who did a great deal of fieldwork among the native population of the area.

The story is particularly interesting in preserving details about Gaelic communities near the Lowland border. The tale shows that ordinary Highland folk were in danger from miscreants, and that such behavior was not the norm in Highland communities. The final remark of the storyteller, however, indicates that many innocent Highland men—or, at least, men undeserving of the punishment—were hanged in Crieff due to the anti-Gaelic prejudices that prevailed at the time.

The events of the tale cannot precede the Union of the Crowns (1603), which enabled the sale of Scottish cattle to English markets and galvanized the formation of Highland droving on a massive scale. Crieff became the main cattle market for Highland drovers in the last quarter of the seventeenth century but was surpassed by Falkirk in the 1760s.[42]

The drover went from the west down the side of Loch Earn with his three herd-boys driving the cattle, heading for Crieff where the good man expected to sell his cattle for a good profit the next day, for it was Michaelmas, at the largest market that was in Scotland at that time, and for many years before that or after that.

The big fair day came, and the drover did his best to sell his cattle to an elegant Englishman who was seeking cattle to bring home to England. As was natural, the drover asked more money for his cattle than he expected to get, and the Englishman was offering less than he expected to pay for them before losing the offer.

After they had haggled for a while, the men agreed on the price and the bargain was sealed with a good drink of ale.

The drover got the money and after he and his herd-boys had eaten a meal, they headed west. They arrived at St. Fillans, or as the people of old called it, the Big Port. As that location is twelve miles away from Crieff, you'll understand that they were in need of a drink in the little tavern that was in St. Fillans. When the drover left with two of the herd-boys, one of them stayed behind in the tavern as he was not fully sated.

They took the road until they arrived at the Highlanders' Path, which is over a mile away from St. Fillans, where they had a mishap that left them all in a bad mood. A wild, fierce man lept out in front of them on the path, with a claymore in his right hand and a pistol in his left hand.

He said to them with an unfriendly voice, "Out with your sporrans quickly or I'll take your lives!"

They had no choice but to do that immediately. With a sad and heavy heart, the three of them were left poor and empty-handed indeed, for he took all of their money. The drover lost the price of the cattle and the two herd-boys lost their earnings.

They arrived at the tavern that was at Lochearnhead tired and disheartened. They wished to rest at the tavern, but they didn't have a penny between them for food or drink, and they were complaining to one another about what happened to them.

After a while, the man who had stayed behind at St. Fillans came into the room in which they were. He took a look around and he told them why he was confused, "Why on earth have you not ordered ale? You all look like you have been hanged! Here, here, let's go, and let's get ale now, for I myself am hot and thirsty."

The drover answered, "We don't have as much as a six-pence. A robber stole all of our money."

"Shame, shame! For you to admit such a thing! Three strong men pillaged by one man! Your reputation is totally ruined."

After saying that, he called for ale for them all and he paid for it as well.

The drover asked him, "Did you not come across the robber at all?"

"Oh, indeed I did," said the youth, "but he didn't take a red cent from me. The robber yelled haughtily to me, 'Hand over your money to me.' Without a word, I pulled out my sporran in such a way that most of the money fell out on the path. He stooped down distractedly to gather it but I struck him hard on the skull with my staff, sending him into a faint, as his blood ran thickly from his head and his nose. I robbed him and I took his claymore and his pistol. I am certain that he will not recover from that any time soon."

The news spread and a band of strong, young men went down the road to seize him. They found him where the herd-boy had left him. They tied his hands behind him for fear of what he would do when he regained consciousness. Then they carried him to Monzievaird where he was condemned to death by the famous Macintosh about whom the proverb says, "It's not every day that Macintosh holds court."

Without delay, the robber was hanged on the high scaffold of Crieff that was cursed by the Gaels of old when they passed by it, and indeed, there was good reason for that.[43]

The Massacre of Glencoe

Rt. Rev. Archibald Campbell, a native of the Appin-Glencoe area, contributed this tale to the periodical *An Sgeulaiche* in 1909.[44]

The Massacre of Glencoe is a notorious event in Scottish history that is often misrepresented as an episode in a clan feud. It was instead an action by the central government to make an example of the MacDonalds of Glencoe, considered to be one of the most resistant to the rule of the regime. Clan chieftains were required to swear an oath of loyalty to William and Mary by 1 January 1692 or face severe consequences. MacDonald of Glencoe was delayed by several circumstances but appeared at Fort William on 30 December to swear his allegiance, only to be sent by the resident commander to Inverary, causing a further delay, even though he had proof of his effort to comply.

Robert Campbell of Glenlyon was sent with troops to enact punishment. There are Gaelic traditions that say that this was a duty that he was loathe to carry out and that the family suffered from a curse thereafter. Regardless, Gaels considered the massacre a ominous breach of solidarity among clans and a violation of the sacred duty of hospitality.[45]

This tale seems to assure the listener that it is possible and praiseworthy to resist what is unjust and that we may be ultimately rewarded for acting out of our compassion, even if the road may be long and lonely. The tale also provides a model of reconciliation for those who have been alienated through the machinations of outsiders to recognize their common interests as Gaels and their commitment to a shared set of values and traditions.

Hardly a month had gone by when Captain Campbell of Glenlyon came with a regiment of soldiers to Glencoe. Their excuse was that they came to collect income taxes and other necessary dues.

When MacDonald of Glencoe asked them whether they came as friends or enemies, Campbell answered and he said that they came as friends and as neighbors, and he gave his word that no harm would be done to him or his clan.

On account of this promise, Clan Donald welcomed they warmly, and for fourteen days they received incomparable hospitality from the men of Glencoe.

At last, the night of terrible misfortune came! After MacDonald of Glencoe and Captain Campbell had spent the day in each other's company, they parted at about seven o'clock at night with good cheer and respect for one another.

When MacDonald of Glencoe noticed that the regiment was growing in size, he was struck with suspicion that there was deceit and treachery afoot. But his father and his brother would not listen to any dark doubts against the honor of the Laird of Glenlyon. Iain and Alasdair, the sons of MacDonald of Glencoe, heard the soldiers whispering that the matter did not agree with them at all, that they were willing enough to fight the men of Glencoe face to face, but that it was a shameful thing that was coming to them unawares.

The oral tradition of the people tells us that the matter was bothering one of the soldiers so much that he asked the man of a house to take a walk outside with him, but because he had sworn not to say a word, he spoke as follows to a large stone that was in front of him:

O grey stone that is in the glen
Although, to be here, you have every right,
It is sure that you'd not stay
If you knew what is to happen tonight.

The Glencoe man took off and he went directly to MacDonald of Glencoe, and he told him what happened. MacDonald asked his sons to look outside and see what they could see. But before they went very far, they saw and heard plenty.

Before they returned to speak to their father, they saw that the house was surrounded by the soldiers. They heard the ammunition of the guns, and the screaming, crying, and lamenting of the women and children.

They were completely unprepared to struggle against the soldiers who were all armed. The soldiers went into the chamber of MacDonald of Glencoe. They fired at him, the bullet went through his skull, and he fell dead in the arms of his wife.

All hell broke loose. The slaughter began. Before it was six o'clock in the morning, forty Glencoe natives had been sent to Eternity.

The houses were set on fire. There was a strong regiment in every pass. The poor wretches could not escape in any direction. There was heavy snow on the ground. They were unable to travel out through Bealach an Innein or even through Gleann Lic na Muidhe.

Every one of their earthly possessions was stolen. Their cattle and their sheep, and all livestock, were driven out of the glen. That is the meaning of the bagpipe tune:

O women of this glen, of this glen, of this glen,
O women of this glen, it is time for you to arise,
The cattle have been stolen, the cattle have been stolen,
The cattle have been stolen, and the men have been slaughtered.

The soldiers went into every house, where they left no one but widows and orphans. In one house, a little boy hid under the bed and when the soliders told him to come out, he answered and said, "Wait until I chew this bone."

It seems as though the boy was chewing a bone with some meat on it when the soldiers burst indoors. An officer saw a woman in great sorrow standing in the shelter of a craig, with an baby on her arm. He immediately ordered one of his men to go and kill the baby before it could become a boy.

It was indeed a baby boy but the soldier was compassionate and warm-hearted, and he didn't have the courage to do harm to the child.

He returned to his commander and explained the matter to him. He received an order to go back and kill the baby, and as proof that he carried out his responsibility, he had to show the officer that his sword was smeared with the blood of the baby.

But alas! The command was merciless, and the heart of the man who gave it was merciless. But there was no avoiding it.

The solider left with a heavy heart, but when he approached the unfortunate, ill-fated woman, he noticed that there was a little puppy greeting him, who was standing at the feet of the woman.

"This is my chance!" said the soldier to himself.

He took his sword of out its scabbard, and he thrust it through the dog. And with pomp, as it were, and ostentatiously, he took his sword smeared with blood to the captain, who was fully satisfied that his order was fulfilled.

Many years after this, a very old man was seen taking the road in the strath of Appin. It was nightfall. Snow showers and sleet were pouring down across the moors of Gèarrloch Glen. The old man was very weak. He was a stranger in his own homeland.

Night came. It was a dark, cold, miserable night. The road was remote but the old man saw a light in the distance, and though it was far away, it did not take him long to reach it. This was the house at Dail na Tràighe.

He reached the guest house at last, and he received a welcome that warmed him to the depths of his heart.

But before he went inside, he stood on the threshold, and he blessed the house according to the old Highland custom:

May the house and all in it be blessed,
All wood, rock, and beam,
May those inside have much food
Plenty of clothing and good health.

After he sat down, and ate some food, the chatter and conversation began. The old man gave an account of how he had spent his life. He had been a red-coat soldier, although he was now without a home or a friend in the world.

The man of the house realized that this was one of the murderers at the Massacre of Glencoe, and he considered killing him.

But the old man indicated that he was not a Campbell and that he did not shed a drop of blood in the glen. He explained how he saved the life of a baby that was on the arm of its poor, unfortunate mother, even though he received an order to kill it.

The man of the house changed his mind, and rather than stabbing him with a knife, he instead leaped up, put his arm around the old man's neck, and kissed him.

He explained to him that he was that baby, and that his mother often told him the same story.

The old man had a warm home that night, and for every other day and night as long as he lived.[46]

Chapter Five

Tales of the Otherworldly

Legends of the so-called "supernatural" are the most interesting type of Gaelic oral narrative. Like other legends, they are believed to describe events that actually happened and often refer to specific people, places, and times that validate them. Some are based on plots, and use motifs, that are found in other cultures[1] but they still offer fascinating insights into the specifics of the Gaelic worldview and ontology.

The lexicon of symbols, beliefs, and practices revealed by these tales provide further evidence of a shared culture and mentality in Gaelic-speaking communities from Kintyre to Caithness and St. Kilda. No one ever wrote a guidebook to this lexicon or needed one: instead, the keys to unlocking their meaning were encoded by and contextualized in these oral narratives, the nuances of the language in them, and the patterns that recur across them that would have been heard and absorbed countless times since birth.

The English term "supernatural" assumes that beings, forces and phenomena can be subjected to the principles of science and rationality to determine which are merely absurd figments of imagination. There is no such native concept in Gaelic. The word traditionally used to describe such entities and phenomena is *ana-ghnàthaichte*, simply meaning "unusual, extraordinary."[2]

When studied as a whole, these Gaelic tales suggest that everything is alive, that there is a plethora of entities and energies hidden behind surface appearances, that there are protocols and rules of engagement, and that the universe has order and meaning if we can read its subtle cues and clues. They help to answer questions such as: When do the signs indicate that there are forces antithetical to our well-being at work? How can we put ourselves in alignment with benevolent forces and beings, and avoid or counteract the malevolent?

What may seem to be a single, simple thing has the potential to be understood as many different things: a grassy hillock might also be an entrance to the Otherworld, or the resting place of the ancestral dead, or a source for creativity, or a place of ceremony where the mundane rules of time and limitation are suspended, or all of these things at different levels of reality. Whether we are to understand a bird as simply being a creature or an omen to be to read or the shape assumed by a friend or foe depends on the time we encounter it, the way it behaves, the song it sings, the color and textures of its appearance, and our own intentions, among other things.

The supernatural being from Gaelic tradition best known in the anglophone world is the *sìdhiche* ("fairy"), although the connotations in Gaelic are quite different from the fairy in modern English. Fairies, according to Gaelic definition, are not small, winged or pixie-like but are virtually identical to humans. The ancestral dead are often seen among them. They can be capricious and dangerous. There is a great deal of variability and ambiguity in tales of the supernatural, and that malleability is part of what gives them their power and imaginative potential. The fairies chiefly reside in the Otherworld, and yet that place can take the form of an alternate reality that intersects and mingles with our own, especially on the liminal days of *Samhain* ("Halloween") and *Bealltainn* ("Beltane, May Day").

The fairies are only one sort of supernatural being that feature in Gaelic folktales. There is also the *glaistig* or *gruagach*, an earthly caretaker of specific territories and ruling families; the *uruisg*, an awkward beast that resides around waterfalls and corries on the mainland; the *each-uisge* ("water horse") that lives in lochs; and many others.[3]

Gaelic beliefs and tales about the Otherworld and extraordinary beings cannot be explained or rationalized with any singular unifying theory. They consist of many layers and strands accumulated over a very long time period serving many different purposes.[4]

First of all, we know from early medieval texts and from their very name that the *sìdhichean* ("fairies") are in origin the pre-Christian gods of the Gaels.[5] Some aspects of fairy lore are remnants of ancient beliefs that resonate with the qualities of myth as described by Karen Armstrong:

> All mythology speaks of another plane that exists alongside our own world, and that in some sense supports it. Belief in this invisible world but more powerful reality, sometimes called the world of the gods, is a basic theme of mythology. It has been called the "perennial philosophy" because it informed the mythology, ritual and social organisation of all societies before the advent of our scientific modernity, and continues to influence more traditional societies today. According to the perennial philosophy, everything that happens in this world, everything that we can hear and see here below has its counterpart in the divine realm, which is richer, stronger and more enduring than our own.[6]

Perhaps the most significant vestige of the divine origin of the fairies in Gaelic tradition is their association with nature, especially in the undomesticated wilderness, as recently summarized by Meg Bateman and John Purser:

> The land is where the divine resides, so there is no division between the physical and the spiritual. The gods and goddesses, and later the fairies, give an animism to the earth: they are the spiritual element that unites the manifest forms of nature. There is an uneasy truce between man and the land. Temporarily under his control, the land and the gods are still a potentially destructive force.[7]

Gaelic oral narratives of the supernatural consist of potent symbols and metaphors that relate to the ineffable, the mysterious, the profound, and the mundane. It is implied in some tales that the Otherworld is the source of human creativity, leading to the metaphor of the fairy hill representing the subterranean aspects of our psyche, the unconscious.[8]

Tales about the Otherworld and its inhabitants sometimes explore, by means of comparison and contrast, what it means to be human in the same way that modern science fiction probes the human experience by comparing and contrasting us with robots and "little green men" from outer space. Stories were also used to discuss a range of tensions, abuses, jealousies, and inequalities between individuals, families, the sexes, and social classes. In a highly interdependent society where most people in a community were closely related, one had to be careful not to comment too pointedly about others' behavior.

Supernatural tales allowed people to use coded language to discuss delicate matters, to reflect on social norms and expectations, and to offer insights about the human condition. In our age of relative material stability and comfort it may be difficult to appreciate the mental and emotional toll of high levels of injury, sickness, death, endemic violence, and precariousness. There was a need to express grief, release anxieties, integrate difficult realities, repress anti-social responses, and foster resilience.[9]

Observations about the nature of myth testify to the rich symbolic potential of these stories and their therapeutic and explanatory functions.

> Our modern alienation from myth is unprecedented. In the pre-modern world, mythology was indispensable. It not only helped people to make sense of their lives but also revealed regions of the human mind that would otherwise have remained inaccessible. It was an early form of psychology. The stories of gods or heroes descending into the underworld, threading through labyrinths and fighting with monsters, brought to light the mysterious workings of the psyche, showing people how to cope with their own interior crises.[10]

It must also be emphasized that belief in the Otherword and supernatural beings was not confined to the uneducated peasantry: the élite of the Gaelic world that spanned Highland Scotland and Ireland cultivated these creeds because they cast an aura of mystique around their social status and legitimated their political authority.[11] It is thus not surprising to find chieftains mingling with the fairy folk in the tales, and poets and artists involved in complicated relationships with the Otherworld, and receiving their talents from its representatives.

The Origin of the Fairies

Alexander Carmichael transcibed this tale from Roderick MacNeill of Mingulay in 1871, when the storyteller was ninety-two years old. Carmichael only gives the original Gaelic text for the verses, with the prose text translated into English.

From the establishment of Christian institutions in the Gaelic world in the early medieval period, there was a strong desire to accommodate Gaelic beliefs and traditions predating Christianity within a Christian framework. This synthesis survived, if awkwardly at times, until recent times. There are many variants of this tale in Gaelic which attest to the malleability of oral tradition to sustain this compromise.[12]

The Proud Angel fomented a rebellion among the angels of heaven, where he had been a leading light. He declared that he would go and found a kingdom for himself. When going out at the door of heaven the Proud Angel brought prickly lightning and biting lightning out of the doorstep with his heels.

Many angels followed him—so many that at last the Son called out, "Father! Father! the city is being emptied!" whereupon the Father ordered that the gates of heaven and the gates of hell should be closed. This was instantly done. And those who were in were in, and those who were out were out; while the hosts who had left heaven and had not reached hell flew into the holes of the earth, like the stormy petrel birds.

These are the Fairy Folk—ever since doomed to live under the ground, and only allowed to emerge where and when God permits. They are never allowed abroad on Thursday, that being St. Columba's day; nor on Friday, that being the Son's day; nor on Saturday, that being Mary's Day; nor on Sunday, that being the Lord's day.

Dia eadar mi 's gach sìdhe
Gach mì-rùn is gach druidheachas,
An-diugh an Daorn air muir is air tìr,
M' earbs', a Rìgh, nach cluinn iad mi.

God be between me and every fairy,
Every ill wish and every magic spell
Today is Thursday on sea and land
I trust, o God, that they do not hear me.

On certain nights when their mounds are open and their lamps are lit, and the song and dance are moving merrily, the fairies may be heard singing light-heartedly:

Chan ann a shìol Àdhaimh sinn
S chan Àbram ar n-athair,
Ach shìol an aingeil uabhraich
Chaidh fhuadach á flathas.

We are not of the see of Adam
And Abraham is not our father,
But the seed of the proud angel
Who was exiled out of heaven.[13]

Dispirited Fairies in Ross-shire

An anonymous contributor from Ross-shire sent two anecdotes in Gaelic about the fairies to the newspaper *The Highlander* in 1881, saying that they happened "a few years ago."

The encounter between the man and the fairies happens, as is often the case, in the liminal time between day and night and in the wild, away from human habitation. People sometimes utilize symbols of Christianity to ward off the threats posed by supernatural beings in Gaelic folktales, but this text reflects the increasing domination of church orthodoxy over traditional secular Gaelic culture, the role of the written word in establishing that authority, and an awareness that older beliefs were fading away as a result.

In an area of Ross-shire not long ago there was a certain religious man named Iain. He happened to have a pregnant mare. She had been on the high moor and the time was approaching when she was supposed to have a foal. The man went out to the high moor very early on the Sabbath to see if she had given birth to the foal yet, and if she hadn't, he was going to wait for her to do so, keeping watch.

He found her after he had looked for her for a while, but she hadn't given birth yet. He had brought his Bible and he sat at the side of the mare and began to read it. While he was reading, he heard a loud sound around him, and suddenly there were large, grey-haired people standing at his feet.

"What is that book that you are reading?" asked one of them.

"It is the Bible," said Iain.

"Do you see any promise for my kind of being in it?" said the man.

"What kind of being are you?" asked Iain.

"I am," said the man, "one of the angels who fell down from the heavens."

"Oh," said Iain, "I don't see any sign of a promise for your kind in it."

When he heard that there was no promise at all for his kind in the Bible, he left crying and roaring, telling the sad tale to the others.[14]

The Stuff of Life

The Rev. James MacDougall had amassed a huge collection of folktales in Gaelic from western Argyll by 1893. He did not leave a record about the people who told him the tales, however.

This short anecdote suggests that recognizing the presence of the fairies requires being highly attuned to the environment. It also intimates the close association between the fairies and the fecundity of the land, and suggests that there is rivalry between humans and fairies over the bounties of nature.

There was once a farmer's son in Rannoch who became ill, and he would go to the high ground, morning and evening, to see if he could recover.

When the summer came, and the cattle went to the shielings, he followed them, and he stayed with them until they returned home to the strath at the beginning of harvest time.

On a calm, misty day, he went away to gather them to the milking pen, but he got lost in the mist, and he spent a long time seeking them before he came upon them. He found them at last grazing in a big, beautiful corrie with nutritious, green grass up to their eyeballs. The day was warm and dewy, and the grass was bursting up briskly from the ground.

As he was tired with the warmth and with traveling the high ground, he sat down on a green hillock to take a rest.

He was not there for long when he heard a voice coming from the root of every blade of grass at his feet, saying: "Some of it for me, some of it for me!"

He then listened a while, and now the same voice was coming from the root of every blade of grass in the corrie. He looked to see if he could find out where the voices came from, but there was no one, big or small, to be seen. He listened again, and when he heard the same clamor the third time he understood that it came from the fairies. And so he cried as loud as they did, "And some of it for me too!"

The clamor stopped immediately, and then he drove the cattle to the pen.

The milk-maids were waiting for them, and wondering what had kept them so long. They began to milk the cattle, but before they had milked half of them, every vessel in the pen was overflowing with milk. They could not understand how the milk became so abundant so quickly. They eventually began to praise the weather and say that it was the reason for the abundance.

The farmer's son listened patiently to all that he heard, but he said to himself that the milk was not so plentiful on every farm as it was on theirs that day, and that it would not be so plentiful there either, had he left the fairies alone when they were drawing it to themselves in the corrie.[15]

The Fairies and the Farmer's Gift

This is one of many tales collected in Gaelic from anonymous storytellers on the Isle of Arran in the late nineteenth century. This tale relates two common ideas in tales of the supernatural. The first is to be careful of what you wish for, as it may entail costs that may be difficult to pay. The second is to be cautious of the fairies, as they are powerful beings who can bring great harm to those cross them. An equation between the fairies and the well-being of the soil is suggested the offerings of grain by and to the fairies, and the ploughing field as the theater of action.

There was once a certain farmer that had a lease of land in this island in the past. One day in the beginning of spring, as he was in the field following the horses in the plough, he was struck, as often happened, with hunger.

He said to himself, "If I just had a bite of bread, it would sustain me until noon."

As he came to the head-rig, he smelled a pleasant aroma which whetted his appetite even more: the smell of a newly-made bannock. He said, "I would like to eat a bit of that bannock," and he continued on behind the horses in the plough until he again returned to the head-rig, and what did he see but a newly-made bannock lying on the ground in front of him.

This astonished him, but he picked up and ate the bannock, and he had never eaten a tastier bannock.

"Indeed," he said, "I would like to get a boll of the meal from which that bannock was made."

He made another pass with the horses, and having again come to the same place, he sees a boll of meal sitting on the ground.

He released the horses from the plough and brought the boll of meal home, and he had he never eaten such meal: it was so sweet and tasty.

He started to contemplate the matter, and he came to the conclusion that this was the work of the fairies, and that it was his duty to reward their kindness. When his own meal came from the mill, he left a boll of it at the head-rig where he had previously got the bannock and meal of the fairies, and they took away the meal of the farmer with them.

A short time after this, the fairies met him in the field and their kindness had turned into anger, for they seized him and thrashed him severely with flails.

They asked him, "Why did you give us that sort of meal?"

"I gave you," said the farmer, "the best meal I had."

"But," they said, "the meal which we gave you was made from the top-grain on the stalk."

"If that is the way it is," he said, "I will give you meal as good as the meal you gave me."

With this promise, they released the farmer and he went home as fast as his legs would take him, and he threshed the top-grain on the stalk, sent it to the mill, and left a boll of the meal where the fairies would get it.

From then until he died, he and the fairies were good friends.[16]

Great MacMhuirich and the Fairies

This tale was published by Elizabeth Carmichael (1870–1928) in *The Celtic Review* in 1908 based on the fieldwork of her father, Alexander Carmichael. This tale was drawn from the materials he collected from the descendants of the MacMhuirich literary dynasty living in South Uist in the nineteenth century.

Great MacMhuirich is a composite figure in Gaelic folklore representing the stature and power of the professional poets.[17] The misfortunes Great MacMhuirich experiences prompt him to listen carefully for clues about restoring proper relations with the fairy world and nature, which are essentially equated here. Having realized the need to ensure the organic cycles of nature, returning nutrients to the soil (a theme also shown in the previous tale), he teaches the lesson to members of his household.

The people apply the term *frìde* and its derivatives *frìdean, frìdeag, frìdich* to creatures which they allege dwell in the internal rocks and in the innermost parts of the earth. They say that these gnomes eat and drink like men, and that it is not right to deprive them of the crumbs that fall to the ground. When crumbs of food or drops of milk fall on the floor, the old people deprecate removing them, saying, "*Gabh ealla ris, is ioma beul feumach tha feitheamh air*" ("Leave it alone, there are many needy mouths waiting for it").

Great MacMhuirich of Stadhlaigearraidh was losing his cattle through *dosgaidh* ("mischance, accidents"). As he sat on a fairy hill musing over his losses he heard weeping and wailing in the hill below him:

Ist a lurain, Uist a luaidh,
Ist a chuilein nan cas luath,
Duair a shuidhichear clàr MhicMhuirich,
Gheobh mo luran iodh is uachdar.

Hush, o lovely, hush, o darling,
Hush, o pet of the restless feet,
When MacMhuirich's table is set,
My darling will get grain and cream.

MacMhuirich went home, and though he never went into his kitchen before, he went in that day. His baking woman was making bread, and bits of dough and grains of meal were falling from her in the process.

She took no notice of these until a piece fell from the bannock on her palm, and then she stooped down and lifted it. MacMhuirich noticed her, and he went over and gave her a tap on the back of the hand with the switch he had, saying, "Leave it alone, o dear, many a needy mouth is waiting for it. And as long as you are in my house, never again remove the fragments of food from the floor, there are many needy mouths waiting for it."

And as long as MacMhuirich lived, he went daily to the fairy hill with an offering of crumbs of bread and drops of milk and never again did Great MacMhuirich lose his kine or his sheep or his horses.

We must remember the smallest of God's creatures if we are to thrive in this world below and to live in the world beyond, and the aged narrator had acted on her belief throughout her long life, though she had never once seen nor heard the recipients of her bounty.[18]

The Glaistig of Glen Duror

This tale comes from the collection made by the Rev. James MacDougall by 1893 from anonymous sources. Some tales such as this suggest considerable overlap between female fairies and *glaistigs* (there is no direct translation in English). Some tales also reflect thematic connections with the goddesses depicted by medieval Gaelic literature who personify territories and look after the interests of the land and the beings that are sustained on it.

There was a *glaistig* in Glen Duror who was called "the Maiden." She was a human woman at first. Two or three hundred years ago she was a dairy-maid between Glen Duror and Glenachulish and her name and surname, and even the farmstead where she was raised, are still remembered.

She was taken away by the fairies during child-birth, and she never returned. But according to tradition, she was changed into a fairy woman, or a *glaistig*, who took shelter in the ravines and recesses of the craigs between the two glens. She frequented, in particular, the Robbers' Ravine on the south side of Ben Vehir, and there she was often seen by the travelers on the road.

It seems that she retained as a *glaistig* the affection she had for cattle and all kinds of livestock previously. She was often to be seen in the middle of the cattle, as if she were counting them, before market time, and when tenants changed residence, as if she were setting aside the stock that was leaving, or taking possession of those that were coming in. If she preferred one of the tenants over the others, she was very careful of his livestock, and when the livestock had to be relocated, she would place every obstacle between him and their removal from the premises.

According to tradition, the last time this happened was about thirty years ago. At any rate, from that day to this, the *glaistig* has been neither seen nor heard. Perhaps she was driven out of the glen by the screaming of the whistles of steamers passing up and down Loch Linnhe, or by the blasts fired by the quarriers of the quartz rock at the foot of the Dogs' Ravine.

She has departed anyway, and no one misses her.

Many a tale was told about her, and many a pail of milk was offered to her by the dairymaids at the shielings of the glen. For the night they left the pail full of milk for her, they would find everything right the next day. But the night they neglected to do this, the calves would be let out of the pen, and the cows would be sucked dry the next morning.[19]

The Gruagach Stones

This information was printed by Elizabeth Carmichael in 1908 from the fieldwork of her father Alexander Carmichael in the nineteenth century. Tales such as this demonstrate a large degree of overlap beween the personas and roles of the *ban-sìdh* ("fairy woman"), *glaistig*, and *gruagach*.[20] Although many ministers claimed that the practice of pouring milk as a votive offering came to an end in the nineteenth century due to the triumph of orthodox Christian beliefs and practices, there is testimony in both Scotland and Nova Scotia that some people continued it well into the twentieth century.

The *gruagach* was a supernatural female who presided over cattle, and took a kindly interest in all that pertained to them. In return she was offered a libation of milk when the women milked the cows in the evening. If the oblation were neglected, the cattle, notwithstanding all precautions, were found broken loose and in the corn, and if still omitted, the best cow in the fold was found dead in the morning.

The offering was poured on *clach na gruagaich* ("the gruagach stone"). There is hardly a district in the Highlands which does not possess *leac na gruagaich* ("a gruagach flagstone") where on the milk libation was poured.

All these oblation stones are erratic ice blocks. Some of them have a slight cavity into which the milk was poured, others have none, the libation being simply poured on the stone. In making the oblation the woman intoned a rune.

There is probably no district in the Highlands where the *gruagach* could not be fully described.

A woman living in the remote island of Heisgeir described her so graphically and picturesquely that her interested listener could almost see her moving about in the silvery light of the kindly moon: the *gruagach* with her tall conical hat, her rich golden hair falling about her like a mantle of shimmering gold, while with a slight swish of her wand she gracefully turned on her heel to admonish an unseen cow.

At intervals he seemed to hear her mellow voice in snatches of eerie song as she moved about among the grassy ruins of the old nunnery—all silent now of the holy orisons of gentle sisters.

The Red Hand of Kincardine

The Rev. William Forsyth (1825–1907) collected local Gaelic traditions from the parishes of Abernethy and Kincardine in Speyside during the time he was minister there, which he published in 1900. Forsyth's texts are primarily in English, although he leaves many names and phrases in their original Gaelic form.

This tale forms part of Forsyth's description of Loch Morlich. Although this Otherworld being named *Làimh Dhearg* ("Red Hand") is a male, he seems to function similarly to Gaelic chthonic goddesses who are connected to a local dynasty. There are many other Gaelic folktales about female beings who prevent hunters from having a greater impact on the wildlife than they ought to.

The concluding comment from the spectre about two different forms of a place name highlights the distinction between an anthropocentric worldview and a nature-focused one, as Forsyth himself notes. *Glacan Bealaidh* means "the Hollow of Broom," whereas *Glacan Beadaidh* means "the Hollow of Beattie," and refers to a local family.

There are fairy hills at both ends of the lake. Those at the west are said to be the abode of *Dòmhnall Mór Bad an t-Sìdhein* ("Big Donald of the Thicket of the Fairy Hill"), King of the Fairies. The sands and thickets at the east are the haunt of the *Làimh Dhearg*, the Spectre of the Bloody Hand, which was believed to be connected with the Stewarts of Kincardine.

Robin Òg, son of one of the Barons of Kincardine, was once out hunting in Glenmore. He killed a hind, and was proceeding to gralloch it. Happening to lay down his *sgian dubh* ("dagger") beside him, it disappeared. Then he took the knife from his dirk, and when he laid it down it too vanished. He finished his work the best way he could, and went away wondering.

Some time after he met an old man on the sands of Loch Morlich, wrapped in a grey plaid, but with one hand red and bloody exposed. It was the *Làimh Dhearg.*

"Is this you, Robin?" he said. "You are too often in the Glen, slaughtering my poor innocents. Do you remember the hind you killed in Glacan Bealaidh? You call it Glacan Beadaidh, but we call it Glacan Bealaidh. Here are your knives, but I counsel you to be more sober in the Glen in the future."[21]

The Specter of the Tay and the Fairy-Fort of Kincraigie

A man who identified himself only as "E. Cameron" contributed the following letter to *The People's Journal* in 1886 about traditions on the eastern border of Highland Perthshire near Dunkeld. It was written in English but contains Gaelic names and phrases. This short text demonstrates that the same clusters of beliefs about the fairies and inhabitants of bodies of water held just as strongly here as elsewhere in the Highlands into the nineteenth century.

In the last generation a strong notion prevailed that the Tay river was haunted by a weird old man called *Bodach an Abhainn* "the Specter of the River," who bellowed loudly at night, and seized upon the lonely traveler passing his watery abode. It is said that one night a young farmer coming home by the river at Logierait, fortified with a stock of "Dutch courage," sent back a derisive echo to the *bodach*'s roaring. He was immediately pursued, but escaped after a smart run to his own door, leaving one tail of his coat in the hand of *Bodach an Abhainn*.....

In Kincraigie there was a knoll with a sandy slope and large old fir trees growing toward the summit which was always held sacred to supernatural influences. It was observed that anyone who ploughed on this mound was certain to die afterwards.

When a farmer's cattle were dwindling away and dying, a mystic fire was raised here and the cattle driven through the fire, as an antidote to supposed witchcraft. The kindling was specially got by rubbing two sticks together. The fire was called *teine éiginneach* ("need fire") and the knoll itself the *dùn* ("fort").

Once a large tree disappeared from the *dùn* and was supposed to have been spirited away by the fairies to a neighboring hillock or fairy mound. From the inhabitants of the hillock a local violinist named MacKillop professed to derive some of his best tunes.[22]

The Tailor of Rannoch and the Fairy

This tale comes from the collection made by the Rev. James MacDougall by 1893 from anonymous sources. There are many tales about fairies stealing babies and leaving changelings—fairies who were insatiable, sickly, and bad-tempered—in their place. There was a relatively high rate of child mortality and breast-feeding does not come easily to all mothers. This kind of narrative might enable parents to detach emotionally from a child who does not seem to respond to their best efforts to provide him or her with all of the care and attention they are able. The defiant cry of the changeling as it departs may be a projection of the mother's own frustrations and resentments.

The red-haired tailor lived in Rannoch. Like the others of his occupation, he would go from house to house to make clothing from the cloth that judicious women made for their men and for their sons in the old days.

Once, as he was coming close to a house where there was several days of work to do, the afternoon came upon him and in the gloomy twilight he saw a being that looked like a very small child running in front of him, and keeping out of sight behind every bush and hillock at the side of the road.

The tailor fortified his gait expecting to catch up with the strange little man before him, but rather than getting ahead, he was falling further behind with every step he took. As soon as he noticed that, he began to run with all of his might, but despite that, he could not lessen the distance between them.

He finally lost patience so badly that he threw a large pair of scissors at the nimble little man in front of him, and it struck him in the knee joints. The fairy, for that is what he was, fell down on his face, and before he could get up, he was in the grasp of the tailor, with the scissors across his chest.

"Tell me where you are going, my good lad," asked the tailor.

"I'm on my way from the Big Fairy Hill to the house that is in front of you, to get some breast-milk from the woman of the house," answered the little ruffian.

This was the very same house to which the tailor was going.

"And what will you do to the woman's own child?" he said then.

"Oh! I will put him out through the back window of the house to my own people and they will take him to our place," answered the other man.

"And will they send him home when you get enough of the breast-milk of his mother?"

"Oh, not at all. Never."

"All right, that will do," said the tailor. And he let his prisoner go.

As soon as he was back on his feet, the fairy set out for the house, and he was inside before the tailor. He had the house to himself, for the man and woman of the house were in the byre milking the cows, and no one was inside but the baby in the cradle. He lifted the baby into his arms and stretched him outside the back window to what he thought were the other fairies. But the tailor was there before them, and he took the baby silently into his arms and he took him to his sister's house which was close by, and he left the child in her care.

When he returned, he found the woman there before him, and the changeling was in the cradle, ready to burst with crying. The woman lifted him up and gave him a drink from her breast and then she put him back into the cradle. It was not long before he began to cry and scream again. She lifted him up and gave him another drink. It seemed that nothing satisfied him but to be left sucking on her breast.

This game went on for a few days. But after the tailor's patience ran out, he finally leaped from his working table and he brought in a full creel of peat, and he made a big fire on the hearth.

When the fire was burning hotly, he leaped over to the cradle, and he lifted the changeling up, and before anyone could interfere, he threw it into the very middle of the flames.

But the little ruffian leaped up and out through the chimney, and from the top of the house he cried out to the woman, "I took the juice of your breast, despite you."

And he went his way.[23]

The Fairies and the Stolen Wife

This is one of many tales collected in Gaelic from anonymous storytellers on the Isle of Arran in the late nineteenth century. It incorporates two very common motifs: humans use metal to assert power against Otherworld forces, and fairies steal women and leave wooden logs resembling them in their place.

The simplest interpretation of the tale is that it describes, in a rationalized or repressed way, a wife who has died through childbirth, which was a very common occurrence. Alternatively, she may have left her husband, which has long happened for many reasons, including being abducted by another man.

It could also be a coded way for a husband to describe the death of his wife's love for him: he may feel that she has been inexplicability replaced by an object incapable of reciprocating his affection in that most intimate of spaces, the bed. Finding her again and returning her home in this case would correspond to recovering the connection of intimacy in their marriage, or at least the hopes of doing so.

A long time ago there was a band of fairies who lived in in Cnoc 'ic Eoghain in Drumiginar. They and a certain farmer named MacMurchie were very friendly with each other. He would often go visiting with them, but always took the precaution to thrust a knife, a darning-needle or a piece of iron of that sort above their door so as to keep the way clear for him to come out.

On one of the nights on which he went to visit them, he found them all assembled on the top of the hillock, busily preparing for an urgent trip. Each one of them pulled a ragwort, and after repeating some secret words, they went astride the ragwort, and up they went into the air as light as a feather.

MacMurchie did the same thing: he pulled a ragwort, went astride on it, and, repeating the secret words, up he goes after them as fast and light as any of them. They steered their course over beyond the Mull of Kintyre by the shortest route to Ireland.

In a short while, MacMurchie found himself in the kitchen of a farmer in Ireland, where the woman of the house was lying in bed at the brink of death, and every old woman in the neighborhood was tending to her.

In the twinkling of an eye, the fairies snatched the poor woman away, and they left in her place a log of wood that resembled a woman. Then they took off back home in the same way they left, with MacMurchie and the farmer's wife in their company.

When they reached the fairy hill in Drumiginar, they gave the woman to MacMurchie because he accompanied them to Ireland, and she stayed with him as his wife.

Seven years later, on a warm summer evening, an Irish beggar came their way, and being tired, he sat down on the knocking-stone beside MacMurchie's door.

The housewife was milking the cows, and every time she went past, between the byre and milkhouse, the beggar would say, "Well, if I had not put my wife in the coffin with my own two hands, I would swear that you were her."

The end of the story was that the woman departed with the Irish beggar: her rightful husband.[24]

The Chanter from the Fairies of Loch Roag

This tale was one of many about the Otherworld collected in Lewis from unnamed informants. As it appeared in *The Celtic Review*, which was edited by Elizabeth Carmichael, it was most likely taken from the nineteenth-century fieldwork of her father, Alexander Carmichael. This tale seems to have been transcribed in English only, apart from one term.

It is after humans spoil the integrity of the fairy habitation that a female representative of the Otherworld instigates an encounter. She suggests a deal: she will bestow a magical reed if the lad will restore the soil to the fairy hill. These are two common motifs to the tale: humans should not disturb the dwelling places of the fairies, and Otherworld beings are capable of granting talent and skills upon humans.

In an island in Loch Roag there is a conical hillock said to have been the favourite resort of Fairies. The people of the island began building a turf fence for the purpose of keeping the cattle from coming in on the arable land. The line of the fence passing near the base of the hillock, they cut a quantity of turf off the side of the knoll.

On the day following that on which the sods were cut a young lad—an amateur bagpipe-player—was employed in boring a piece of wood in order to make a chanter of it, when a strange woman came to him, and saluting him, told him that she would put him in the way of getting a much better chanter than he could ever make, provided he would place the sods which were cut in yonder hill yesterday in their original places.

He had scarcely come back from replacing the sods when the strange woman made her appearance, and after expressing her approbation of the manner in which he had executed the work, she told him to get *Maide nan Cuaran*—a stick stuck in the wall on which brogues were hung—and work it down to the shape of a chanter, and bore it, and after he had finished to put in the mouthpiece a reed which she handed him.

He finished the chanter to the best of his ability and inserted the Fairy's reed. The music played on the bagpipes with that chanter excelled all other pipe music. The chanter was kept for many generations by the descendants of the lad in Uig till they emigrated to America, when they took the chanter with them.[25]

MacCrimmon's Fairy Sweetheart

The Rev. Neil Ross (1873–1943) was a native of Skye who had a particular interest in bagpipe music and published numerous accounts about music and musicians from Gaelic oral tradition. This is an extract from a long essay about the MacCrimmons that Ross contributed to a periodical in 1910.

There were professional bagpiping dynasties who dominated the art between the seventeenth and eighteenth centuries in various districts of the Highlands, and each had stories explaining their prowess as a result of gifts from the fairies, including the MacCrimmons, the Rankins, the Chisholms, and the *Clann an Sgeulaiche* MacGregors. In this tale, as in many others, however, this gift did not come for free: the MacCrimmon bagpiper was obliged to follow the fairy woman into the Cave of Gold and never return.

When the brown-haired youth from the clan of the worthy musicians played on the multi-droned bagpipe at the bottom of Sloc nam Pìobairean ("the Pit of the Bagpipers"), his eyes were struck were amazement and his veins pulsed with joy to see the magical nymph, more beautiful than any other living maiden. The likes of her could not be found in the four corners of the world. She had a silver chanter in her hand and she held it out to MacCrimmon.

She told him that the chanter would give him success over all of the musicians on earth. But after a year and a day he would have to go to the Cave of Gold.

The youth grabbed the silver chanter and he was quickly enchanted. He would not part with it even if he got all of the wealth in the world. When he played on the instrument of the melodious notes, music was heard that was unlike any before. The lark and the thrush came to listen and they all remained silent. The deer came from the misty mountain to listen to the melodious marching music. The brown otter came to the stream bank and the seal of the waves came to land to eavesdrop. The sickly became whole and the sad became joyous. The golden age had come.

The solace lasted for a year and a day. But the hour and the minute came. On a joyous summer's morning, the youth made ready to travel. He turned his back to his kin and he left the land of the living. He turned toward the Cave of Gold and he played a tune whose only testimony are the words:

I will not come, I will not arrive,
I will not come out of the Cave of Gold;
The little kids
Will be craig-climbing goats
And the feeble children will be soldiers;
The infants at the breast
Will be grown men
Before I come out of the Cave of Gold.[26]

The Uruisg's Reward

This tale was sent by an anonymous contributor to the Gaelic periodical An *Deò-Gréine* in 1910 and seems identical to a story sent to John F. Campbell in 1860.[27] It explains that a place name in Kintyre was called after an *uruisg* (water-dwelling monster) that lived there. The choice presented to the human protagonist of the tale between either talent or success occurs in other Gaelic folktales, although it is most frequently offered by a fairy woman. Such stories offer the perceptive insight that exquisite artistry does not always coincide with material prosperity.

In a corner of Kintyre there is a stream running through a hollow that is called Allt na Béiste ("the Stream of the Beast"), and this name was supposed to have been given to the stream because, according to tradition, there was a terrible *uruisg*, or some monster of that sort, inhabiting the recesses of the stream.

This monster was terrifying the entire area, and no one would go near the place where the *uruisg* was living. From time to time, the bellowing and roaring of the monster would be heard at a distance, frightening both young and old, and they would travel for miles to go around it rather than going across the stream near that place.

But there was one man in the area who made up his mind—come what may, victory or defeat—to challenge the monster, and should he succeed, the place would be free of this terror. This was Big, Black-haired Iain, a brave, vigorous, valiant man.

Iain was advised many times to leave this terrible thing alone, that it would be better to leave things as they were than to put his life in danger, but he turned a deaf ear to all advice.

It was on a summer afternoon that he equipped himself to battle the *uruisg*, and he left for the residence of the creature. When Iain was nearing that place, the *uruisg* heard the sound of feet, and it released a roar that would split the craigs, and it shook up Iain, even as brave as he was.

He reached the edge of the stream and he challenged the monster to come out of the holes.

He got a frightening roar in response. He took a step or two forward to the middle of the stream, and he stood on a wide stone that was there. The *uruisg* came out to meet him with a fierce expression on its face. Iain was not sure whether it was monster or human, or both, but even if it were the Devil himself, he would not take a single step back. He prepared himself for battle with his sword in his hand.

"Strike me," said the *uruisg*.

"I will not, strike me yourself," said Iain.

"I will not," said the *uruisg*, "but you strike me."

"I will not," said Iain, "but if you strike me, I will strike you."

They went on like this for a long time, without one of them making the first strike. The *uruisg* finally gave the first blow to Iain. Even so, Iain stood his ground like a man, and he delivered more than he received, beating and stabbing with all of his strength. They had a rough and hard fight, until they were both so tired that they stopped the battle so that they could rest. Iain stood up like he was ready to start the battle again, but apparently the monster got more than it wanted.

After a moment, it spoke. "I see," it said, "and I have proof in my own body that you are a valiant man, and that your heroism has triumphed over me. I never thought that there was a single person in this area, or any other area, who was audacious enough to come against or challenge me like you did. I will not fight you anymore, but for your courage I will offer you a choice between two things, and you will have it accordingly."

"Let me hear those two things," said Iain.

"Which will you take," said the *uruisg*, "talent or success?"

Without thinking about it too much, Iain responded, "I will take talent without success."

"So shall it be," said the *uruisg*, "I will not bother a single living soul from now on, and I will not been seen or heard here or anywhere else again."

The *uruisg* disappeared in the blink of an eye, and Iain took the road homeward.

He explained what had happened, and although Iain was an honest man, many neighbors doubted the account, until they proved to themselves that they were indeed free of the source of fear that had bothered them for many years, and that Big Black-haired Iain was the brave hero who had rescued them.

After that happened, Iain began his daily work as usual, and he himself and all of his neighbors were greatly surprised that the work of his hands came out so neat and artistic. Every task, every craft, every project that he would take on would be completed so well, deftly, and fully that his reputation and the achievements of his work spread far and wide throughout the land. A variety of work of every sort suited his hands every day.

But even though Iain's work was a great benefit to the country round about, no matter what he did, no success for himself or his family resulted from his efforts. Even if reward for his labor came to his hands, it would not stick to him. Iain was as poor at the end of the week as he had been at the beginning.

For as famous as he was for the talents of his hands, no success followed him, and he realized when it was too late that he had made a poor choice for himself when he chose talent without success.[28]

The Cloven-Hoofed Sweetheart

This is one of many tales collected in Gaelic from anonymous storytellers on the Isle of Arran in the late nineteenth century. This is a Gaelic variant of the widespread Rumpelstiltskin folktale, classified as tale type ATU-500. The plot has, however, been refashioned in a Gaelic context through the influence of traditions about young women whose suitors turn out to be fairies, *each-uisge* ("water-horses"), or other non-human entities. The message of these tales is to be certain of the true nature of your sweetheart before you are bound to them in marriage. The name of something is often the key to unlocking its identity.

There was once a young girl who had a handsome sweetheart. He would often go to see her alone, but he would not tell his name, nor where he lived. Every time he went to see her he would always find her spinning. He was keen for her to run away with him and was always asking her to go with him, but she refused to.

One of the times that he went to see her, she was about to begin to spin a sack of wool. He offered to spin the sack of wool if she would promise to leave with him. She was tired of the work, and she promised him that she would leave with him on the condition that she would be free from her promise if she found out his name before the sack of wool was spun.

So what happened is that he put the sack on his back and went on his way.

On a certain night after that, as she was going to a friend's house, and crossing a deep stream in an isolated place, she heard the sound of a spinning-wheel and a ditty of a song coming from the bottom of the stream.

This astonished the girl, and she drew near the place from which the sound came. What did she see and hear but an old, dark-complexioned, shrivelled man sitting at a large spinning-wheel, spinning intensely and singing cheerfully:

"Little does my sweetheart know
That 'Cloven-Hoofed' is my name."

The girl now understood what kind of a sweetheart she had, and that his dwelling place was in the deep hollows of the stream. When he had finished the work he went again to see the girl, and to ask for the reward of his labor. As soon as she saw him, she repeated the words she had heard:

"Little does my sweetheart know
That 'Cloven-Hoofed' is my name."

No sooner had "Cloven-Hoofed" heard those words than he disappeared in a shower of red sparks up the chimney, and he never troubled the girl again.[29]

The Last Each-Uisge in Lewis

This tale was one of many about the Otherworld collected in Lewis from unnamed informants, most likely by Alexander Carmichael in the nineteenth century.

There are many short tales about the *each-uisge* in Gaelic tradition which describe him as courting a female in the shape of a human male, keeping his animal nature in disguise. The young woman eventually discovers his true, dangerous character and escapes from his clutches just in time. This tale is longer and more elaborate than most. In this case, he is represented as not just a sexual predator but an economic one as well, threatening the well-being of the kin group.

An element of the hero tale genre has also been incorporated into the story by bringing in the MacLeod bowman. The special arrow that he reserves in his quiver until the end of his confrontation with the *each-uisge* is named the *Badhbhag* after a monstrous fairy woman who first appears in the Celtic canon as a goddess of war.

This is how the last *each-uisge* that was in Lewis came to his end: A man lived in Erista, in the parish of Uig, who was the tenant tacksman not only of that and the neighboring village but of the extensive tract of land between Loch Roag and Loch Langabhat.

In the summer season he used to send his cattle to graze on the moor with two females to look after them. The women lived in a shieling in Glen Langabhat, where the ruins of the shieling are still to be seen.

The women were frequently visited by the *each-uisge* in human form, but as he conducted himself in no way disagreeably they did not feel any repugnance to his visits. In the course of time, however, he seems to have undergone a change of disposition, inasmuch as his conduct towards them became highly offensive. He not only insulted and ill-treated themselves, but committed great depredations among their master's cattle, killing some of them on the spot and carrying some of them away. But, says my informant, he always had the form of a quadruped when he killed them on the spot, but of a man when taking them away and visiting the women.

His indignities towards the women and his depredations amongst the cattle increased to such an extent that the women left the field to himself, and made their way to Erista, where they told their master how matters stood. Their master, not believing their reports, and deriding their cowardice, sent two servants to the moors to see what was the real state of matters.

When the servants came in sight of Glen Shanndaig they saw the *each-uisge* in the act of taking one of the cattle away. This satisfied them, and they returned and told their master what they had seen. The owner of the cattle saw that he must get the *each-uisge* killed or else his cattle would be all lost to him.

There was a man in Earshadir on the shores of Loch Roag who was a famous archer and who had killed some time before two *each-uisges*, one in Skye and another in the parish of Lochs. To him, then, the owner of the cattle went and offered him a great reward if he could kill the *each-uisge*.

The archer, whose name was MacLeod, agreed to go at once. He accordingly took his bow and arrows and started for the glen, accompanied by his son, who did not know where they were bound for till they were half-way on their journey.

When the son heard the object of the journey he would not by any means go, but wished to return home and let his father go alone. The father would not permit this, but bound his son with cords and left him there.

MacLeod proceeded alone on his way, and when he came in sight of the glen he saw the *each-uisge* coming up from the loch and making for him. He held himself in readiness, and when the beast was within range he let fly the arrow, which stuck in the creature's side, but did not in the least impede his progress. As he came still nearer, the man let go a second arrow, which caused the *each-uisge* to stagger, but still he came on with his mouth wide open and his eyes glaring.

The man saw he was in danger and took out the *Badhbhag*, and placing it waited till the creature was near, when he fired it so that it went in at its mouth and through its heart. The beast fell dead, and MacLeod cut off its tail as a pledge that he had killed the *each-uisge*, and picking up the *Badhbhag* returned to the tacksman, who rewarded him generously.[30]

MacPhee's Black Hound

The Rev. John G. Campbell transcribed this tale from the recitation of Donald Cameron of Ruag, Tiree, in 1863. Campbell collected several folktales from Cameron and expressed huge admiration for him. Cameron had become impoverished after the Duke of Argyll deprived him, and others, of land: "the writer cannot but express his admiration of Cameron as the best reciter he has ever fallen in with."[31]

The story of MacPhee's black hound was a very popular one in Gaelic and there are several different versions, but this is the longest and most interesting. The tale led to a common saying in the Highlands: *Thig là a' choin duibh fhathast* ("The black hound's day has yet to come"), used of something that had not yet been of use but might still be in the future.[32]

The character of MacPhee himself is key to unlocking some of the puzzles in this text, as this surname derives from *MacDhubhShìthe* ("the son of the Black-haired Fairy") and this association with fairies was never completely forgotten in Gaelic tradition. The shape-shifting female at the beginning of the tale is one of the manifestations of the Gaelic chthonic goddess and this motif of her appearing to a hunter alternately as a deer or women is told in many tales across the Highlands. According to some tales, *Cailleach na Beinne Brice* was in love with MacPhee and would not let him part from her.[33]

The verbal exchange between MacPhee and the fairy woman is particularly interesting. Like many highly charged dialogs in Gaelic tales, it is in the form of loose poetry (as is clear in the original Gaelic text but not in translation).[34] MacPhee exposes her identity as a fairy-woman, in order to try to asset control over her, and accuses her of cavorting with Diarmaid and other members of the Fianna. She, in return, calls him "Brian Brugh," a name that has an echo of the name of the Irish warrior-king Brian Boru (†1014) but also refers directly to the dwelling-place of the fairies (*brugh*). She accuses him of cavorting with fairy women, going from one fairy hill to another. This obviously rattles him, as he shuts down the dialog and calls for violence against her.

The group of men that MacPhee encounters at night after hunting, from whom he gets the black hound, can also be inferred to be members of the Otherworld.

This tale integrates multiple plots and motifs. A disembodied hand that reaches in through a window, door or hole to grab someone is a migratory motif found in many narratives and is best known from its appearance in the Grendel episode of Beowulf.[35] There are variants of a tale across the Highlands about young men who spend the night in a bothy, wish for the company of young women, and then get ripped apart by supernatural females who seem to be answering their call for romance. The title "Àirigh na h-Aon Oidhche" ("The One-Night Shieling") is generally used for this tale type in Gaelic.[36]

The chief of Clanranald in Arisaig, the Laird of Moidart, went out hunting in his deer forest when he was young and unmarried. He saw a full-grown stag before him, as beautiful as he had ever seen. He set his sights to his gun, and the stag turned into a woman, the most beautiful he had ever seen. He let down the gun from his eye, and it was a full-grown stag as it was before. Every time he set his sight to the gun, the animal became a woman, and every time he let it down to the ground, it became a full-grown stag.

He then put the gun to his sight, and he went over until he was against her chest. He made a leap, and he grabbed her between his two hands.

"You will not be separated from me," he said. "I will marry no one but you."

"Do not do that, o chief of Clanranald," she said. "You have no business with me. I will not suit you. You will have to kill a cow for me every day that you have me."

"You will have that," said the Lord of Moidart, "even if you want two a day."

But the chief of Clanranald's herd began to grow thin. He then started to send her away but was unable to. Then he went to an old man in the settlement who was his counsellor. He told him that he would be ruined and did not know by what means he could get rid of her. The kindly old man said that if MacPhee of Colonsay could not get rid of her, there was not a man alive who could.

That very minute a letter was sent off to MacPhee. MacPhee answered the letter, and came to Arisaig.

"What is this business you have with me," said MacPhee, "o chief of Clanranald?"

The chief of Clanranald explained to him how the woman had restricted him so that he could not send her away.

"You go on," said MacPhee, "and kill a cow for her today as usual, send her dinner to her room as usual, and give me my dinner on the other side of the room."

The chief of Clanranald did as MacPhee asked him to do. She began her dinner, and MacPhee began his own dinner. When MacPhee was done with his dinner, he looked across at her

"What is your news, o Fairy?" he said.

"What is that to you, o Brian Brugh?" she said.

"I saw you, o Fairy," he said, "when you were meeting with the Fianna, when you went away with Diarmaid Ó Duibhne, traveling with him from one rough fur-coverlet to another."

"I saw you," she said, "o Brian Brugh, when you rode on an old black horse, as the sweetheart of the slim fairy woman, while you were constantly chasing her from fairy-mound to fairy-mound."

"Set hounds and lads after the beast," said MacPhee. "Long have I known her."

Every hound and man in Arisaig was called, and they were sent after her. She fled away out to the headland of Arisaig, and they didn't see her again.

MacPhee then went home to his own Colonsay. He went out hunting one day, and night came upon him before he got home. He saw a light and made straight for it. He saw many men sitting within the place, and an old grey-haired man along with them in their midst.

The old man spoke and said, "O MacPhee, come forward."

MacPhee stepped forward, and what came his way but a female hound as beautiful as he had ever seen, and she had young pups. He saw one of her pups that was black in color, and he had never seen a pup as black or as beautiful as it was.

"This hound will be mine," said MacPhee to the man.

"No, it will not," said the man. "You can take your choice of her pups, but you will not get that one."

"I will not take any of hers," said MacPhee, "but this one."

"Since you are determined to take it with you," said the man, "it will only be of use to you on a single day, and it will do well. Come here on a particular night and you will get it."

MacPhee came to the place on the night he had promised to come. They gave him the hound, "And take good care of him," said the old man. "He will only ever be of use to you on one day."

The black hound began to grow into a beautiful pup, and no one had ever seen a hound so large or so beautiful as it was. When MacPhee would go out to hunt, he would call the black hound, and the black hound would reach the doorway, and then it would go back and lie down where it was before. The noblemen who used to come to MacPhee's house would ask him to kill the black hound, as it was not worth feeding. MacPhee would tell them to leave it alone, that the black hound had not yet had its day.

Then many noblemen came over from Islay to visit MacPhee, and to ask him to go to Jura to hunt. Jura was a wilderness at that time, with no one living there, and there was no place in the world like it for hunting deer and roe. There was a place there called the Big Cave where noblemen who went hunting would usually stay.

They prepared a boat to go across the sound that day. MacPhee got up to leave, with sixteen young noblemen along with him. Each one of them called the black hound, and he reached the doorway, and returned and lay down where he was before.

"Use the gun on him," said the young noblemen.

"I won't," he said. "The black hound has not had his day yet."

They made their way to the shore, and the wind picked up, but they did not get across that day.

The next day they made ready to go. The black hound was called, and he reached the doorway, and went back where he was before.

"Kill him," said the noblemen, "and don't feed him any longer."

"I will not kill him," said MacPhee. "The black hound's day has yet to come."

But they failed to get across that day also, because the weather was so rough, so they returned.

"The black hound has foresight," said the noblemen.

"He knows that his own day has yet to come," said MacPhee.

The weather was beautiful on the third day. They made their way to the harbor, and they did not say a word to the black hound this day. They launched the boat to leave. One of the noblemen looked and said the black hound was coming, and that he had never seen such a creature, because it was looking so ferocious. It leaped, and was the first creature in the boat.

"The black hound's day is approaching," said MacPhee. They took food and sleeping gear with them, and came ashore in Jura. They spent that night in the Big Cave. And the next morning they went out to hunt the deer. When it approached evening, they came home. They prepared supper. They had a fine fire and light in the cave. There was a big hole in the very top of the cave that was just big enough for a man to go through it. After they ate their supper, the young noblemen stretched themselves out on the beds.

MacPhee stood up and began to warm the back of his legs against the fire as he stood. Each one of the young men said that he wished his own sweetheart was along with him there that night, and if she were, he would be well off.

"Well," said MacPhee, "I myself would prefer my wife to be in her own house. It is enough for me to be here myself tonight."

MacPhee looked in the distance, and he saw sixteen women coming in through the opening of the cave. The light went out, and the only light they had was what came from the fire.

The women went over to where the noblemen were in their beds. MacPhee could not see a speck of light because the cave had become so dark. He didn't hear a sound from any of the men, off in the distance.

The women stood up, and one of them looked at MacPhee. She stood across from him, as though she were going to attack him. The black hound arose, and looked ferocious. It lunged at them. They left for the opening. The black hound leaped after them to the mouth of the cave. When they left, the black hound returned and lay down at MacPhee's feet. A little after that, MacPhee heard a clamor on the ceiling of the cave above him, such that he thought the cave would fall down about his head. He looked up, and he saw a human hand coming down from the hole, as though it were going to grab him, and take him out through the hole in the top of the cave.

The black hound lunged, and it seized the hand between the shoulder and the elbow, and lay on top of it.

The contest began between the hand and the black hound. Before the black hound let go of its grip, it chewed the hand until it fell on the floor.

The thing that was in the top of the cave went away, and MacPhee thought that the cave might fall about his head. The black hound rushed out after the thing that was outside. As the black hound was leaving him, MacPhee was feeling most uneasy.

When the day was dawning, the black hound returned. He lay down next to MacPhee. Within a few minutes, it was dead.

When day-light came, MacPhee looked, and not a single man of those who had been with him in the cave had survived. He took the hand with him, and went to the boat on the shore. He went on board. He went to Colonsay, with neither hound nor man.

He brought the hand with him, so that people could see the horror he had experienced that night that he was in the cave. No one in Islay or Colonsay had ever seen such a hand, or had ever imagined that such a thing existed. They sent a boat to Jura, to take home the corpses that were in the cave.

That was the end of the day of the black hound.[37]

The Old Wife of Laggan

An anonymous contributor sent this tale to the Gaelic periodical *An Deò-Gréine* in 1916. Iain Garve MacLeod died in 1671 and his death is attributed in Gaelic traditions to the work of witches, but there are many variants of this tale across the Highlands that are not tied to this particular witch or historical episode.[38] The motif of the swelling hag was so well known from these folktales that it led to a common proverbial expression: *Tha thu ag at, mar a bha a' chailleach* ("You are swelling, like the hag"), used of someone who is exaggerating or bragging.[39]

The Old Wife of Laggan was the last witch I have heard about in the region, and as for the fairies, there's no one in Badenoch who has ever seen one. Well, I haven't heard about it anyway.

It may be that some of your readers have not heard the story of the Wife of Laggan, and for that reason, I'll say a word or two about the creature. If all of the tales are true, she is the one who got rid of Iain Garve MacLeod of Raasay. But on the day that she did that, she got the pain and sickness of death. After she returned, after drowning Iain Garve, she headed for the mountains and she went into a bothy in which one of her neighbors was staying.

This man went hunting often, and if there was a storm, as happened on that day, he would have a rest there, and maybe spend the night in the bothy that I mentioned.

On this day, he was indoors with a good fire before him, and he was drying and warming himself. He looked at the doorway, and what did he see but a shaggy grey cat and it was so sickly it could hardly follow him in. The hunter had two hounds, and they jumped on the creature as soon as it came into the doorway.

As soon as the hounds jumped on it, it screeched, and at the same time, it asked the hunter to show it mercy. The hunter was greatly surprised that the cat spoke to him. And so that he could see what kind of animal he had there, he held back the hounds. And when he did, the cat looked just as it had been at first.

"Come to the fire and warm yourself," says the hunter.

"I won't," said the cat, "for I am afraid that your hounds will rip me apart."

Then the cat gave a long hair to the hunter, asking him at the same time to tie up the hounds with it to the wall-beam of the bothy.

The hunter put the hair around the wall-beam and he made it appear to the cat that he also put it around the hounds. Then the cat came to the fire and as soon as it did, it began to get bigger.

The hunter noticed this, and he said, "Curse you, you lousy creature, you are getting bigger."

And in the blink of an eye, the cat was as big as a greyhound, and at the next glance, the creature shape-shifted, and who was there with him but one of his female neighbors, who was commonly called "The Wife of Laggan," who he was as familiar with as the back of his hand.

"O mountain hunter," she says, "your days have come to an end. You have long hated me and my kind, but now we will win."

She jumped on him, and she grabbed him by the throat, but as soon as she did, the hounds jumped on her.

"Tighten and choke, o hair!" she said, thinking that the hair was around the throats of the hounds, and as soon as she said it, the hair sliced through the wall-beam.

The hounds attacked her, ripping out her flesh, but she finally escaped from them, and in the blink of an eye, she flew off in the shape of a raven.

To make a long story short for you, she died that night. Two walkers happened to be going at that very time past the Monadhliath mountains between Strathdearn and Badenoch, and what did they see but a woman running quickly coming straight for them, and she passed by them without saying a word. They didn't get much further when they encountered two black hounds following the woman in hot pursuit. Shortly after that, they saw a black-haired man riding a black horse. The black-haired rider stopped and he asked them if they had seen a woman pursued by hounds.

They said that they had.

"Do you think that they will catch up with her before she reaches the graveyard?"

The men said that they wouldn't be far behind, in any case. And then the rider left. It wasn't long until he encountered them on the way back with the woman in front of him in the saddle, with one hound clinging to her thigh on the left side of the horse and the other hound clinging to a stone on the right side.

"You caught her."

"I did," said the rider, "right at the entrance of the graveyard."

The men came to Badenoch and they explained what happened to them on the way. And it was sad, for there is no doubt that it was not the spirit of the Old Wife of Laggan who they saw running toward the graveyard, for it was a sacred place, and the Devil came after her.[40]

The Witch of Braemar

John Grant of Glengairn printed this story in his 1861 collection of folktales from Braemar in Aberdeenshire. Although he translated the story into English, the names of people and places remain in Gaelic.

Witches can summon wind and storms, and overturn boats, in many Gaelic tales. They could also shapeshift, although usually into hares, cats or crows, rather than mice. The name of the witch suggests that either she or her family had some connection to France. Many of the Highland élite spent time in continental Europe, especially France, before the mid-eighteenth century.

Caitir Fhrangach ("French Kate") was a strong witch, and sometimes a wee witch, for she could transform herself into a mouse to evade her pursuers. But Robert McKeiry was a strong and swifter wizard, who took the shape of a weasel when he pursued the mouse, and caught her.

Such was the chase, when Ketty of France was taken to be burnt for drowning the Laird of Abergeldie.

The deed was done at his own wife's instigation. Ketty had told the lady that her lord smiled on strange women. Yes, more, she by her art enabled the lady to see this gallant Gordon, while at sea, on his way home from France, paying pressing suit to another lady fair. Oh, fie, Abergeldie! The sight so enraged her that she begged the witch to drown him.

Who can make the wind blow, and the stormy surges rise, if a witch can't? She ordered a large vessel to be filled with water. She had it put into a dingy dark garret at the top of the castle. She placed an empty wooden dish on the water, which floated as beautifully as ever ship on summer sea.

But bide a wee: down went Ketty to the lowest cellar of the castle, and began her incantations. There was a slight tremor, a movement of the water. Nay, a few miniature waves ran across its surface. The wooden vessel came to rock the least bit. The incantations proceeded, and the motion increased. Higher and higher rose the tiny billows.

The little vessel laboured now and tossed, and the water broke over its lip. The lady looked on with death-pale face and blood-shot eyes. There was a boiling, a hissing of the troubled little sea, and its wooden coast was lashed with foam-crested waves. There was no peace for the frail craft, which, with every lurch, was gradually filled with water.

Alas! One great wave, the lady fled to her chamber, and the little bark was at the bottom. Ketty sent to tell her that her husband was to the bottom now.

Not long after word came that the vessel was wrecked on which he was, and that all on board had perished. The lady's heart changed on hearing this, and her wrath fell upon the witch.

Caitir Fhrangach was caught and burnt on *Creag nam Ban* ("The Rock of the Women"), near Abergeldie. Had the lady been made to keep company with Ketty in the flames, Creag nam Ban would proclaim to the world a tale of truer justice.[41]

MacLeod of Dunvegan and the Witches

A contributor identified only as "A.M." sent this short Gaelic tale to the periodical *An Gàidheal* in 1944. As the writer comments, not all female practitioners of magic were evil or worked maliciously. There were two battles at Inverlochy, but this tale most likely relates to the battle fought in 1645.

When there was witchcraft in the land, and both aristocrat and peasant gave heed to magic, it was malice that was attributed to witches. But if the tale is true, there were some of them who did kindly deeds.

The chieftain of the MacLeods of Dunvegan encountered one of each sort at the time of the Battle of Inverlochy. On the day that MacLeod left the fortress with his men, the people of the area came out to see the soldiers on their way to the battle and to wish the men farewell.

There was a particular woman sitting on the stone wall of a house, with her back to the thatch, spinning with a distaff. As MacLeod passed by her, she shouted, "My best wishes to you, o MacLeod!"

"Best wishes to you yourself," he responded, and at the same time, he tossed a silver coin on the road. She made such a rush to grab the silver that she fell down from the wall and the pointed end of the distaff went into her face. The power of the money turned her ill-intent against her.

On the day of the Battle of Inverlochy, MacLeod noticed that there was a crow hovering above him while the battle was happening. Many of the MacLeods fell in battle, but the chieftain returned safely to the fortress.

A little while after that, the women of the area began to complain that the milk was losing its nutrients. An unusual number of the cattle were dying and falling over the craigs. Suspicion fell on a particular woman and she was taken to court before the chieftain of the MacLeods.

He sentenced her to be hanged.

"If you would remember, o MacLeod," she said, "when I was a black crow keeping the bullets away from you at the Battle of Inverlochy, you wouldn't do this."

"That is true, o woman. Let her go," said MacLeod.[42]

Hugh of the Wee Head

John Dewar collected this tale about Hugh of the Wee Head for John F. Campbell in about 1860. Hugh of the Wee Head lived in the early sixteenth century and his ghost is seen when descendants of the MacLeans of Lochbuie are near death.[43] It was considered "the best known and most dreadful spectre in the West Highlands" in the nineteenth century.[44] It followed the family far beyond Scotland, for it was seen in Cape Breton in the twentieth century.[45] This tale provides an account of Hugh's difficult marriage and hapless death.

As hospitality and generosity are the cardinal virtues of Gaelic society,[46] the selfishness and miserliness of the MacDougall woman emphasize her anti-social nature. The heron, after whom she is named, is a thin and wiry bird, and has long been associated with stinginess and death in Gaelic tradition.[47] Seeing a heron when setting off for a journey was considered a bad omen.[48]

Getting butter without asking for it was considered, on the other hand, a sign of good luck.[49] The fact that Hugh's wife will not look after his physical sustenance or metaphysical fortune, even after he has gone so far as to draw her attention to the stores of butter by throwing a shoe, seals his fate for the worse.

The fairy woman who washes a bloodied shirt is a very old omen of death in Gaelic tradition, often referred to in English as "the washer at the ford." She is closely related to the banshee of Irish tradition and is ultimately derived from the chthonic sovereignty goddess.[50] Claiming her as a foster-mother by sucking at her breast, and thus gaining her protection, evokes the strong bonds between foster-mothers and foster-sons in Gaelic tradition.[51]

There was once a chief of Lochbuie in Mull who was called Gap-Toothed Iain MacLean. He had a son named Hugh. They called him Hugh of the Wee Head. When Hugh of the Wee Head grew up to be a man, he married the daughter of a nobleman of the MacDougalls of Lorne. Hugh's wife was an terrible miser, and very bad tempered. The people of Mull called her the Black Heron MacDougall.

The Black Heron MacDougall did not at all like visitors coming to bother her, nor did she like to give hospitality to any one.

She managed to make Hugh of the Wee Head build her a house in a loch called Loch Sguabain and there was a causeway of stepping stones between the Isle of Loch Sguabain and the lake shore to keep people from going to the house frequently.

When Hugh of the Wee Head and his wife had been living for a while in the Isle of Loch Sguabain, she began to be jealous seeing her father-in-law living in a grand castle while she lived in an inferior house in the Isle of Loch Sguabain. And she gave Hugh of the Wee Head no rest, day or night, but said to him constantly, "It seems to me that you could get more land than you have now from your father, and I think that your father has been living in the castle for a long time. It seems to me that he could give you the castle now, and a lesser house would suffice for him now. You are the heir, anyway.

The castle and all of the estates and everything will come to you eventually. And the sooner you get more land and the castle, the better."

She did not grant Hugh of the Wee Head rest or peace, day or night, until he went to his father to ask for more land and the castle from him.

His father replied to him, "I will keep the castle myself, and all the land that I have as long as I live, and after that you will get them, but I will keep what I have as long as I live."

Hugh of the Wee Head went home, and as soon as he did, his wife began to pester him for being so weak as to capitulate to a man as old as his father. Hugh of the Wee Head went back two or three times to his father to plea for more land and the castle from him.

But his father would not yield to giving anything at all to Hugh of the Wee Head, except for what he already had. On one of these occasions Gap-Toothed Iain went out along with his son, Hugh of the Wee Head, and when they were at a place named the Field of the Horsemen, they had a terrible falling out, Hugh struck his father in the mouth and knocked him over, knocking out two of his teeth. That caused quarreling and bad blood between Hugh of the Wee Head and Gap-Toothed Iain his father.

Gap-Tooted Iain left and arrived at MacLean of Duart, and voiced his complaint to him about what his son had done to him.

MacLean of Duart gathered his men and went to take vegeance out on Hugh of the Wee Head for striking his father. Hugh gathered men together, and he and MacLean of Duart fought a battle at Dàil a' Bhroinein at Cùl a' Ghàra Mhóir. Hugh of the Wee Head lost, and his men were routed. The Black Heron MacDougall was not happy about it. She got men from her father in Lorne, and she would not be satisfied unless another battle was fought. They appointed a day to fight a battle at Ceann a' Chnocain in Glen Forsa.

A day or two before the day of battle, Hugh went to Beinn an t-Sealbh to hunt. Mist descended on the mountain and he didn't kill anything or procure venison, but got lost in the mist on the mountain.

At dusk, he came to a stream that was red with blood. He climbed up the moor, following the stream to see what was causing the blood in the stream. After climbing up to a little gorge that was there, he saw a fairy woman with a pile of bloody shirts that she was washing in a pool in the stream. She had stretched-out breasts that were slung over her shoulder.

Hugh of the Wee Head came up behind her unawares. He took hold of her breast and put it in his mouth, and sucked it, and said, "I claim your fosterage. I declare to you that I have sucked your breast."

She said, "I'm afraid that will not be of much use to you. You have a very bad wife at home. If you had a good wife at home, I might have been able to do you some good, but your wife is so bad that I'm afraid that I cannot do you much good."

"What are you doing here?"

"I am washing the bloody shirts of those who will fall on the day of the Battle of Ceann a' Chnocain in Glen Forsa, and I think I have your shirt here among the others."

"Am I to fall in the battle?"

The fairy woman said, "If your wife gives you butter without you asking for it on the day that you go to battle, you will come home alive. But if she does not give you butter without you having to ask for it, you will not come home alive from the battle."

When the day of the battle came, the wife of Hugh of the Wee Head was rushing him to go to the battle. Hugh went and brought his men together to her so that she could feed them before they departed. She prepared barley bread and white whey for them, and she prepared barley bread and burnt eggs for Hugh of the Wee Head himself. Hugh of the Wee Head sat for a while at the meal without eating it. At last, he threw his shoe at the place where the butter was kept, but she paid no attention.

He said, "Neither shoe nor talk can change a bad wife," standing up at the same time and putting on his shoe.

She said, "Sit down and eat before you leave."

"I will not eat. It will not be said that barley bread, burnt eggs and white whey spilled out of my guts today," and he went away without eating anything. And the men who were with him did not eat anything either.

They went to the battle, and they met their enemies at a place called Ceann a' Chnocain in Glen Forsa. MacLean of Duart was leading his own men, and he was eager to find Hugh of the Wee Head in order to kill him.

The battle was fought, and Hugh of the Wee Head lost. His men were routed. Hugh of the Wee Head himself was on horseback, and the foot of the horse was cut off, and he was captured as a prisoner, but MacLean of Duart cut his head off.[52]

The Washing Woman and the Chieftain of Clanranald

Alexander Carmichael collected this short tale no later than 1875, probably in Benbecula. Although the previous tale about Hugh of the Wee Head mentions the building of a fortified residence on an island—what is now usually called a "crannog"—this tale offers even more interesting details about how they were constructed in order to protect the security of the inhabitants. The location of crannogs in water seems to have invited the presence of the washer at the ford, who in this tale is called by the nickname *Luideag an Uillt* ("the Ragged Lady of the Stream"). As the story makes clear, omens were taken seriously by all.

A long time ago, the chieftain of Clanranald lived in a lake fortress called Dùn Buidhe in Dùn Gainmheacha in Benbecula. There was a stone causeway between the shore and the fortress, and people would travel back and forth on it. In the middle of this causeway, a flagstone had been arranged in such a way that it would make a loud booming sound with just a foot stepping on it, and so the people in the fortress would be warned about the coming of a friend or foe. The causeway of every loch fortress had a stone like this. They called this stone the "warning stone" or the "detecting stone."

One of the retinue of the chieftain of Clanranald was returning home once late at night, and as he was going over the detecting stone, who did he startle but the washing woman as she was busily washing a shirt at the side of the stones.

"For whom are you washing that shirt?" asked the footman.

"For the chieftain of Clanranald," said the Ragged Lady of the Stream. "His death omen has been seen, and he will not cross this causeway again alive."

The footman reached the bedside of the chieftain of Clanranald as quickly as his legs would take him, to relate the prophecy of the Ragged Lady, and when he did, it caused a great commotion. When the news made the rounds, it was understood that it would be better to abandon and relocate without a moment's hesitation. The canoe was made ready, and the chieftain of Clanranald left the fortress, himself, his family and his men, immediately.

Then the chieftain of Clanranald built Borve Castle on a small craig in the middle of a small loch in the west of Benbecula, but that loch is now filled with sand-drift. That was more than six hundred years ago.[53]

The Midwife and the Queen of the Fairies

This is one of many tales collected in Gaelic from anonymous storytellers on the Isle of Arran in the late nineteenth century. The tale reflects the some of the ambiguities concerning the Otherworld in Gaelic tradition: although the fairies and their realm are often portrayed as quintessially beautiful, youngful, artful, and appealing, sometimes these charms turn out to be nothing but illusion and deception.

The term *Sealladh an Dà Shaoghail* ("the Sight of the Two Worlds") appears in a number of Gaelic narratives. This tale implies that this facility gives the seer the ability to see both the mundane, human world and the fairy world as it actually is, rather than how the fairies trick humans into seeing it.

A long time ago, an old woman lived in Ballymichael who was a midwife. One day as she was reaping with one of the neighbors, what did she come across but a big, ugly frog that was heavily pregnant.

"I beg and implore you," said the old women, as she put the frog aside with the point of the sickle, "not to part with your burden until my two hands are around you."

Nothing more happened at the time, but a night or two thereafter who should come to her door but a young man on horseback in great haste, calling to her to get up quickly to aid and assist a woman in childbed.

She hurried up and mounted the horse behind the youth, but instead of keeping to the main part of the road, he went by the back road of Ard Bheinn.

"Where in the world," said the old woman, "do you intend to go, or how far do you have to go?"

"It is the hastiness of your tongue that set your feet into motion tonight. You put the Queen of the Little Fairies under a spell when she was in the shape of a frog, and she will get neither help nor relief until your two hands are around her, but by the soul in your body, do not accept either food or drink or payment, or else you will become as I am, under the dripping of the torches, powerless to return to house or family."

They reached the cave of Ard Bheinn, and they went into a room so beautiful that there was nothing like it to be seen on earth. The Queen of the Fairies was in bed, and many of the little fairies were waiting on and serving her.

The old women did everything that was needed, and it was not long until a big, strong son was born.

When the infant boy was cleaned and clothed, they gave an ointment to the midwife to anoint his eyes so that he would get the Sight of the Two Worlds. But it happened that the old woman scratched her eyebrow while the ointment was on her fingers, and as soon as she did that, she got the Sight of the Two Worlds in one of her eyes. And now, the room which looked so beautiful with the one eye, she saw as a dark hole full of spider-webs with the other eye.

Since everything was finished, food and drink were set before her, but she refused it entirely. They were compelled, then, to pay her for her labor, and they offered her a handful of gold. But the gold that was so yellow and beautiful to the one eye looked like manure to the other, and she would not take it at all.

When the fairies saw there was no use in dealing with her, they set her on the horse, and it was then that she recognized the youth: he was the son of a neighbor who was stolen by the fairies, and his family thought that he had died.

The old woman reached her own bothy when the cock was crowing, and no sooner had the cock crowed than the youth and horse disappeared, and she never saw them again.[54]

The MacGlashens of Lismore

This tale comes from the collection made by the Rev. James MacDougall by 1893 from anonymous sources. This tale accounts for the way in which the Sight of the Two Worlds became established within a particular family. It implies that aspects of the Otherworld co-exist and intersect with the mundane human world but are usually hidden or disguised for all but those with this facility. The tale also demonstrates ways in which seers put their abilities to use in people's lives. Like anecdotes about the Second Sight, this tale mentions that the facility can be temporarily shared with another person through physical touch and looking over the shoulder of the seer.[55]

According to oral tradition the MacGlashens of Creaganich in Lismore had the Sight of the Two Worlds. One of them acquired this ability in the following way.

When his parents were taking him to the Parish Church for baptism, they sat down to rest for a few minutes on a hillock at Allt Aogain, a place reputed to be particularly haunted by the fairies.

While they were resting, they laid the child down beside them, wrapped in a tartan plaid, and fast asleep. And when they went away again, the woman who had charge of him forgot to take him with her.

As soon as he was missed they returned and found him fast asleep where he had been left. There was no change to be seen in his appearance. Nevertheless the fairies had been with him and left him with the Sight of the Two Worlds.

This ability which he was given then passed down from him to his descendants for many generations. One of them, who was alive at the beginning of this century, is still remembered as a remarkable seer.

Here is one of many stories that were once told about him.

His brother-in-law lost his first wife in childbirth, and he was inconsolable for some time afterward. One evening, as he was returning home in MacGlashen's company, and lamenting his loss, MacGlashen said, "You don't need to lament like that for your wife. If you wish, I can bring her back to you quickly."

But the man of sorrow begged him not to.

"Well," said MacGlashen, "there she is, hopping from knoll to knoll in front of us in the form of a grey bird. And if you do not allow me to bring her back to you before the end of the year comes, you will never see her again. For she is with the fairies, and they are going to relocate to a new residence soon, and once they leave, I can never bring her back."

The widower stopped his lamentation for his wife, and he married another woman before the end of the year had come.

On the night of the wedding, MacGlashen, who was present there, said to his friend, "Look over my shoulder and you will see the first wife standing between the second wife and her husband."

But his companion declined the offer.[56]

The Farr Seer

W.A. Craigie transcibed this tale from an unnamed Gaelic speaker in Farr, Sutherland, in the late nineteenth century. The informant uses the term *fiosaidheachd* to refer to the power to receive portents of things to come in the future, which related most commonly to death.

There is a man in the parish of Durness who is still alive who has the power of foresight. He has seen and heard many unusual things: lights, coffins, funerals, knocking noises, and the cries of drowning people.

One night he and a neighbor were coming home very late at night. They took a shortcut and came to the side of a small bay. While they passed it, the man made a great gasp, as though a heavy burden was thrust on his back.

His companion asked him what bothered him.

He answered, "O man, did you not see that corpse being lifted on my back?"

The other man ran away, yelling, "I will never go out with you again after night has fallen!"

A short while after this, a sailing vessel was lost on the shore and all of the hands were drowned. One of the bodies came to land in this same bay, and in order to get it to a place where a coffin could be made for it, the corpse was lifted onto this man's back at the very same spot where he felt it coming on top of him before.

When the corpse was lifted onto his back, the man made the same kind of gasp as he made before. His neighbor, who was there, remembered what had happened previously when they were coming home late.[57]

The Dream of the Dead in Strath Tummel

This tale was sent by an anonymous correspondent to *The Highlander* newspaper in 1878. This account contains fascinating commentary about beliefs in omens, what might be interpreted as an omen, and the functions of these beliefs in Gaelic society.

The world has become so clever now that a person who speaks about wraiths, *uruisgs* or dreams will hardly be listened to. When my grandfather walked the earth, he saw and heard amazing things. Every time he went out at night, he would see a light going to the graveyard, and if he went close to the graveyard, he would heard the hollow sound of soil falling on the coffin that would indicate the spot in which the first grave would be opened.

Lying in bed, he would hear screaming and bellowing going by on the main road and he would know that one of his neighbors was to be carried (to the grave) in a short while to come.

There was no stranger who would come to the door about whom he didn't know a short while before, given the cockrel. There was no news that came his way that he didn't say explained the meaning of a dream he had. Nothing ever happened to him about which he didn't have a dream beforehand except for the accident whose meaning he didn't interpret in his dreams before it came to pass. The wraiths and dreams have departed and they are only mentioned in old stories.

There was a young lad in Strath Tummel and when he tried going through the river, he was swept away and he was drowned. All of the people in the neighborhood gathered and they went to search for his body all around the river. For a week, his kin and friends were searching for him intensely in every way but he was not found.

The search for him was now abandoned and his grieving mother said that if she had the body of her son that she would be fully resigned to the loss that came upon her.

A few nights after this, the woman was alseep and she thought that her son came to her bedside. The shadow of death was on his face and he was shaking from the cold.

"O my beloved mother," he said. "I am so cold, stretched out over there and there is no friend who will lift my head."

"My child, where is your body, can you still be found?" responded his mother.

"Search for me and you will find me. I can be found and no man or boy can find me. We will be of the same lineage."

The woman awoke, and she didn't think that it was an idle dream. She urged the people to try one more time.

Some people believed that the body would have to be found by a dog, but it said in the dream that the person who would find him would be of the same lineage. Among those who went out, there was a midget and when he looked under an embankment, he saw the body. This was the person who was neither a man or a boy, and he was of the same lineage as the boy who was lost.[58]

Epilogue

Reclaiming Our Voices

Those responsible for undermining Scottish Gaelic oral tradition over the last few centuries have rationalized their cultural vandalism in many ways. The assimilationist British State saw it as an obstacle to the anglonormative imperial project. Church authorities saw it as too worldly: its popular appeal distracted Highlanders from the message of the Gospel. Besides that, they thought that it contained too many relics of paganism and "superstition." Educational authorities saw it as a sign of being primitive, parochial, and unambitious. Schools emphasized the English language and skills deemed to be practical and useful for moving workers around an industrialized world serving the needs of empire and capitalism, like interchangeable cogs in a well-regulated machine.

There has been all manner of further collateral damage. The native inhabitants of large portions of the Scottish Highlands were ruthlessly evicted from the second half of the eighteenth century onward. Communities were dispersed and traditions uprooted. Those families that did remain were put into individuated allotments and subjected to new economic imperatives, fragmenting older patterns of communal living. Written literature—especially that in English—was perceived as an unstoppable force replacing older genres and commanding greater prestige and utility. The Scottish Gaelic language—the key to unlocking the literary tradition—was driven to the brink of extinction. Mass media were broadcast from the studios of London and Hollywood who professionalized the business of storytelling, chose what stories were deemed worthy of telling, and how they would be told.[1]

> I am reminded, finally, of an old man in Barra who, in 1970, tired of returning home to an empty house as television took over from the ceilidh, one night painted THE END in large white letters on the end of his thatched cottage. It remains an appropriate symbol for the passing of one tradition and the arrival of the brave new world.[2]

These losses and tragedies will sound familiar to those attuned to the plight of marginalized communities, whether their disenfranchisement has come through the naked imposition of empire and colonialism, or through more the subtle and insidious directives of modernity and capitalism. A society that loses its own stories inevitably takes on the stories dictated by someone else. That act of ventriloquism can result in alienation from the past, from the lived environment, from a sense of self and agency. It can result in disorientation and the self-destructive denial of the worth of one's own culture and identity. When that is coupled with the loss of language and the loss of territory and community, the consequences can be devastating at a social and personal level.

> As cultures wither away, individuals remain, often shadows of their former selves, yet denied any real possibility of securing a place in a world whose values they seek to emulate and whose wealth they long to acquire. This creates a dangerous and explosive situation, which is precisely why the plight of diverse cultures is not a simple matter of nostalgia or even of human rights alone, but a serious issue of geopolitical stability and survival.[3]

Scottish Gaeldom has been rocked by these catastrophes over the last two and a half centuries, and the crises have only continued to mount as the tolls of empire, environmental destruction, and economic inequity become increasingly manifest all around us. How can we break the spell of materialism, of alienation from nature, of disconnection from community, and the corresponding drive to over-compensate through consumption and power over others?

Becoming aware of the myths that inform our conscious and unconscious lives, and restoring the ancestral wellsprings of indigeneity to the heart of culture, rather than as an optional and decorative afterthought, are necessary steps for recovery. We need stories that shift our focus away from materialism, domination, and individualism, and toward spiritual and communal values, collaboration, and stewardship, if we are to survive and thrive on this planet into the future.

An old Gaelic proverb asserts "*Is fheàrr na 'n t-òr sgeul innse air chòir*" ("A tale well told is worth more than gold").[4] The Gaelic peoples of Scotland and Ireland are renowned for their banter, word play, and verbal flair, and this is no accident but the result of centuries of investment in literary activity at the highest levels of society. Whereas some civilizations strive to attain their crowning glories in the form of palaces, paintings, sculptures, or armies, Gaeldom has always laid the greatest emphasis on poems, songs, and stories. These are monuments that have minimal impact on the environment and strengthen social bonds.

None of this should be taken to mean that there is single, pure, fixed canon of tales that can be reinstated so as to restore a clear vision of the past and future to Scottish Gaeldom. Storytelling traditions are always dynamic, always adapting to the needs of each community, reflecting contemporary conditions and concerns. The cardinal rules of the *céilidh*, in fact, call for inclusivity and invite fresh ideas: *A' cheud sgeul air fear an taighe agus sgeul gu latha air an aoigh* ("The host tells the first tale and the guest tells tales until dawn"). The hosts open their homes and hearts to those who come to them and the community can then determine which new materials are worth adapting into their own lives, after contemplation and discussion.

In his writings about community empowerment, land reform, and political activism in Scotland, Alastair McIntosh has amplified Hugh MacDiarmid's summoning of the Gaelic bardic tradition and its ability to reveal the hidden layers of archetype and psychosis:

> The bard at most *invokes* awareness or opens up consciousness to that which is already present in mythopoesis. As such, the bard mediates between consciousness and the Jungian collective unconscious.... The function of the shaman or bard, as we have seen, is to step outside of consensus trance reality, observe the psychodynamics of individual or social disease, and then step back in to protest for change.... Action for transformation, then, starts with becoming truly aware of how we feel: within ourselves, in our communities and in relation to nature. It faces up to the reality of disease—the spiritual dis-eases of disequilibria,

> stunted growth and cancerous growth. Rather than pushing away or masking existential pain with consumption or addictions, it recognises its value. The pain is the mantra. It is the signal that points us to where healing is called for. That's why we need to feel it, to go into it, to see where it's coming from and to find what it asks of us. Healing then becomes a process of re-creation, opening up the channels of creativity.[5]

Some efforts to undo some of the damage done to the Scottish Gaelic community and its language and culture are underway, however small and tenuous they may currently be. Stories play a key role in them. Màiri McFadyen and Raghnaid Sandilands have used the metaphor of "cultural darning and mending" for their work to restore the connections between community, tradition, land, and language in the Highlands.

> It was beautiful to hear the songs, warm and soaring and about love of place, brought back into the airspace. At the end of that night, a friend said to Raghnaid, "if you know the stories, you love the place, and if you love the place you look after it." This simple sentiment is at the heart of why such activism is important: it invites people into an ethical and reciprocal relationship with the land, its past, people and their stories. It asks people to take agency in their own place, to "dig where they stand," to be part of a story that is slowly accruing and unfolding.[6]

This is the power of stories: to connect us to one another, to ourselves, to the land, to the deep past, to the ground of being, and so find a life worth living.

Appendix

Original Gaelic Sources

A' Bhànrigh a Dh'Iarr Deoch á Tobar Àraid

Bha bànrigh ann roimhe seo a bha tinn agus bha triùir nighean aice.

Thuirt i ris an té bu shine, "Falbh do'n tobar fhìor-uisg' agus thoir do m' ionnsaigh deoch gu m' leigheas."

Dh'fhalbh an nighean agus ràinig i an tobar. Thàinig losgann a-nìos a dh'fharraid di am pòsadh i e nam faigheadh i deoch d'a màthair.

"Cha phòs mis' thu, a chreutair ghrànnda, air aon chor!"

"Ma-tà," ars' esan, "chan fhaigh thu an t-uisge."

Dh'fhalbh i dhachaigh agus chuir a màthair air falbh a piuthar a b' fhaisge dhi a dh'iarraigh deoch de'n uisge. Ràinig i an tobar agus thàinig an losgann a-nìos, agus dh'fharraid e dhi am pòsadh i e nam faigheadh i an t-uisge.

"Cha phòs mis' thu, a chreutair ghrànnd'," ars ise.

"Chan fhaigh thu an t-uisge ma-tà," ars esan.

Thill i dhachaigh, agus chaidh a piuthar a b' òige dh'iarraidh an uisge. An uair a ràinig i an tobar, thàinig an losgann a-nìos mar a b' àbhaist, agus dh'fharraid e dhi am pòsadh i e nam faigheadh i an t-uisge.

"Mur am bheil seòl eile agam air leigheas fhaotainn do m' mhàthair, pòsaidh mi thu," ars ise, agus fhuair i an t-uisge, agus shlànaicheadh a màthair.

Bha iad an déidh gabhail mu thàmh 's an oidhche an uair a thàinig an losgann do'n doras ag ràdh,

"A chaomhag, a chaomhag,
an cuimhneach leat
an gealladh beag
a thug thu aig an tobar dhomh?
A ghaoil! A ghaoil!"

An uair a bha e gun tàmh ag ràdh mar seo, dh'éirich an nighean agus thug i a-staigh e, agus chuir i cùl an dorais e, agus chaidh i a laighe. Ach cha robh i fada 'na laighe an uair a thòisich e a-rithis air a ràdh, a-chaoidh,

"A chaomhag, a chaomhag,
an cuimhneach leat
an gealladh beag
a thug thu aig an tobar dhomh?
A ghaoil! A ghaoil!"

Dh'éirich i an-sin agus chuir i fo noigean e. Chum sin sàmhach e tacan. Ach cha robh i fada 'na laighe nuair a thòisich e rithis air a ràdh,

"A chaomhag, a chaomhag,
an cuimhneach leat
an gealladh beag
a thug thu aig an tobar dhomh?
A ghaoil! A ghaoil!"

Dh'éirich i a-rithis agus rinn i leabaidh bheag dha taobh an teine. Ach cha robh e toilichte. Cho luath agus a bha i 'na leabaidh, thòisich e a-rithis air a ràdh,

"A chaomhag, a chaomhag,
an cuimhneach leat
an gealladh beag
a thug thu aig an tobar dhomh?
A ghaoil! A ghaoil!"

Dh'éirich i an-sin agus rinn i leabaidh dha làmh ri 'leabaidh fhéin. Ach bha e gun tàmh, ag ràdh,

"A chaomhag, a chaomhag,
an cuimhneach leat
an gealladh beag
a thug thu aig an tobar dhomh?
A ghaoil! A ghaoil!"

Cha robh i a' toirt feairt air a ghearan gus an tuirt e rithe, "Tha sean chlaidheamh meirgeach cùl do leapa leis an fheàrra dhuit an ceann a thoirt dhìom, na bhith 'gam chumail am péin nas faide."

Ghabh i an claidheamh agus gheàrr i an ceann deth. An uair a bhoin an stàilinn da, dh'fhàs e 'na òganach dreachmhor, agus thug e iomadh buidheachas do'n òg-bhean a bha 'na meadhon an draoidheachd, fo'n robh e ré ùine fhad a' fulang, a chur dheth. Fhuair e an-sin a rìoghachd, oir bu rìgh e, agus phòs e a' bhana- phrionnsa, agus bha iad fada beò gu subhach còmhla.

Craobh-Airgid agus Craobh-Òir

Bha ann roimhe seo rìgh aig an robh bean d'am b' ainm Craobh-Airgid agus nighean d'am b' ainm Craobh-Òir. Latha de na làithean, chaidh Craobh-Òir agus Craobh-Airgid do ghleann, far an robh tobar anns an robh breac.

Arsa Craobh-Airgid, "A bhricein, a bhalaich bhig bhòidhich, nach mise an aon bhànrigh is brèagha anns an t-saoghal?"

"O! gu dearbh, cha tu."

"Có eile?"

"Tha Craobh-Òir, do nighean."

Chaidh Craobh-Airgid dachaigh agus an caothach 'ga dalladh. Laigh i air an leabaidh, agus cha bhiodh i slàn gu bràth gus am faigheadh i cridhe agus grùthan Chraoibh-Òir, a h-inghean, ri'n ithe.

Aig beul na h-oidhche, thàinig an rìgh dhachaigh, agus dh'innseadh dha gun robh Craobh-Airgid, a bhean, glé thinn. Chaidh e far an robh i, agus dh'fhaighnich e dé bha cearr oirre.

"O! Chan eil ach rud a dh'fhaodas tusa a leigheas ma thogras tu."

"Gu dearbh, chan eil rud sam bith a b' urrainn domhsa dèanamh riut nach dèanainn."

"Ma gheobh mi cridhe agus grùthan Chraoibh-Òir, mo nighean, ri'n itheadh, bidh mi slàn."

Dh'fhalbh an rìgh agus chuir e a chuid ghillean d'an bheinn-sheilg a dh'iarraidh boc-goibhre, agus thug e a chridhe agus a ghrùthan d'a mhnaoi ri'n itheadh; agus dh'éirich i gu slàn fallain.

Dé thachair mu'n àm seo ach gun tàinig mac rìgh mhóir thairis a dh'iarraidh Chraoibh-Òir ri pòsadh. Dheònaich an rìgh ris a seo, agus dh'fhalbh iad thairis.

Bliadhna an déidh seo, chaidh Craobh-Airgid d'an ghleann far an robh an tobar anns an robh am breac.

"A bhricein, a bhalaich bhig bhòidhich," ars ise, "nach mise an aon bhànrigh is brèagha anns an t-saoghal?"

"O, gu dearbh, cha tu."

"Có eile?"

"Tha Craobh-Òir, do nighean."

"O, ma-tà, is fhada sin bho nach eil ise beò. Tha bliadhna ann bho'n a dh'ith mi a cridhe is a grùthan."

"O! gu dearbh, is ise nach eil sin marbh. Tha i pòsta aig prionnsa mór thairis."

Chaidh Craobh-Airgid dhachaigh, agus dh'fheumadh an rìgh an long fhada a chur air dòigh, gun robh ise a' dol a choimhead a h-eudail, Craobh-Òir, agus gur fhada bho nach fhaca i i. Chaidh an long fhada a chur air dòigh agus dh'fhalbh iad.

Is i Craobh-Airgid fhéin a bha air an stiùir, agus stiùir i an long cho math agus nach robh fada sam bith gun thairis a ruigheachd.

Bha am prionnsa a-mach anns a' bheinn-sheilg. Dh'aithnich Craobh-Òir long fhada a h-athar a' tighinn.

"O," ars ise ris na seirbhisich, "tha mo mhàthair a' tighinn agus marbhaidh i mise."

"Cha mharbh idir. Glaisidh sinn a-staigh ann an seòmar thu far nach fhaigh i 'nad chòir."

Is ann mar seo a bha agus an uair a thàinig Craobh-Airgid air tìr, agus a thòisich i air éigheachd, "Thig an coinne do mhàthar fhéin, agus i air tighinn gad choimhead."

Thuirt Craobh-Òir nach b' urrainn di, gun robh i air a glasadh anns an t-seòmar agus nach fhaigheadh i ás.

"Nach cuir thu," ars Craobh-Airgid, "do mheur bheag a-mach air toll na h-iuchrach, agus gun toireadh do mhàthair fhéin pòg dhi?"

Chuir ise a-mach a meur, agus dh'fhalbh Craobh-Airgid agus stob i bior nimhe innte, agus thuit Craobh-Airgid marbh.

An uair a thàinig am prionnsa dhachaigh agus a fhuair e Craobh-Òir marbh, chaidh e gu mór mhulad uamhasach, agus leis cho brèagha agus a bha i, cha do thìodhlaic e idir i, ach ghlais e a-staigh ann an seòmar i, far nach faigheadh gin sam bith 'na còir.

An ceann ùine, phòs e a-rithist, agus bha an taigh uile fo làimh na mnà seo ach aon seòmar, agus bha e fhéin a' gléidheil iuchair an t-seòmair sin. Latha de na làithean, dhì-chuimhnich e an iuchair a bheir leis, agus fhuair an darna bean a-staigh do'n t-seòmar. Dé chunnaic i an-sin ach an t-aon bhoireannach a bu bhrèagha a chunnaic i riamh.

Thòisich i air a tionndan agus a feuchainn, agus thugadar an aire do'n bhior nimhe 'na meur. Thug i am bior aiste agus dh'éirich Craobh-Òir beò, cho brèagha agus a bha i a-riamh.

Am beul na h-oidhche, thàinig am prionnsa dhachaigh ás a' bheinn-sheilg, a' coimhead gu math tùirseach.

"Dé an geall," ars a' bhean, "a chuireadh tu rium nach toirinn gàire ort?"

"O, gu dearbh, cha tugadh nì sam bith gàire ormsa ach Craobh-Òir a thighinn beò."

"O, ma-tà, tha i beò sìos an-sin anns an t-seòmar."

An uair a chunnaic am prionnsa Craobh-Òir beò, rinn e toileachas mór agus thòisich e air a pògadh, is a pògadh, is a pògadh.

Ars an darna bean, "Bhon is ise a' chiad té a bha agad, is fheàrr dhut leantail rithe, agus falbhaidh mise."

"O, gu dearbh, chan fhalbh, ach bidh an dithis agaibh agam."

An ceann na bliadhna, chaidh Craobh-Airgid d'an ghleann far an robh an tobar anns an robh am breac.

"A bhricein, a bhalaich bhig bhòidhich," ars ise, "nach mise an aon bhànrigh is brèagha anns an t-saoghal?"

"O, gu dearbh, cha tu."

"Có eile?"

"Tha Craobh-Òir, do nighean."

"O, ma-tà, chan eil ise beò. Tha bliadhna ann bhon a chuir mi am bior nimhe 'na meur."

"O, gu dearbh, is ise nach eil sin marbh; is i nach eil."

Chaidh Craobh-Airgid dhachaigh, agus dh'fheumadh an rìgh an long fhada a chur air dòigh, gun robh ise a' dol a choimhead a h-eudail, Craobh-Òir, agus gur fhada bho nach fhaca i i. Chaidh an long fhada a chur air dòigh agus dh'fhalbh iad.

Is i Craobh-Airgid fhéin a bha air an stiùir, agus stiùir i an long cho math agus nach robh iad fada sam bith gun ruigheachd.

Bha am prionnsa a-mach anns a' bheinn-sheilg. Dh'aithnich Craobh-Òir long a h-athar a' tighinn.

"O," ars ise, "tha mo mhàthair a' tighinn agus marbhaidh i mise."

"Cha mharbh idir," ars an darna bean. "Is ann a théid sinn sìos a coinne."

Thàinig Craobh-Airgid air tìr. "Thig sìos, a Chraoibh-Òir, a ghaoil," ars ise, "agus do mhàthair fhéin air tighinn gad ionnsaigh le deoch phrìseil."

"Tha e 'na chleachdamh anns an dùthaich seo," ars an darna bean, "gun toir an neach a bheir seachad deoch balgam e fhéin an toiseach."

Chuir Craobh-Airgid a beul ris, agus dh'fhalbh an darna bean agus thug i dòrn da sìos a craos, agus thuit i marbh. Cha robh aca ach giùlan na closaich mhairbh dhachaigh, agus a tìodhlacadh.

Bha am prionnsa agus a dhà mhnaoi beò fada an déidh seo, gu toilichte agus gu rianail. Dh'fhàg mise an-sin iad.

Buachailleachd Chruachain

Bha triùir mhac aig buachaille Chruachain, agus dh'fhàs e tinn an galar a bhàis, agus chuir e fios air a mhac a bu shine 'thighinn a bhruidhinn ris. Thàinig a mhac an-sin a bhruidhinn ris agus thuirt 'athair ris, "A mhic, 's e mun do chuir mi fios ort gu bheil a' choltas ormsa nach bi mi fada 's an t-saoghal seo, agus tha mi toileach, gun gabhadh tusa buachailleachd Chruachain."

Thuirt a mhac ris, "Cha ghabh mi no taing dhuits' air a shon."

Agus thuirt 'athair, "Abair ri d' bhràthair meadhanach tighinn an-seo a bhruidhinn riumsa."

An-sin thàinig am mac meadhanach agus thuirt e, "Athair, gu dé am feum a th' agad ormsa?"

Thuirt 'athair ris, "Tha, dh'fheuch an gabh thu buachailleachd Chruachain?"

Thuirt a mhac, "Cha gabh no buidheachas dhuibh air a shon."

Thuirt 'athair ris, "Abair ri d' bhràthair òg tighinn an-seo."

Thainig am mac òg an-sin is thuirt e ri 'athair, "Gu dé am feum a th' agaibh orm an-diugh, a dhuine?"

Agus thuirt 'athair ris, "Tha 'choltas ormsa gum bheil am bàs dlùth orm a-nis."

Agus thuirt a mhac, "Gabhaidh mise buachailleachd Chruachain."

Agus thuirt 'athair an-sin, "Nuair a shiubhlas mise 's a thìodhlaiceas sibh mi, théid thu an ceann là no dhà a chuairteachadh Chruachain; agus cuairtichidh tu Cruachan mu h-aon agus Cruachan mu dhà, agus suidhidh tu air tulachan taitneach taobh-uaine air an éireadh grian gu moch agus air an laigheadh i gu h-anmoch; agus an-sin thig far am bi thu gruagach òg casurlach donn le ball òir is le caman airgid, agus their e riut, 'Feumaidh tu dol a chluich an-diugh rium, a mhic òig. Chaill thu Cruachan.' Their thusa ris an-sin, 'Có theireadh nach imireadh?' agus cluichidh sibh an là sin, agus their esan riut, 'Tog brìgh do chluiche' agus their thusa an-sin, ''S e brìgh mo chluiche-sa 'bhean as fheàrr a th' ann 'nad fhearann-sa.' An-sin bheir e gu 'fhearann thu is leigidh e fhaicinn duit mnathan cho brèagha 's a chunnaic thu riamh ach cha ghabh thusa gin diubh sin. Chì thu té bheag loireach odhar a' cartadh a' bhàthaiche, agus their thu ris a' ghruagach, ''S i sin a' bhean a bhios agamsa'; agus bheir e dhuit i, agus pòsaidh tu i agus bheir thu leat dhachaigh i; agus innsidh ise dhuit a h-uile nì is còir dhuit a dhèanamh. Mo bheannachd leat a-nis, agus guma math a shoirbhicheas Cruachan duit."

Shiubhail 'athair an-sin agus thìodhlaic iad e; agus a' cheud là chaidh esan a chuairteachadh Chruachain, chuairtich e mu h-aon e agus chuairtich e mu dhà e agus shuidh e air tulachan taitneach taobh-uaine air an éireadh grian gu moch 's air an laigheadh i gu h-anmoch; agus thàinig an gruagach casurlach donn far an robh e le ball òir is le caman airgid agus thuirt e ris, "An imir thu dol a chluich an-diugh rium, a mhic òig? Chaill thu Cruachan."

Thuirt am buachaille òg, "Có theireadh nach imireadh?"

Chluich iad an là gu teth, togarrach.

Bhuidhinn mac òg rìgh Chruachain, agus thuirt an gruagach, "Tog brìgh do chluiche."

Agus thuirt esan ris, "'S e brìgh mo chluiche a' bhean as fheàrr a th' ann 'nad fhearann."

Thug e an-sin e gu mnathan cho brèagh 's a ghabhadh faicinn; agus chunnaic e té bheag loireach odhar a' cartadh a' bhàthaiche, agus thuirt e, "Sin an té bhios agamsa." Thug e an-sin dhachaigh i, 's phòs e i.

An làrna-mhàireach chaidh e 'chuairteachadh Chruachain a-rithis, agus chuairtich e mu h-aon e agus chuairtich e mu dhà e agus shuidh e air tulachan taitneach taobh-uaine air an éireadh grian gu moch is air an laigheadh i gu h- anmoch; agus thàinig an gruagach òg casurlach donn far an robh e le ball òir is le caman airgid agus thuirt e ris, "An imir thu dol a chluich an-diugh rium, a mhic òig? Chaill thu Cruachan."

Thuirt am buachaille òg, "Có theiradh nach imireadh?"

Chluich iad an là gu teth togarrach. Bhuidhinn mac rìgh Chruachain agus thuirt an gruagach, "Tog brìgh do chluiche."

Agus thuirt esan ris, "'S e brìgh mo chluiche an loth as fheàrr a th' ann 'nad fhearann."

An-sin thug an gruagach e dh'ionnsuidh lothan cho brèagh 's a b' urrainn da 'fhaicinn agus chunnaic e loth loireach odhar agus thuirt e, "Sin an té bhios agamsa."

Thug e leis an loth 's thill e dhachaigh.

Thuirt a bhean ris, "Ciamar a chaidh dhuit an-diugh?"

"Chaidh gu math," ars esan. "Bhuidhinn mi an là."

An làrna-mhàireach thog e air a chuairteachadh Chruachain agus chuairtich e Cruachan mu h-aon agus chuairtich e mu dhà e agus shuidh e air tulachan taitneach taobh-uaine air an éireadh grian gu moch 's air an laigheadh i gu h-anmoch agus thàinig an gruagach òg casurlach donn far an robh e, agus thuirt e ris, "An imir thu dol a chluich rium an-diugh? Chaill thu Cruachan."

Thuirt am buachaille ris, "Có theireadh nach imireadh?"

Chluich iad an là sin gu teth, togarrach; agus chaill buachaille Chruachain an là, agus thuirt e ris a' ghruagach, "Tog brìgh do chluiche."

Thuirt an gruagach ris, "'S e brìgh mo chluiche gum faigh thu dhomhsa an claidheamh geal solais a th' aig Rìgh na Sorcha."

Chaidh am buachaille dhachaigh feasgar an là sin; agus an uair a ràinig e an taigh, cha robh a bhean no an loth loireach odhar r'am faotainn aige. Thàinig am famhair mór,Rìgh na Sorcha, agus ghoid e leis a bhean is an loth. Chuir e seachad an oidhche seo 'na thaigh fhéin, chaidh e 'laighe. Nuair a thàinig a' mhadainn, thàinig e 's rinn e 'bhraiceas, agus thog e air ás déidh na mnà agus na lotha dh'fheuch am faigheadh e iad. Dheasaich e bonnach a bhiodh aige 'na chuideachd, agus tharraing e air falbh. Bha e 'falbh an-sin fada cian agus trian agus tamull gus an robh dubhadh air a bhonnaibh agus tolladh air a ghruaidhean, gach eun ceanna-bhuidhe a' gabhail tàimh am bun nam preas is am bàrr nan dos, neula dorcha na h-oidhche 'tighinn air, agus neula an là 'dol dheth; agus chunnaic e taigh fada bhuaidhe, 's ge b' fhada bhuaidhe, cha b' fhada 'ga ruighinn e. Chaidh e a-staigh, is shuidh e ann an ceann uachdair an taighe, 's cha robh duine a-staigh; agus bha teine air ùr-fhadadh is taigh air ùr-sguabadh, is leab' air ùr-chàradh. Agus có thàinig a-staigh ach seobhag Ghlinne Cuaiche.

Is thuirt i ris, "Am bheil thu an-seo, a mhic òig Chruachain?"

"Tha," ars esan.

Thuirt ise ris, "Am bheil 'fhios agad có bha an-seo an-raoir?"

"Chan eil," ars esan.

"Bha," ars ise, "am famhair mór, Rìgh na Sorcha, do bhean, agus an loth loireach odhar, agus bha e a' maoidheadh ort gu fuathasach nam faigheadh e greim ort gun tugadh e dhiot an ceann."

"Ma-tà tha mise 'gad chreidsinn gu math," ars esan.

Thug i dha biadh is deoch an-sin, is chuir i a laighe e. Dh'éirich i 's a' mhadainn, is rinn i dha 'bhraiceas, agus dheasaich i bonnach dha a bhiodh aige air an rathad, agus dh'fhalbh e. Feasgar chunnaic e taigh fada bhuaidhe, 's ge b' fhada bhuaidhe, cha b' fhada 'ga ruighinn e. Chaidh e a-staigh, 's shuidh e an ceann uachdrach an taighe; 's bha teine air ùr-fhadadh, is taigh air ùr-sguabadh, is leab' air ùr-chàradh. Thàinig a-staigh lach a' chinn uaine 's thuirt i ris, "Am bheil thu an-seo, a bhuachaille Chruachain?"

"Tha mi," ars esan.

"Am bheil 'fhios agad," ars ise, "có bha an-seo an-raoir?"

"Chan eil," ars esan.

"Bha an-seo," ars ise, "am famhair mór, Rìgh na Sorcha, agus do bhean, agus an loth loireach odhar, agus e a' maoidheadh ort nam biodh tu aige gun cuireadh e an ceann diot."

"'S mi 'tha 'gad chreidsinn," ars esan.

Rinn i biadh is deoch dha, 's chuir i a laighe e. 'S a' mhadainn an làrna-mhàireach, dh'éirich i, 's rinn i 'bhraiceas, agus dheasaich i bonnach a chuir i leis airson an astair. Dh'fhalbh e an-sin, is tharraing e. Bha e a' coiseachd air aghaidh fad an là, agus 's an fheasgar chunnaic e taigh beag fada bhuaidhe, 's ge b' fhada bhuaidhe, cha b' fhada 'ga ruighinn e. Chaidh e a-staigh, 's shuidh e an ceann uachdrach an taighe, agus bha teine air ùr-fhadadh, is taigh air ùr-sguabadh, is leab' air ùr-chàradh. An-sin thàinig a-staigh madadh-ruadh na coille crìonaich, agus thuirt e ris, "Am bheil thu an-seo, a bhuachaille Chruachain?"

"Tha mi," ars esan.

"Am bheil 'fhios agadsa," thuirt am madadh-ruadh, "có bha an-seo an-raoir?"

"Chan eil," ars esan.

"Bha an-seo," ars am madadh, "am famhair mór, Rìgh na Sorcha, agus do bhean, agus an loth loireach odhar, agus bha e a' maoidheadh ort gu fuathasach nam biodh tu an-seo gun cuireadh e an ceann dhiot."

"'S mise 'chreideas," arsa buachaille Chruachain.

Thug e biadh dha an-sin, biadh is deoch, is chuir e a laighe e. 'S a' mhadainn dh'éirich am madadh-ruadh, is dheasaich e bonnach a chuir e leis airson an astair. Dh'fhalbh e an-sin, is tharraing e. Feasgar chunnaic e taigh fada bhuaidhe, 's ge b' fhada bhuaidhe, cha b' fhada 'ga ruigheachd e. Chaidh e a-staigh, 's shuidh e an ceann uachdrach an taighe. Bha teine air ùr-fhadadh, taigh air ùr-sguabadh, is leab' air ùr-chàradh, agus thàinig a-staigh dòbhran donn an uillt, is thuirt e ris, "Am bheil thu an-seo, a bhuachaille Chruachain?"

"Tha," ars esan.

"Am bheil 'fhios agadsa," arsa dòbhran donn an uillt, "Có bha an-seo an-raoir?"

"Chan eil," ars am buachaille.

"Bha an-seo," ars an dòbhran donn, "am famhair mór, Rìgh na Sorcha, agus do bhean, agus an loth loireach odhar agus bha e a' maoidheadh nam biodh tusa aige an-seo gun tugadh e an ceann dhiot."

"'S mi a chreideas sin," arsa buachaille Chruachain.

Thug e dha biadh is deoch an-sin, is chuir e a laighe e; agus a' cheud dùsgadh a rinn e 's a' mhadainn, chunnaic e seobhag Ghlinne Cuaiche, lach a' chinn uaine, madadh-ruadh na coille crìonaich, agus dòbhran donn an uillt, agus bal dannsa aca air an ùrlar. An-sin rinn iad a' bhraiceas a chur an òrdugh, is ghabh iad am braiceas uile còmhla, agus thuirt iad ris, "Ma thig éiginn sam bith ort, cuimhnich oirnn-ne, agus cuidichidh sinn thu"

Dh'fhàg e beannachd aca an-sin, is dh'fhalbh e.

Feasgar an là sin, ràinig e an uamh 's an robh am famhair mór, Rìgh na Sorcha, 'fuireach; agus có bha a-staigh roimhe ach a bhean fhéin. Bha am famhair mór air falbh a' sealgaireachd. Thug ise dha biadh an-sin, agus chuir i am falach e an ceann-uachdair na h-uamha, agus aodaichean thairis air 'ga chumail am falach.

Thàinig am famhair mór dhachaigh, 's thuirt e, "I! O! Hoghagaich! Tha boladh an fharbhalaich a-staigh."

"Chan eil ann ach eun beag adhair a ròst mi, agus 's e sin am fàile a tha thusa 'faireachdainn."

"U! Mas e sin a th' ann," ars esan, "tha mi coma."

An-sin thuirt i ris, "B' fheàrr leam gun innseadh tu dhomh càit' am bheil do bheatha 'ga gléidheil is gun gabhainn cùram math dhi."

"Tha i ann an cloich ghlais," ars esan, "a tha thall an-sin."

Nuair a dh'fhalbh esan a-màireach, thug i a-staigh a' chlach ghlas agus dhress i gu math i, 's chuir i ann an ceann uachdrach na h-uamha i. Nuair a thàinig am famhair dhachaigh 's an fheasgar, thuirt e rithe, "Gu dé th' agad air a dhressadh an-sin?"

Thuirt ise ris, "Do bheatha fhéin, agus feumaidh sinn a bhith cùramach uimpe."

"Tha mi 'faicinn gum bheil thu ro thoigheach orm; ach chan ann an-sin a tha i fhathast," ars esan.

"Càit' am bheil i?" ars ise.

"Tha i ann an caora ghlais a th' air a' bhruthach sin thall," ars esan.

Nuair a dh'fhalbh esan an làrna-mhàireach, fhuair i greim air a' chaora ghlais, is thug i a-staigh i, 's dhress i gu math i, 's chuir i ann an ceann uachdrach na h-uamha i. Nuair a thàinig esan dhachaigh 's an fheasgar thuirt e rithe, "Gu dé a th' agad air a dhressadh an-sin?"

Thuirt ise, "Tha, ghaoil, do bheatha fhéin."

Agus thuirt esan, "Chan ann an-sin a tha i fhathast."

"Ma-tà," ars ise, "tha thu 'gam chur-sa gu dragh mór a ghabhail cùraim dhi agus cha d' innis thu an fhìrinn an dà uair seo."

Thuirt esan an-sin, "Tha mi a' smuaineachadh gum faod mi innseadh dhuit a-nis. Tha mo bheatha-sa fo chasan an eich mhóir anns an staball; agus tha àite gu h-ìosal ann an-sin 's am bheil lochan uisge, agus air muin sin, tha seachd seicheanan glasa, agus air muin nan seicheanan seachd fòidean réisg, agus fodhpa sin uile, tha seachd plancaiche daraich. Tha breac air an loch sin, agus tha lach am broinn a' bhric agus tha ugh am broinn na lacha, agus tha bior de dhroigheann dubh am broinn an uighe, agus gus an téid am bior sin a chagnadh gu mìn, chan urrainn iad mise 'mharbhadh. Aon uair is gum bean iad do na seachd seicheanan glasa, na seachd fòidean réisg, is na seachd plancaichean daraich, mothaichidh mise e ge b' e àit' am bi mi. Tha tuagh agamsa bràigh an dorais, agus mur téid na bheil an-sin a ghèarradh troimhe le aon bhuille, cha ruigear an loch, agus nuair a ruigear, mothaichidh mise e."

Dh'fhalbh esan an-sin do'n beinn shìthne is sheilg an làrna-mhàireach, agus thuirt a bhean ri buachaille Chruachain, "Nach fheàrra dhuinn a-nis oidheirp a thoirt leis an tuaigh air sin a ghèarradh."

"'S fheàrr," ars esan.

An-sin chaidh iad a-mach do'n staball, agus rug buachaille Chruachain air an tuagh a dhol a bhualadh an àite, agus thuirt an t-each breac mór, "Cum thusa an tuagh, 's buailidh mise i."

Chum buachaille Chruachain an tuagh air muin nan seachd seicheanan glasa, nan seachd fòidean, agus nan seachd plancaichean daraich. Dh'éirich an t-each breac mór air a chasan toisich, agus chuir e i trompa gus an d'ràinig i an loch. Thug am breac leum a-mach ás an loch ann an abhainn a bha dol seachad; agus cha b' urrainn iad breith air.

"A! Nam biodh agamsa dòbhran donn an uillt, cha bhiodh e fada 'breith air a' bhreac."

Thàinig dòbhran donn an uillt is thuirt e, "Dé tha dhìth ort, a mhic òig? Chaill thu Cruachan."

"Tha dhìth orm am breac a leum a-mach ás an abhainn gum faigh thu dhomh e."

A-mach air an abhainn a ghabh an dòbhran donn agus fhuair e am breac, agus thug e do bhuachaille Chruachain e. Dh'fhosgail buachaille Chruachain am breac agus leum lach á broinn a' bhric is thug i na speuran orra air a sgiathan, is cha b' urrainn da faotainn; agus thuirt e, "Nam biodh agamsa seobhag Glinne Cuaiche, cha bhiodh i fada a' breith air an lach."

Thàinig an t-seobhag is thuirt i ris, "Dé tha thu ag iarraidh, a bhuachaille Chruachain?"

"Tha mi ag iarraidh gum beir thu air an lach a tha a' falbh air a sgiathan an-sin," ars am buachaille.

Dh'fhalbh an t-seobhag an-sin, is chaidh i ás déidh na lacha, 's rug i orra. Dh'fhosgail esan broinn na lacha an-sin is leum ugh ás a-suas do na speuran.

Thuirt an-sin buachaille Chruachain, "Nam biodh agamsa lach a' chinn uaine, cha bhiodh i fada 'faotainn an uighe dhomh."

Thàinig i, 's thuirt i ris, "Dé tha dhìth ort, a bhuachaille Chruachain?"

Thuirt esan, "Falbh is faigh an t-ugh a leum suas 's na speuran cho luath 's as urrainn duit: tha am famhair mór a' tighinn an-seo."

Dh'fhalbh lach a' chinn uaine 's fhuair i an t-ugh, 's dh'fhalbh esan, agus bhris e an t-ugh, agus leum am bior droighinn a-mach, agus chaidh e ann an tom droighinn a bha làmh ris; agus chan aithneadh esan am bior seach bior eile de'n droighinn nuair a thòisich e air iarraidh. Bha am famhair a' tighinn, is a' casadh air; agus thuirt am buachaille, "A! Nam biodh agamsa madadh-ruadh na coille uaine, cha biodh e fada 'faotainn a' bhior dhomh."

Thàinig am madadh-ruadh, is thuirt e ris, "Dé tha dhìth ort, a bhuachaille Chruachain?"

Thuirt esan ris, "Falbh is faigh dhomh cho luath 's a rinn thu riamh am bior droighinn a leum ás an ugh; tha e 's an tom droighinn sin."

Dh'fhalbh am madadh-ruadh, is fhuair e am bior, agus thug e do bhuachaille Chruachain e, agus chagainn buachaille Chruachain am bior, agus bha am famhair cho teann air ri fichead slat, agus thuit e fuar, marbh ann an-sin. Chuir am buachaille 's a bhean an oidhche sin seachad 's an uaimh mar bh' aca. Agus thug iad leò na bha de dh'òr is de dh'airgead aig an fhamhair, agus an claidheamh geal solais a bh' aige. Agus thug iad leò an t-each breac mór, agus an loth loireach odhar. Agus mharcaich ise dhachaigh air an loth, agus mharcaich esan air an each do Chruachan.

An làrna-mhàireach bha iad a dol a chuairteachadh Chruachain, is thug e leis an claidheamh geal solais agus thuirt a bhean ris nuair a bha e 'falbh, "Thig an gruagach òg 'ad choinneamh, agus sìnidh tu dha an claidheamh, agus their esan an-sin riutsa, 'Càit' a-nis am bheil leithid mo chlaidheimh an roinnean ruadh an domhain?' Agus their thusa, 'Chan eil mur bhi aon mheang bheag a th' ann.' Agus their esan riut, 'Leig 'fhaicinn am meang.' A chionn gun cuir esan an ceann diot, beiridh tu air a' chlaidheamh a dhol a leigeil fhaicinn a' mheang a' th' ann, agus tàirnidh tu an claidheamh, is bheir tu an ceann deth, agus their thu, 'Sin agad am meang a th' ann.'"

Dh'fhalbh e an là seo, 's chuairtich e Cruachan mu h-aon, is Cruachan mu dhà, 's shuidh e air tulachan taitneach taobh-uaine air an éireadh grian gu moch 's air an laigheadh i gu h-anmoch. Agus chunnaic e an gruagach casurlach donn a' tighinn.

"An tàinig thu, a bhuachaille Chruachain?" thuirt an gruagach.

"Thàinig mi an t-aon uair seo fhathast," ars am buachaille.

"An d'fhuair thu an claidheamh geal solais dhomh?" ars an gruagach.

"Fhuair," ars esan, is shìn e dha e.

Thuirt an gruagach, "Càit' a-nis am bheil leithid mo chlaidheimh an ceithir roinnean ruadh an domhain?"

"Chan eil," ars am buachaille, "mur bhi aon mheang bheag a th' ann."

"Leig fhaicinn domh am meang," ars an gruagach.

"Thoir dhomhs' 'am làimh an claidheamh," ars am buachaille,"'s leigidh mi fhaicinn duit e."

Tharraing am buachaille an-sin an claidheamh, 's thilg e an ceann deth, 's thuirt e ris, "Sin agad am meang a th' ann."

Dh'fhàg e marbh an-sin e, 's thill e dhachaigh agus bha buachailleachd Chruachain aige fhad is a bha e beò.

Cànan nan Eun

Bha seann ridire Frangach ann is cha robh aige ach aona mhac, is cha robh fios aige dé mar a bheireadh e dha ionnsachadh os cionn feadhnach eile. Is e an t-ainm a bha air a' ghille, Alastair.

Smaointich e, an déidh a h-uile ionnsachadh a thoirt da, gun cuireadh e do dh'Eilean nan Eun e, a dh'ionnsachadh cainnt nan eun.

Chuireadh do'n Eilean e, is lòn latha is bliadhna leis, is gun ionnsaicheadh e cainnt nan eun. Thugadh ás an ceann bliadhna e is thuirt 'athair ris, "Gu dé a th' agam an ceann bliadhna air son thu bhith an Eilean nan Eun?"

Thuirt an gille, "Chì mi rud."

"Am bheil dad idir agam air a shon ach sin?" ars 'athair.

"Chan eil," ars esan.

"Cuiridh mi bliadhna eile ann thu," ars 'athair ris.

"Chuir e bliadhna eile ann e, is an ceann na bliadhna an uair a thàinig e air ais, thuirt 'athair ris, "Gu dé a th' agam an ceann bliadhna air son thu bhith an Eilean nan Eun?"

"Chì mi rud, is cluinnidh mi rud," ars esan.

"Am bheil tuilleadh agam air a shon?" ars 'athair.

"Chan eil dad," ars esan.

"Cuiridh mi an treas bliadhna ann thu," ars 'athair.

Chuir e an treas bliadhna ann e, is an ceann na treas bliadhna, thug e ás e.

"Gu dé a th' agam air son thu bhith an treas bliadhna ann?" ars an Ridire.

"Chì mi rud, cluinnidh mi rud, is tuigidh mi rud."

An làrna-mhàireach, leum glaisean dha'n uinneig, is e 'ceileireadh. Thuirt an Ridire an-seo ri 'mhac, "Gu dé tha e ag ràdh?"

"Cha mhór is fhiach gu dé tha e ag ràdh," ars esan.

"Gun géilleachdainn da sin, chan eil dad agad ach na bheir thu dha chionn gus an innis thu e," ars an Ridir ris, "Siud a' cheud cheist a chuir mi ort, is feumaidh tu a fuasgladh."

"Ma-tà, mas fheudar domh a fuasgladh, is e bha an glaisean ag ràdh gum bi sibhse a' fuasgladh barr-iall mo bhròige fhathast le ur fiaclan, is gum bi mo mhàthair a' cumail a' bhasain rium, is an searbhadair 'na dòrn."

"Mas e sin e, gum fàs mise cho bochd sin anns an t-saoghal," ars 'athair, "cha bhi thusa ann gus an tàmailt sin a thoirt domh."

An làrna-mhàireach, chuir an Ridir fios air a cheathar chomhdhaltan air son gum bàthadh iad e. Bu duilich le a chomhdhaltan sin a dhèanamh, ach air a iarrtas fhéin, chuir gach aon dhiubh deth ball de 'aodach, is chòmhdaich iad an gille, chum 's gun tilleadh 'aodach dhachaigh chun 'athar, is chuir iad gu Eilean nan Eun e far an robh e roimhe. Agus bha e an-sin fad trì bliadhna eile.

An uair a bha na h-eòin 'ga aithneachadh, is ann an-sin a bha iad a' tighinn timcheall air is bha e 'gan itheadh is 'gam marbhadh, chor is ma bha an còrr uaidh de chainnt nan eun, gun d'fhuair e na trì bliadhna eile e.

Chunnaic e soitheach a' dol seachad an ceann nan trì bliadhna, is 'fhalt is 'ìnean sìos air dol thairis. Bhuail e air éigheachd ris na daoine, is le cho grannda 's a bha e, ghabh iad eagal roimhe, is cha tugadh iad leò idir e.

Thuirt a h-aon diubh ged a bha e cho grànnda gum bu choltas duine a bh' ann, is thàinig e fhéin air a thòrachd.

Dh'fhaighnich e, an uair a thug e air bòrd e, "Gu dé a' choire a rinn thu?"

"Cha d'rinn dad," ars an gille. "Bha mi air soitheach eile is ghabh mi air tìr an-seo, is dh'fhàg an soitheach mi ann."

"Ma-tà, tha mi gun duine-cloinne riamh," ars an sgiobair. "Ma ghabhas tu rium mar mhac, gabhaidh mi riut mar athair."

Thàinig iad air tìr ann am Pàrais na Frainge far an robh an rìgh. Thug an sgiobair leis a dha 'thaigh is thuirt e ri a mhnaoi, "Tha mac dìolain agam: cha tug mi dhachaigh riamh e gus a seo; thug mi dhachaigh an-dràsta e."

Agus 's ann air a mhnaoi a bha an othail an uair a chunnaic i an gille. Dh'innis a' bhean do a fear gun robh naidheachd mhór anns an rìoghachd, gun robh trì fithich gheàrr dhubh a' cur dragh air lùchairt an rìgh o chionn trì bliadhna. Dh'fhalbhadh iad a h-uile là is thigeadh iad a h-uile oidhche a' sgreadail is a' sgreuchail do shimilear an t-seòmair 's an robh an rìgh a' cadal. Chuir an rìgh fios a-mach nam faigheadh e duine sam bith a chaisgeadh na fithich gum faigheadh e a nighean ri a pòsadh agus leth na rìoghachd.

"Ma-tà," ars esan, "a-réir nan cùmhnantan sin, chaisginnsa na fithich."

"Ma-tà," ars an sgiobair, "ma chaisgeas, tha mise sona gu bràth, is faodaidh mi sgur de'n mharachd."

Dh'fhalbh am maraiche a dh'ionnsaigh an rìgh is thuirt e ris, "A-réir nan cùmhnantan, tha mac agamsa a chaisgeas na fithich."

Thuirt an rìgh ris a thoirt an-siud. Chaidh esan an-seo air ais gus an taigh is thug e leis an gille far an robh an rìgh, is fhuair e na cùmhnantan sgrìobhta o làimh an rìgh.

Thuirt an gille an-seo ris an rìgh: "Bha bliadhna ghort agaibh o chionn trì bliadhna is bha i a' gortachadh air eunlaith nan speur mar a bha i air daoine. Bha fitheach boireann is fitheach fireann còmhla, is rug am fitheach boireann trì uighean. An déidh a bhith a' gur nan uighean, is gun roimhe ach seachdain, thuirt am fitheach boireann gum falbhadh e is gum fàgadh e iad o chionn gum feumadh e e fhéin a chumail beò. 'A leobhra,' ars am fitheach fireann, 'tillidh mi fhéin, feuch an toir mi a-mach na h-eòin.' Thill am fitheach fireann is thug e a-mach aon fhear de na h-eòin is bhàsaich fear eile dhiubh. An uair a thàinig a' phailte, thàinig am fitheach boireann is bhuail e air toirt a-mach an treas eòin, agus bhàsaich an treas eun air an fhitheach bhoireann, is bha e an-sin gun ugh gun eun. Bhuail e an-sin air a bhith ag agairt còir air a' cheud eun, ag ràdh gum bu leis fhéin e, is gur h-e rug an t-ugh. 'Ma-tà, nam fàgainn e mar a dh'fhàg thusa, bhàsaicheadh e mar a rinn càch,' ars am fitheach fireann, 'is chan eil cuid agad deth.' Is gus an dèan sibhse, a rìgh, ceartas, có dhiubh am fear leis an leis an t-eun, bidh iad a' tighinn chugaibh mar siud."

"Agus có dhiubh," ars an rìgh, "am fear do'n chòir an t-eun 'fhaotainn?"

"'S ann agaibh fhéin a tha an ceartas ri 'dhèanamh," ars an gille.

"Tha mi fhéin a' smaointeachadh," ars an rìgh, "gur h-ann aig an fhitheach fhireann as còir an t-eun a bhith, on is e a dh'fhan dha ghur."

"Chan eil agaibhse," ars an gille, "ach an uair a thig na fithich a-nochd a ràdh, 'Fhithich fhireann, is leat an t-eun; chan eil cuid aig an fhear bhoireann deth.'"

An oidhche sin fhéin, an uair a thàinig na fithich, rinn an rìgh ceartas daibh, is chleachd e briathran Alastair. Dh'fhalbh am fitheach fireann is an t-eun an-seo, is chuir iad cuairt deiseil mu'n lùchairt is dh'fhalbh am fear boireann is chuir e cuairt tuathail air.

Bha na cùmhnantan ri'm faighinn an-seo: cha do dh'fhan iad riamh tuilleadh. An uair a chunnaic an rìgh gun do shìn an ùine is nach tàinig iad a chur cogaidh air tuilleadh, thuirt e gum feumadh an gille na cùmhnantan fhaighinn. Bu dearbhta gum faigheadh e na cùmhnantan is phòs e fhéin is nighean an rìgh. Cha robh e an-seo fada pòsta is leth na rìoghachd aige an uair a bhàsaich an rìgh is chrùnadh 'na rìgh air an Fhraing e.

An déidh da pòsadh, is gun fhios có a bh' ann, cha do leigeadh a chòir na mnatha e, ach chuireadh gu ceann bliadhna e chun rìgh a bha ag ionnsachadh modh do chlann rìghrean. Bha dithis de chlann rìghrean ann—b' e sin Ludovic, mac Rìgh na Spàinte, agus Daibhidh, mac Rìgh na Gréige.

Bha nighean bhrèagh aig an Rìgh (Rìgh nam Modh) is bha Ludovic, mac Rìgh na Spàinte, a' dèanamh suas rithe. Nam faigheadh a h-athair a-mach gun robh iad a' leannanachd ris an nighinn, gheobhadh iad an sgiùrsadh.

Rinn Ludovic, mac Rìgh na Spàinte, companas risan (ri Alastair), an uair a thàinig e, is dh'fhàg e companas mhic Rìgh na Gréige. On a bha fios gun robh esan pòsta, cha robh amharas air a bhith leannanachd ri té sam bith. Dh'fhalbh air Alastair a bhith dèanamh suas rithe air son an fhir eile. Bha esan a' dèanamh eatorra fad na bliadhna; an ceann na bliadhna, chaidh e dhachaigh.

Dh'innis mac Rìgh na Gréige gun robh iad a' dèanamh suas ri chéile. An uair a chuala a h-athair seo, chuir e a dh'fheuchainn a chéile iad, a' creidsinn gum biodh am fear breugach fodha.

Ars ise ri mac Rìgh na Spàinte, "Is bochd nach robh Alastair ann; tha eagal orm gum bi thu fodha."

Dh'fhalbh e is ràinig e an Fhraing is chaidh e far an robh Alastair is an uair a chunnaic Alastair e, dh'fheòraich e dheth gu dé bha ceàrr, is dh'innis e da.

Cha d'rinn e dad ach chuir e dheth an t-aodach a bha air fhéin is thuirt e ris, "Siuthad, agus seas m' àite gus an till mi."

Dh'fhalbh Alastair agus ràinig e. Bhuail e buille air mac Rìgh na Gréige is leòn e e is thuirt e ris an rìgh, "Am fòghnadh siud?"

Thuirt an rìgh gum fòghnadh is cha robh ach am fear a dh'innis a' bhreug a sgiùrsadh dhachaigh do'n Ghréig.

Thill Alastair do'n Fhraing is thug e dà oidhche air an rathad. Thàinig e dhachaigh. Chaidh e a laighe dà oidhche le a mhnaoi. Thàinig an treas oidhche. Chaidh e a laighe an oidhche sin le a mhnaoi is thuirt i ris, "Cuime nach eil thu a' dèanamh a-nochd mar a rinn thu an-raoir is air a bhòn-dé?"

"Gu dé sin?" ars esan.

"Claidheamh rùisgte bhith eadar mi is thu an-raoir is air a bhòn-dé."

"Cha bhi sin ann tuilleadh," ars esan. "Cha robh an-sin ach bòidean beag a chuir mo mhàthair ormsa, fuireach o'n mhnaoi an fhad ud; is cha bhi an claidheamh ann tuilleadh."

Gu dé a bhuail daoine dona air a ràdh ach nach robh fios có a b' athair no a bu sheanair da, nach robh ann ach duine a fhuaireadh air eilean mara. Bha iad a' toirt oirrese seo a chreidsinn. Thug iad oirre mu dheireadh a bhith dèanamh puinnsinn is a bhith 'ga thoirt da, gus an d'fhalbh a' ghruag deth. Sgiùrsadh a-mach ás an rìoghachd e is phòs ise rìgh eile.

Bha e a' falbh fad ceithir bliadhna gus an d'fhuair e a-mach far an robh mac Rìgh na Spàinte. Ràinig e ceàrn mac Rìgh na Spàinte is chan fhaigheadh e fuireach ann.

"Mum falbh mi," ars esan, "abair ris a' bhean-mhuinntir tighinn far am bheil mi."

Thàinig a' bhean-mhuinntir far an robh e is dh'iarr e oirre an ainm Dé a thoirt far an robh mac Rìgh na Spàinte no far an robh a bhean.

"Rud sam bith," ars ise, "a dh'iarras tu orm an ainm Dhé, nì mise e."

Chaidh a' bhean-mhuinntir far an robh a bana-mhaighstir is dh'iarr a bana-mhaighstir oirre a thoirt far an robh i. Bha esan air fàs cho grànnda is cho duaichnidh is meud bhrann air, leis a' ghnàthachadh a fhuair e. Chaidh e a-staigh far an robh i is bha ise agus gloine 'na làimh. Lìon i gloine dha is dh'òl e e is an uair a dh'òl, leig e tuiteam do'n fhàinne 'na ghrunnd. An uair a mhothaich ise e a' cur an fhàinne 'na ghrunnd, thog i am fàinne is bha a h-ainm ann.

"Có thug seo dhutsa?" ars ise.

"Thug sibh péin," ars esan.

"Is e sin ri ràdh," ars ise, "gur tu Alastair."

"O, is mi!" ars esan.

Chuala iad anns gach ceàrn mar a rinn na Frangaich air. Dh'òrdaich iad a ghlanadh is chuir iad deise a dh'aodach an rìgh air is chuir iad ann an seòmar e. An uair a thàinig an rìgh dhachaigh, thuirt a' bhànrigh ris, "Có an duine bu duileacha leis a bhiodh anns an rìoghachd 'na ghille maol carrach le meud bhrann?"

"An leobhra," ars esan, "tha Alastair."

"Ma-tà," ars ise, "is e a th' ann gu truagh."

Chaidh iad far an robh e 'nan dithis is bhuail iad air caoineadh 'nan triùir. Air cho grànnda is gun robh e, cha dèanadh dad an gnothach ach dol còmhla riutha ghabhail tràth-nòin. Chuir iad a-rithist a chadal e.

Chaidh Rìgh na Spàinte a chadal cuideachd.

Gu dé chuala Rìgh na Spàint 'na chadal ach guth a' cantail ris, "Nam biodh fuil do thriùir chloinne air a toirt á an trì bràghadan is a ghlanadh leatha, bhiodh e fo mhìn dreachd mar a bha e roimhe."

Dh'éirich an rìgh tràth is gheàrr e na trì sgòrnain aig a chloinn, is nigh e Alastair leis an fhuil, is bha e fo mhìn-dreachd mar a bha e riamh. Chaidh an rìgh an-sin far an robh a bhean is thuirt e rithe, "Gu dé luthaigeadh tu air son Alastair a bhith cho mìn gheal is a bha e an latha a bhuail e mac Rìgh na Gréige air mo shonsa?"

"Chan fhaca mi nì," ars a' Bhànrigh, "nach luthaiginn da ach thu fhéin."

"An luthaigeadh tu do thriùir chloinne a chur gu bàs?" ars an rìgh.

"Luthaigeadh," ars ise.

Dh'fhalbh iad far an robh Alastair is chaidh an triùir a chaoineadh nam pàistean far an robh iad is bha trì muinealan air na pàistean is iad a' mireag anns an leabaidh. Dh'aithnich iad an-sin gur mìorailt o Dhia a bh' ann is thug iad taing do Dhia is bha iad gu subhach sòlasach còmhla, an triùir, an uair a chunnaic iad gun robh na pàistean beò.

Bha Rìgh na Spàint o'n taigh an làrna-mhàireach is an earar is an eararais, is cha robh fios gu dé bha e a' dèanamh is bha e o'n taigh na trì làithean an déidh a chéile. An ceann an treas latha thàinig e is thuirt e ri Alastair, "Thalla; bith 'gad sgioblachadh fhéin; tha mise an déidh arm a thogail a thoirt do rìoghachd a-mach dhut."

"Cha téid," ars esan, "cha dealaich mi riut gu bràth."

Cha riaraicheadh seo Rìgh na Spàint ach falbh leis an arm. Thàinig e air an Fhraing gun fhios, sgrios e gach duine, is mharbh e an rìgh mo choinneamh na bànrigh. Dh'iarr ise bàigh dhi fhéin; nach robh i latha riamh gun aithreachas on a dhealaich e rithe.

Chrùnadh Alastair 'na rìgh air an Fhraing mar a bha e roimhe. Bhiodh e an-seo a' dol do'n bheinn-sheilg a h-uile latha is bhuail e air feòraich an robh an seann ridire ('athair) a bha ann an ceàrn de'n Fhraing beò. Fhuair e an-seo gun robh e beò ach gun deachaidh e ás a chuid cho mór is gun robh e am feum na daonnachd.

Dh'fhalbh Alastair an-seo is sgrìobh e chun an ridire gun robh Rìgh na Frainge gus a bhith aige gu cuid oidhche. Chuir an seann ridire fios-freagairt chuige gun robh esan cho bochd is nach b' urrainn da cuid oidhche a thoirt da, gun robh e uair is gum b' urrainn da cuid oidhche a thoirt da, ach nach b' urrainn da a-nis a thoirt do dhuine sìos uaidhsan.

Ghabh an rìgh a dh'ionnsaigh taigh an ridire. Bha an ridire a-staigh is b' éiginn da gabhail ris an uair a thàinig e.

"Ma bha thu 'nad ridire air an àite seo," ars an rìgh, "nach tu a ruith a-mach!"

"O, is mi!" ars an ridire.

"An robh duine de shliochd idir agad?" ars an rìgh, "a chumadh suas do ghnothach na b' fheàrr na sin?"

"O, cha robh," ars esan, "ach aon mhac is dh'fhalbh e is chan eil e maireann. Chan ioghnadh mise a bhith bochd, co-dhiù!"

Ge b' e air bith mar a bha, ghabh e leabaidh an oidhche sin is chaidil e. An uair a dh'éirich e 's a' mhadainn, thug an seann ridire làmh air brògan an rìgh 'fhuasgladh is bha cruaidh shnaim air a' bharr-iall, is chuir e 'fhiaclan air ga fhuasgladh. Thàinig bean an ridire a-nuas agus searbhadair aice agus basan uisge.

"O, a mhàthair!" ars an rìgh, "Cuir air an làr i is cuir an searbhadair uat. Tha cainnt a' ghlaisein air a coilionadh."

Thuit i ann an neul.

"Mas ann mar sin a tha e," ars an ridire, "bu chòir mise a mharbhadh."

"Chan eil fios," ars esan, "am bithinnsa 'nam rìgh mur am biodh a h-uile dad mar sin ach chan fheum sibh an déirc tuilleadh."

Is dhealaich mi riutha.

Seanchan Mór an Éirinn is Gobha nan Sgeul an Albainn

Bha siud ann roimhe Éireannach iomraideach a bha cho foghlaimichte is gun tugadh Seanchan Mór mar fhar-ainm air. Bhiodh uaislean is sgoilearan a' tighinn ás gach ceàrn gu bhith a' cur an comhairle ris, agus b' ainneamh a rachadh ceist a chur ris nach fhuasgladh e.

Ach bha gu sònraichte trì rudan ann air an robh e aineolach, agus cha robh fios gun robh duine beò air an t-saoghal aig an robh eòlas orra, ach a-mhàin am fear ris an cainte Gobha nan Sgeul, a bha a' fuireach ann an Albainn.

Bha aig Seanchan Mór triùir mhac a bha dleasnach cliùiteach agus bha e a' cur dorran orrasan cuideachd gum biodh duine air talamh a bheireadh bàrr an eòlais air an athair.

Latha de na làithean, 's e thuirt Dòmhnall Òg, am mac a b' òige, "'S e mo bheachd gur còir dhuinne ar deagh dhachaigh 'fhàgail agus a dhol a dh'iarraidh cosnaidh. Tha e air iomradh gum bheil Gobha nan Sgeul a' gabhail ghillean, agus chan eil fios nach faigh sinn uaidhe fastadh agus còrr."

Le cead is beannachd an athar, thog an triùir orra. An deagh ùine, ràinig iad an ceann-uidhe. Dh'fharraid Gobha nan Sgeul de dh'Iain, am mac a b' aosta, gu dé an obair a b' fheàrr leis, agus fhreagair esan gum b' e còcaireachd.

Dh'fhaighneachd e sin de Dhòmhnall, am mac meadhanach, gu dé bu toigh leis-san agus thuirt e gum b' e gàirnealaireachd.

Nuair a chaidh a' cheist cheudna 'chur air Dòmhnall Òg, fhreagair e, "Cha robh mise riamh ach a' leughadh is ag innse naidheachdan do m' athair."

"Tha coltas tapaidh oirbh, 'illean," ars Gobha nan Sgeul. "Bheir mi fastadh do'n triùir agaibh agus cuiridh mi gach aon a dhèanadh an dleasnais as toigh leis."

Aig àm freagarrach, chaidh na seirbheisich ùra a sheòladh dha'n àite-cadail is an-sin chaidh gach aon a bha a-staigh gu tàmh. Nuair a fhuair an triùir a bhith leò fhéin, thug Dòmhnall Òg earal do dh'Iain gu dé bu chòir dha dhèanamh air an ath latha.

Tràth 's a' mhadainn, bha gach aon aig a dhreuchd fhéin agus chaidh gach nì air adhart gu rianail. Ach air àird feasgair, thàinig aon de na seirbheisich 'na bhoil dha'n Ghobha, is thuirt e ris gun robh an còcaire ás a cheann.

"Thigibh an-seo," ars esan, "agus faicibh fhéin gu dé tha e ris."

Ghabh Gobha nan Sgeul a-mach agus fhuair e Iain beagan astair o'n taigh agus bior-ròstaidh aige 'na làimh. An darna uair, spàrradh e am bior a's talamh cho fada 's a ghabhadh sin dèanadh. An uair eile, tharraingeadh e air ais e, sheasadh e air a chorra-biod is chuireadh e am bior an àird cho fad is a b' urrainn dha.

Dh'fhaighneachd an Gobha gu dé bu chiall do'n dol a-mach a bha an-sin.

"Chan eil ach seo," ars Iain. "Bha m' inntinn air luasgan a chionn nach robh fios agam có dhiubh as doimhne, an dìleann fodhainn no 's àirde an t-adhar os ar cionn."

"Ma-tà, 'laochain," ars Gobha nan Sgeul, "ge b'i dé chualas mu'n dìleann fodhainn, cha d'fhuaras riamh iomradh air an adhar os ar cionn."

Nuair a chaidh an taigh mu thàmh an oidhche sin, shuidhich Dòmhnall Òg mar bu chòir a dhèanamh air an ath latha. An déidh dol gu gluasad 's a' mhadainn, chaidh cùisean air an adhart gu gasta gus an tàinig fios gu fear an taighe gun robh an gàirnealair air dol ceàrr. Ghreas an Gobha a-mach agus fhuair e Dòmhnall gun suim dha dhleasnas ri obair gun tùr. Chuireadh e air a chòta, ach cha luaithe air e na spàrradh e dheth e, is chuireadh e air a pheiteag. Ach an ceart uair, spìonadh e dheth a pheiteag agus chuireadh e air a chòta.

"Gu dé as ciall do'n obair a tha an-seo?" ars an Gobha.

"Tha sin furasta innse," ars Dòmhnall. "Tha agam còta a thug m' athair dhomh agus peiteag a fhuair mi o m' mhàthair, agus tha mi fo iomagain a chionn nach eil fhios agam có dha as còir dhomh am barrachd urraim a thoirt, do m' athair no do m' mhàthair."

"Urram dha t' athair," ars Gobha nan Sgeul, "agus ùmhlachd dha d' mhàthair."

Air an treas latha, b' e Dòmhnall Òg fhéin a bha ris a' chleasachd neònach. Bhiodh e tacan aig a leabhraichean is an-sin bheireadh e leum a-mach air an doras. Thilleadh e a-staigh, shuidheadh e is thòisicheadh e rithist ri leughadh, ach cha b' fhada gus am biodh e a-mach ás ùr.

Air do Ghobha nan Sgeul tighinn a-staigh do'n t-seòmar, dh'fharraid e gu dé bha ceàrr.

"Gabhaibh mo lethsgeul," ars Dòmhnall Òg. "Is cinnteach gun robh mi tro chéile. Bha ceist an-siud a' cur trioblaid orm agus is gann gum bi mi saor o luasgan gus am faigh mi fuasgladh oirre. Ged is iomadh leughadh is seanchas a rinn mi, cha d'fhuair mi riamh eòlas air có bu chòir a' cheud sgeul innse, fear an taighe no an t-aoigh."

"A' cheud sgeul air fear an taighe, agus o oidhche gu latha air an aoigh," ars Gobha nan Sgeul.

Nuair a chaidh an triùir ghillean a chadal an oidhche sin, thuirt Dòmhnall Òg, "A-nis, fhuair sinn na trì sgeòil a bha dhìth air ar n-athair! Ach nuair a théid Gobha nan Sgeul a laighe 's a nì e meòrachadh air mar a rinn sinne, tuigidh e gun deach an car a thoirt ás. Is fheudar dhuinne, ma-tà, bhith falbh. Tha deagh each aig a' Ghobha agus chan eil dòigh againn air teicheadh ach an t-each a thoirt leinn agus a mharcachd gus an toir e thairis. Cha bhi fada gus an tig an Gobha a-staigh an-seo agus bheir e beum de'n chlaidheamh tarsainn na leabadh. Nuair a chì e nach eil sinn innte, gabhaidh e ás ar déidh. Tha each eile am falach aige a tha cho luath ri coileach an t-sruth."

Mar a thuirt, rinn, ach cha robh an triùir fada 'marcachd gus an do thuit a' bhrùid bhochd a bha fodhpa leis an sgìos. Thug iadsan an-sin na buinn riutha ach cha b' fhada gus an tuirt Dòmhnall Òg, "Cluinnibh! Tha an Gobha a' tighinn agus cha bhi sàbhaladh againn mur an cuir sinn innleachd air a bonn. Cuireamaid nas urrainn dhuinn de dh'atharrachadh air ar coltas agus tòisicheamaid ri aimhreit mun cuairt air a' chraoibh seo. Nuair a thig esan is a dh'fhaighneachdas e gu dé tha ceàrr, freagraidh tusa, a Dhòmhnaill, gum bheil craobh an-seo a thug t' athair dhut is gum bheil sinne 'ga toirt uat. Nuair a dh'fharraideas esan gu dé chòir a thug e dhut oirre, abraidh tu gun tug na tha cam is dìreach dhi. An-sin, canaidh tusa, Iain, gum bheil do chòir-sa a cheart cho math, gun tug e dhut na tha grod is ùr dhi. Nuair a gheibh mise cothrom labhairt, abraidh mi gum bheil mo chòir-sa nas fheàrr na ur còir-se, gun tug e dhomh na tha fo thalamh is na tha os cionn talmhainn. Cuiridh seo fo imcheist e. Tionndaidh e 'aghaidh ris na siantan is bidh e fad cheithir-uairibh-fichead a' beachd-smuaineachadh. Gheibh sinne fada air falbh mun tig e uige fhéin."

'S ann mar seo a bha, ghabh an triùir air tuasaid is air sabaid mun cuairt air a' chraoibh. Ràinig am fear a bha an tòir orra agus thachair gach nì mar a thuirt Dòmhnall Òg. Nuair a thug Gobha nan Sgeul 'aghaidh ris na siantan, thug na gillean an casan ás.

An ceann nan ceithir-uairibh-fichead, thàinig an Gobha uige fhéin. Thug e 'aghaidh ri aitreamh Sheanchain Mhóir an Éirinn agus ge b' fhada uaidhe i, cha b' fhada 'ga ruigheachd. Chaidh e a-staigh 's e an riochd déircich agus nuair nach d'fhuair e roimhe ach Seanchan Mór 'na aonar, dh'fhaighneachd e càit' an robh na gillean.

"Chan eil iad aig an taigh," fhreagair Seanchan.

"Tha mise an déidh tighinn air astar fada," ars an Gobha, "agus tha mi feumach air biadh."

"Ma-tà, tha poit shlabhagain agam a' bruich, ach tha an teine gu dol ás," ars Seanchan. "Tha bàta an-siud aig a' chladach air an robh mi ag obair agus tha gu leòr de shliseagan mun cuairt air. A-nis, tha mise cuagach agus chan eil e furasta dhomh a dhol a dh'iarraidh nan sliseag. Is fheàrr dhut fhéin ultach diubh a thoirt dhachaigh, agus greasaidh iad a' phoit."

Cha luaithe bha an Gobha a-mach air an doras na thug Seanchan uige pòca na buidseachd. Nuair a ràinig am fear eile am bàta, chrom e air son na sliseagan a thogail agus chuir e 'uchd air an t-sileadh air son tacsa. Ach nuair a thog e 'cheann, bha am bàta a-muigh air a' chuan. An ath shùil a thug e, bha e an éideadh is an dreach boireannaich. Cha b' fhada gus an d' ràinig am bàta tìr air nach robh e eòlach agus bha roimhe air a' chladach sreath de fhleasgaich dhreachmoire, is iad uile a' glaodhaich á beul a chéile, "Am pòs thu mise?"

Thagh ise aon a chòrd rithe. Phòs iad is an ceann bliadhna bha urra mic aca. An ath bhliadhna, fhuaras leanabh gille eile agus an treas bliadhna, rugadh an tritheamh fear.

Bha na gillean a' fàs gu inbhe dhaoine agus latha bh' ann, chaidh an teaghlach air fad a-mach a dh'iarraidh éisg. Bha an triùir ghillean an toiseach a' bhàta, agus nuair a ràinig iad an grunnd iasgaich, dh'iarr athair air a mhac a b' aosta an t-acair a chur a-mach.

Rinn esan siud, ach thuit e fhéin an comhair a chinn an déidh an acair.

Thug an ath mhac an roid ud gus a bhràthair a theasraiginn, ach siud a-mach thuit e fhéin.

Dh'éirich a' cheart nì do'n mhac a b' òige agus an-sin do'n athair.

An uair sin, thog Gobha nan Sgeul a cheann agus bha a' chualag shliseag aige. Thug e dhachaigh gu Seanchan iad. Ghoil a' phoit agus fhuair e pairt de'n t-slabhagan.

"Am bheil thu toilichte le d' thuras?" dh'fhaighneachd Seanchan Mór.

"Toilichte no diombach, foghnaidh siud dhiotsa," fhreagair Gobha nan Sgeul.

Agus dhealaich mise riutha.

Eachdraidh Mhànuis

Bha Rìgh Lochlainn ann, is phòs e, 's rugadh dithis mhac da. 'S e Oireal a bha air an dàrna fear agus Iarlaid air an fhear eile. Dh'eug an athair is am màthair. Shuidh Pàrlamaid air son cilleadaireachd a chur air an rìoghachd gus an tigeadh a' chlann gu h-aois, is gus an gabhadh iad bòidean na rìoghachd orra fhéin.

Chuir iad fios air na gillean; 's bha Oireal 'na dhuine meata; 's e Iarlaid a bu mhotha. Thuirt Oireal ris a' Phàrlamaid nach gabhadh e gnothach fhathast ris an rìoghachd.

"Ploc cha bhi agaibh di," ars a' Phàrlamaid, "mur an gabh sibh an-diugh i."

Ars Iarlaid ri Oireal, "Gabh thusa an dara leth 's gabhaidh mise an leth eile."

"Ma-tà," ars Oireal, "nì mi sin."

Sgrìobhadh an rìoghachd air na gillean. Ann am beagan bhliadhnachan, phòs Iarlaid nighean Rìgh na Gréige, 's phòs Oireal nighean Rìgh Sgiath Sgial, Rìgh na h-Arcainn. Thug Sgiath Sgial seisear mhnathan coimhideachd le a nighinn 's thug Rìgh na Gréige leithid eile le a nighinn fhéin.

Trì ràithean o'n oidhche sin, bhuail anacair cloinne nighean Rìgh na Gréige, 's cuideachd bhuail anacair chloinne nighean Sgiath Sgial, 's rugadh mic dhaibh, 's rugadh dà mhac dheug do na mnathan coimhideachd. Thugadh "Mànus" air mac Oireil, is "Eochaidh" air mac Iarlaid. Thòisich na mic air tighinn air an aghaidh. Bha Mànus a' fàs mór, 's cha robh Eochaidh ach beag. Chuireadh do'n sgoil iad, 's bha a chomhdhaltan fhéin còmhla ris a h-uile fear aca.

Bha iad ag iomain air an fhaiche tighinn ás an sgoil, is chuir Mànus am ball air Eochaidh.

"Bidh rìoghachd m' athar fhéin agamsa," arsa Mànus.

Thuirt nighean Rìgh na Gréige, "B' e mo thoil crìoch mhoirt, agus mhillidh, agus mharbhaidh, a chur air Mànus."

"Ma-tà, b' e sin a bu mhór am beud a chur air mac mo bhràthar fhéin," ars an Rìgh.

"Mur an dèan thusa e, nì mise e," ars ise.

Dh'fhalbh i staigh 's bhuail i leideag air a mac fhéin, 's chuir i mach ás an taigh e.

"Falbh," ars ise, "'s thoir ceithir ranna ruadha an t-saoghail ort, 's na faiceam air do bhonn air an fhonn chiadna thu fhad 's a bhios an saoghal air suidheachadh. Bheir mise leam Mànus 's bidh e 'na mhac agam fhéin."

Thug i Mànus a-staigh leatha fhéin agus chuir i mac fhéin air grianan àlainn aon-chasach, far am faiceadh e a h-uile duine, 's nach fhaiceadh duine e. Bha Mànus a-staigh aice 's cha robh e a' faighinn dol a dh'amharc a mhàthar idir. Thuirt a mhàthair, an-siud, gun rachadh i far an robh a muime 's gun gabhadh i a comhairle. Ann an ceann bliadhna, chuir i fios air Mànus.

Ann am beagan bhliadhnachan, chuir bean bhràthar athar fios air Mànus.

"Dé, a Mhànuis," ars nighean Rìgh na Gréige, "a tha thu a' smaointeachadh a dhèanadh an-diugh? Ma phòsas tu gheibh thu an treas cuid de'n rìoghachd; fonn, is fearann, agus ionmhas."

"Ma-tà, chan eil aois pòsaidh agams' ann," ars esan.

"Cha ruig thu leas sin," ars ise, "tha aon fhear air an fhearann agam fhéin a fhreagras duit. Théid thu a dh'iarraidh a nighinn agus pòsaidh tu i. 'S e Iarla na Fiùghaidh a th' ann. Pòsaidh tu nighean Iarla na Fiùghaidh."

Dh'fhalbh i 's thug i leatha corra-theaghlach, is bheireadh i leatha cóig ceud fear. Ràinig i taigh Iarla na Fiùghaidh a' toirt do Mhànus a pòsadh.

Thuirt bean Iarla na Fiùghaidh rithe, "Chan eil aois pòsaidh aig mo nighinnsa fhathast, 's chan eil aois pòsaidh aig Mànus."

"Ma-tà," ars nighean Rìgh na Gréige, "taigh na tulach cha bhi agad air an fhearann agamsa mur an toir thu do nighean da."

Smaointich an duine nach robh math dha a diùltainn, 's phòsadh Mànus agus nighean Iarla na Fiùghaidh ri chéile. Chaidh iad a laighe an oidhche sin an taigh bhràthar athar.

"An tu seo, a Mhànuis, a mhic àidh agus a dhuine dhona? Am bheil fios agad dé a' bhean a thug i siud do dh'Eochaidh, a mac fhéin? Thug a' ghaoth luimneach Mhàirt. Chan ann ri mnaoi shaoghalta a phòs i e; gus an tugadh e an ceann dìotsa. Thusa agus bean agad air do leabaidh tràth oidhche! Bidh thu dol ás a h-uile latha, 's cha chum thu cath ris-san."

"An ann mar seo a tha?" ars Mànus.

Chaidh e far an robh ise.

"Bi fàgail na rìoghachd," ars bean bhràthar athar ris, "air neo cha bhi agad ach na bheir thu ga chionn."

"B' e," ars esan, "an treas cuid a gheall thu domh de'n rìoghachd."

"Ploc cha bhi agad an-seo," ars ise; "tha do chuid fo chlachan agus fo gharbhlach anns an t-seana Bheirbhe."

"Ma-tà, on a tha thu 'gam chur air falbh, thoir dhomh seisear chomhdhaltan Eochaidh, 's gum biodh a dhà dheug agam."

Fhuair e siud. Dh'fhalbh e 's thug e air an t-seana Bheirbhe. Nuair ràinig e an t-seana Bheirbhe, cha robh a chridhe aig duine dol a chòir a' chaisteil. Bha caoraich anns an t-seana Bheirbhe agus 's e "na caoraich chorrachar" a theirte riutha. Bhuail iad air dèanadh sluic 's an talamh. Bha na caoraich a' dol 's an t-sloc 's iad a' breith orra; 's bha iad 'gam marbhadh 's a' cumail feòla riutha fhéin. Bha iad bliadhna mar seo 's an t-seana Bheirbhe.

"Bhuais e! Bhuais e!" ars Mànus. "Tha bliadhna on a chunnaic mi mo mhuime. 'S fheàrr dhomh dol a faicinn."

"Chan e mo chomhairle duit dol ann," ars iadsan; "ach ma tha thu a' falbh, tha dà chomhdhalta dheug agad, 's thoir leat iad."

"Cha chuideachadh suarach dhomh fhéin iad a bhith leam," ars esan.

Ghabh e air falbh agus bha nighean Rìgh na Gréige ag amharc a-mach air uinneig 's mhothaich i do Mhànus a' tighinn. Chaidh i sìos far an robh bràthair athar.

"Tha mac do bhràthar a' tighinn an-seo," ars ise, "le criosan dùinte daite air a thaobh clì, air am faighte gaol ban òg agus gràdh mhaighdeannan." Gum b' ann ga toilse crìoch mhoirt, agus mharbhaidh, agus mhillidh a chur air. Thuirt bràthair athar gum bu mhòr am beud siud; 's nach biodh esan an làthair siud a chur air.

"Mura dèan thusa e, nì mise e," ars ise.

Chaidh i mach ás an taigh 's thug i a dhà chomhdhalta dheug uaidh 's mhionnaich i iad di fhéin. Dh'fhalbh esan air ais gus an t-seana Bheirbhe leis fhéin gu dubhach deurach brònach; 's bha an t-anmoch ann. Dé a chunnaic e ach fear earraidh deirg.

"An tu seo, a Mhànuis?" ars esan.

"'S mi," ars Mànus.

"Tha mi smaointeachadh nam biodh olc no mhath de dh'airm agad, gum faigheadh thu 'nad rìgh air Lochlainn."

"Chan eil sin agam," ars esan.

"Ma-tà," arsa Fear an Earraidh Dheirg, "nan tugadh tu gealltanas domhsa, bheirinn airm dhuit."

"Dé an gealltanas a bheir mise dhuit? Chan eil dad agam ri thoirt duit."

"Ma-tà chan iarr mi móran ort; bha mi 'nam fhear pasgaidh arm aig do sheanair 's aig do shinnseanair; nan tugadh tusa gealltanas domh gum bithinn 'nam fhear pasgaidh arm agad, bheirinn airm duit a-nochd."

"Bheir mise sin duit mas e gum bi mi gu bràth 'nam rìgh."

Dh'fhalbh iad 's ràinig iad an taigh. Thug Fear an Earraidh Dheirg iuchair a-mach is dh'fhosgail e an dorus, 's nuair a dh'fhosgail e e, bha an taigh sin làn arm; 's gun bìdeag ann ach airm.

"Siuthad a-nis 's tagh airm," ars fear an earraidh dheirg. Rug Mànus air claidheamh 's bhrist e, a h-uile fear a bha e breith air, bha e 'ga bhristeadh.

"Na dèan, a Mhànuis,—na bi a' bristeadh nan arm, 's gun fhios nach bi feum agad orra fhathast. Nuair a bha mise 'nam dhuine òg bha cogadh aig do sheanair, 's bha seana chlogad, agus seann lùireach orm. Feuch iad," ars Fear an Earraidh Dheirg.

Rug Mànus air a' chlaidheamh 's dh' fhairtlich air a bhristeadh. Chuir e an clogad 's an lùireach uime. Dé a chunnaic e an-sin ach brat a-nuas á druim an taighe.

"Dé air am math am brat ud?" ars Mànus.

"Tha," ars esan, "nuair a sgaoileas tu oirean air seilbh bìdh agus dibhe, gheibh thu e mar a chosgas tu. Tha buaidh eile air; nan coinnicheadh nàmhaid thu, a' gabhail seachad, bheireadh e pòg do chùl do dhùirn."

Thug e am brat do Mhànus, 's phaisg e am brat 'na achlais. Dé a chunnaic e ach slabhraidh iarainn a-nuas á druim an taighe.

"Dé air am math an t-slabhraidh ud?" ars Mànus.

"Chan eil creutair, air an t-saoghal, a chuirte siud mu 'amhaich nach biodh còmhrag ceud fear air," ars Fear an Earraidh Dheirg.

Thug Mànus leis an t-slabhraidh. Nuair a bha e a' falbh dé a chunnaic e ach dà leòmhann agus cuilean aca. Thàinig na leòmhainn mu choinneamh, 's iad gus itheadh, 's gus a sgath. Sgaoil e am brat, 's thàinig na leòmhainn 's phog iad cùl a dhùirn, 's ghabh iad seachad air. Dh'fhalbh an cuilean leòmhainn feadh a' bhruit 's phaisg e am brat mun cuairt air. Phaisg e am brat mun cuairt air 's thug e leis gus an t-seana Bheirbhe e.

Nuair a ràinig e an t-seana Bheirbhe, bha nighean Iarla na Fiùghaidh a-staigh. Chuir e an t-slabhraidh mu amhaich a' chuilean leòmhainn. Dh'fhalbh an cuilean leòmhainn 's ghlan e an caisteal, 's cha d'fhàg e creutair na uile-bheist beò ann. Chuir e teine anns a' chaisteal. Bha e bliadhna an-seo ann 's cha robh dìth air. Chaidh e a-mach latha 's thuirt e gun rachadh e dh'amharc a mhuime.

Thug e leis an cuilean leòmhainn 's dh'fhalbh e. Mhothaich ise dha a' tighinn. Bha claidheamh air a thaobh an latha sin. Thàinig i mach na choinneamh 's bha measan donn aice. Ghabh e an coinneamh Mhànuis, 's a bheul fosgailte, gus Mànus a sgath agus itheadh. Dh'fhalbh an cuilean leòmhainn 's ghabh e air thoiseach air Mànus, 's chuir e spòg ann an cùl a' bhràghaid aig a' mheasan aice-se, 's leig e mhionach a-mach gu talamh.

"Siuthad, a Mhànuis," ars' ise, "ach cuir do chuilean a-staigh air druim taigh nan leòmhann."

Chuir e an cuilean leòmhainn a-staigh air druim an taighe, 's chuir e an t-slabhraidh mu mhuineal, 's cha d'fhàg e leòmhann fo dhruim an taighe gun mharbhadh, 's leig e e fhéin 'na shìneadh marbh còmhla riutha.

Chaidh Mànus dhachaigh, gun chuilean gun duine, an oidhche sin. Dé an obair gus an do chuireadh a dhà chomhdhalta dheug ach a chartadh taigh nan leòmhann. Nuair a chuireadh a-mach iad, cha robh leòmhann fo dhruim an taighe nach robh sgòrnan air a gheàrradh. Bha an cuilean leòmhainn agus gun bhoinne fallais air, 's an t-slabhraidh iarainn, a chuir Mànus air, mu amhaich. Thuirt fear dhiubh gum bu neònach leis an leòmhann a bha an-siud; gun bhoinne fallais air, seach càch.

"Sin cuilean leòmhain fir mo ghaoil," arsa fear de'n chuideachd, "cuilean leòmhainn Mhànuis!"

"Ma-tà," arsa fear dhiubh, "ged a tha mionnan oirnn gun falbh ás a' bhaile; mun éireadh esan, dh'fhalbhamaid agus bheireamaid brath seachad."

"Chan eil duine a théid a-mach ás a' bhaile seo," ars càch, "an déidh do'n oidhche tighinn, nach eil goirteas sheachd bliadhna air ás a dhéidh."

Chaidh iadsan chun na h-uinneig; 's nuair a chaidh iad chun na h-uinneig dh'fhosgail an cuilean leòmhainn a shùilean, 's thàinig e beò.

Dh'fhalbh ise far an robh a fear 's thuirt i ris, an garbh-shiubhlach a chur air dòigh agus cóig ceud fear ann.

Thuirt esan gum biodh goirteas seachd bliadhna air neach a rachadh a-mach an déidh thuiteam na h-oidhche.

Thuirt ise ged a bhiodh goirteas sheachd bliadhna deug ann gum falbhadh iad a dh'iarraidh ceann Mhànuis.

'S e am Bodhar Bacach a theireadh iad ris an fhear a bha a' dìon na rìoghachd anns an àm sin, 's cha chluinneadh e smid gus am biodh naoidh naoinear ag éigheachd 'na chluais. Mharbhadh e naoidh naoinear air ais, 's naoidh naoinear air adhart, leis a' chlaidheamh. Dé a dhùisg e ach stoirm a' gharbh-shiubhlaich a' tighinn, agus shaoil e gur h-e nàmhaid a bha ann. Dh'éirich e air a' gharbh-shiubhlach, 's cha d'fhàg e mac màthar de'n chóig ceud beò; e fhéin agus an cuilean leòmhainn. Dh'fhalbh an cuilean leòmhainn, 's dà chomhdhalta dheug Mhànuis, do'n t-seana Bheirbhe.

"Coma leat," ars ise, "ged a rinn Mànus siud ormsa tha an Gruagach Dearg, mac Rìgh na Gréige ann, 's bheir e ceann Mhànuis ás an t-seana Bheirbhe."

Dh'fhalbh a mhàthair an-seo, 's chuir i soitheach thun Mhànuis gus an t-seana Bheirm, 'ga thoirt air falbh, mun tugadh an Gruagach Dearg an ceann deth. Dé a rinn a mhuime ach muir-tiothachd a chur air a' chuan air alt 's nach faigheadh Mànus falbh. Chuir a màthair mairnealaiche anns an t-soitheach. Dé a rinn an soitheach ach stad anns a' mhuir-tiothachd.

"Am bheil soitheach air an t-saoghal a bheir ás an-seo sinn?" ars Mànus ris a' mhairnealaiche.

"An leabhra, tha; long bhreac MhicBhalcain gobha," ars am mairnealach.

Bha iad air bòrd 's cha b' urrainn iad gluasad.

Am beul na h-oidhche, spàrr an cuilean leòmhainn a cheann fo achlais Mhànuis, 's ghabh e mach bhàrr na luinge, 's Mànus air a mhuin. Dh'fhalbh e 's ràinig e sgeir. Dh'fhàg e Mànus air an sgeir 's gheàrr e fhéin leum leis an taobh eile di. Thuit Mànus 'na chadal; agus bu mhath leis am bàs fhaighinn le càch, seach fhàgail leis fhéin air sgeir. Thàinig guth ga ionnsaigh 's thuirt e ris, "Éirich." Dh'éirich e 's chunnaic e soitheach.

Có a bha an-seo ach long MhicBhalcain gobha, agus an cuilean leòmhainn 'na riochd air an stiùir, 's mac MhicBhalcain gobha, 's a dhà sheòladair dheug, marbh air a h-ùrlar. Ràinig e an soitheach, 's chuir e dhà chomhdhalta dheug, 's nighean Iarla na Fiùghaidh ann an long MhicBhalcain gobha. Bhuail e air seòladh air feadh na tiothachd.

Dé a chunnaic e ach fearann; 's nuair a chunnaic e am fearann chunnaic e an aona chaisteal a bu bhrèagha a chunnaic e riamh. Ghabh e air tìr 's chuir e MacBhalcain gobha 's a dhà sheòladair dheug air tìr air rubha. Ràinig e an caisteal, 's chaidh e a-staigh, 's bha boireannach brèagha a-staigh an-sin 's a dhà dheug de nigheana maola ruadha. Shuidh a dhà chomhdhalta dheug làmh ris na nigheana maola ruadha. Shuidh a dhà chomhdhalta dheug làmh ris na nigheana maola ruadha, 's thuirt iad, nach fhalbhadh iad gu bràth gus am faigheadh iad ri'm pòsadh iad.

Cha b' fhada gus an tàinig an Gruagach Bàn, mac Rìgh na Sorcha, dhachaigh 's buinnseach ruadh na màthair dha.

"Có seo ag amharc," ars esan, "air mo dhà dheug de nigheana maola ruadha an clàr an aodainn? 'S nach fhaca mi duine riamh a bhiodh ag amharc orra nach tugainn an ceann an aghaidh na bràghad deth."

"Tha dà chomhdhalta dheug agamsa 's tha iad an déidh gaol a ghabhail air do nigheana maola, ruadha, 's feumaidh tu an toirt daibh am pòsadh," ars Mànus.

"Ma-tà," ars an Gruagach Bàn, "an cumhnant air an dèanainnsa sin, tha mi cinnteach nach dèanadh tusa rium e; sin mise a chur a-staigh air m' athair, 's mi a-muigh air o chionn seachd bliadhna."

"Nì mi sin," ars Mànus, "ach thu fhéin a dhol còmhla rium."

An làrna-mhàireach dh'fhalbh iad. Ràinig iad Rìgh na Sorcha. Thàinig Rìgh na Sorcha a-mach, 's thug e làmh dheas da mhac fhéin, 's a làmh thoisgeal do Mhànus. Dh'fhalbh an cuilean leòmhainn 's rug e air, 's leag e e.

"Caisg dìom a' bhiast mun toir e mo bheatha dìom," ars Rìgh na Sorcha.

"Nì mi sin," arsa Mànus, "ach sgrìobh le boinne de t' fhuil gur h-e do mhac t' oighre dligheach."

"Ma-tà 's fhada on a dhèanainnsa sin nan tigeadh e fhéin ga iarraidh."

Dh'fhalbh e an-seo agus sgrìobh e 's dh'fhalbh iadsan an-seo gu tighinn dhachaigh. Nuair a bha iad a' tighinn an-seo bha nighean Iarla na Fiùghaidh ann an allt.

"O," ars an Gruagach Bàn, "tha mise marbh."

"Dé a th' ort?" ars Mànus.

"Tha clach," ars esan, "anns an allt, 's tha trì bric fo'n chloich, 's tha iad ann an apran na mnatha agad. Fad 's a bhiodh na bric beò, bhithinn-sa beò. Tha fear aca 's an teine an-dràst' aig do mhnaoi-sa."

"Am bheil dad air an t-saoghal," ars Mànus, "a dhèanadh feum dhuit?"

"Tha," ars esan, "beannach nimhe aig Rìgh an Domhain Mhóir 's nam faighinn 'fhuil, bhithinn cho math 's a bha mi riamh."

Ràinig iad an taigh 's bha an Gruagach Bàn marbh.

Dh'fhalbh Mànus an-seo, 's bha an long bhreac an déidh a goid air, 's cha robh fios air an t-saoghal có a thug uaidh i. Thuirt fear da chomhdhaltan gun tug Brodram, mac Rìgh an Domhain Mhóir, leis i.

Ghabh e air falbh gu Brodram. Dh'fhaighneachd e dheth dé a thug dha an soitheach a thoirt uaidh. Thuirt esan gur h-e goid a rinn e fhéin roimhe, 's nach robh còir aig urra. Thuirt e gun robh beannach nimhe aig athair, agus fhad 's a bhiodh am beannach nimhe beò gum biodh 'athair beò, 's nam marbht' am beannach nimhe gum biodh an rìoghachd aigesan.

Dh'fhalbh e le Brodram, 's bha am beannach nimhe a-staigh ann am pàirc. Chaidh an cuilean leòmhainn a-staigh do'n phàirc, 's chuir e a spòg ann an lag a' bhràghad aig a' bheannach nimhe. Thuit am beannach nimhe marbh 's thuit an rìgh marbh a-staigh. Bha Brodram an-seo 'na rìgh air an domhain mhór, 's fhuair Mànus an fhuil, 's thill e, 's thug e beò leatha an Gruagach Bàn.

"Chan fhaod e bhith nach téid thu fhéin leam a-nis 'gam chur a-staigh air an rìoghachd," ars e ris a' Ghruagach Bhàn.

Thuirt an Gruagach Bàn gun rachadh. Ràinig e Brodram 's thuirt Brodram gun rachadh e leis. Bha Balcan 's a dhà fhaolainn deug ag obair 's a' cheàrdaich 's dh'ath-bheòthaich e a dhà sheòladair dheug. Dh'iarr e air dol leis 's thuirt Balcan gun rachadh.

Dh'fhalbh Balcan, 's an Gruagach Bàn, is Brodram, 's Gruagach an Tùir, mac Rìgh Siginn leis. Ràinig iad Lochlann. Choinnich Fear an Earraidh Dheirg iad.

Thòisich an Gruagach Bàn agus an Gruagach Dearg:

Gu fiachach, fuachach, meanmnach.
Chuireadh iad tri dìthean diubh
Ann an cleitibh adhair agus iarmailt.
Chruinnich mialchoin Fialchoin
A ghabhail aighir air na biastan;
Bheireadh iad air an fhairge traoghadh;
Air an talamh sgàineadh;
Air na rionnagan tuiteam.

Mharbhadh an Gruagach Dearg, 's chuireadh a cheann air stob, 's chrùnadh Mànus 'na rìgh air Lochlainn, 's cha d'fhàg iad duine beò ann an Lochlainn.

A' Chailleach Bheur

Bha ann, o chian fhada an t-saoghail, cailleach mhór mhór a thàinig a-nuas á Lochlann. Bha cliabh air a druim agus slacan draoidheachd 'na làimh. Anns a' chliabh, bha ùir is creagan, gu Albainn a dhèanamh.

Air an rathad a' tighinn, thuit cuid de'n ùir is de na creagan 's an loch. 'S e sin a rinn na h-eileanan.

Bu nighean do Ghrianan a' chailleach seo. Cha robh ach aon sùil ghlogach aice an clàr an aodainn, ach bha sealladh na sùla sin cho luath ri rionnach a' chuain. Bha neul a h-aodainn dubh-ghorm agus bha fiaclan sgòrach ruadh 'na craos.

Bha bréid air a ceann,—mar a bhiodh air na mnathan o shean,- ach an àite bhith geal, 's ann a bha e breac ballach is bha a ciabhan glasa mar chritheann fo chrith-reòdha, a-sìos m'a guailnean.

Cor uair bhiodh osain oirre is cor uair mogain liatha ach chan fhacas riamh i gun sùmag de phlaide odhar m'a slinneinean.

Bha treudan fhiadh aig a' chaillich agus iomadh ealtainn de ghabhair is de chaoraich cho geal ris an t-sneachd. Shiubhladh i leò thairis air mullach nan càrn is a-nuas na sléibhte. B' i a' Chonathuil an clacharan thairis air am biodh na gabhair air an iomain a-nuas bho Chruachan ach b' ann a-nuas Gleann Nibheis a bu bhitheanta bha i ag iomain nam fiadh.....

Bha tobar fìor-uisge air mullach Chruachain far am biodh a' Chailleach a' fuireach 's an oidhche le a treudan. B' e a dleasdanas faire thairis air an fhuaran seo agus clach a chur air beul an tobair aig àm dol fodha na gréine.

Ach aon oidhche, air dhi a bhith sgìth ag iomain nan treud, thuit i 'na cadal gun a' chlach a chur air beul an tobair. Ruith an t-uisge thairis gus an do bhris e mar bheum-sléibhe tro na creagan aig Bealach a' Bhràn Shruith 's thaom e sìos air a' chòmhnard, a' toirt léir-sgrios 'na lorg air gach duine 's ainmhidh a bha 'tighinn beò air. Tha am bealach an-sin fhathast far am bheil Atha a' ruith á Loch Odha. Agus b' ann mar sin a rinneadh Loch Odha.

Iolaire Loch Tréig

Bha roimhe seo seann iolaire mhór a' tàmh an Àird-Mheadhain Loch Tréig, far am minig a bha a seòrsa. Bha i liath leis an aois, bhon a bu chuimhne leatha fhéin. Is bha i, uime sin, an dùil gum b' i creutair bu shine bha beò ri 'linn.

Ach an earalas nach faodadh a comh-aois a bhith maireann an àiteigin, chuir i roimhpe, an ceud chothrom a gheibheadh i, sgrìob a thoirt air chuairt.

Bliadhna a bha sin, thàinig an aon Oidhche Bhealltainn a b' fhuaire 'dh'fhairich no chunnaic i riamh agus smaoinich i gum bu mhath an leithsgeul di e air a rùn falaich a chur an gnìomh. Agus 's a' mhadainn mhoich Latha Bealltainn sin fhéin, seach latha sam bith eile, mun do bhlais na h-eòin eile an t-uisge, togar oirre air cheann a turais.

Cha robh dùil bheò a thachradh oirre, ach neul na h-aoise bhith oirre, nach farraideadh i, "Am faca thu Oidhche Bhealltainn riamh cho fuar ris an oidhche an-raoir?"

Ach chan fhac' a h-aon. Coma, bha an latha ás a thoiseach, is bha i mar seo a' cumail air a h-adhart gun chluain, gun chlos, gus an do thachair seann dreathan donn còir oirre.

"Fàilte air an dreathan, Latha Buidhe Bealltainn," ars ise. "Am faca thu riamh Oidhche Bhealltainn cho fuar ris an oidhche an-raoir?"

Ach sean is gun robh tuar is dreach an dreathain, cha b' fhiosrach e gum faca. Cha robh eòlas aige air creutair bu shine na e fhéin ach chuala e gun robh seann ghobha dubh bho chian am Bun Ruaidh, is ma bha e fhathast beò, gum bu dualach, ma thàinig a leithid, gum faca esan i. Agus sheòl e an rathad dhi.

Thug i taing do'n dreathan, agus togar oirre gu ceàrdach Bhun Ruaidh.

Ràinig i ach cha robh roimhpe ach làrach fhuar: thriall gach mith 's gach math, ach an gobha dubh is bha esan fhéin bho chian dall leis an aois, agus an déidh toll a dhèanamh 's an innean a' glanadh a ghuib.

Chuir i fàilte na Bealltainn air a' ghobha, 's dh'innis i fàth a turais: "Am faca thu riamh," ars ise, "Oidhche Bhealltainn cho fuar ris an oidhche an-raoir?"

Thug an gobha glaomadh bochd air fhéin, is thuirt e nach faca riamh, agus nach cuala e iomradh air a leithid ach gun robh seann ùdlaiche, bho chionn chan eil fhios cuin, a' tathaich Choille Innse 's gun robh a chalg air liathadh leis an aois bhon a bu chuimhne leis-san a bhith 'na bhùta beag a' sgiathais air feadh nam preas.

"Bu tric leis ùine 's aimsir 'na dhéidh sin," ars esan, "tighinn a-nall air chéilidh orm a chur seachad na h-oidhche faide geamhraidh, agus a thoirt sgeòil domh air cor na dùthcha. Ach sguir sin. An turas mu dheireadh a bha e bhos, bha an aois cho trom iar laighe air is gum bheil eagal orm nach eil e an urrainn gluasad mór a dhèanamh. Thug sinn cho fad an coimhearsnachd a chéile 's gun dèan mi, mar a thuigeas tusa, sogan ri a sheann langan, tùchanach mar a tha, an uair a chluinneas mi e 's a' chamhanaich. Is e creutair as sine tha làthair an-diugh fad m' aithne 's m' eòlais agus ma nì thu guth aige 's an dol seachad, innis dha fàth do thurais agus gum faca thu mise. Is mur tàinig caoc-hladh air, nì e do làn di-beatha."

Dh'aithris e an-sin di gnothaichean àraid a thachair ri linn nan triath bu chuimhne leis am faicinn, mu euchdan a shinnsrean agus mu bhuil a mhuirichinn. Nuair a bha iad a' gabhail "madainn mhath" le chéile, dh'earb is dh'earail e oirre tadhal aige an ath uair a bhiodh i togail oirre do Choille Innse.

Is fhuair i an t-ùdlaiche 'na chrùban am fasgadh seann stuic fheàrna agus spidean-nan deighe le cuinneannan a shròine.

Chuir i fàilte na Bealltainn air, agus dh'innis i fàth a turais: "Am faca thu riamh," ars ise, "Oidhche Bhealltainn cho fuar ris an oidhche an-raoir?"

Bha an t-ùdlaiche cho sean is gun do leig e an cabar air an t-slinnean ach thuirt e air a mhìn-athais nach bu chuimhne leis gum faca riamh.

Fhuair i gu faoilteach furanach e, agus dh'fhiosraich e gu coibhneil mu'n ghobha dhall. Thug iad an-sin treallan air seanchas agus air sloinntireachd, is bha an iolaire dol a thagairt urram na h-aoise. Ach an uair a bha iad a' dealachadh, thuirt an t-ùdlaiche gun robh breac cam ann an lochan Choire na Ceanainn, air an do chuir e eòlas an tràth a bha e 'na laoighean òg an cois a mhàthar a' tighinn a-nall an Làirig Leacach á Beinn a' Bhric.

"Bha smalaich na h-aoise air an uair sin fhéin," ars esan, "agus ma tha ùine agad, is fiach dhuit dol 'dha choimhead: is cnacaiche gasta e."

Is e bh' ann gun do thog i a-rithist oirre 's gun do ràinig i an lochan.

Chuir i deoch eòlais air a' bhreac cham agus dh'innis i fàth a turais: "Am faca thu riamh Oidhche Bhealltainn cho fuar ris an oidhche an-raoir?"

Thuirt am breac gum faca: aon oidhche eile 's gun robh i cho fuar, is ged a bha e an teas fhala 's an tréine a neirt, gum b' fheudar dha tòiseachadh air geàrradh shùrdag air feadh an uisge a chumail teas air fhéin.

"Agus," ars esan, "sùrdag dha'n tugas, leumar ás an uisge, 's buailear mo leth-che-ann ris an lic dhuibh ud thall. Ach bha nimh an reòthaidh cho dian, is mun d'fhuair mi mi fhéin a thoirt air m' ais, gun do lean mo shùil ris an lic is dh'fhàg sin an-diugh mise cam!"

An tràth chuala an iolair seo, thug i modh is urram na h-aoise do'n bhreac. Agus thill i air a h-ais a dh'Aird-Mheadhain a dh'aithris a sgeòil do'n àlach òg.

Chunnaic iad ioma latha geal grianach 'na dhéidh sin ach cho fad is a b' urrainn di sgiath a ghluasad, cha deachaidh Latha Bealltainn fuar no teth seachad oirre nach deachaidh i tacan air chéilidh air na h-aostaidh còire: an gobha, an t-ùdlaiche, agus am breac.

Teicheadh ro'n Bhràth

Chaidh Duan Torra Tealaich latha do'n tràigh 's chuala e sgrìob-sgrab nam partan, is dh'fhalbh e theicheadh ro'n Bhràth.

Cha b' fhada bha e a' falbh gus an do thachair Dabhach nighean an Dabhaich ris. Dh'fhaighneachd i dheth, "Cà'il thu a' dol?"

"Tha mi a' teicheadh ro'n Bhràth!"

"Có chuala e?"

"Mise a chuala is a chunnaic e, agus 's ann air mo bhonnaibh fhéin a thàinig e!"

"Tha mise a' falbh!"

"Biodh, nara biodh, tusa a' falbh, tha mise a' falbh!" is dh'fhalbh iad.

Cha b' fhada a-rithist gus an do thachair Cromach nighean a' Chromaich riutha.

"Cà'il sibh a' dol?" ars ise.

"Tha sinn a' teicheadh ro'n Bhràth!"

"Có chuala e?"

"Mise a chuala is a chunnaic e, agus 's ann air mo bhonnaibh fhéin a thàinig e!" ars Duan.

"Tha mise a' falbh."

"Biodh, nara biodh, tusa a' falbh, tha sinne a' falbh!" is dh'fhalbh iad.

Thachair an-seo riutha Dà Mhac Gille Mhàsaich.

"Cà'il sibh a' dol?" ars iadsan.

"Tha sinn a' teicheadh ro'n Bhràth!" fhreagair càch.

"Có chuala e?"

"Mise a chuala is a chunnaic e, agus 's ann air mo bhonnaibh fhéin a thàinig e!" ars Duan.

"Tha sinne a' falbh!"

"Biodh, nara biodh, sibhse a' falbh, tha sinne a' falbh!" is dh'fhalbh iad.

Có choinnich an-sin iad ach Fàsach Cùl an t-Sionnaich.

"Cà'il sibh a' dol?" ars esan.

"Tha sinn a' teicheadh ro'n Bhràth!"

"Có chuala e?"

"Mise a chuala is a chunnaic e, agus 's ann air mo bhonnaibh fhéin a thàinig e!" ars Duan.

"Tha mise a' falbh."

"Biodh, nara biodh, tusa a' falbh, tha sinne a' falbh!" is dh'fhalbh iad.

Có an-sin a thàinig 'nan còmhdhail ach Am Fear Liath 's a mhac.

"Cà'il sibh a' dol?" ars iadsan.

"Tha sinn a' teicheadh ro'n Bhràth!"

"Có chuala e?"

"Mise a chuala is a chunnaic e, agus 's ann air mo bhonnaibh fhéin a thàinig e!" ars Duan.

"Tha sinne a' falbh!"

"Biodh, nara biodh, sibhse a' falbh, tha sinne a' falbh!" is dh'fhalbh iad.

Choinnich an-sin iad an Cliamhainn is a Chruit.

"Cà'il sibh a' dol?" ars iadsan.

"Tha sinn a' teicheadh ro'n Bhràth!"

"Có chuala e?"

"Mise a chuala is a chunnaic e, agus 's ann air mo bhonnaibh fhéin a thàinig e!" ars Duan.

"Tha sinne a' falbh!"

"Biodh, nara biodh, sibhse a' falbh, tha sinne a' falbh!" is dh'fhalbh iad.

B' e an ath aon a choinnich iad Sagart Gille Glic.

"Cà'il sibh a' dol?" ars esan.

"Tha sinn a' teicheadh ro'n Bhràth!"

"Có chuala e?"

"Mise a chuala is a chunnaic e, agus 's ann air mo bhonnaibh fhéin a thàinig e!" ars Duan.

"Tha mise a' falbh!"

"Biodh, nara biodh, tusa a' falbh, tha sinne a' falbh!" is dh'fhalbh iad.

Ràinig iad an-seo Dithis Mhnaoi an Dath.

"Cà'il sibh a' dol?" dh'fharraid iad.

"Tha sinn a' teicheadh ro'n Bhràth!"

"Có chuala e?"

"Mise a chuala is a chunnaic e, agus 's ann air mo bhonnaibh fhéin a thàinig e!" ars Duan.

"Tha sinne a' falbh!"

"Biodh, nara biodh, sibhse a' falbh, tha sinne a' falbh!" is dh'fhalbh iad.

Thachair an uair sin riutha Bloigh Mise is Cùl-Càise.

"Cà'il sibh a' dol?" ars iadsan.

"Tha sinn a' teicheadh ro'n Bhràth!"

"Có chuala e?"

"Mise a chuala is a chunnaic e, agus 's ann air mo bhonnaibh fhéin a thàinig e!" ars Duan.

"Tha sinne a' falbh!"

"Biodh, nara biodh, sibhse a' falbh, tha sinne a' falbh!" is dh'fhalbh iad.

Cha b' fhada gus an do choinnich iad a' Chearc Bhreac is a linn.

"Cà'il sibh a' dol?" ars ise.

"Tha sinn a' teicheadh ro'n Bhràth!"

"Có chuala e?"

"Mise a chuala is a chunnaic e, agus 's ann air mo bhonnaibh fhéin a thàinig e!" ars Duan.

"Tha mise a' falbh!"

"Biodh, nara biodh, tusa a' falbh, tha sinne a' falbh!" is dh'fhalbh iad.

Mu dheireadh thall, có thachair 'nan rathad ach An Gearran Bacach Bàn.

"Cà'il sibh a' dol?" ars esan.

"Tha sinn a' teicheadh ro'n Bhràth!"

"Có chuala e?"

"Mise a chuala is a chunnaic e, agus 's ann air mo bhonnaibh fhéin a thàinig e!" ars Duan.

"Tha mise a' falbh!"

"Biodh, nara biodh, tusa a' falbh, tha sinne a' falbh!" is dh'fhalbh iad.

Bha iad a' falbh 'nan ruith 's 'nan leum gus an do ràinig iad abhainn. B' fheudar stad gu'n comhairle chur ri chéile feuch ciamar a gheibheadh iad tarsainn. 'S e rinn iad suas gun dìreadh gach aon aca air muin a' ghearrain agus gun grunnaicheadh esan dha'n taobh eile.

Sin mar a rinneadh, chaidh iad a mharcachd a' Ghearrain Bhacaich Bhàin: Duan Torra Tealaich, Dabhach nighean an Dabhaich, Cromach nighean a' Chromaich, Dà Mhac Gille Mhàsaich, Fàsach Cùl an t-Sionnaich, am Fear Liath 's a mhac, an Cliamhainn is a' Chruit, Sagart Gille Glic, Dithis Mhnaoi an Dath, Bloigh Mise is Cùl-Càise, agus a' Chearc Bhreac is a linn.

Rinn an truaghan sin a dhìcheall gu faighinn tarsainn ach nuair a bha e mu mheadhan na h-aibhne, bhris a dhruim, thuit iad uile 's an uisge, is chaidh am bàthadh!

Sgrìob Chloinn Uisnigh

Bha triùir mhac Uisnigh 'nan laighe còmhla marbh gun deò, taobh ri taobh, air a' mhachair mhìn ghuirm agus Deirdre crom os an cionn a' fras-shileadh nan deur.

Chladhaicheadh uaigh is shìneadh an triùir bhràithrean taobh ri taobh innte. Arsa Deirdre an-sin, "Teann a-nall, a Naois, a ghràidh."

Is an uair a rinn na mairbh àite dhi, leum ise sìos do'n uaigh, shìn si i fhéin 's an aon uaigh ri Naois, agus b' e a rinneadh gun d' adhlaiceadh Deirdre leatha fhéin air taobh eile an locha.

Dh'fhàs an-sin crann giubhais ás gach uaigh is ri ùine, choinnich an cuid mheanglan, is chuir iad snaim os cionn meadhan an locha.

Gheàrr Conchobhar iad sìos le chéile, ach dh'fhàs iad an dara h-uair is chuir iad snaim. Gheàrr an rìgh iad a-rithist, ach cha do chinn iad an treas uair. Cha d'fhàs na croinn ghiubhais na bu mhò. Ach an oidhche sin fhéin, an déidh iad a bhith air an geàrradh sìos an dara h-uair, oidhche rionnagach chiùin, gun leud boise de neul air speur, mu mheadhan oidhche, no mu'n àm 's am biodh daoine a' gabhail mu thàmh, chunnacas boillsgeadh anabarrach an cop nan speur.

Bha strìoch shoilleir gheal a' dìreadh an dà àird an adhar a bha co-choimeas ris an dà thaobh 's an robh Deirdre is Naois 'nan laighe is iad a' coinneachadh 'nan solas blàth an àirde na h-iarmailte os cionn meadhan an locha: Sgrìob Chloinn Uisnigh! B' e sin a h-ainm a' cheud oidhche a chunnacas i agus is e sin a h-ainm a-nochd.

B' ann an-sin is an-sin féin a chunnaic Conchobhar nach robh e gu feum dha a bhith a' strì ri Naois is Deirdre a sgaradh bho chéile, is leig e dheth a dhroch obair.

Am beul-aithris nan Gàidheal, tha cuimhne fhathast air maise is màldachd Dheirdre, air neart is air gaisge Naois.

Mar an ceudna, tha Sgrìob Chloinn Uisnigh ri a faicinn gach oidhche mar chrios mun cuairt a' Chruinne-Ché, is gach gath solais a chithear a' boillsgeadh innte mar phlosgaibh gaoil a' sìor-shiubhal is ag ath-shiubhal eadar an spioradan, nach faodar an sgaradh bho chéile ri là no linn.

An Teine Mór

Cha robh na Gàidheil riamh air dheireadh air sluagh sam bith eile ann a bhith a' toirt cunntas air na h-adhbhair air son gun robh nithean iongantach ri'm faicinn air an talamh. Mar bu trice cha robh na beachdan a bh' aca mu nithean iongantach an t-saoghail dad na bu ghlice, no na b' amaidiche na na beachdan a bh' aig sluagh eile an t-saoghail. Tha a' chùis coltach gun robh iad fhéin glé riaraichte le'n cuid bheachdan, agus air an adhbhar sin, fàgaidh sinn beachdan nan seann daoine còire far an d'fhuair sinn iad, agus mar a fhuair sinn iad. Ged a tha sinne gu math glic 'nar barail fhéin, is dòcha gum bheil cuid de ar beachdan a cheart cho amaideach is a bha am beachdan-san.

O chionn còrr is dà cheud bliadhna bha an àireamh bu mhó de shluagh na Gàidhealtachd air am beathachadh agus air an còmhdachadh le toradh na dùthcha do'm buineadh iad. Cha robh na marsantan ach glé thearc anns an àm, agus air an adhbhar sin, dh'fheumadh an sluagh cur suas leis na nithean a gheibheadh iad anns an dùthaich.

Bhiodh iad aig an àm ud a' dath le dathan na dùthcha. Dhèanadh iad dath uaine agus dath buidhe cho brèagha 's a b' urrainn duine fhaicinn le bàrr an fhraoich.

Ann an àiteachan boga 's a' mhòintich, gheibheadh iad talamh ris an abradh iad "dubhach." Is cuimhne leam feadhainn de na sluic ás am biodh iad a' cladhach na dubhcha fhaicinn.

Is minic a chuala mi mu'n chothlamadh a bha seann bhean àraidh a' dèanamh uair dha'n robh an saoghal. Seo na dathan a bh' ann: "Dubh na dubhcha, ciar na caorach, is glas aotrom, is glas trom."

Tha e air aithris gun robh sluagh nan Eileanan an Iar déidheil air dathan dearga. An uair a bhiodh na marsantan-paca 's an àm a dh'fhalbh a' siubhal air feadh na Gàidhealtachd, bu ghnàth leotha bhith reic dhathan dearga, mar a tha càrnaid agus màdar.

Bha aon nì ri 'fhaotainn anns an dùthaich a dhèanadh dath dearg, agus b' e sin "rudh." Is e freumhan feòir a th' anns an rudh. Chan fhaighear e ach ann am bruthaichean tiorma gainmhich. Bhiodh mnathan a' dol a bhuain an ruidh anns an oidhche air eagal gum faigheadh am maor, no h-aon sam bith eile de'n luchd-riaghlaidh, fios air.

Tha e coltach gun robh an t-uachdaran fada an aghaidh a bhith buain an ruidh, do bhrìgh gun robh móran de'n mhachaire thioram air a chladhach an àm a bhith 'ga bhuain, agus gun robh móran de ghainmhich thioraim nam bruthaichean air a siabadh air feadh a' mhachaire an uair a thigeadh tiormachd an earraich.

Bha tuathanach ann am Beinn na Faoghla ris an abradh iad gu cumanta "Calum Sagart." B' ann de Chloinn 'ic Carmaic a bha Calum Sagart a thaobh cinnidh. Bu mhath a b' aithne dhomhsa ogha dha, Iain mac Aonghais 'ic Caluim Shagairt. Cha chuala mi an t-adhbhar air son an tugadh Calum Sagart mar fhar-ainm air. Ach ma thachair gun robh e air mhuinntireas aig sagart, bhiodh e nàdurra gun canadh iad Calum an t-Sagairt ris. An-sin thigeadh an t-ainm gu bhith mar a chuala mi e.

Tha e coltach gun robh Calum Sagart 'na dhuine cho modhail is cho iomchaidh 's a gheibhteadh anns an dùthaich gu léir. Ach a-réir mar a chuala mi, is ann aige a bha an aon bhean bu mhiosa a bh' ann an Uibhist. Is e badhbh a bh' innte. Tha e air a ràdh, ma gheibh badhbh a guidhe nach fhaigh a h-anam tròcair.

A-réir choltais gun d'fhuair bean Chaluim Shagairt a guidhe aon uair co-dhiù. Bha nighean aig Calum Sagart a bha, mar a thachair a dh'iomadh té roimpe 's an déidh, an geall air dathan annasach a bhith anns an aodach aice.

Chuir i roimpe gun rachadh i bhuain ruidh gu snàth no clòimh a dhath. Chan fhaodadh i a dhol 'ga bhuain air an latha, air eagal gun tugteadh suas do'n mhaor i, agus a chum a' chùis a chumail cho falachaidh 's a ghabhadh dèanamh, chuir i roimpe gun rachadh i 'ga bhuain air oidhche Luain-Dòmhnaich, is e sin ri ràdh, an déidh dà uair dheug oidhche Dhòmhnaich.

Bha a màthair anabarrach fada an aghaidh dhi a dhol a bhuain an ruidh. Ach cha tugadh an nighean cluas no géill a dh'aon fhacal a theireadh a màthair rithe. Ma bha a màthair 'na baidhbh, tha e coltach gun robh an nighean a cheart cho rag ris a' mhac-mhollachd. On a chuir i roimpe falbh a bhuain an ruidh, dh'fhalbhadh i ged a rachadh am muir h-ear thar a' mhuir h-iar.

An uair a chunnaic a màthair i a' dol a-mach air an doras, thuirt i, "Tha thu a-nis a' falbh agus mollachd do mhàthar air do cheann. Nam bu tig an là a chithear aghaidh do bhonn."

Tha a' chùis coltach gun d'fhuair a màthair a guidhe, oir cha d'fhuaras beò no marbh nighean Chaluim Shagairt riamh, aon chuid air muir no air tìr. Ach an uair a thugadh dùil thairis nach robh i a' tighinn dhachaigh, dh'fhalbh na càirdean agus na coimhearsnaich 'ga marbh-iarraidh, agus fhuair iad pairt de 'h-aodach air a' mhachair far an robh i a' buain an ruidh.

An ceann beagan ùine an déidh dha seo tachairt, chunnacas an solas ris an abrar "An Teine Mór." A-réir choltais gun do chreid gach neach a chuala mar a thachair gun d'fhuair bean Chaluim Shagairt a guidhe, agus gum b' e nighean Chaluim Shagairt An Teine Mór.

Rìgh nan Eun

Aon uair dh'éirich còmhstrìth eadar na h-eòin mu có dhiubh bu chòir a bhith 'na rìgh thairis orra. Thuirt an iolaire gum bu chòir an t-urram a thoirt do'n eun a b' àirde a dhìreadh air iteig gus na speuran.

Chaidh latha a shònrachadh air son feuchainn có an t-eun a gheibheadh an t-urram. Latha brèagha samhraidh, chruinnich gach eun anns an ealtainn gu aon àite. Thàinig iad o cheithir àirdean an adhair, beag is mór, is gach dath.

Air an aon chraoibh bha an smeòrach, an lòn-dubh, an gealbhonn, is am brù-dearg, agus bheireadh an ceòl sonas do neach sam bith a chluinneadh e.

Thàinig eòin a' mhonaidh is an t-sléibhe mar tha a' chearc-fhraoich is an coileach-dubh, an easag is an naosg.

Bha ann cuideachd eòin-mhara: an fhaoileag, an steàrnal, gèadh is lacha, còrr is gille-brìghde.

Thàinig an iolair is dh'amhairc i gu pròiseil air na h-eòin bheaga. Agus mu dheireadh có thigeadh ach an dreathan-donn, agus an uair a chunnaic na h-eòin eile i, rinn iad uile gàire.

Rinneadh deiseil air son na farpais is dh'éirich na h-eòin uile air sgéith 's an adhar. Ach cha b' fhada chaidh a' chuid bu mhò dhiubh, is an ceann ùine, thill iad uile gu talamh ach an iolair.

Fuirich ort, cha do thill iad uile: fhuair an dreathan-donn cothrom agus leum i air druim na h-iolaire is an-sin chrùb i eadar an dà sgéith mhór.

Nuair a shaoil an iolair gun robh i cho àrd is a b' urrainn di a dhol is i a-nis a' fàs sgìth, ghlaodh i, "Is mise rìgh nan eun."

Dh'éirich an dreathan suas gu h-àrd o dhruim na h-iolaire.

"Cha tu idir," ars ise. "Is mise rìgh nan eun. Tha mi an-seo fada os do chionn."

B' fheudar do'n iolair cromadh gu talamh agus aideachadh gun d'rinn an dreathan-donn an gnothach oirre.

Is e an dreathan-donn rìgh nan eun o'n latha sin gus an-seo.

An t-Adhbhar mun Abairear Iasg Rìgh ris an Dallaig

Dé ach Rìgh Lochlainn a thighinn gu Rìgh Éireann gu bhith treis còmhla ris.

Chaidh Rìgh Lochlainn is Fionn latha dh'iasgach is bàta beag aca, 's cha robh duine aca ach iad fhéin. Thug iad a' chuid a bu mhò an latha ag iasgach is cha d'fhuair iad dearg.

Laigh an-siud beathach air Fionn is bhuail e air iasgach air chor is gun do chuir e an dubhan ann. Thug e a-staigh an t-iasg, is dé an t-iasg a bha ann ach dallag! Bha dubhan Rìgh Lochlainn anns a' ghoile aice fo dhubhan Fhinn is dubhan Fhinn anns a' bheirbheul. Bhuail Rìgh Lochlainn an-siud air toirt a-mach na dallaig, on is e a dhubhan a b' fhaide sìos innte.

Bhuail iad air coiteachadh air a chéile, 's cha leigeadh Fionn leis bìdeag gus an rachadh iad gu lagh.

Chaidh iad an-siud gu tìr leis a' bhàta 's chaidh iad gu lagh 's rinn an lagh an t-iasg do dh'Fhionn is gum bu chòir càin a chur air Rìgh Lochlainn on nach d'fhairich e an t-iasg an uair a bhuail e an toiseach e.

Leis an àrdan a ghabh Rìgh Lochlainn, chaidh e dhachaigh do Lochlann is dh'innis e d'a mhuime 's d'a oide mar a thachair. B' i a' Mhuilghheartach a mhuime agus b' e Gobha nan Duan a bha pòsta aice, 'oide.

Thuirt ise gur h-i a bheireadh dìoghladh siud a-mach. Thàinig i an-sin gu ruig Éirinn is Rìgh Lochlainn leatha agus Gobha nan Duan.

Cha tuirteadh ris an dallaig riamh ás a dhéidh sin ach "iasg rìgh."

O, Àdhaimh!

Bu thoigh le Rìgh Seumas a Cóig seachdain a chur seachad an-dràsta 's a-rithist ann an Lùchairt Sgàin. Agus nuair a bhiodh e an-sin, bu ro thaitneach leis e fhéin uidheamachadh, chan ann mar rìgh, ach mar dhuine bochd agus sgrìob a thoirt air feadh Gàidheil Shrath Bhreamhainn.

Aon latha nuair a bha an rìgh air a rathad troimh Ghleann Sìth is a' dlùthachadh air Srath Bhreamhainn, chunnaic e bodach mór reamhar de mhuinntir an t-sratha sin a' spìonadh fraoich. Bha am bodach a' gabhail a' ghnothaich gu ro shocrach. An déidh na h-uile bad riamh a spìonadh e, chuireadh e 'làmh air a chruachainn is theireadh e "O, Àdhaimh!"

Sheas an rìgh is bheachdaich e air grabhann mhath, ach cha robh gaoisean fraoich a' tighinn ás a bhun nach robh "O, Àdhaimh!" a' tighinn ás a' bhodach.

A-nis, bha gu leòr Ghàidhlig aig an rìgh mar a bha aig 'athair is aig a sheanair roimhe agus bha briathran an duine, uime sin, a' cur iongnadh nach bu bheag air.

Mu dheireadh, dh'fharraid e, "Car-son a tha thu ag ràdh, 'O, Àdhaimh!?'"

Fhreagair an duine gu dàn dalma, gun fhios aige có bha 'bruidhinn ris, "Nach mi a dh'fheudas 'O, Àdhaimh!' a ràdh! Mur biodh gun d'rinn e ball-magaidh dheth fhéin ann an gàradh Edein. chan ann am fallas mo ghnùise a bhiodh mise ag itheadh m' arain an-diugh."

"Am bheil thu a' saoilsinn, ma-tà," ars an rìgh, "gun dèanadh tusa na b' fheàrr anns a' ghàradh sin na rinn Àdhamh?"

"Na b' fheàrr, mo chreach!" ars am bodach, "cha b' urrainn domh na bu mhiosa a dhèanamh ged a dh'fheuchainn ris."

"Cha dèan do ghearan mu'n eas-ùmhlachd aig Àdhamh," ars an rìgh, "feum sam bith dhuit fhéin no do dhuine eile. Ach innsidh mise dhuit rud a nì. Cuir thusa luchd-cartach de'n fhraoch bhòidheach sin gu Lùchairt Sgàin a-màireach is bheir mise mo ghealladh gun téid do phàigheadh gu math air son do shaothrach. Feòraich an-sin air son Seumas Stiùbhart, oir tha mise ro eòlach air agus cuiridh esan ceart thu. Dèan mar a tha mi ag iarraidh ort is bidh do dhuais 'nad dhòrn a-màireach. Slàn leat!"

Thog an rìgh air agus chuir e seachad a' chuid eile de'n latha sin is an oidhche an caoimhneas blàth nan Gàidheal aig taobh Abhainn Bhreamhainn nam breac bòidheach. Air an ath mhadainn bha an rìgh is bodach an fhraoich air an rathad gu Lùchairt Sgàin ach cha robh iad an cuideachd a chéile, oir bha an rìgh a' geàrradh tro gach aithghearr is 'ga chumail fhéin á sealladh an fhir eile. An uair a ràinig am bodach le 'each is le 'chairt, bha an rìgh a' feitheamh air aig doras mór na lùchairte, agus e sgeadaichte ann an còmhdach meallta eile, air chor is nach d'aithnich am Breamhannach bochd gum faca e riamh roimhe e.

Dh'fheòraich am bodach, "Am bheil Seumas Stiùbhart a' fuireach an-seo?"

"Tha," fhreagair an rìgh, "is mise an duine sin agus bheir mi deagh luach saothrach dhuit air son an fhraoich sin, mur eil e reicte agad cheana."

"'S e am fraoch a reiceadh riutsa ceann-fàth mo thurais," ars an duine, "agus fàgaidh mi breith na prìse agad fhéin."

Sméid an rìgh air gille-stàbaill. Chuir e am beothach eich fo 'chùram agus sheòl e an duine a-staigh do sheòmar-aoigheachd mór. Bha bòrd brèagha an-sin air an robh dìnneir bu ghasta 'chunnaic an duine ré fad a bheatha.

"A-nis," thuirt an rìgh, "tha agamsa ri dol a-mach car tiotan, ach dèan thusa thu fhéin aig an taigh. Sìn do làmh, is gabh de gach nì is àill leat. Ach air na h-uile cor, na bean do'n t-soitheach airgid sin a tha air teis-meadhan a' bhùird. Chan eil duine sam bith aig am bheil de chridhe corrag a chur air an t-soitheach sin ach an rìgh a-mhàin."

Chaidh an rìgh an-sin a-mach ás an t-seòmar, dhruid e an doras, agus chuir e 'shùil ri toll na h-iuchrach.

"Chan eil mi a' tuigsinn," thuirt am bodach ris fhéin, "ciod e idir as urrainn a bhith anns an t-soitheach airgid sin. Rìgh an-seo no rìgh an-siud tha am breamas 's a' chùis ma nì sealltainn air na th' ann dolaidh."

Dh'éirich e is thog e am brod. Cha bu luaithe rinn e sin na leum luchag gheal ás an t-soitheach. 'S ann an-sin a thòisich an ruaig dhian. Déidheil is mar bha an rìgh fhéin air an t-sealg, cha robh e riamh na bu déine an déidh gille nan cròc na bha am Breamhannach air tòir na luchaig. Bha i a' ruith 's a' leumadh am-measg nan soitheach, agus am bodach le 'chrògan móra faobach a' cur cuid dhiubh sin bun os ceann is 'gam briseadh ann am braise na tòrachd. Chuir na tubaistean sin, is an t-eagal gum biodh am fear a chaidh a-mach air ais, an duine bochd 'na bhreislich. Ach, mu dheireadh thall, leum an luchag ann an soitheach beag cumhang. Fhuair e an-sin greim oirre is dhùin e suas i gu grad 'na h-àite fhéin.

Cha mhór nach do chaill an rìgh a lùths aig cùl an dorais a' gàireachdaich ris na thachair ach nuair a dh'fhosgail e an doras, ghabh e air fhéin a bhith feargach, agus thuirt e, "Air chinnte, cha robh thu cho mì-mhodhail is cho beag nàire 's gun do ghabh thu gnothach ri soitheach airgid an rìgh?"

"Cha do ghabh, cha do ghabh," ars am bodach, "cha do chuir mise corrag air."

"A sheann eucoraich," ars an rìgh, "tha thu ag innseadh na tul-bhréige dhomh ás an aodann! Tha thu nas miosa na Àdhamh, oir ghabh esan ri 'chiont ach dh'aicheadh thusa. Na cluinneamsa 'O, Àdhaimh' no 'O, Eubha' a' tighinn tuilleadh ás do chraos. Mach á mo shealladh, a thrustair, is thoir do dhachaigh ort!"

Bha am bodach truagh an leithid de bhrath-cheò leis na h-uile dad a bh' ann, is nach do ghabh e umhail nuair a bha e a' dol a-mach air an doras, gun deach sporan a chur 'na phòc' anns an d'fhuair e an déidh-làimh cóig buinn òir.

Cha robh naidheachd bu docha leis an rìgh fhéin innseadh, nuair a bhiodh gean math air an cuideachd nan Gàidheal, na "O, Àdhaimh!"

Sliochd nan Trì Fichead Burraidh

Chan eil fhios agam an cuala do luchd-leughaidh seann sgeulachd a b' àbhaist a bhith 'ga aithris ann an cuid de cheàrnan d'an Ghàidhealtachd mu dhà bhràthair a thog orra air an aon latha 's a dh'fhàg taigh an athar is a thug an saoghal mu'n cluasan a dh'fheuchainn ciamar a shoirbhicheadh leò. Chaidh fear dhiubh aon rathad, agus am fear eile rathad eile.

An déidh daibh a bhith ùine mhór air falbh, agus iad le chéile air beairteas a dhèanamh, tha e coltach gun do bhuail e an ceann an dà bràthair aig an aon àm gun tilleadh iad air an ais d'an dùthaich fhéin a-rithist.

Thog iad orra le'n sliochd is le'n cuid spréidh agus a-réir na h-eachdraidh, bha deich fir fhichead de shliochd aig gach fear dhiubh. Ge b' e ciod am fortan no mì-fhortan a bha 'gan stiùireadh, thachair an dà bhuidheann air a chéile ann an gleann air bun cnuic ris an abrar, mas math mo bheachd, Sliabh an Tuim, ann an Creignis. Bha a' ghrian air dol fodha agus am feasgar air claonadh air a lethid de dhòigh is ma chunnaic an dà sheann duine a chéile nach d'aithnich an darna bràthair am bràthair eile.

Shuidh an dà chuideachd a leigeil an sgìos agus a ghabhail greim bìdh, sliochd an darna fir crioman beag a-suas am bruthach, agus càch aig ìochdar a' ghlinne.

Tha e coltach gun do thilg fear de'n fheadhainn a bha gu h-àrd rudeigin a-nuas orrasan a bha gu h-ìosal, aon chuid d'a dheòin no gun fhios, no gun tug e adhbhar faoin air choireigin daibh a' smaoineachadh gun robh iad a' dèanamh tàire orra agus ciod a bha air no dheth ach gun d'éirich na fearaibh.

Rùisg iad an claidheamhan is am badaibh a chéile a ghabh iad "gun fhios có bu Chalum." Is e bu deireadh do'n chòmhstri nach d'fhàgadh duine beò de na bha an-sin ach an dà sheann duine. An uair a chunnaic iad an sgrios a rinneadh am-measg an cuid cloinne, mheas iad gun robh an t-àm sgur.

Shuidh iad air cnocan agus thòisich iad air feòraich mu eachdraidh càch a chéile, an uair, ciod a b' iongantaiche leò 'fhaicinn na gum b' iadsan an dà bhràthair a dhealaich bho chionn ùine cho fada. Ma bha seòrsa toileachaidh aca a chéile 'choinneachadh, bha mulad gu leòr orra bhith faicinn an léir-sgrios a thug an gòraich 's am braisead air an trì fichead òigear a bha 'nan laighe gun chlì aig an casan.

Riamh uaidh sin, theirear "Sliochd nan trì fichead burraidh" ris an fhine Ghàidhealach a tha a' giùlan an aon ainme riutha. Nan innsinn có iad, chan eil fhios agam nach cuirinn mì-thlachd air Cloinn Chaluim!

Tòrachd na Tàine

Bha duine uasal ann an Éirinn ris an canadh iad an Dubhaltach. Cha bu tighearna fearainn idir e ach bha cuid mhór an t-saoghail aige agus ionnsachadh math agus e o theaghlach measail, agus leis a sin, bha àite suidhe aige ann an cuideachd uaislean. Cha robh air a theaghlach ach aona ghille mic d'am b' ainm Cù Chulainn. Bha e fhéin agus Iarla Ghlinn Chuilisg còmhla anns a' cholaiste agus bha iad 'nan càirdean 's nan companaich.

Bha nighean an iarla a' posadh agus chuir an t-iarla cuireadh chun na bainnse dh'ionnsaigh an Dubhaltaich seachdain ro'n àm. Dh'fhalbh an Dubhaltach agus a bhean chun na bainnse le'n gillean is le'n eich dhìolta. Bha Cù Chulainn a' sireadh falbh ach cha leigte leis. Nuair a dh'fhalbh iadsan, dh'fhalbh esan ás an deaghaidh. Bha ball is caman aige is bha e 'ga iomain fad fìn foineach an là air an rathad.

Am beul na h-oidhche, an dol fodha na gréine, ràinig iad an drochaid mhór bha dol chun pailios an iarla. Bha cù air an drochaid 'ga gléidheadh 's cha leigeadh e duine seachad gun phàigheadh. Cha robh airgead aig a' ghille.

Smaointich e aige fhéin gum bu tàmailteach dha tilleadh dhachaigh agus chuir e am ball air sorachag agus bhuail e a-staigh air an dala ceann a' choin is a-mach air a' cheann eile e is chuir e an cù na 'bhuta leis an drochaid.

Sin a' cheud euchd a rinn Cù Chulainn.

Ghabh e a-staigh dha'n bhaile is chunnaic e gillean ag iomain agus thòisich e air iomain còmhla riutha.

Nuair thàinig an oidhche, thuirt e ri fear dhe na gillean bha ag iomain còmhla ris, "Nach ann an-seo," ars esan, "a tha taigh an iarla?"

"'S ann," ars an gille eile. "Dé seo do ghnothachsa ris?"

"Nach eil banais mhór ann?"

"Tha."

"B' fheàrr leam gun ionnsaich tu dhomh e."

"Cha leig iad a-staigh thu."

"Tha m' athair is mo mhàthair air a' bhanais agus feuchaidh mi an leig."

Bha an caisteal air a lasadh le craoslach chraobhach sholais. Ghabh e a-staigh is ghabh e am-measg na cuideachd is thug e ruith a-null is chaidh e eadar dà ghlùn 'athar.

"An tu a tha seo, a Chù Chulainn?" ars athair.

"Is mi," ars Cù Chulainn.

"Ciamar a fhuair thu a-staigh is an cù air an drochaid?"

"Mharbh mi an cù."

Dé bh' ann ach fear do stiùbhartan an iarla 's an rùm agus falbhar agus innsear dha mhaighstir cainnt Chù Chulainn. Leum an t-iarla a-nuas.

"Có tha seo," ars esan, "a mharbh mo chù air an drochaid?"

Cha tuirt duine diog: bha eagal orra.

Thuirt an Dubhaltach, "Seo e, tha e ag ràdhainn rium gun do mharbh e do chù."

"Cha chreid mi sin, gum marbhadh giullan beag mar sin mo chù."

"O! Is mi a mharbh e gu dearbh is cha chuir thu gu duine sam bith eile e ach mise," ars Cù Chulainn.

"Bhuel," ars an t-iarla, "feumaidh tu fuireach seachd bliadhna air an drochaid 'ga gléidheadh gus an tog mise cù 'nad àite, neo pàighidh tu £700 Sasannach dhomh."

"An-tà, pàighidh mise sin air son mo mhic," ars an Dubhaltach, "ach ma phàigheas, cha mhór as fhiach mi fhéin 'na dheaghaidh. Ach nam faighinn ùine, phàighinn sin is mi fhéin bhith mar bha mi roimhe."

Dh'éirich Cù Chulainn 'na sheasadh agus thuirt e, "Cha phàigh thu, athair, aon sgillin, ach théid mise chun na drochaid ga gléidheadh dha, agus fuirichidh mi bliadhna, agus feumaidh esan ceartas a' choin a chumail riumsa."

Bha Cù Chulainn an-sin bliadhna air an drochaid. Bha e fuasach air son sgoil, agus a chuile duine a thigeadh chun na drochaid, theireadh e ris, "Cha leig mi a-null thu mur toir thu dhomh leasan." Agus nuair a thigeadh duine uasal, bheireadh e dha am pàigheadh, agus an leasan còmhla ris. Leis cho dìcheallach is a bha e 'ga togail, dh'ionnsaich e mar seo moran sgoile. Thàinig e an-sin dachaigh.

Bha anns an àm sin dha'n t-saoghal colaiste ann an Dùn Sgàthaich 's an Eilean Sgitheanach agus cha robh fear ris am b' fhiach fear a ràdh an rìoghachd na h-Alba, an Sasainn no an Éirinn, nach cuireadh a mhac ga ionnsachadh ann. Cha robh meas air fear ach fear a gheibheadh ionnsachadh an Dùn Sgàthaich. Cha robh sgoil no foghlum no math-chleas nach faighte ann, is cha robh meas air cleas ach cleas a gheibhte ann. Cha bhiodh Cù Chulainn beò mur leigte air falbh a sgoil Dhùn Sgàthaich e, agus leigeadh air falbh e.

Bha e naoidh bliadhna an-sin. Bha uasal Albannach d'am b' ainm Am Feardiag mac Daimbain anns an sgoil ri linn Chù Chulainn agus b' e ceud ghaisgeach an t saoghail e r'a linn fhéin.

Bha am Feardiag agus Cù Chulainn a' laighe is ag éirigh còmhla fad nan naoidh bliadhna agus iad nan companaich aig a' chéile. An àm a bha iad a' dealachadh, mhionnaich iad dha chéile nach cuireadh an dala fear trioblaid air an fhear eile gu bràch. Cha robh sian a dh'ionnsaich an dala fear nach d'ionnsaich am fear eile ach aon chleas a bh' aig Cù Chulainn ris an cante an Gath Balg.

Mar a Thòisich an Fhéinn

Aig sìn-sinnseanair Rìgh Éirinn o'n chóigeamh glùn, 's ann a lìonsgair na Fiantaichean. 'S e dithis agus triùir bha iad a' faighinn a h-uile bliadhna de dhaoine móra agus boireannaich anns an robh sia troighean. Bha iad 'gam pòsadh sin ri chéile agus an sliochd a bha tighinn bhuapa, bha meudachd mhór mhór annta gus na rinn iad reiseamaid mhór dha na Fiantaichean.

Nuair a fhuair iad a-nise na Fiantaichean cruinn, 's ann air son a bhith 'nan saighdearan agus 'nan luchd-dìon air a rìoghachd air na Lochlannaich. 'S ann air son cur ás do na Lochlannaich a chaidh an togail an toiseach.

Nuair a fhuair iadsan iad fhéin cho làidir, chuir iad litir gu Rìgh Éirinn nach ruigeadh e leas dùil a bhith aige ri'n cuideachadh-san ri 'bheò no ri 'bhàs. Rinn iad rìgh dhaibh fhéin an-sin air Cumhall. Bha naoi naonan ann dhiubh an toiseach ge b'rith am barrachd a bh' ann nuair a rinneadh rìgh de Chumhall.

Cha chuala mi riamh có bhuaidhe thàinig Cumhall ach bha Diarmad, Goll is Osgar 'nan clann peathar do dh'Fhionn. Nuair a thàinig an triùir-sa bho Rìgh Éirinn gu ruige an t-Eilean Sgitheanach a chumail nam fiadh bho na Fiantaichean, ach an aona fhear bu dona air a ghreigh, 's e sin an aon fhear bh' air a chur a-mach dhaibh gus a mharbhadh dhaibh fhéin.

Cha robh iad ach leigeadh greim dha fheòil agus balgam dhe shùgh dha na h-uile fear do na Fiantaichean. B' fheudar dhaibh a bhith cur deilgnean daraich 'nam broinn 'ga cumail a-staigh. Bha iad mar sin riamh gus an tàinig Fionn orra.

A' chlann a thàinig bho nighean Chumhaill, piuthar Fhinn, b' iad sin Diarmad is Goll is Osgar. Bha iad càirdeach do Fhionn ged nach robh iad càirdeach do na Fiantaichean. B' e Fionn bràthair am màthar.

Nuair a bha Cumhall 'na rìgh orra, cha robh de chridhe aig duine an tilleadh ged a bha gu leòr air feadh an t-saoghail na bu treasa na iad.

Chuir an rìgh Cumhall a-mach lagh nach robh duine dhèanadh cron nach sgaradh iad 'bheatha. Bha aon fhear an-sin, ciod e rinn e ach laighe le mart. Rug iad air a' bhoin agus mharbh iad i agus chuir iad cuid na bà (seach, arca na bà) mu 'amhaich, agus dh'fhuaigh iad e air chor is nach tugadh duine sam bith ás e. Chuir iad air falbh bhuatha buileach e agus cha chanadh iad facal ris ach Arca Dubh.

Chaidh e gu pàilis Rìgh Éirinn e fhéin is a bhean. Chuir e brath a-staigh thun an rìgh gun robh gnothach beag aige ris. Thàinig an rìgh a-mach agus mhothaich e dha agus dh'fhaighneachd e dheth gu dé an duine bh' ann.

Thuirt Arca an-sin gum b' esan fear dha na Fiantaichean.

"Nach tu a chaill do nàire nuair a thàinig thu 'nam aodann, an déis dha m' shìn-shinnseanair ur cur cruinn agus sibh a dhealachadh bhuam a-rithist, is nach leigidh sinn leas dùil a bhith againn cuideachadh fhaighinn bhuaibh?"

"An-tà," ars esan, "a chionn gur e mise bha ag iarraidh orra thusa a leantail, chuir iad seo mu m' amhaich mar thàmailt is chuir iad bhuatha mi. Thàinig mi far robh sibh fhéin gus sibh a thoirt dhomh cuideachadh."

"Chan urrainn domhsa cuideachadh a thoirt dhut, a leithid de dhuine mór."

"Chan iarr mi ach iasgach na h-aibhne agus cumaidh mi iasg ribh fhéin air ur bracaist."

"Gheibh thu sin – agus innis dhomh ciamar a chuirear Cumhall gu bàs?"

"Cha do thog Cumhall," ars Arca, "sùil ri gin riamh ach boireannach ro bhrèagha."

"An-tà," ars an rìgh, "'s ann agamsa tha an aon bhoinne-fala as àille tha fo'n ghréin. 'S còir dhuinn litir a chur ga ionnsaigh."

Sgrìobh Rìgh Éirinn litir an-sin gu Cumhall, e 'thighinn far an robh e gum faigheadh e maithte na rinn e 'na aghaidh.

Dh'fhalbh Cumhall an-sin agus chaidh e dha'n phàilis aig Rìgh Éirinn. Is nuair a ràinig e, chuireadh dinneir gu feum dhaibh. Shuidh iad aig bòrd is cha robh Cumhall a' leigeil a shùl bhàrr nighean Rìgh Éirinn.

"Cha chreid mi nach eil thu air gaol a ghabhail air an nighinn."

"An-tà," arsa Cumhall, "'s i an aon bhoinne-fala as docha leam a chunnaic mi riamh."

"Mas i, pòs thu fhéin is i fhéin, ma-tà."

Phòs iad an-sin agus oidhche na bainnseadh aca, chuireadh Arca Dubh an aon seomar riutha a' falach. Nuair a chunnaic Arca sin an t-àm (gun robh a thrì meanmachd fir 'ga chall air muin na mnatha), thug e an ceann bhàrr Chumhaill le 'chlaidheamh fhéin, Mac an Luin. Bhuail a bhean a basan. Nuair a chunnaic Bran Mac an Luin aig Arca, lean e Mac an Luin agus Arca.

Dh'fhàs a bhean trom is chuir an rìgh a-mach achd, nam b' e nighean a bhiodh ann gum biodh iad coma mu déidhinn, nach togadh i tòrachd a h-athar. Ach nam b' e gille 'bhiodh ann gun rachadh a mharbhadh cho luath is a thigeadh e dh'ionnsaigh an t-saoghail.

Ann an ceann nan trì ràithean, thuisleadh ise air leanabh nighinn agus le toileachadh is le toil-inntinn a rinn an rìgh, cha robh duine bha mu'n champa nach robh marbh leis an daoraich.

A' bhean-ghlùin bu ghiorra dhith, thuirt i rithe, "Seall gu dé th' agam an-dràsta?"

"Tha agad an-dràsta," ars ise, "pàiste-gille."

"Éirich thusa," ars i fhéin, "agus falbh leis agus tog e."

"An ann," ars ise, "is mi air mo mhionnachadh nam b' e gille bhiodh ann gun rachainn a thoirt suas dha'n rìgh gur e gille bhiodh ann?"

"Falbh thusa agus tog e, is cho fada 's is bonnach dhomhsa e, is bonnach dhutsa e, no nì eile a bhios agam, is leatsa do chuid dheth, ach tog an gille."

Dh'fhalbh a' bhanaltrum, a bhean-ghlùine, is thog i leatha am pàiste is a-mach a ghabh i.....

Cha robh fios aige (aig Fionn) air an t-saoghal dé dhèanadh e ach 's e sgeuma rinn e, lean e an abhainn a thachair ris is chunnaic e duine mór mór ag iasgach air an abhainn agus chaidh e far an robh e.

"Gu dé do naidheachd, 'ille bhig?" ars an duine mór a bha sin.

"An-tà, chan eil agamsa guth," ars an gille, "ach b' fheàrr leam nan tugadh tu dhomh breac dhe'n iasg a th' agad, is mi gu bhith marbh leis an acras."

"An-tà," ars esan, "ma tha 'shealbh ort fhéin is gum marbh mi breac an-dràsta, gheibh thu e."

Mharbh e an-sin breac is cha do mharbh e leithid riamh cho mór ris.

Ars an duine, "Chan fhaigh thu am fear-sa idir. Cha do mharbh mi leithid riamh o thàinig mi agus bidh e ro mhór ann an sùilean an Rìgh leithid seo dh'iasg thoirt thuige. Ach gheibh thu an ath fhear a mharbhas mi," ars e fhéin.

Mharbh e an-sin fear is bha e na bu mhotha na 'chiad fhear a mharbh e. "Chan fhaigh thu am fear-sa idir," ars e fhéin.

"Ud," ars an gille, "cumaidh tu mise gu bràch gun bhreac thoirt domh, a' gealltainn a h-uile fear a thoirt dhomh 's gun thu 'ga thoirt dhomh."

"An-tà, 'ille, mionnaichidh mi air bàrr na slaite, ged a bhiodh e uiread ris na dhà, gum faigh thu am fear-sa."

Mharbh e an-sin breac, is bha e na bu mhotha na gin a mharbh e.

"An-tà, 'ille mhath," ars e fhéin, "seo dhut a-nist e. Cuiridh tu an teine air an taobh ud dha'n allt agus cuiridh tu am breac air an taobh-sa dheth. Ma leigeas tu ball dubh na losgadh air, chan fhaigh thu sgath dheth."

Chuir an gille an teine air an taobh thall dha'n allt agus am breac air an taobh-sa. Mar a bha am fiodh cho leumach, dé bha ach splang a dh'fhalbh ás an teine agus bhuail e air taobh a' bhric. Leum an gille a-null air an allt is chuir e 'mheur air a phoc a dh'éirich air a' bhreac agus dh'fhàisg e a-staigh am poc ris an iasg agus loisg e 'mheur is chuir e 'mheur 'na bheul is fhuair e fiosachd gur e siud am fear a mharbh 'athair Cumhall is gur e an cù bh' aig 'athair, an cù bha còmhla ris aig an abhainn is gun robh an claidheamh bh' aig 'athair, Mac an Luin, fo'n leabaidh aige.

Nuair a bhruich esan an-sin am breac, thug e taing do dh'Arca Dubh a chionn a thoirt dha. Dh'fhalbh e an-sin is chaidh e gu ruig taigh Arcaidh is thuirt e ri bean Arcaidh gun do chuir Arca e dh'iarraidh a chlaidheimh.

Thuirt ise an-sin ris, "Chan eil dùil leam gu bheil claidheamh aige ach an claidheamh a th' air a thaobh."

Thuirt esan an-sin rithe-se gun robh e fo 'leabaidh. Dh'fheuchadh fo 'leabaidh 's cha d'fhuaradh e. Chaidh e an-sin a-mach is bha e a' nòdachadh gur e rud air choireigin a chaidh 'na cheann fhéin nuair a smaointich e air a leithid.

Chuir e 'mheur a-rithist 'na bheul agus fhuair e a-mach gur ann fo phosta na leapa bha e air a thìodhlacadh. Thill e a-staigh an-sin is thuirt e rithe gun robh e ag ràdh gur ann fo phosta na leapadh a bha e air a thìodhlacadh. Thog iad an leaba, fhuair iad Mac an Luin. Rug e air Mac an Luin agus dh'fhalbh e sìos far an robh Arca Dubh.

"Tha thu air tilleadh a-rithist, 'ille," ars Arca.

"Tha," ars an gille.

"Dé tha thu ag iarraidh niste?"

"Chan eil ach gum bheil iad ag ràdh gur thu fhéin a mharbh Cumhall."

"An-tà, is mi," ars esan. "An ann dol a thogail a thòrachd tha thusa?"

"Chan ann, ach tha mi cinnteach gur ann agad a bha spòrs air."

"Leabhar, is ann," ars e fhéin:

> "Bhéiceadh e mar mhuic,
> Bhramadh e mar ghearran,
> Is ceann mo shleagh 'na thiompan."

"An-tà," ars esan, "a mhic na galladh," is e a' toirt tarraing air Mac an Luin, "Ma bha sin agadsa air m' athair, bidh e agamsa ortsa," is e a' leigeil ceann Arca leis an abhainn.

Nuair a chunnaic Bran an-sin Mac an Luin, ghrad dh'éirich e agus lean e Fionn. Bha an-seo Fionn a' smaointeachadh co-dhiù a rachadh e gu baile na dh'fhanadh e ás. Ach chaidh e dha'n choillidh a dh'fheuchainn gu dé stuth bha Mac an Luin. Thòisich e air na craobhan is bha e leagail nan craobhan mar gum biodh an t-arbhar fo fhaobhar na spealadh.

Fionn agus am Bradan

Cha robh de chridhe aige 'aghaidh a thoirt air aon àite leis am bu ghnàth le 'mhuime bhith tathaich. Dh'fhalbh e air fainneoladh agus gun fhios gu math aige càite agus cam gach rathaid dha ach gabhail seachad air eas dha'm b' ainm Eas Ruaidh.

Agus chunnaic e fear ag iasgach air an eas, agus thuirt Fionn ris, "Tha mi," deir esan, "ann am fàillinn mhóir, tha mi a' guidhe ort, thoir dhomh beathach beag do na h-iasgaibh sin a dh'itheas mi."

"Cha toir," deir an t-isgair.

"Nam biodh tu cho math," arsa Fionn, "agus gun cuireadh tu a-mach an t-slat air mo shealbhaidh."

Rinn an t-iasgair sin agus air ball, dh'iasgaich e làn-bhradan.

"Cha toir mi am beathach-sa dhuit, tha e ro mhòr agus ro mhath. 'S ann a tha an-seo iasg rìgh."

"Nam biodh tu cho mhath is gun tugadh tu dhomh fhéin an t-slat."

"Gheibh thu sin," ars an t-iasgair.

Air do dh'Fhionn an t-slat-iasgaich fhaotainn, thilg e a-mach an dubhan agus tharraing e gu tìr bradan a bha na bu mhò na bradan an iasgair.

"Chan fhaod mi am beathach-sa 'thoirt dhuit," deir an t-iasgair, "ach bheir mi beathach beag nas lugha na seo dhuit. Ach feumaidh tu 'ròstadh air taobh eile an eas, agus an connadh air an taobh seo, agus ma bhios ball amh no loisgte air, caillidh tu do cheann ris, agus," ars an t-iasgair, "théid mise 'chadal, agus biodh e ròsta mun dùisg mi."

Ged bu chruaidh seo, b' fheudar aontachadh leis. Thòisich Fionn air teinidh 'fhadadh is air an iasg a ròstadh is chaidh an t-iasgair a chadal. Bha Fionn 'ga shàrachadh a' brasnachadh an teine is a' ròstadh an éisg. Ach uair do na h-uairibh, dh'éirìch balg loisgte air a' bhradan, agus cho luath 's a b' urrainn da, leig e 'mheur air is loisg gu cnàimh e. Chuir e 'mheur 'na bheul le gradadh agus fhuair e Fios an Dà Shaoghail, mar a their iad. Fhuair e fios 's a' mhionaid sin gum b' e an t-iasgair a mharbh athair Fhinn is gum b' e Forca Dubha ainm an iasgair is gun robh claidheamh athar làmh ris ann am falach.

Dh'éirich e le cabhaig agus fhuair e claidheamh athar is thug e an ceann de dh'Forca-Dubha, is ri siubhal 'na dhéidh sin ghabh Fionn. 'S ann uaidhe seo a fhuaireadh sgreubhadh a' bhradain ri Eas Ruaidh, cha b' fhuar e is cha bu teth.

Air ball an déidh an ceann a thoirt dhe'n iasgar, ghabh Fionn a thuras agus stad no fois cha d'rinn e gus an d'ràinig e taigh a' ghobhainn, a sheanair.

Garaidh agus na Mnathan

Ma-tà, bha na boireannaich a bh' aig na Fiantaichean—na mnathan aca gu tuiteam ás a chéile le blonaig is le saill. Bha na Fiantaichean air ion is a bhith air thogail. Cha robh fios ciod e bha toirt do na mnathan a bhith cho lag fann is a bha iad. Bha na Fiantaichean a' dol do'n tràigh o'n cheud tràghadh gu leathach lìonaidh: fhad is a gheibheadh iad maorach ann.

'S i an sgeilm-sa 'rinn Garaidh, "Leigidh mi orm gum bheil mi bochd an-diugh, 's gheibh mi a-mach ciod e an seòl-bidhe th' aig na boireannaich a bhith cho reamhar is a tha iad, is sinne cho caol is a tha sinn."

Chaidh na Fiantaichean do'n tràigh, is feadhainn dhiubh gu tìr-mór do Ghleann Eilge, is feadhainn eile do'n fhearann a tha mu choinneamh Chaol Arcainn.

Bha Garaidh an-seo anns an leabaidh, is e bochd. Chruinnich na boireannaich, is dh'fhalbh iad do'n tràigh. Bha maorach beag anns an tràigh—'s e maorach Moire 'their sinne ris—is lìon iad an sgùird leis a' mhaorach a bh' ann an-sin. Thug iad leò ultach an-sin de'n dubh-stamh, agus sgrìob agus ghlan iad carraig an dubh-staimh. Bhruich iad am maorach, thug iad am biadh ás, is phronn iad carraig an dubh-staimh. Bhruich iad carraig an dubh-staimh is am maorach ann am-measg a chéile, is rinn iad miasan air. Agus 's e sin a-nis am biadh a bh' aig na mnathan a bha 'gam fàgail cho reamhar—is fhad on a chuala sibh gun robh smior-conaig an fhéidh an carraig an dubh-staimh.

An uair a dh'ith iad sin, thug Garaidh an-seo smoisleachadh ás, agus sìos bha na boireannaich air a mhuin. Is bha iad ag ràdh nan leigteadh bheò leis gun innseadh do na Fiantaichean am biadh a bh' acasan, is nuair a gheibheadh na Fiantaichean a-mach sin, chan fhàgadh iad maorach air tràigh nan dubh-stamh ri cloich gun a thoirt ás, agus a bhith 'ga bhruich.

Rug iad an-sin air Garaidh, is rinn iad naoi gadan figheachain air a ghruaig, agus dh'fhuaigh iad ris an ùrlar ceann Gharaidh le naoidh deilgne daraich. Rug iad air a' chlaidheamh aige fhéin gus an ceann a thoirt dheth.

Thug e cruinn leum ás, is lean craiceann a chinn agus a ghruaig ris an ùrlar, agus dh'fhalbh e, is cha robh mac bothaig a bh' aig na Fiantaichean an Sléibhte nach do chuir e 'na theine.

Bha sneachd òg o'n oidhche ann, is chunnaic na Fiantaichean na bothagan 'nan teine, is a-mach a ghabh Reatha is thug e an caolas air, is chuir e an t-sleagh fo 'uchd agus le 'chudthrom fhéin am meadhan a' chaolais, bhrist an t-sleagh agus bhàthadh e; agus riamh o'n latha sin, lean "Caol-Reatha" air a' chaolas sin.

Agus Caol Arcainn: bhrist an t-sleagh le Arca fo 'chudthrom, agus am meadhan a' chaolais, bhàthadh e fhéin, agus o'n latha sin, tha "Caol Arcainn " air a' chaolas sin.

Thàinig an-seo na Fiantaichean dhachaigh, is cha robh bothag riamh a bh' aca nach robh 'nan teine.

"'S e," arsa Fionn, "Garaidh Dubh a rinn seo."

Ach fhuair iad sràbh na fala bha 'cheann a' sileadh air an t-sneachd, agus lean iad sràbh na fala riamh gus an d'ràinig iad beul uamha.

Bha Garaidh air a dhol a-staigh an comhair a chùil, is nuair a chaidh e a-staigh greis, thionndaidh e 'aghaidh air ceann na h-uamha, agus ciod e rinn e ach gun d'rug e air calman, agus choisich e a-staigh astar beag eile, agus rug e air dà chalman eile. Chaidh e fhéin do cheann na h-uamha an-sin. Is nuair a thàinig na Fiantaichean thun na h-uamha, thuirt Fionn an-seo ri Aodh Mac Garaidh: "Falbh, agus thoir a-mach t' athair ás an uaimh."

Dh'fhalbh Aodh is nuair a chrom e thun na tràghad, thill e far an robh Fionn.

"Tha lorgan m' athar," ars esan, "a' falbh ás an uaimh."

"O, falbh thusa," arsa Fionn, " 's gum bu shuarach air mìorailtean Gharaidh Dhuibh a dhol a-staigh an comhair a thòin."

Chaidh Aodh a-staigh, is air dha dhol a-staigh, leig 'athair ás calman, is thill Aodh an-seo a-mach far an robh Fionn, agus thuirt e ris, "Nam biodh m' athair-sa 's an uaimh, nach biodh calman beò innte."

"O, falbh thusa," arsa Fionn, " 's bu shuarach air mìorailtean Gharaidh Dhuibh breith air calman beò innte."

Chaidh Aodh an-seo a-staigh, is, air greis dha dhol a-staigh, leig 'athair ás na dhà còmhla.

Thill Aodh gu Fionn, is thuirt e ris, "Ged a bheireadh m' athair air calman, cha bheireadh e air a trì bheò."

"Falbh thusa," arsa Fionn, "agus thoir a-mach t' athair."

Dh'fhalbh e sin, is fhuair e 'athair an ceann shuas na h-uamha.

"Siuthad a-nis, Aoidh!" arsa Fionn, "is thoir an ceann bhàrr t' athar le Mac an Luin."

"Am bheil idir," ars Aodh, "gin ann a bheir an ceann bhàrr m' athar ach mise?"

"Chan eil," arsa Fionn. "Bheir thusa dheth e, is gheibh thu t' iarrtas."

"Ma gheibh mise m' iarrtas," ars Aodh, "cuir thusa ceann m' athar air do shliasaid."

Cha do dh'fhàg Mac an Luin fuigheall beuma riamh a chaidh m'a choinneamh. Nan cuireadh Fionn ceann Gharaidh air a shliasaid, rachadh Mac an Luin tro shliasaid Fhinn. Is bha Fionn bho fheum an uair sin.

"An-tà," arsa na daoine, "cladhaichidh sinn fad agus leud cas Fhinn anns an tràigh. Cuiridh sinn trì sailthean daraich ar muin cas Fhinn, agus cuiridh sinn ceann Gharaidh air muin nan sailthean."

Rinneadh sin, agus rug Aodh Mac Gharaidh air Mac an Luin, is tharraing e e, is chuir e an ceann bhàrr 'athar, is chaidh e tro na tri sailthean gus an do choinnich an tràigh bàrr Mhic an Luin. Ghabh Aodh an-sin misg-chatha, is dh' fhoighnich e de dh' Fhionn, "Có air a dhiùbhlas mi mo chath?"

"Diùbhlaidh," ars Fionn, "air an làn sin a' tighinn a-staigh."

Thòisich Aodh an uair sin air an làn air ceud lìonadh gu ceud tràghadh, is thuit e fhéin marbh an-sin air ceud tràghadh.

Is e sin an rud bu duilghe le Fionn a rinn e riamh: an gaisgeach a b' fheàrr a bh' aige a chur mu làr.

Fionn an Taigh a' Bhlàir Bhuidhe

Là dha'n robh Fionn mac Cumhaill 's a' chuid eile de'n Fhéinn anns a' bheinn-sheilg, dh'éirich cur is cathadh; is mun d'fhuair iad an t-sealg a chur cruinn, thàinig an t-anmoch orra. Sgìth, airtealach mar a bha iad, thog iad orra gu teàrnadh gu baile.

Mar a bha iad a' gabhail air an adhart gu trom athaiseach, thàinig iad air bothan fàs am bràighe glinne agus ghabh iad gu tàmh ann. Dh'fhadaidh iad teine, is chaidh na gillean air sùrd gréidheidh is gus am biodh an t-eunbhruich ullamh, thòisich iad air iomairt nan còrn, is air seanchas mu'n àm bho shean. Chuir cuimhne air cliù an sinnsire togail fodhpa mar a b' àbhaist; is thuirt iad uile cruinn a' còmhluath gum b' e mo thru-aighe duine no beathach a thigeadh a chur dragh air an Fhéinn an oidhche sin, no a the-annadh ri tàire a thoirt do dh'Fhionn.

An teis-meadhain na bruidhne seo, thigear maigheach chaol ruadh a-staigh; agus, gun fhiamh gum umhail, cairear car no dhà dhi air a' chagailt, is togar an luath mu na sparran, agus thugar a-mach oirre!

Ma thug, cha deachaidh sin air mhì-thapadh dhaibhsan. Thug iad daoidh-leum a-mach ás a deoghaidh. Ach chaidh iad 'nam brath-cheò cho mór le dorchadas a thàinig orra, 's nach bu léir dhaibh a chéile.

Lean Fionn is a dhà ghille dheug i a bhun is a lorg thar guallainn a' ghlinne. Is cha do chaill iad sealladh oirre gus an do leum i a-staigh air sgùid de thaigh ùdlaidh a thachair orra aig bun sìdhein. Dé an taigh a bha an-seo, ach Taigh a' Bhlàir Bhuidhe, famhair a bha 'tighinn beò air tuirc nimhe 's air feòil dhaoine!

Rachar a-staigh, is gabhar sgeul, ach cha d'fhuaras forfhais air a' mhaighich. Cha robh a-staigh ach a' bhean is i a' fuineadh. Cha tàinig am Blàr Buidhe dhachaigh ás a' bheinn-sheilg. Thug i biadh is deoch dhaibh is thuirt i gum b' fheàrr dhaibh a-nis a bhith 'falbh, mun tigeadh am Blàr Buidhe dhachaigh.

Thuirt Fionn nach do theich iad ro dhuine riamh, agus nach dèanadh iad toiseach de'n Bhlàr, is theann iad na b' fhaide a-staigh.

"Feith ri dheireadh," ars a' bhean.

Mar a b' fhìor, cha d'fhuair iad iad fhéin a shocrachadh ach gann, tràth a dh'fhairich iad stuirn-stairn aig an doras. Có bha an-siud ach am Blàr Buidhe 's a ghillean, is torc nimhe mór fiaclach aige air a mhuin! Thug e crathadh beag mór air fhéin a chur an t-sneachda dheth, is chuir e crith fo'n ursainn is fo shuidheachan an taighe.

"Tha mi a' faireachdainn fàilidh fharbhalach romham, a bhean. Có seo th' agad a-nochd?" ars am Blàr.

Dh'innis a bhean na h-aoighean a thàinig air choimheadachd oirre bhon a dh'fhalbh e.

"A-mach do ghillean, 'Fhinn, a thoirt na h-eallaiche dhiom," ars am Blàr.

Cha tug Fionn an t-euradh do dhuine riamh, agus cuirear sianar a-mach dhiubh far an robh am Blàr. Mu'n gann a bha iad seach an stairsneach, bhuail am Blàr slat na draoidheachd orra, 's bha iad 'nan colbh-cloiche. Is chuir e air taobh tuath an dorais iad a chur stad air a' ghaoth dheathaich! Dh'fhàg e an-sin iad is thug e fhéin is a ghillean a-staigh an torc. Cha d'fhuirich iad ach ri robladh lomaidh a thoirt air, is chuir a' bhean air e 's a' choire mhór, 'na chlosaich mar a bha e!

Mun d'fhuair e ach goil is leth-goil, spàrr am Blàr bior na feòla ann, is bha siud aige air an ùrlar. Is gun tuille dàlach, shuidh e fhéin is a ghillean mun cuairt da. Gach cnàimh mar a chreimeadh iad, thilgeadh iad siud gu Fionn is gu 'ghillean. B' olc a' bhiatachd e, ach cha robh comas air.

Bha Fionn 'na thost is 'na chuimhne 's b' ion<gnadh> dà sin. An uair a bha an ròic thairis, is cha b' fhada chuige, dh'iarr am Blàr Buidhe air a mhnaoi an t-ubhal òir a thoirt a-nuas gus an oidhche fhada gheamhraidh a chur seachad air Fionn. Thug i a-nuas an t-ubhal, is thug i dha e. Thòisich iad air a chéile leis an ubhal, is ma thòisich, cha b' fhada gus an do chuir am Blàr ás do'n iomlan de ghillean Fhinn.

Thuig am Blàr nach dèanadh e an gnothach air Fionn leis an ubhal, is thuirt e gum feumadh iad dol a ghleachd. An dromannan a chéile gabhar iad, ach, ged a bhiodh iad fhathast a' gleachd, cha tugadh e glideachadh air Fionn. Tràth a chunnaic am Blàr gun do thachair a sheise ris, dh'iarr e air a mhnaoi a' ghreideal a chur air gus an rachadh casan Fhinn a gharadh, gur cinnte gun robh e fuar, is an oidhche chruaidh reòdhte a bh' ann. Chaidh a' ghreideal a chur air gus an robh i 'na caoir dheirg. Is dh'iadh iad uile mu Fhionn (sin tràth a thuirt e, "Cha duine, duine 'na aonar"), agus spàrr iad air a' ghreideil e gus an do loisg a chasan gu ruig nan sléistean!

Bha e a-nis gun chomas suidhe. Leig am Blàr rochd gàire ás, agus spàrr e stob na feòla tro chòrn a dhà mhàis. Is bha e an-sin gun chomas éirigh no suidhe. Shaoil leis a' Bhlàr gun robh e gun phlosg analach, is thilg e seachad 's a' chùil e.

Cha robh Fionn riamh roimhe an gaile na bu mhutha na seo, ach an uair a bha e eadar an t-euradh is aimbeairt, agus cuimhnichear e gun robh còrn nam fiù aige, is gun cluinnteadh e an cóig chóigean na h-Éireann.

Nuair a ghabh an taigh gu fois, mhàgair e a-mach gu dubh balbh sàmhach gu mullach cnuic is shéid e an còrn trì uairean. Fad an ama seo, bha 'chuid eile de'n Fhéinn gu dubhach deurach air tòir Fhinn. Cha d'fhàg iad cùil no cèal gun sireadh, is iarraidh-mhairbh aca air.

Mu dheireadh thall, nuair a thug iad géill is dubh-ghéill, chuala Diarmaid Donn mac a pheathar an còrn. Is ma chuala, cha bu rabhadh gun fhreagairt. Bha fios aige gur h-éiginn-bhàis a bheireadh air Fionn a shéideadh. Thuig e gun robh an gnothach gu h-olc is thug e bòid is briathar air a chlaidheamh nach rachadh biadh no deoch thar 'anail gus an coibhreadh e air bràthair a mhàthar.

Thog e air e fhéin is a ghillean, is bu cham gach dìreach leotha thar chnoc is shloc. Is ge b' fhada bhuapa e, cha b' fhada ga ruighinn iad.

Fhuair iad Fionn 'na dheòiridh truagh gun chomas éirigh no suidhe am fasgadh tuim. Dh'fharraid Diarmaid dheth ciod a dh'fhairich e.

"Is coma sin," ars Fionn. Is dh'innis e dha gach car mar a thachair: mar a mharbh am Blàr Buidhe na gillean, agus an droch ghiullachd a fhuair e fhéin bhuaidhe. Is chomhairlich e dhasan tilleadh dhachaigh mun éireadh an cleas ceudna dha; gun robh esan mar a bhiodh e cia-dhiubh.

Bhòidich is bhriathraich Diarmaid nach tilleadh e gus an tugadh e a-mach an aicheamhail is gun tuilleadh a ràdh, thug e taigh a' Bhlàir Bhuidhe air.

Cha robh a-staigh ach a' bhean is i a' fuineadh. Thug i biadh is deoch dhaibh agus ghabh i an sgeul. Dh'innis i dhaibh gun robh am Blàr Buidhe 's a' bheinn-sheilg is gum b' fheàrr dhaibh a bhith falbh mun tigeadh e dhachaigh, no gun éireadh dhaibh mar a dh'éirich do dh'Fionn.

"A roghainn biodh dha," ars Diarmaid, "ach chan fhalbh sinn gus an toir sinn a-mach an aicheamhail."

Is shuidh iad a-staigh.

"Feith ri dheireadh, ma-tà," ars ise.

Cha robh iad ach goirid mar sin tràth a dh'fhairich iad stuirn-stairn aig an doras.

Có bha siud ach am Blàr is a ghillean, is torc nimhe mór fiaclach aige air a mhuin. Thug e togail bheag mhór air fhéin a chrathradh an t-sneachda dheth, 's chuir e crith fo'n ursainn is fo shuidheachan an taighe!

Ghlaodh e: "Tha mi a' faireachdainn fàilidh fharbhalach romham, a bhean. Có seo a th' agad a-nochd?"

Dh'innis a bhean gun robh Diarmaid is a chuid ghillean.

"A-mach do ghillean, a Dhiarmaid, a thoirt dhiom na h-eallaiche," ars am Blàr.

Leum Diarmaid e fhéin a-mach agus mun d'fhairich am Blàr thall no bhos e, mharbh e an darna leth dhe 'ghillean, is chuir e turach iad air taobh deas an dorais mu choinneamh gillean Fhinn!

"Is olc an t-aoigh thu," ars am Blàr.

"Mur faic thu nas miosa na siud dhiom mun tig an latha, na bith a' gearan," ars Diarmaid.

Is gun tuilleadh bruidhne, thug e a-staigh an torc. Ghréidh iad an torc gu math 's gu ro mhath, is ghabh e fhéin is a ghillean an leòr dheth. Gach cnàimh mar a lomadh iad, thilgeadh iad siud do'n Bhlàr is dha 'ghillean.

"Is olc an t-aoigh thu," ars am Blàr.

"Mur faic thu nas miosa na siud dhiom mun tig an latha, na bith a' gearan," ars Diarmaid.

Is dh'iarr e an t-ubhal a thoirt a-nuas gus an oidhche fhada gheamhraidh a chur seachad air a' Bhlàr Bhuidhe. Thug a bhean a-nuas an t-ubhal, agus thòisich an cleas. Air a' cheud tilgeadh a thug Diarmaid do'n ubhal, mharbh e dithis de na bh' air làimh dheis a' Bhlàir.

"Is olc an t-aoigh thu," ars am Blàr.

"Mur faic thu nas miosa na siud dhiom mun tig an latha, na bith a' gearan," ars Diarmaid.

Thilg am Blàr air ais an t-ubhal, ach cha d'rinn e dochann sam bith air gillean Dhiarmaid. Thug Diarmaid an t-ath-thilgeadh do'n ubhal is mharbh e dithis de na bh' air làimh chlì a' Bhlàir agus mar sin gus an do mharbh e am fear mu dheireadh dhiubh.

Is am Blàr gun tàmh ag ràdh, "Is olc an t-aoigh thu."

Agus amhuil sin, Diarmaid 'ga fhreagairt.

Mu'n uair a bha iad sgìth de chluich an ubhail òir, thuirt Diarmaid ris a' Bhlàr gum b' fheàrr dhaibh dol a chur car gleachd. Chaidh na fir a ghleachd. Is ma chaidh, cha robh an gleachd fad air chumail, tràth a bha am Blàr air claisneach a dhroma air leacan loma an ùrlair.

"Is olc an t-aoigh thu," ars am Blàr, is thug e cnead ghointe ás!

"Mur faic thu nas miosa na siud dhiom mun tig an latha, na bith a' gearan," ars Diarmaid, is dh'iarr e air a mhnaoi a' ghreideal a chur air gus an rachadh casan a' Bhlàir a gharadh gur cinnte gun robh e fuar an déidh tighinn dachaigh ás a' bheinn sheilg.

Chaidh a' ghreideal a dhèanamh dearg is thug Diarmaid togail do'n Bhlàr, is bha e an-siud 'na sgug buidhe air a' ghreideil!

"Oiteag, oit, oit," ars am Blàr.

"Gabh air do shocair e," ars Diarmaid, "creinidh do chnàimhean buidhe air mun cobhair mise ort."

Is chum e air a' ghreideil e gus an do loisg a chasan gu bun nan sléistean! Bha am Blàr a-nise gun chomas suidhe, agus ghrad-spàrr Diarmaid stob na feòla tro chòrn a dhà mhàis, is bha e an-sin gun chomas éirigh no suidhe. Is thilg e air shlisnich 's a' chùil e!

Tràth bha iad seachd sgìth ag éisteachd oiteagail a' Bhlàir, rug Diarmaid air sprogan air, is thuirt e, "Am bàs air do mhuin, a bhodaich. Ciod é t' éirig? Is tog dhiom brìgh do chluich."

"Oiteag, oit, oit!" ars am Blàr, "chan eil a dh'éirig agams', ach cuach ìocshlaint a tha am bun na creig ud thall, agus leighisidh i Fionn!"

Nuair a chuala Diarmaid mu'n chuaich, cha d'fhuirich e ri tuille chumhlaid iarraidh bu ro fhada leis a bha bràthair a mhàthar 'ga chuaradh aig bun an tuim, is chaidh e do'n uamha.

Thugar a' cheud làmh air a' chuaich, is buailear leatha gu Fionn. Ionnlaidear a chreuchdan aiste trì uairean. A' cheud uair, dh'fhàs a chasan gu ruig nan glùn; an dàrna h-uair, dh'fhàs iad gu ruig nan aobrann; is an treas uair, bha Fionn gun chron, gun chiùrram, cho beò slàn is a bha e riamh!

Rinn aon bhoiseag do dh'uisge na cuaiche geasan nan gillean a bhristeadh, is thug e am Blàr air.

"A chulaidh-thruais," ars Diarmaid ris, "bòidich nach iomair thu tuille de gheasan no 'chleasan air an Fhéinn."

Bhòidich am Blàr siud is ioma rud eile a bharrachd, is thug Diarmaid gu suairce dha fhéin is dha ghillean an dìol dh'uisge na cuaiche is ghabh iad an cead dheth chéile. A dhèanamh sgeula goirid dheth, lean a' chuach ris an Fhéinn is dh'fhàg mise aca i!

Diarmaid agus Gràinne

Nuair a bhiodh an Fhéinn a' folbh a shealg, bhiodh h-aon diubh daonnan a' fantail aig an taigh a choimhead nam ban. Thuit e air Diarmaid an latha ud gur h-e a dh'fhanadh. Bha rud ris an canadh iad "sùgh seirc" an aodann an duine 's bha clogad air nach fheumadh e thogail, chionn cha robh bean a chìtheadh an sùgh seirc nach tuiteadh ann an gaol air, is bha fios aig Diarmaid gun robh na buadhan seo air fhéin.

An latha a dh'fhan e aig an taigh, bha dùil aige nach robh neach 'ga fhaicinn, is thug e togail air a' chlogad, 's faicidh Gràinne nighean Rìgh Chóige Ullainn aodann Dhiarmaid. Cha bhiodh an t-anam blàth innte mur am falbhadh i le Diarmaid.

Arsa Diarmaid, "Cha fhreagair domhsa sin: falbh leatsa."

"O, falbhaidh sinn air neo sracaidh mi m' aodach is bheir mi suas thu do dh'Fhionn."

"Chan eil àicheadh agam ort nach creid e thu, chionn gur tu a bhean dhìleas fhéin, gu dearbh."

Dh'fhalbh iad, is bha e còmhla rithe trì làithean is trì oidhchean, ach bha e saor <aiste>. Dh'fhalbh iad air an aghaidh. Bha iad a' dol a-null air abhainn, is thog ise a h-aodach suas mum fliuchte i, 's dh'éirich breac beag an uair sin, is bhuail e suas air a sliasaid.

"Mo laochan thu fhéin, a bhric bhig bheadaidh! Uiread is a thug dhomh de thoil-inntinn, cha tug Diarmaid domh o cheann nan trì làithean is nan trì oidhchean a tha e leam. Is nam biodh tu air chomas falbh air tìr leam, bu choltach gur h-ann mar a bu lugha an duine a b' fheàrr e."

"Ma-tà," ars esan, "na dh'fhulaing mise air son geanmnaidheachd de thàmailt, chan fhulaing mi nas fhaide e."

[Dh'fhàgadh freagairt Gràinne ás]

"Tha Fionn a-nis," ars esan, "air tighinn dachaigh 's chan fhaigh iad sinn a-staigh. Thig iad an-sin air ar tòir is gheibh iad sinn."

"Chan fhaigh," ars ise. "Co-dhiù a gheibh no nach fhaigh, bheir sinn ionnsaigh air sinn fhéin 'fhalach. 'S e an rud a nì sinn, théid sinn do'n choille seo shuas 's falachaidh meanganan is duilleach na craoibhe sinn."

Dhìrich iad do'n chraoibh an-sin, is chaidh iad ann an cridhe na craoibhe, 's tharraing iad meanglain is duilleach na craoibhe mun cuairt orra.

Thàinig an Fhéinn ionnsaigh an taighe 's cha d'fhuair iad Diarmaid no Gràinne aig an taigh.

"Seo, seo, ghillean," ars Fionn, "tha mise gun bhean is tha an Fhéinn gun Dhiarmaid is còir duinn falbh gus am faigh sinn iad."

Dh'fhalbh iad air an tòrachd, is chaidh iad a-null air a' cheart abhainn. Nuair a chaidh iad a-null, ars Fionn, "Tha sinn an déidh treis-choiseachd a dhèanadh, is on a tha, leigidh sinn anail bheag aig bonn na craoibhe seo shuas."

Ghabh iad comhairle Fhinn is shuidh iad aig bonn na craoibhe.

Ars Fionn, "'S còir duinn teannadh ri cluiche, ghillean."

"Tha sinn deònach," ars iadsan.

B' àbhaist do dh'Fhionn is do dh'Osgar a bhith 'nan dà cheann stoc. 'S e Diarmaid daonnan a b' àbhaist a bhith còmhla ri Fionn. Bha fios aig Fionn gun robh buaidhean air Diarmaid aig cluichean. Bha nis Osgar agus dh'fheumadh e duine a bhith leis, agus 's e 'athair fhéin a b' àbhaist a bhith leis.

Thòisich iad a' cur nan cluichean. A h-uile cluiche a bha 'dol, 's ann air Fionn a bha e a' dol, is bha Osgar a' buidhinn. Chuir iad trì chluichean.

Ars Fionn, "Tha mi ag ionndrainn uam Dhiarmaid gu trom, chionn b' ainneamh leamsa cluich a dhol am aghaidh nuair a bhiodh Diarmaid leam. Ach tha iad a-nis a' dol am aghaidh on a dhealaich e rium. Ach théid mi uair eile riut."

Bha Diarmaid ag éisteachd. Dh'fhalbh e 's chuir e ri 'thaobh deas mar siud a làmh, is rug e air té de na caora dearga a bh' air a' chraoibh, is leig e sìos ris a' chraoibh i, 's druim Fhinn ris a' chraoibh. Dh'fhairich e rud a' bualadh air a dhruim, is chuir e a làmh air a chùlaibh, is rug e air a' chaora, 's chuir e 'na phòca i. Thòisich iad air cluiche 's chaidh an cluiche seo le Fionn.

"Tha h-aon agam," ars Fionn.

"Tha," ars Osgar, "ach tha a dhà gu d' dhìth."

"An téid thu tuilleadh ann?" ars Osgar.

"Théid, théid," ars Fionn. "Feuch a-rithis e."

Leig Diarmaid sìos an ath chaora 's bhuidhinn Fionn am fear seo.

"An téid thu ann tuilleadh?" ars e.

"Théid," ars Osgar. "Ma tha a dhà agad, tha fear gu d' dhìth."

Leig Diarmaid a-nuas an treas té agus bhuidhinn Fionn an treas fear.

"Tha sinn a-nis," ars Osgar, "cothrom is cothrom. Na bhuidhinn mi, thug thu fhéin air t' ais a-rithis e."

"An téid thu ann tuilleadh?" ars Fionn.

"Théid," ars Osgar. "Bidh fios a mhath no uilc againn air an t-siubhal seo."

Chaidh iad ann a-rithis. Leig Diarmaid a-nuas an ceathramh té, 's bhuidhinn Fionn.

"Ge b' e air bith mar a bha fad is a bha thusa gun Diarmaid leat, bha mise a' buidhinn. Ge b' e air bith mar a tha a' chùis, tha gnothaichean a bhoineas do Dhiarmaid mun cuairt ortsa an-diugh, mum bheil thu air buinig a' cheathramh uair.

Ars Oisean, "Cha do chuir m' athair oirnn, a mhic, le ceartas idir."

"Chuir," ars Fionn.

"Cha do chuir," ars Oisean.

"Chuir: a dhearbhadh gun do chuir, tha ceithir caoran ann am' phòca mu choinneamh a h-uile cluich a bhuidhinn mi."

Thug e a-mach na ceithir caoran, is nuair a thug e a-mach iad, thuirt e, "Thig a-nuas á sin, a Dhiarmaid, thu fhéin agus Gràinne, nighean Rìgh Chóige Ullainn, chionn tha sibh an-sin còmhla."

Thàinig Diarmaid agus Gràinne a-nuas. Roinneadh a' chuideachd ás ùr, is chaidh Fionn is Osgar thar a chéile. Thòisich na h-airm, is thòisich an sgath, 's bha iad a' dèanadh móran coire air a chéile. Bha a' chuid eile de'n Fhéinn a' faicinn gun robh Osgar a' brath buinig air taobh a sheanar.

Arsa Goll mac Morna, "Ged nach robh cuid againne de'n aimhreit, is còir dhuinn réite 's eadraiginn a dhèanadh eadar Clanna Treunmhor."

Ars Conan, "Leig le Clanna Baoisge cuirp a chéile a gheàrradh."

Thuirt Fionn an-sin ri Osgar casg a chur air armaibh, mum biodh Clann Morna fhathast 'nan déidh an Alba.

Thug Fionn aire do Dhiarmaid is thuirt e:

> Tha mo ghrunnd, is mo làmh, is mo shùil
> Deònach cùirt a dhèanadh dhuit;
> A Dhiarmaid O Duibhne, fhir thréin!
> Falbh le m' chéile gun fhios domh!

Bha boireannach ann ris an cainte Mala Lìth, 's bha speil mhuc aice, 's bha torc nimhe air an ceann, is chaidh iomadh gille math a shealg nach tàinig riamh slàn o'n torc.

Ars Fionn ri Diarmaid, "A Dhiarmaid, theirig a shealg an tuirc aig Mala Lìth air shealbh mhuc. Is iomadh fear a chaidh ann nach tàinig ás an allt thar bhreac."

Dh'fhalbh Diarmaid a shealg an tuirc.

Diarmaid agus Bran

Bha an Fhéinn latha a' sealg an Càrn na Béiste, cnoc cruinn àrd ann am monadh Ach' an Allt mu choinneamh an Uillt Dheirg, far an robh biast fhiadhaich ris an tuirteadh an torc nimhe a' còmhnaidh, agus on d'fhuair an càrn an t-ainm, 's mar an ceudna loch beag faisg air a' chàrn ris an canar Loch na Béiste.

Chunnaic an Fhéinn a' bhéiste 's a' chàrn, is chuir Fionn a chù Bran an aghaidh na béiste, ach nuair thàinig e faisg air an torc is a chunnaic e 'fhiamh oillteil fiadhanta, dhiùlt e aghaidh 'thoirt air, agus thill e air ais is 'fheaman 'na ghobhal.

Chuir Fionn air ais an darna uair e, ach nuair ràinig e mu choinneamh na béiste, cha rachadh e 'na còmhdhail idir. Thill e le geilt agus nàire a' sgugadh tro'n fhraoch gu cùl-coise a mhaighstir 'ga dhìon fhéin. Ach las corraich Fhinn, is thionndainn e air a' chù, 's thug e breab dha le 'chois air son a gheilteachd.

Thàr an cù ás le nàire 's tàmailt sìos le bruthach, gus an d'ràinig e lon an t-sratha air bruach na h-aibhne far an do chladhaich e toll dha fhéin 's an deachaidh e gu grad ás an t-sealladh, leis an tàmailt gun deachaidh a bhualadh.

Lean an Fhéinn air tòir a' choin, is nuair ràinig iad an toll, bha an cù á fradharc. Dh'fheuch iad a thàladh a-mach, ach cha fhreagradh e. Is nuair thug iad thairis a' feitheamh, thòisich iad air cladhach air a shon. Ach mar bu doimhne chladhaicheadh iadsan, is ann bu doimhne tholladh esan, gus fo dheireadh, dh'éirich an t-uisge orra 's b' éiginn dhaibh stad. Lìon an toll le uisge, is tha loch beag ann gus an latha an-diugh ris an abairear Loch Brain, is fhuair an srath uile an t-ainm Srath Bhrain o'n àm sin.

Phill an Fhéinn an-sin air an ais gus a' chàrn air tòir an tuirc a-rithis, is thug iad fhéin aghaidh air le'n cuid airm, is mharbhadh e le Diarmad.

Bha Diarmad 'na dhuine ro mhaiseach, is ball seirc air clàr 'aodainn a bheireadh air na h-uile boireannach a chitheadh am ball seirc tuiteam ann an trom ghaol air.

Bha Fionn ag eudach air air sgàth a mhnatha fhéin, is a' sireadh dòigh eigin air cur ás da gun a làimh fhéin a bhith ann.

Bha ball-dòbhrain air sàil chlì Dhiarmaid a bha ro leòntach, is b' fhiosrach Fionn air seo. Air an adhbhar sin, dh'àithn e dha a dhol a thomhas an tuirc gu mion air a dhruim an aghaidh nam frioghan. Ghon am frioghan nimheil am ball-dòbhrain, is thug an nimh bàs Dhiarmaid.

Calum Cille agus Dòbhran a Bhràthair

Thòisich Calum Cille air togail na h-Idhe. Chruinnich e móran sluagh. Ach na thogadh e air an latha, leagte air an oidhche e.

Bhuail e sin air daoine a chur a dh'fhaire na h-Idhe. A h-uile madainn, bhiodh iad sin marbh aig bonn na h-Idhe.

Cha do lean e fad air daoine a chur ann, ach bhon a bha e fhéin 'na dhuine naomh, chaidh e agus dh'fhan e a dh'fhaire na h-Idhe, feuch am faiceadh e no am faigheadh e ciod é a bha tighinn ceàrr oirre.

Bha e a' coimhead thuige agus bhuaidhe, agus bha iad ag ràdh gur ann air sgurr na creige, faisge air a' mhuir, a bha i (chan fhaca mise i). Chunnaic e biast a' tighinn bhàrr a' chladaich is an dala leth dhi 'na h-iasg agus an leth eile an coltas boireannaich. Bha i sean le slignich.

Nuair a chrath i i fhéin, chuir i crith air an Ì 's air an talamh. Leig i gliog dhith fhéin mar gum biodh pigeachan 'gan crathadh.

Chaidh Calum Cille sìos 'na coinneamh agus bhruidhinn e rithe agus dh'fhaigh-neachd e dhith am b' fhiosrach i gu dé bha a' marbhadh na daoine bha esan a' cur a dh'fhaire na h-Idhe anns an oidhche.

Thuirt i ris gum b' fhiosrach.

"Ciod a bha ag éirigh dhaibh?" ars e.

Thuirt ise nach robh sian ach an t-eagal a bha iad a' gabhail roimpe: nuair a bha i a' tighinn gu tìr gun robh an cridhe a' leum ás a' chochall aca.

"An fhiosrach dhuit," ars e, "ciod e a tha leagail na h-Idhe a tha mise a' togail?"

"Is fhiosrach," ars ise. "Bidh an Ì a' tuitim mar sin gu bràth, a Chaluim Chille nao-imh. Cha mhise a tha 'ga leigeil ach 'na dhéidh sin, thathar 'ga leagadh."

"An aithne dhuit a-nise an aon dòigh air an cuir mi air aghaidh an Ì?"

"Is aithne," ars ise. "A Chaluim Chille naoimhe, a-màireach cuiridh tusa ceist air na bheil de dhaoine 's an obair agad, feuch có am fear a dheònaicheas e fhéin a thìodhlacadh beò fo'n talamh, agus bidh 'anam sàbhailte ma dheònaicheas e sin a dhèanamh, agus chan fhaic iad mise seo gu bràth 'na dhéidh. Theid an Ì air adhart gun umhail sam bith."

An làrna-mhàireach, chuir e ceist air an t-sluagh mhór an robh a h-aon sam bith dhiubh a dheònaicheadh a thìodhlacadh beò air chumhnanta gum biodh 'anam sàbhailte ann am flathanas. Cha robh gin sam bith deònach gabhail dha'n t-sloc ged a bha e air innis gum biodh 'anam sàbhailte le òrdugh Dhia.

(Dh'innis ise dha cuideachd gum feumadh seachd fhaid dhoimhneachd a bhith 's an t-sloc.)

Bha Dòbhran bochd a bhràthair ann an iomall an t-sluaigh. Thàin' e a-nall agus sheas e air cùlaibh Chaluim Chille a bhràthair agus thuirt e gun robh esan uile dheònach a bhith air a thìodhlacadh uile bheò fo'n talamh air chumhnanta gun gabhadh an Ì togail do Chalum Cille a bhràthair naomh, agus e a' toirt creideas do Chalum Cille gum biodh 'anam sàbhailte le òrdugh Dhia.

Ars Calum Cille, "Ged nach eil bràthair agam ach Dòbhran bochd, tha mi toilichte gur e a dheònaich a dhol dha'n t-sloc. Agus nach motha na sin a chìte a' bhiast a' tighinn thun a' chladaich gu bràth."

Rinneadh an sloc seachd àirdead duine. Nuair a chunnaic Dòbhran an t-sloc, thi-onndaidh e ri Calum Cille 's dh'iarr e mar fhàbhar ceann a chur air an t-sloc agus esan 'fhàgail 'na sheasamh cho fada 's a thogradh Dia 'fhàgail beò.

Fhuair e iarrtas, a chur sìos beò dha'n t-sloc. Dh'fhàgadh an-seo e. Thàinig Calum Cille is thòisich e air an Ì 's bha e fichead là ag obair is bha an Ì a' dol air aghaidh uamha-sach. Bha e toilichte an gnothach a bhith dol leis.

Ann an ceann an fhichead latha, nuair a bha h-uile nì air thuairim a bhith dol air adhart gu math, thuirt e gum bu chòir sealltainn dé a' chrìoch a chaidh air Dòbhran bochd, agus an sloc 'fhosgladh.

Bha Dòbhran a' coiseachd air ùrlar an t-sluic. Nuair a chunnaic Dòbhran gun do dh'fhosgladh an t-sloc is a mhothaich e an saoghal gu léir mu choinneamh, thug e cru-inn-leum ás gu beul an t-sluic is chuir e 'dhà bhois air beul an t-sluic gu h-àrd. Chroch e e fhéin ris an t-sloc. Bha lèana mhór réidh suas o'n Ì agus móran luachrach oirre. Na chunnaic Dòbhran dhe'n luachar, dh'fhas e ruadh agus tha am bàrr beag ruadh sin air an luachar riamh.

Dh'éigh Calum Cille 's e thall: "Ùir, ùir, air sùil Dhòbhrain, mum faic e an còrr dhe'n t- saoghal is dhe'n pheacadh."

Chuir iad an ùir air agus thill iad a dh'ionnsaigh an cuid obrach. Is cha deachaidh car an aghaidh Chaluim Chille tuilleadh gus an d'fhuair e crìoch air an Ì.

Naoimh Chinn-Tàile

Bha triùir naomh ann an dùthaich Chinn-Tàile, triùir naomh urramach ainmeil: b' e Còmhghan Naomh Loch Aillse agus b' e Faolan Naomh Chill Fhaolain agus b' e Dubhthach Naomh Chinn-Tàile, dà thaobh Loch Dubhthaich.

Bha an triùir naomh 'nan càirdean gràdhach caoimhneil mar bu dual do naoimh a bhith. Bhiodh iad a' coinneachadh agus a' còmhradh, ag ùrnaigh agus a' cràbhadh, an-dràsta agus a-rithist. Bhiodh an triùir a' seanchas air dìomhaireachd na diadhachd agus air giamhachas a' pheacaidh, air staid nan saoidh ann an nèamh agus air cor nan daoidh ann an ifhrinn. Bha na daoine 'nan càirdean caomha anns gach dòigh mar bu chòir do chràbhaich agus do choimhearsnaich.

Ach latha dhe na làithean, gu dé mì-shealbhadh ach a choinnich a' bhò aig Naomh Còmhghan agus a' bhò aig Naomh Faolan ann an ceum cumhann a' chadha am bràigh a' bheàrraidh. Cha do sheachain té seach té an ceuma anns a' chadha chumhann agus, gun smid á bus, gun ghuth á beul mór, gun droch fhacal, am badaibh a chéile 'ghabh iad! Shabaidich agus charraidich iad ann an-sin fad finn foineach an tràth là ghil shamhraidh, gu greimil geanail mar bu dual do Ghàidheil a dhèanamh, bò no duine.

Mu dheireadh thall, anns a' charachd a bh' ann, chuir a' bhò aig Naomh Còmhghan a' bhò aig Naomh Faolan an comhair a cùil leis a' chreig chorraich os cionn amar na h-aibhne. Bha a' bhò 'na glog marbh: na spaidean agus a ceithir casan os a cionn ann an amar carach na h-aibhne.

Bha an ceòl feadh na fìdhle, a rùin, agus cha b' ioghnadh e, ach cha robh atharrach air.

Choinnich an dà naomh mu dhéidhinn na dà bhò, choinnich, a rùin, agus throid iad, throid gu dubh dona geur guineach searbh salach, a ghràidh, an dà naomh gheal mar dhà pheacach dhubh.

Bha Dubhthach a' strì ri sìth a dhèanamh eadar na daoine ach chan éisteadh iad ris agus cha bu diù leò a chainnt. Mar is minig a thachair do luchd eadraiginn, is ann bu bheag a thaing a dhol anns an làdar-miot a bh' ann.

Ghuidh Naomh Faolan mar fhàgail air Loch Aillse nach d'readhadh boinne mara, no breac buinne, a-suas air Nostaidh gu suthainn sìor. Agus cha deachaidh bho'n latha sin a chun an latha an-diugh: braon mara no breac buinne a-suas air abhainn Nostaidh.

Agus ghuidh Naomh Còmhghan mar fhàgail air Cill Fhaolain nach tigeadh pòr no piseach nan tonn toraidh gu bràtha air càraid a rachadh chum stòl pòsaidh ann an Cill Fhaolain. Agus cha tàinig riamh bho'n latha sin a chun an latha an-diugh: pòr no piseach nan tonn toraidh air càraid riamh a phòs ann an sgìre Chill Fhaolain.

Bho'n latha a throid an dà naomh a dh'ionnsaigh an latha a th' againn, d'uair tha dithis ann an Cill Fhaolain a' dol a phòsadh, is ann thig iad a-sìos bog balbh gu stòl pòsaidh aig ministeir Loch Aillse, no aig ministeir Chinn Tàile no aig sagart na Dòrnaidh. Cha phòs iad an Cill Fhaolain idir. Is cuimhne liom fhìn càraid a phòs ann an Cill Fhaolain agus cha tàinig tonn toraidh, pòr no piseach orra latha riamh. Is ann a chaochail iad le chéile an taobh a-staigh do cheann na bliadhna an déidh dhaibh pòsadh.

Is dona an troid! Is dona an troid, a rùin, aig naomh no aig nàbaidh, aig cràbhach no aig peacach. Och, a Mhoire nan gràs, is dona an troid!

An Caoineadh-Magaidh

Nuair a bha Tiriodh fo chumhachd nan Lochlannach, bha bean uasail Lochlannach (their muinntir an eilein gur h-i nighean Rìgh Lochlainn a bh' innte) a' fuireachd anns an eilean le a fear agus a dithist chloinne. Ged a bha i uasail, bha i air a shon sin fhéin 'na boireannach fuathasach crosta, agus bha na Tiristich fo mhór eagal roimpe. Ach ged a bha i de nàdar cho borb agus gun robh eagal aig na fir fhéin roimpe, bha gaol mór aice air a dithis chloinne, balach agus caileag.

Chan eil cuimhne agam a-nis ciamar a thachair dhi tighinn do Thiriodh an toiseach, co-dhiù am b' ann le a toil fhéin no ann an cuideachd a fir agus a dhaoine a ghabhail fasgaidh ro ànradh sìde (tha mi am beachd gur h-ann air son an adhbhair mu dheireadh a thàinig i ann), ach coma co-dhiù, ghabh i gaol mór do'n àite agus rinn i a dachaigh ann.

Cha do dh'iarr i an t-eilean fhàgail aig àm sam bith ged a bha a fear 'ga fàgail glé thric leatha fhéin nuair a bhiodh e a' falbh le a luchd-leanmhainn, feuch càite am faigheadh e creach ri thogail no daoine a mhort agus a mharbhadh, gus an do thuit aon latha air an tàinig fios cabhagach á Lochlainn ag iarraidh oirre tilleadh dhachaigh cho luath agus a b' urrainn dhi.

Co-dhiubh am b' ann o h-athair, an Rìgh, no o a fear a thàinig am fios, chan eil cuimhne agam a-nis, ach b' éiginn dhi falbh leis na h-uiread de chabhaig agus nach d'fhuair i cothrom air na pàistean a thoirt leatha, agus dh'fhàg i iad air cùram muinntir an eilein, ag earalachadh orra a h-uile cùram a b' urrainnear a ghabhail dhiubh agus a' maoidheadh orra nan éireadh beud sam bith dha'n chloinn gun diùladh a h-uile aon aca air a shon.

Bha na Tiristich glé thoilichte a bhith saor o'n Bhana-Lochlannach car ghreis, oir dh'fhuiling iad móran cruadail bhuaipe, ach bha iad deònach gu leòir deagh chùram a thoirt air a cloinn, oir tha e coltach gur h-e pàistean laghach a bh' annta agus gun robh spéis mhór aig muinntir an eilein dhaibh.

C'a b'e'r gu dé an t-adhbhar a thug a' Bhana-Lochlannach air falbh o Thiriodh, ghléidh e i nas fhaide na bha dùil aice agus bha còrr is dà bhliadhna air dol seachad mun do thill i a-rithist.

Beagan mun do thill i, chaochail an dà phàiste a dh'aindeoin gach cùram a fhuair iad o'n fheadhainn a bha 'sealltainn ás an déidh. Bha bròn gu leòr air na Tiristich air son bàs an dà phàiste, ach bha iomagain nas mó orra air son na dh'fhaodadh tachairt dhaibh fhéin nuair a thilleadh am màthair.

Tha e coltach gur h-ann toiseach an t-samhraidh a thill a' Bhana-Lochlannach. Mun do ràinig i an t-eilean, fhuair na Tiristich fios air dhòigh air choireigin gun robh i aig làimh, agus thuit eagal mór orra, oir bha iad cinnteach mur an rachadh bacadh air choireigin a chur air a fearg nuair a chluinneadh i mu bhàs a dà leinibh, nach fhàgadh i taigh no aitreabh gun a chreach is gun a losgadh, no duine no creutair gun a mhort no gun a mharbhadh.

Uime sin, nuair a chualas gun robh a' Bhana-Lochlannach a' dlùthachadh ris an eilean, chruinnich a h-uile duine de mhuinntir an eilein an ceann a chéile, feuch an rachadh aca air seòl sam bith 'fhaotainn chum fearg na Bana-Lochlannaich a sheachnadh.

An déidh dhaibh ioma comhairle a chluinntinn agus a dhiùltadh, thàinig seann fhear liath air adhart agus thuirt e nach robh e gu feum sam bith dhaibh feuchainn ri iad fhéin a dhìon le fearas-airm, gun robh na Lochlannaich gu mòr na b' fheàrr air an armachadh agus gun robh iad nas ionnsaichte ann an cogadh na bha na Tiristich, agus a dh'aindeoin gach euchd a dh'fhaodadh iad a dhèanadh, gun rachadh am mort agus am milleadh aig a' cheann mu dheireadh.

"A luchd dùthcha," ars esan, "tha mi a' smaointinn, ged a tha sinn fo mhór eagal air son na dh'fhaodas tachairt dhuinn air tàilleibh bàs dà leinibh nighinn Rìgh Lochlainn, tha mi an dùil nach eil aon againn nach eil a' caoidh an dà leanabh bhòidheach a shiubhail, a chionn is e pàistean laghach a bh' annta, agus bha gaol mór againn uile orra, agus tha fhios is cinnte aig a h-uile neach a tha làthair an-seo an-diugh nach do dhiùlt sinn riamh dhaibh nì sam bith a bheireadh sòlas dhaibh fhad is a bha iad leinn, agus nach do chaomhainn sinn nì sam bith a dhèanadh feum dhaibh nuair a bha iad tinn, agus gum bheil ar cridheachan air an lìonadh le bròn a chionn gun do shiubhail iad. Nis, a chàirdean, tha mise a' smaointinn nam b' urrainn sinn am bròn a tha sinn a' faireachdainn a leigeil ris do'n Bhana-Lochlannach ann an dòigh a dhrùidheadh air a h-inntinn agus air a cridhe gum faodamaid tilleadh a thoirt air a corraich agus gum faigheamaid saor ás a' chàs anns am bheil sinn. Uime sin, is e a tha mise a' comhairleachadh dhuibh gun cruinnich sinn a dh'ionnsaigh a' phuirt aig an tig i air tìr gach mart agus laogh, gach caora agus uan, anns an dùthaich, agus gun sgair sinn bho chéile iad, na mairt agus na caoraich air aon chnoc agus na laoigh agus na h-uain air cnoc eile, far am faic iad a chéile ach far nach faigh iad a chòir a chéile, agus tha mise a' cur mo cheann an geall gun cluinnear an-sin tuireadh a dhrùidheas air cridhe na Bana Lochlannaich, ged a bhiodh e nas cruaidhe na a' chreag air am bheil an t-eilean seo stéidhichte."

Ghabh na Tiristich ri comhairle an t-seann duine, agus fada mun d'ràinig long na Bana-Lochlannaich port, bha i air a lìonadh le ioghnadh agus le iomagain mhóir leis a' chaoineadh mhuladach a bha i a' cluinntinn air tìr.

Cho luath agus ràinig an long am port, chuir a' Bhana-Lochlannach fios air seanairean an eilein agus dh'fharraid i dhiubh dé bu chiall do'n chaoineadh seo a bha i a' cluinntinn on thàinig i ann an sealladh air tìr?

Fhreagair fear de na seanairean i gun tàinig call mór air an eilean o chionn ghoirid, call cho mór agus cho muladach agus gun robh na creutairean fhéin ann an co-fhaireachdainn ris na daoine air a shon.

Chuir an fhreagairt seo am barrachd ioghnaidh air a' Bhana-Lochlannach agus nuair a dh'amhairc i mun cuairt oirre agus a chunnaic i cho tùrsach brònach a bha gach coltas, thuirt i gu coibhneil gun robh i duilich air son a' chall a thàinig orra agus nan rachadh aice-se air nì sam bith a dhèanamh chum am bròn a thogail, gum biodh i ro thoilichte a dhèanamh.

Ghabh na seanairean an-sin misneach agus ann am briathran ciùin agus stòlda, dh'innis iad dhi mar a thachair do'n dà leanabh a dh'fhàg i ás a déidh, mar a thuit iad aon ás déidh a chéile ann an tinneas, mar a chaidh gach leigheas a b' urrainnear fhaotainn fheuchainn chum slàinte aisig air ais dhaibh, agus mu'n bhròn a thuit air muinntir an eilein nuair a chaochail iad.

Fada mun do sguir an seanair d'a iomradh, bha a' Bhana-Lochlannach a' caoidh is a' tuireadh mar gum bristeadh i a cridhe, agus an àite mort agus milleadh a dhèanamh air na Tiristich, mar a mhaoidh i nuair a dh'fhàg i, is ann a thug i taing agus beannachadh dhaibh air son an coibhneis d'a cloinn.

Innis Eabhrach

Tha an Innis Eabhrach, a-réir beul-aithris, 'na eilean a tha fo dhrùidheachd, agus 'na laighe fo'n fhairge dlùth do dh'Eilean an Iarainn a-mach o thràigh Choire Chraoibhidh. Air uairean, bhiodh e an sealladh cho soilleir is gum faicteadh na h-adagan arbhair air na h-achaidhean, agus na mnathan a' cur an luideagan a-mach air thiormachadh.

Tha e nis mu leth-cheud bliadhna bhon chunnacas mu dheireadh e. Aon latha, air do thuathanach a bhith mach ag amharc ás déidh a spréidh, dé chunnaic e ach an t-eilean ag éirigh ás an fhairge dlùth do'n chladach, agus a chum is gum faigheadh e sealladh a b' fheàrr dheth, ruith e thun a' chladaich.

Car tiotan chaill e sealladh air an fhairge ann an lagan tro'm b' éiginn da siubhal, agus air dha an àirde ruigheachd bho'm faiceadh e a' mhuir, cha robh an t-eilean r'a fhaicinn—chaidh e ás an t-sealladh gu buileach.

Air do bhàta Arannach aon uair a bhith fàgail ceadha Ionar Àir, agus dìreach mun do sheòl i, tha e air a ràdh gun tàinig duine àraidh—coigreach—le lothag ghlas air taod, ag iarraidh turas-mara.

Thug an sgiobair air bòrd iad, is chuireadh am bàta mach gu fairge. Nuair a thàinig iad dlùth do dh'Eilean an Iarainn, thòisich an lothag ri sitrich, agus chualas sitreach eile 'ga freagairt o dhoimhne na fairge.

An-sin dh'iarr an coigreach air an sgiobadh a tilgeil thar an taobh, agus air dhaibh sin a dhèanadh, thug e cruinn-leum ás a déidh agus chaidh iad, ar-aon, ás an t-sealladh.

Bliadhna 'na dhéidh seo, có a thachair air an sgiobair aig margadh Ionar Àir ach an duine ceudna do'n tug e turas-mara.

"Chunnaic mi thusa roimhe seo," ars an sgiobair.

"Ma chunnaic," ars an duine, "chan fhaic thu fear eile gu bràth," agus am priobadh na sùla, thugar sgailc le 'bhois do'n sgiobair 's an aodann, 'ga fhàgail dubh dall.

Tha e air a ràdh gun cluinneadh na h-iasgairean, 's iad a' feitheamh an lìontan a thogail, air oidhchean ciùin sàmhach, crònan tiamhaidh ciùil agus ranntachd òran ag éirigh suas á Innis Eabhrach, mar seo:

Càit an d'fhàg sibh na fir gheala, Ho ró 's golaidh u lé
Dh'fhàg sinn iad 's an eilean mhara. Ho ro 's golaidh u lé
Cùl ri cùl is iad gun anail, Ho ró 's golaidh u lé

Mas fìor an sgeul, thàinig tuathanach a bha an Cille Phàdair aon latha air maighdean-mhara á Innis Eabhrach agus i 'na suain chadail air an tràigh, 's a cochall-drùidheachd ri 'taobh.

Rinn e greim air a' chochall agus ghabh e a rathad thun a thaighe, 's cha robh aic' air ach gum b' éiginn dhi dhol leis. Thàinig iad a-réir a chéile cho math 's gun do phòs iad, agus bha mac is nighean aice dha.

Seachd bliadhna 'na dhéidh sin, air dha bhith anns an eaglais air là sàbaid àraidh, agus air tilleadh dhachaigh, cha robh a bhean air thoiseach air.

'S e bh' ann gun robh na pàistean ri cleasachd anns an t-sabhal, agus thàinig iad tarsainn air rud a chuir ioghnadh orra. 'Nan deann-ruith, chaidh iad thun am màthar a' glaodhaich "A mhàthair! A mhàthair! Thigibh agus faicibh an rud bòidheach a tha aig m' athair falaichte anns a' chùil-mhosain."

Is math a thuig am màthair dé an "rud bòidheach" a bh' ann, agus thuirt i ris a' chloinn, "Thoiribh a-steach an-seo e agus bheir mise ceapaire math òrdaig dhuibh."

Rinn na pàistean mar dh'iarradh orra, agus mar bha dùil aice, 's e an cochall-drùidheachd a bh' ann da-rìreabh. Rinn i greim air a' chochall, is cha luaithe fhuair i 'na làmhan e na thugar aiste gus a seann dachaigh anns a' mhuir.

Air uairean, thigeadh i gu Rudha an Lòin a' gairm air a pàistean, agus chunnacas iad 'na cuideachd is i a' cìreadh am fuilt agus a' seinn dhuanagan daibh.

Aon latha, lean am balachan a mhàthair air a' mhuir, agus chan fhacas sealladh tuilleadh dheth, ach thill a' chaileag dachaigh. Dh'fhas i suas 'na h-inghinn eireachdail, phòs i, agus a-réir an sgeòil, tha cuid d'a sliochd an làthair gus an là an-diugh.

An Gobhainn Mór

Bha roimhe seo duine àraidh ann am Poll Mhàilidh ris an canadh sluagh "an Gobhainn Mór." Bha seachd mic aig a' Ghobhainn, agus bha e fhéin is a chuid mac cho maith air inneil airm a dhèanadh ri duine a bhuail riamh òrd air innean. Gu h-àraidh bha cliù orra air son na claidheamhan fuar-iarann a rinn iad. Bha na claidheamhan seo air an dèanadh gun teine idir, le teas a chur 's an iarann le buillean nan òrd.

Agus bha meas mór aig na Gàidheil orra a thaobh is gun do lean buaidh mhór iad. Chan e a-mhàin gun robh cliù air a' Ghobhainn Mhór mar ghobhainn, ach is mór an cliù a bh' air fhéin is a sheachd mac mar laoich.

Bha crodh aig a' Ghobhainn ann am Poll Mhàilidh a bha air leth brèagha, ach ann an ùine ghoirid, dh'fhàs iad cho bochd is gun gann a dh'éireadh iad 's a' bhàthaich. Is a dh'aindeoin na gheibheadh iad ri ithe, cha ghabhadh iad coltach ni b' fheàrr.

Faisg air Poll Mhàilidh tha Tòrr na Sìdh, torran bòidheach a bha, ann an làithean a' ghobhainn, 'na àite còmhnaidh aig na sìdhichean. Tha iad a' cur air a' ghobhainn gun robh sìdheach 'na leannan aige ged a bha 'bhean beò.

Là air an robh e fhéin is ise 's a' choille, dh'innis i dha gun do ghoid na sìdhichean an crodh brèagha, agus gum b' iad crodh sìdh a bha nise 's a' bhàthaich.

Ann am fearg mhór, rinn an gobhainn air a' bhàthaich agus thòisich e air a' chrodh leis an tuagh. Ach ann am priobadh na sùil, thug iadsa an cinn á na buailidhean agus mach ás a' bhàthaich a ghabh iad.

Rinn an gobhainn greim cruaidh air earball na bà fo dheireadh agus lean e rithe gus an tàinig iad gu Càrn an Ràth ann am Beinn a' Gharbhlaich, faisg air Achadh na Bà Bàine. Dh'fhosgail an càrn agus chaidh an crodh a-staigh. Agus ma chaidh, lean an Gobhainn gus an tàinig e gu seòmar àlainn anns an robh gach nì bu luachmhor na chéile. Agus chaidh iarraidh air an nì bu docha leis ainmeachadh is gum faigheadh e e.

Ann an oisean uaigneach de'n t-seòmar bha loth bheag pheallagach air an cuala an Gobhainn a leannan sìdh a' bruidhinn mar an loth a b' fheàrr 's an rìoghachd. Agus thuirt e gun gabhadh e an loth.

"Fiacail á beul t' iompaidh," ars na sìdhichean, oir dh'aithnich iad gun d'fhuair e comhairle mhaith. Ach thug iad an loth dha, le àithne gun a cur an cairt gu bràth, oir fhad is a chumadh e ann an crann i, nach biodh loth eile 's an tìr a threabhadh rithe:

Threabhadh i Achadh nam Bò,
Is an Lurga Mhór bho cheann gu ceann;
Mar sin is an Gortan Ceapagach
Mun leigeadh i ás an crann!

Bha an loth pheallagach iomadh là aig a' Ghobhainn Mhór, agus b' fheumail i dha fhéin is dha muinntir na dùthcha gu léir. Ach mu dheireadh, chaidh lòban a chur oirre a dh'innearadh. Agus riamh an déidh sin, cha robh i nì bu treise na loth eile.

Bha seachd mic a' ghobhainn a' cadal anns an t-sabhal air cnoc ris an abairear fhathast Torran nan Gillean. Bha nighean a' Ghobhainn pòsta aig fear air an robh Gille Phàdraig Gobha mar ainm. Anns na làithean sin, thachair dha Camshronach 'mharbhadh ann an Loch Abar agus theich e gu Urchadan, far an d'fhuair e obair ann an ceàrdaich a' Ghobhainn Mhóir.

Chuala Mac Dhòmhnaill Duibh gun robh am mortair 's a' ghleann, agus chuir e daoine a dhèanadh greim air.

Nuair a chuala an Gobhainn gun tàinig na h-Abaraich, thug e air an duine air an robh iad an tòir 'fhalt agus 'fheusag a gheàrradh. Thàinig na h-Abaraich 'na cheàrdaich a dh'fhaighneachd air son an duine, a bha aig an àm buaileadh an ùird.

"Buail an t-òrd, a Ghille Mhaoil," ars an Gobhainn.

Bhuail an Gille Maol an t-òrd mar fhìor ghobhainn agus cha d'aithnich na daoine e. Thill iad dhachaigh agus dh'innis iad nach do theach an turas leò. Greis an déidh seo, fhuair Mac Dhòmhnaill Duibh a-mach gum b' e am fear air an robh e an tòir a bha da-rìribh 's a' Ghille Mhaol, agus lasadh 'fhearg an aghaidh a' ghobhainn agus sluagh a' ghlinne. Agus chuir e roimhe sgiùrsadh a thoir orra!

Thàinig e fhéin agus moran sluaigh, agus ghlac iad Caisteal Urchadain. Bha an-seo an dùthaich fo 'chasan ach an gobhainn is a chuid mac, agus cha robh 'chridhe aige feuchainn riuthsa le sabaid. Agus smuainich e gun gabhadh e dòigh eile.

Chuir e fios air Gille Phàdraig Gobha, cliamhainn a' ghobhainn, agus gheall e dha nam faigheadh e seòl air an gobhainn is a mhic a chur gu bàs, gum faigheadh e talamh a' ghobhainn ann am Poll Mhàilidh.

"Tagh buidheann dhe na fir is tapaidh a th' agad," ars Gille Phàdraig Gobha, "agus leanadh iad mise am meadhan na h-oidhche nochd."

Mar sin a bha, agus dh'fhàg an Gille agus na h-Abaraich an Caisteal am meadhan oidhche, agus rinn iad air an t-sabhal 's an robh mic a' ghobhainn, a' smuaineachadh nam faigheadh iad cur ás daibh-se, gum biodh e farasta an seann ghobhainn a chur gu bàs.

Sheas cuid diubh aig doras an t-sabhail, agus chaidh an còrr a-staigh agus bhuail iad air na gillean. Dh'fheuch na gillean ri faighinn mach, ach mar a bha iad dol thairis air starsainn an dorais, bha na h-Abaraich a' cur nan eanchann ásta le cabair.

Nuair a bha an obair seo aig an t-sabhal, bha bean a' ghobhainn a' faicinn bruadar gun robh muc mhór dhubh, is cuain chuilean aice, a' bùrach fo clach-bhuinn an taigh. Chunnaic i am bruadar seo trì uairean agus an-sin dhùisg i an gobhainn, is thug i air a dhol gus an t-sabhal a dh'fhaicinn ciamar a bha na gillean.

Thug an gobhainn an claidheamh mór aige leis, agus air dha tighinn gus an t-sabhal agus na h-Abaraich 'fhaicinn, thòisich e orra. Theich iadsa, agus lean esa, a' marbhadh air na h-uile beum. Bha e a' dèanamh gu cruaidh air a chliamhainn, agus nuair a chunnaic an gealtair sin seo, thòisich e air éigheachd, "Is mi fhéin a th' ann! Is mi fhéin a th' ann!"

"Tha fios agam gun tu fhéin a th' ann," fhreagair an gobhainn.

Mu dheireadh, rug an gobhainn air a chliamhainn air dhaibh bhith 'dol thairis air allt ris an abairear fhathast Allt Gille Phàdraig Gobha agus gheàrr e a chluais de.

"Sin litir agad," ars esa, "a bheir thu dha Mac Dhòmhnaill Duibh, agus innis dha gum bi mise aig mo bhiadh-maidne a-màireach cuide ris."

An-sin thill e gus an t-sabhal agus fhuair e a chuid mac marbh, ach am fear a b' òige. Chaidh druim an fhir seo a bhristeadh, agus riamh an déidh sin, chaidh e fo'n ainm "an Gobha Crom."

Ghabh an Gobhainn Mór bàs a mhic cho mór gu cridhe, is gun do chaochail e an ùine ghoirid. An déidh a bhàis, chuir an Gobha Crom a chuid acfhainn air srathair Ghàidhealach air muin each, agus dh'fhàg e Urchadan, ag ràdh gun stadadh e far am bristeadh an t-srathair. Cha do bhrist an t-srathair gus an d'ràinig e Peart.

Anns a' bhaile sin, thog e ceàrdaich, agus tha muinntir Urchadain a' cumail a-mach gum b' e an Gobha Crom a bha 's an t-sabaid fhuilteach a bh' eadar Clann Dhaibhidh is Clann Chatain an làthair an Rìgh, air Innis Pheairt, 's a' bhliadhna 1396.

Tha feadhainn gus an là an-diugh ann an Urchadan a tha a' creidsinn gur h-ann dhe sliochd a' Ghobhainn Mhóir a tha iad, agus tha e air a ràdh gur h-ann bho'n Ghille Mhaol a thàinig Clann 'ic Ille Mhaoil a tha 's a' Ghleann.

Calum Garbh mac Eòghainn

Bha e uaireigin roimhe seo 'na fhasan ann an Gàidhealtachd na h-Alba, tràth thigeadh droch chòrdadh sam bith eadar dithis de na fineachan, gun rachadh an darna h-aon agus thogadh e creach o fhearann an aoin eile.

Rachadh tòir a chur air an déidh, agus bu tric a chuireadh luchd na creiche 's an tòir cath.

Thàinig aon uair buidheann de cheatharnaich o Shuaineart, agus thug iad air falbh creach ás an Eilean Leamhaineach.

Anns an àm sin, is e Triath an Araire a bha a' togail a' mhàil duibh anns an Eilean Leamhaineach. Agus bha mar fhiachaibh air, nan rachadh beathaichean air bith a ghoid anns an Eilean, gum pàigheadh e air an son, air neo, am faotainn a-rithist is an toirt a dh'ionnsaigh na feadhnach do'm buineadh iad.

Nan rachadh creach a thogail ás an Eilean, bha e mar fhiachaibh air Triath an Araire a' chreach a thilleadh, air neo, beathaichean eile a chur 'nan àite. Chuir Triath an Araire buidheann de a dhaoine a thilleadh na creich agus is e Calum Garbh MacEóghainn e bu cheannard orra.

Lean Calum Garbh is a dhaoine na ceatharnaich gus gun deach iad seach Taigh an Droma, Leac an Dogha aig Bràigh Ghlinn Urchaidh, agus Inbhir Dhobhrain. Agus fhuair iad na beathaichean air aodann beinne ag itheadh feòir, is gun a h-aon air bith a' toirt an aire orra. Bha na Camshronaich á Suaineart 'nan cadal.

Chaidh Calum Garbh is a dhaoine mun cuairt air na bà, agus dh'iomain iad an crodh air an ais gu dol dachaigh leò. Agus tràth bha iad aig àite do'n ainm Leac an Dogha, sheall fear de dhaoine Chaluim Ghairbh air ais agus chunnaic e na Camshronaich a' tighinn air an déidh.

Bha na Camshronaich 'nan cadal tràth thàinig MacEóghainn is a dhaoine, 's an uair a thug iad air falbh an crodh. Agus an uair a dhùisg iad, cha robh an crodh far an d'fhàg siad iad.

Sheall iad air an son, agus chunnaic iad daoine MhicEóghainn is an crodh aca air thoiseach orra, is iad an àird ri aodann Leac an Dogha aig Bràigh Ghlinn Urchaidh. Lean na Camshronaich iad.

Is e duine anabarrach euchdach do'm b' ainm Maol Onfhaidh a bha 'na cheannard air na Camshronaich, agus chuala e iomradh air Calum Garbh MacEóghainn, agus bha e ro thoilichte 'fhaicinn, agus feuchainn có e an laoch bu tréine dhiubh.

Air do dh'fhear de dhaoine Chaluim Ghairbh MhicEoghainn sealladh a thoirt mun cuairt ás a dhéidh, chunnaic e Maol Onfhaidh agus a dhaoine a' tighinn air an déidh, agus thuirt e ri Calum Garbh, "Siud bratach nan Camshronach a' tighinn air 'nar déidh, is i geal."

Thuirt Calum Garbh, "Mas geal a tha, is dearg a bhios mun till i."

Bha Calum Garbh air cluinntinn iomradh air Maol Onfhaidh, agus bha e ro thoilichte 'fhaicinn, agus gum biodh fios aca có e an gaisgeach bu tréine dhiubh.

Dh'fharraid Calum Garbh có iad na daoine tapaidh a dh'fhalbhadh leis a' chrodh, is gum fuireadh càch aig Leac an Dogha, a thoirt aghaidh air na Camshronaich, is 'gan cumail air an ais.

Cha robh a h-aon air bith toileach falbh leis a' chrodh, air eagal is gun abairteadh cladhairean riu. Fhuair Calum Garbh móran dragh ri a dhaoine, mum faigheadh e feadhainn a dh'fhuireadh leis a' chrodh.

Mu dheireadh, thuirt Calum Garbh gum b' iad an dà dhuine bu shine a bha anns a' bhuidhinn a bha gu dol a dh'iomain a' chruidh air falbh, agus nam biodh feum orra gun robh iad gu tighinn air an ais gu còmhnadh a dhèanamh ris an fheadhainn a bhiodh a' cur a' chath.

Ach b' fheudar croinn a chur agus thuit na croinn air dithis de na daoine bu shine bha 's a' chuideachd. Dh'fhalbh iad a dh'iomain air falbh a' chruidh.

Ach sheas iad air fàireamh, a bha ann an sealladh an àite far an robh an cath ri a chur. Tràth thàinig na Camshronaich air an adhart, cha leigeadh na Pàrlanaich seachad iad, agus thòisich an cath.

Chog iad cho borb is gun do thuit a h-uile duine a bha air an àrfhaich ach Maol Onfhaidh e fhéin. Agus cha robh e leònta. Bha e a' dol air ais is air adhart air feadh na h-àrfhaich ag iarraidh Chaluim Ghairbh. Ach chan innseadh a h-aon air bith de na daoine aig Calum Garbh có e.

Mu dheireadh, ràinig Maol Onfhaidh far an robh Calum Garbh e fhéin 'na laigh. Agus dh'fharraid Maol Onfhaidh de Chalum Garbh an robh Calum Garbh MacEóghainn 'na laigh anns an àrfhaich sin.

Thuirt Calum Garbh gun robh.

Thuirt Maol Onfhaidh gum bu toigh leis 'fhaicinn agus dh'fharraid se càite an robh e.

Thuirt Calum Garbh gun robh pathadh mór air, agus nam faigheadh e deoch gun leigeadh e 'fhaicinn càite an robh Calum Garbh.

Thuirt Maol Onfhaidh nach robh dòigh aige fhéin air deoch 'fhaotainn da ann, nach robh gogan aige.

Bha Calum Garbh 'na laigh, agus troigh na coise geàirrte dheth, agus bha bròg air a chois.

Chum Calum Garbh a chorrag rithe, agus thuirt e, "Thoir an ceap ás a' bhròig agus thoir dhomh deoch ás an t-sruthan ud thall," is e a' sìneadh a làimhe an taobh a bha an sruthan.

Thug Maol Onfhaidh cas Chaluim Ghairbh ás a bhròig, is chaidh e chun taobh an t-sruthain leis a' bhròig, 's thòisich e air nigheadh na fala di, a chum is gun tugadh e deoch de dh'uisge glan chun an duine.

Tràth bha esan 'ga dhèanamh sin, dh'éirich Calum Garbh air a leth ghlùin; agus chuir e saighead 'na bhogha, 's chum e an t-saighead ri Maol Onfhaidh.

Tharraing e an t-sreang, is leig e an t-saighead ri Maol Onfhaidh agus bhuail an t-saighead e mu'n chaol druim.

Tràth mhothaich Maol Onfhaidh an t-saighead 'ga ghuin, chuir e a làmh air a chùlaibh far an do bhuail an t-saighead e.

Ghlaodh Calum Garbh ris, "Ha hó, a chompanaich, iarr air an taobh eile dhiot i. Nuair a leigeas Calum Garbh saighead á bogha, is ann air an taobh is faide uaidhe de'n chomharra a gheobhar i."

Tràth a chuala Maol Onfhaidh sin, tharraing e an claidheamh, agus chaidh e far an robh Calum Garbh. Bha a chlaidheamh tarraingte deas aig Calum Garbh a' feitheamh ris, tràth a thigeadh e. Chòmhraig an dithis ri chéile, agus reub iad a chéile leis na claidheamhnan, gus an do thuit an dithis làimh ri chéile. Cha robh an-sin air an casan de na daoine, ach an dithis a dh'fhalbh leis a' chrodh.

Cha robh aig an dithis sin air, ach fear a dhol le sgeul chun nan càirdean, is am fear eile a dh'fhuireachd a thoirt an aire air na daoine leònta, gus gun tàinig daoine a rinn cobhair orra.

Chaidh na daoine marbha adhlac ann an-sin, agus na daoine leònta a thoirt dachaigh. Chaidh Calum Garbh a thoirt gu Stuc na Cloiche, taobh Loch Laomainn anns an Arar, ach cha d'fhuair mi sgeul ciod e mar a dh'éirich do na Camshronaich a bha leònta air an àrfhaich.

Fionnlagh Dubh MacRath

Bha sealgair ainmeil a' tàmh an Geàrrloch an Siorramachd Rois d'am b' ainm Fionnlagh Dubh MacRath. Bha e a' chuid mhór d'a ùine 'na fhear gléidhidh an fhrìth aig MacCoinnich, ach ri linn marbhaidh anns an robh làmh aige, dh'fhàg e seirbhis MhicCoinnich agus thog e ri saor-shealg air a làimh fhéin air chor is gum b' e sealgair is fearcoille cho ainmeil is a bha riamh 's a' Ghàidhealtachd.

'S ann air na muirt eagalach a chuir e an gnìomh air am bheil mi am beachd iomradh a thoirt an ceartair, ged a rinneadh iomad gnìomh eile leis air am b' fhiach iomradh a thoirt.

Anns an àm anns an robh Fionnlagh an seirbhis MhicCoinnich, bha saor-shealgair a' tàmh an Loch Abar d' am b' ainm Dòmhnall Mór MacUalraig. Bha an duine seo a' dol air astar mór a shealg nam fiadh. Bu mhinig leis dol eadhan cho fada ri frìth MhicCoinnich agus fiadh no dhà a chur 'na shìneadh 's an fhraoch gun fhios do dh'Fhionnlagh Dubh, furachail g'an robh e.

Air a' cheann mu dheireadh, bha a' Bhaintighearna, bean MhicCoinnich, a' cur umhail gun robh tanachadh a' tighinn anns na féidh. Agus aon latha dh'iarr i air Fionnlagh falbh is beagan sìthne fhaotainn "ma bha fiadh air fhàgail 's an dùthaich."

Ghon na briathran Fionnlagh gu ruig an cridhe 's thog e ri monadh. Ach cha deach e fada air aghaidh nuair a thàinig e air fear an lagan ri gualainn na beinne 's e a' greallachadh féidh. Tharraing e na bu dlùithe dha agus cha robh aon eile an-seo ach Dòmhnall Mór MacUalraig á Loch Abar.

"Is leatsa an t-sealg ach is leamsa an t-sitheann," arsa Fionnlagh, agus briathran a bhana-mhaighstir fhathast a' seirm 'na chluasan.

"Is leamsa an t-sealg. Is bu luath mo cheum 'na dàil is MacCoinnich 's a ghillean gun éirigh," arsa Dòmhnull Mór, "agus bidh an t-sitheann leis an fhear aig an fheàrr còir oirre."

Gun an còrr màille bha an dà dhiùlnach am badaibh a chéile, 's co-dhiù am b' ann le tuiteamas no ciamar a thachair e, chaidh biodag Fhionnlaigh Dhuibh an Dòmhnall Mór gu ruig an cridhe, 's thuit e air an raon gun deò.

Dh'fhalaich Fionnlagh an corp 's an fhraoch is thug e 'aghaidh air a' chaisteal le fiadh Dhòmhnaill Mhóir. Ach bu bheag fios a bh' aige air an dosgainn a bha gu mosgladh á obair an latha sin, nuair a leag e am fiadh air beulaibh na baintighearna.

Chuir e iongantas oirrese ciamar a sheilg is a mharbh Fionnlagh e cho luath. Ach dh'innis esan mar a thachair is gun robh Dòmhnall Mór fuar marbh air fhalach anns an fhraoch.

"Ma-tà," ars ise, "ged is mise b' adhbhar air, tha cho math dhuitsa teicheadh, oir dh'fhàg MacUalraig 'na dhéidh an Loch Abar na bheir a-mach dìoghaltas."

'S e sin a rinn Fionnlagh. Thug e air cho fada ri Srath Fàrair far an do thog e bothan dha fhéin is d'a mhnaoi agus 'na dhéidh sin thug e leis a bhràthair is mac a bhràthar a dh'fhuireach còmhla riu, agus theann iad ri beagan àitich a dhèanamh maille ri seilg is iasgach. Is cha robh dìth no deireas orra car tamaill.

Ach aon latha, air do Fhionnlagh tighinn dhachaigh thar a' mhonaidh, fhuair e an taigh gun cheann agus a bhràthair is mac a bhràthar fuar marbh air an achadh far an deach an spadadh ás an seasamh is iad a' treabhadh. Cha robh sgeul air a mhnaoi ach an ùine ghoirid, chunnaic e i is i an impis dol thar a beachd leis an eagal, a' tilleadh a-staigh thar a' mhonaidh far an do theich i le beatha nuair a thòisich an ùpraid.

Dh'innis i an-sin do dh'Fhionnlagh mar a thàinig ceathrar fhear móra, aon dhiubh sean mar gum b' e athair a' chòrra, a-nuas bho thaobh Sgurr nan Lapach, is nuair a chuir iad crìoch air an obair oillteil gun do thill iad an rathad ceudna.

"Cha bhi an gnìomharan gun dìoghaltas," arsa Fionnlagh 's e a' teannadh ri geurachadh na biodaige, agus gun an còrr dàil—eadhon gun na cuirp a bha a' reòthadh 'nam fuil fhéin air an achadh adhlac—thog e 'aghaidh ri Loch Abar oir bha deagh fhios aige gum bu sin ceàrn bhon tàinig na daoine.

Ràinig e is thog e fàth air an taigh a bha e am beachd do'm buineadh iad ach cha robh ri fhaicinn a-staigh ach seann bhean a bha a-mach is a-staigh mar gum biodh a sùil ri cuideigin. Is thuig e leis a sin nach do thill na ceatharnaich fhathast.

Ach mu mheadhan oidhche chunnaic e iad a' tèarnadh a dh'ionnsaigh an taighe 's a' gabhail a-steach. Dh'fheith e gu foighidneach gus an do ghabh iad mu thàmh. Chaidh e a-steach gu socrach sàmhach is bha iad an-siud 'nan sìneadh air an ùrlar air seidean connlaich 'nan trom chadal—cadal gun dùsgadh, mar a thachair, oir rinn biodag Fhionnlaigh Dhuibh nead 'nan cuim.

Is leig e fuil dhearg an cridhe gu làr, fear an déidh fir, is bha e dlùth air Srath Fàrair ceudna mun robh fios an Loch Abar air a' mhort a chaidh a chur an gnìomh 'nam measg.

Ach cha do sguir càirdean Dhòmhnaill Mhóir aig a sin ged nach deach leò na b' fheàrr. Bha Fionnlagh Dubh aon latha air an rathad a dh'ionnsaigh an taighe, 's e tèarnadh bho'n mhonadh, nuair a mhothaich e sèanar choigreach is iadsan mar an ceudna a' dèanamh rathad an taighe. Cho luath is a chunnaic e iad, thuig e ciod a bha 'nam beachd.

Ach rinn e orra mar nach biodh an teagamh a bu lugha 'na inntinn.

"Am bheil fios agadsa," arsa am fear a bu shine, agus a bha, a-réir coltais, mar cheann air a' chòrr, "càite am bheil taigh Fhionnlaigh Dhuibh MhicRath? Tha e coltach leam gum bheil e a' tàmh 's an dùthaich seo?"

"Tha," arsa Fionnlagh, "tha e dìreach far an do dh'fhàg mise e."

"'S aithne dhuit an duine, ma-tà," ars an coigreach is e a' toirt sùla bioraich air Fionnlagh.

"'S aithne gu math," arsa Fionnlagh, "is mise tha a' buachailleachd a threudan a-nis fad iomad bliadhna."

Dh'iarr iadsan air an-sin an taigh a sheòladh dhoibh. Is rinn Fionnlagh air a' bhothan gu lom dìreach.

"Tha fear an taighe tinn air a leabaidh," ars esan nuair a ràinig iad an doras, "ach gabhaibh a-staigh. Bidh e toilichte ur faicinn."

Rinn iadsan sin, fear an déidh fir. Bha nis an doras cho ìosal is gum feumadh neach cromadh cha mhór air a mhàgan, a' dol a-mach no a-staigh, is cha bhuileach a fhuair Fionnlagh am fear mu dheireadh air a mhàgan a' dol a-staigh na tharraing e a bhiodag is bha am fear ud air a spadadh anns an doras.

"Tha fear an taighe an-seo," ghlaodh e an-sin "Có tha 'ga iarraidh?"

Mar phrioba na sùla, thilg a bhean an còrr de'n armachd chuige a-mach air an uinneig, is bha i fhéin a-mach 'na déidh, agus fear de'n t-sianar, cha do dh'fhàg an taigh beò.

Sguir an iomairt aig a seo, agus bu leòr e. Uile gu léir beatha dà fhear dheug air tàilleadh aon fhéidh agus briathran guineach gonach baintighearna!

Dòmhnall mac Fhionnlaigh nan Dàn

A-réir an innse-sgeòil-san, ma-tà, is ann de mhuinntir Ghlinne Comhann a bha e, agus b' e Fionnlagh, 'athair, fear-brataich Mhic 'ic Iain. Is ban-Abrach a bu mhàthair dha. B' e 'sheanair, a thaobh a mhàthar, bàrd agus gìomanach no sealgair Mhic 'ic Raonaill, agus is ann an Creag Guanach a bha e a' fuireach.

Is ann aige a fhuair Dòmhnall 'àrach as 'òige. Air chor is gun d'fhuair e, ionann is bho thùs a làithean, a thogail ris an dàn is ris an t-seilg, mar a tha e fhéin ag ràdh:

Bha mi bhon a rugadh mi riamh,
Ann an caidreamh fhiadh is earb.

An uair a thàinig e gu inbheachd, agus a dh'eug 'athair, chaidh e dh'fhuireach do Ghleann Comhann. Chan eileas cinnteach c' fhad a thug e an-sin. Ach chitear 's an dàn gun do chuir e fhéin is a thriath a-mach air a chéile. Ciod sam bith a bu cheann fàth do'n aimhreit, dh'fhàg Dòmhnall "Eòin á Taigh na Creige," is bhòidich e nach tilleadh e a-chaoidh, is cha mhó na sin a thill.

Thàinig e air a sheann eòlas do Chreag Guanach is fhuair e faoilte 's furan. Thuit gun robh a sheanair air dol bho fheum 's an àm, agus 's e bh' ann gun d'rinn Mac 'ic Raonaill bàrd is gìomanach dha fhéin deth. Thug e dà bhaile dha: Creag Guanach agus an Fheàrsaid Riabhach. Bhiodh e ré an t-samhraidh ionann is air àiridh an Creag

Guanach aig ceann shuas Loch Tréig, agus aig ceann a-bhos an loch bha an Fheàrsaid aige mar bhaile geamhraidh.

An uair a fhuair e e fhéin air a shocrachadh agus air a chothrom mar bu mhath leis, phòs e té de Chloinn Dòmhnaill a' Bhràghad, ach cha do mheal iad ach goirid a chéile. Dh'fhuirich esan tuille 'na bhanntraich, agus an aon nighean a bh' aca—Màiri –, dh'fhan i gun phòsadh a' cumail an taighe ris.

Bha Dòmhnall 'na dhuine cuimte, gun a bhith ro àrd am pearsa. Bha e fuasgailteach fallain is fhuair e saoghal fada.

Cha robh mac-samhailt dha ann air a' bhogha. Ri fear a bhios math air cuspaireachd, theirear gus an latha an-diugh gum bheil e cho cuimseach ri Dòmhnall mac Fhionnlaigh. Bha nì gun chuibheas aige de dhàin is de sgeulachdan, is rinn e fhéin móran òran. Ach chan eileas ag ainmeachadh air ach "Òran na Comhachaig." Cha ghabh "Miann a' Bhàird Aosta" càradh air, mar a b' àill le feadhainn.

Tha ioma sgeul air 'aithris mu 'chuspaireachd, mu 'sheachran-seilge, uime fhéin is mu Mhac an Riochd, mar a thialadh e gu cluais an fhéidh, agus eile, ach fòghnaidh dhomh a h-aon no dithis ainmeachadh.

Ri linn Dhòmhnaill, mar is minig a bh' ann bho sin, bha ùdlaiche ainmeil a' tathaich Gual an Liath-Ghiubhais, agus là 'bha sin, smaoinich e gun tugadh e sgrìob a-null a ghabhail fàth air. Togar air, ma-tà, thair an Uisge Dhubh. Ach mar a bha an rosad an dàn, có bha an latha sin 's a' bheinn sheilg ach Donnachadh Dubh a' Churraic agus a ghillean air an t-slighe cheudna, agus mun d'fhairich Dòmhnall thall no bhos e, bha e an sàs aca.

Cha robh comas air: b' fheudar glacadh a ghabhail, agus falbh leotha do dh'Fhionn-Làirig.

Chaidh ainm Dhòmhnaill fada 's goirid, agus le farmad-cùirte, bha na gillean air lunn cur ás da, ach bu bhàrd an Ridire e fhéin, is cha leigeadh e leotha làmh a chur ann.

Mar a bha iad a' cumail air an adhart, chunnaic iad eilid 'na laighe air fuaran, agus ars iadsan ris, is iad a' fanaid air, "Bheir sinn do chead dhut ma chuireas tu an t-saighead an sùil dheis na h-éilde ud."

Bu rud mì-choltach seo, leis mar a bha an eilid 'na laighe, agus an rathad a bha a' ghaoth. Ach coma, chuir Dòmhnall a bhogha air lugh, is ghèarr e gaoth is talamh air an eilid, ach cha dèanadh e calg dhi. An uair a dh'fhairtlich air tialadh oirre, rinn e seòrsa miamhail de dh'fhead is thog an eilid a ceann. Rinn e a-rithist i is thionndaidh i 's thàinig i 'na choinneimh.

An-sin ghabh e an cothrom, is chum e an t-saighead ri 'sùil, is "cha robh òirleach gun bhàthadh eadar corran a gàine is a smeòirn."

An uair a chunnaic an Ridire cho ro mhath is a rinn e, thug e a chead da. Chan e a-mhàin sin, ach thug e cuireadh dha gu fuireach còmhla ris fhéin fhad is bu bheò e.

Thug Dòmhnall taing dha, is thuirt e ged a bheireadh e dha Fionn-Làirig ás a' ghrunnd, nach b' urrainn da na féidh is Loch Tréig 'fhàgail.

'S an àm ud, bha móran de Loch Abar fo choilltich mhóir, agus gheibhteadh madadh-allaidh ann 'na uaireannan. Bha Dòmhnall latha 's a' ghlasanaich air sgrìob aig taobh an Dubh Lochain (lochan a th' air cùl na Feàrsaide Móire), agus faicear an gòsganach ud air feadh nan clach 's nan sailthean a' tilleadh ás a' mhuileann far an robh e air tòir cobhartaich.

Chum e ris agus leag e e agus cha bu bheag ioghnadh a mhnatha mu'n chiad chòmhlaiche a thachair oirre an craoibh, goirid bho'n doras.

Mharbh e fear eile dhiubh air Lùb a' Choire Chreagaich.

Bha taigh Dhòmhnaill air a' cheart làraich air am bheil Taigh Bàn na Feàrsaid—an-diugh, mo chreach, aig bodach Gallda.

An deaghaidh dha dol bho fheum is nach b' urrainn da dol ach eadar an leaba is an teine, bha e uair an ciaradh nan tràth a' sealltainn a-mach air an uinneig ris a' bheinn, agus thugar an aire do'n ùdlaiche mhór ud ag èaladh thun a' ghàraidh air cùl an taighe.

Bha Màiri 'na suidhe aig an teine, 's chual i spàirn a' tighinn air anail a h-athar. Ghrad-éirich i 's dh'fharraid i ciod a bh' air.

"Uist," ars esan. "Fair mo bhogha."

Shaoil leatha gur breisleach a' bhàis a thàinig air. Bha am bogha air an fharadh bho chionn fhios có an ùine, ach thug i nuas e.

"Cuir air lugh e," ars esan.

"Mo chreach!" ars Màiri. "Chan eil fear air fonn Loch Abar an-diugh a chuireadh air lugh e."

"Feuch thusa ris," ars esan, is e fhéin a' seòladh dhi mar a dhèanadh i, agus 's na cuir a bh' ann. Chaidh am bogha air lugh.

"Càite am beil na saighdean?" ars esan.

Thug Màiri làmh air a' bhalg-shaighead, is chuir i air a ghlùn e.

Thagh Dòmhnall saighead is thuit am fiadh!

"A bhuidhe ri Dia," ars esan, "cha robh dùil agam ri a leithid gu bràch tuille, ach 's siud an t-sealg mu dheireadh dhomhsa."

Dh'òrduich e a thìodhlaiceadh am bian an fhéidh sin, agus uaigh a dhèanamh dha aig doras na h-eaglais agus 'aghaidh a chur ris a' Chròidhearg—beinn a tha am bràigh na Feàrsaid.

Blàr Tràigh Ghruinneart

Bha piuthar de Sheumas Òg Ìle pòsta ri Lachann Dhubhaird agus b' e an Roinn Ìleach an dubhairidh a bha MacGill'Eathain ri faotainn le nighean MhicDhòmhnaill: is e meud na Roinn Ìlich. Tha baile ris an abairear a' Gheàrrach ann an sgìreach Chille Chomain is tha tobar fuarain ann an gàrradh-càil seann taigh na Geàrraich, is tha sruthan a' ruith ás a' dol do'n eara-dheas, is a-staigh do Loch na Dàla aig Port Sgioba (ris an abairear nis Port Charlotte) agus tha sruthan eile dol ás a' cheart tobar is a ruith á làimh na h-àird an iar-thuath 's do'n mhuir aig Cille Chiarain, agus is e na tha eadar an dà shruth sin is a' mhuir am fearann ris an abairear an Roinn Ìleach.

Bha fear de Chlann Aoidh 'na sheanghal aig MacDhòmhnaill, 's b' e an Roinn Ìleach a bha aige airson a sheirbhis, is bha MacDhòmhnaill a' dol chur MhicAoidh ás an Roinn Ìleach, dol thoirt dha Cill Daltain 'na àite, agus bu le MacGill'Eathain an Roinn Ìleach, ach cha do thagair MacGill'Eathain riamh seilbh air dubhairidh na baintighearna, a bha piuthar do MhacDhòmhnaill pòsta ri MacGill'Eathain.

Tràth dh'fhàs Lachann Òg suas, chaidh e do Ìle dh'fhaicinn Roinn Ìleach, is dh'ionndrainn e nach robh port ann gu bàta thoirt gu tìr. Thuirt e ri MacDhòmhnaill, "Bu olc rinn t' athair air m' athair, àite thoirt dha far nach robh làmhraig ann far an gabhadh bàta thoirt gu tìr. Feumaidh tu àite thoirt dhomhsa far am faigh mi mo bhàta thoirt gu tìr."

Thuirt MacDhòmhnaill, "Tabhair do bhàta a-staigh do Loch na Dàla, 's gabh gu tìr aig Port Sgioba. Tha làmhraig glé mhath ann."

MacGill'Eathain: "Cha dèan mi sin, ach gabhaidh mi Port Asgaig is feumaidh mi 'fhaotainn."

MacDhòmhnaill: "Tha thu ag iarraidh tuille na gheibh thu: tha thu toileach fhaotainn na th' eadar Port Asgaig is Loch na Dàla, 's chan fhaigh thu sin."

MacGill'Eathain: "Is ann ri sin a tha m' fhiughair is bidh e agam cuideachd"—is mar sin dhealaich iad gun tighinn gu còrdadh.

Chuir iad batailt air Beinn Bheigeir; chaidh an aghaidh Chlann Dòmhnaill. Chuir iad an ath bhatailte aig àite ris an abairear Muladradh. Chaidh Clann Ghill'Eathain gu léir ach Lachann Mór e fhéin a mharbhadh. Uair eile thàinig Lachann le 'dhaoine gu eileanan Locha Guirm. Chaidh sgrios a thoirt air Clann Ghill'Eathain.

Bha tolman cruinn uaine fa chomhair taigh mór MhicGill'Eathain Dhubhaird, is bha e 'na nòs tràth bhiodh Mac Gill'Eathain a' dol gu cath, gun rachadh e a-mach anns a' mhadainn mum blaiseadh e biadh, is gun rachadh e deiseal trì chuairt air an tolman.

Air a' mhadainn air an robh Lachann Mór dol chur Blàr Tràigh Ghruinneart, thàinig cailleach-fhiosachd a-staigh do thaigh Lachainn. Thuirt i ris, "An d'rinn thu mar a b' àbhaist do d' shinnseara dhèanamh?"

Dh'fharraid Lachann, "Ciod e sin?"

"Dol a-mach anns a' mhadainn mum blaiseadh tu biadh 's dol mun cuairt an tulmain deiseal, trì uairean, 's mur dèan thu sin, cha téid leat."

Thuirt MacGill'Eathain, "Ma-tà, ma b' àbhaist doibhsan dol deiseal, théid mise trì chuairt 'nan aghaidh." Is rinn e sin.

Thuirt a' chailleach, "Tràth ruigeas tu Ìle, na cuir mach t' acair aig Poll Nùstaig, is na h-òl deoch á tobar Néill Neònaich, is na suidhich crann do bhrataich air Cnoc nan Aighean." Gidheadh cha do ghabh Lachann Mór suim.

Tràth ràinig Lachann Ìle, cha robh toil aige dol air tìr aig Tràigh Ghruinneart, air eagal 's gum faiceadh MacDhòmhnaill e, 's gun cuireadh e bac air, is chaidh e gu tìr aig Poll Nùstaig, is chuir e a-mach an acair ann. Chaidh e seach Àrd Neamh, is tràth bha e air an t-slighe dh'fhàs tart air, is thuirt e, "Tha ìot' orm; b' fheàirrde mi deoch."

Sheall na daoine an àird is sìos, is chunna fear dhiubh tobar aig bun tulman beag uaine bha an-sin, is thuirt e, "Tha an t-aon tobar is àillidh a chunnadar riamh an-seo."

Chaidh MacGill'Eathain is dh'òl e deoch ás, 's an déidh dha an deoch òl, dh'fharraid e, "C' ainm a ta air an àite seo?"

Bha fear an-sin a bha eòlach ann an Ìle, 's thuirt e, "Tha an-seo Tobar Néill Neònaich."

"Agus c' ainm a ta air an àite far an do chuir sinn a-mach an t-acair?"

"Tha air an àite sin Poll Nùstaig."

Thuirt Lachann, "Tha an-sin dithis de òrdughan na cailliche seachad."

Chaidh iad air an adhart gu àite far an robh cnoc bòidheach gainneamhachail a bha ann an-sin. Thuirt Lachann, "Suidhich crann na brataich air a' chnocan sin agus sgaoil mach a' bhratach."

Chaidh an crann a shàthadh ann an talamh, is a' bhratach a' sgaoileadh mach, is dh'fharraid Lachann, "C' ainm a ta air an àite seo?"

Thuirt fear de na daoine, "Is e ainm an àite seo, Cnoc nan Aighean."

Thuirt Lachann, "Tha a-nis trì àiteachan na cailliche seachad."

Shuidhich MacDhòmhnaill a bhratach aig ìochdar Chorsabhal, air àite ris an abairear an Creagan, is theirte Crannaig MhicDhòmhnaill ris 'na dhéidh sin.

Bha gille-glic a' dol 'na theachdaire eadar an dà chamb, is a dh'innseadh anns an dàrna an nì rachadh a ràdh anns a' chamb eile. Bha an gille toileach an fhalachd a thogail oir is gum faiceadh e cath, 's tràth rachadh e le sgeul o MhacGill'Eathain gu MacDhòmhnaill, cha b' e 'chainnt a thuirt MacGill'Eathain a dh'innseadh e do MhacDhòmhnaill, is tràth chuireadh MacDhòmhnaill teachdaireachd gu MacGill'Eathain cha b' e na facail thuirt MacDhòmhnaill a dh'innseadh e do MacGill'Eathain is thog e an fhalachd na bu mhiosa na bha i roimhe.

Dh'fhan an dà fhine fa chomhair a chéile ré thrì làithean a strìobh ri còrdadh, ach le foill an teachdaire bha a' dol eadar iad, ghabh an dà fhine fearg r'a chéile, agus b' e bh' ann gum b' éiginn gleachd.

Bha a thrì uimhir sluaigh aig MacGill'Eathain is a bha aig MacDhòmhnaill aig an àm sin, ach bha fiughair aig MacDhòmhnaill ri Raghnall Dubh á Innis Eòghain an Éirinn le bannal de fhir Innis Eòghain an Éirinn, is bha fiughair aige ri fir á Cinn Tìre, 's fir á eilean Arainn gu a chòmhnadh, gidheadh cha robh iad air teachd air an adhart, is b' éiginn do MhacDhòmhnaill dol an aghaidh MhicGill'Eathain gun ach trian de'n àireamh sluaigh a bh' aig MacGill'Eathain.

Bha duine ro bheag, ris an abairteadh "Dubh Sìth MacGilleSheadhanaich," is theireadh cuid Dubh Sleagha ris, 's chaidh e dh'ionnsaigh camb MhicGill'Eathain is dh'iarr e guth de MhacGill'Eathain fhéin. Chaidh Lachann MacGill'Eathain far an robh e, 's dh'fharraid e, "Ciod e do ghnothach riumsa?"

Thuirt Dubh Sìth, "Airm is aodach gu dol leibh do'n chath."

Sheall MacGill'Eathain air le tàir, is thuirt se ris, "Ged bheireadh tu airm is aodach leat, cha tugainnse àite dhuit measg mo dhaoine."

"Seadh, seadh," ars Dubh Sìth 's e falbh. Chaidh Dubh Sìth 's ràinig e camb MhicDhòmhnaill, is dh'iarr e guth do MhacDhòmhnaill.

Chaidh MacDhòmhnaill far an robh e, 's thuirt e, "Ciod e do ghnothach riumsa?"

"Airm is aodach, ma bheir sibh cuid duine dhomh."

Thuirt MacDhòmhnaill, "Bheir mi àite duine dhuit, is b' fheàrr leam gun robh cóig ceud de d' leithid agam."

Thuirt Dubh Sìth, "Ma-tà, ma dh'fhoghnas sibhse do chàch uile, foghnaidh mise do Lachann Mór."

Cha robh MacDhòmhnaill toileach Lachann bhith air a mharbhadh, 's thuirt e, "À, dèan nas urrainn thu air an t-sluagh, ach caomhain Lachann fhéin."

Thuirt Dubh Sìth, "Chaidh am facal a ràdh." Thionndaidh e 'chùl ri MacDhòmhnaill is dh'fhalbh e. Bha gunna aig Dubh Sìth 's cha robh gunna eile aig a' chath ach i fhéin, is chaidh Dubh Sìth am falach, ag iarraidh fàth air Lachann MacGill'Eathain a mharbhadh o fhoill fhalach.

Tràth bha MacDhòmhnaill togairt gu a dhaoine ghluasad chum a' chath, thuirt e ri a phìobaire, "Seinn port ùr dhuinn, a phìobaire, port nach do sheinn thu riamh roimhe." Sheall am pìobaire mun cuairt dh'fheuch am faiceadh e nì-eiginn a bheireadh fonn òrain gu 'chuimhne, 's chunnaic e a' bhanarach aig Roinniche Ruadh a strìobh ris a' chrodh 's na laoigh a thearbadh o chéile, 's iad an déidh faotainn còmhla, 's grad thàinig duanag 'na chuimhne:

O i a thò, dheoghail na laoigh
O i a thò, dheoghail an t-àl,
O i a thò, dheoghail na laoigh,
A bhanarach chaomh, dheoghail an t-àl.

agus is e "Pìobaireachd Thràigh Ghruinneart" theirte ris a' phort sin a-rithist.

Chaidh an dà fheachd an coinneamh a chéile. B' ann an cois na tràgha a chaidh iad, is choinnich iad aig àite ris an abairteadh 'na dhéidh sin Camag a' Chath, agus thòisich an dà fheachd air a chéile leis na saighdean trasd air bun na h-aibhne.

Bha a' mhadainn air bhith ciùin gu sin, ach aig an àm sin, shéid gaoth làidir o'n iar, is bha uisge trom leatha, 's strìobh an dà fheachd có dhiubh gheibheadh mun cuairt an uisg' an toiseach gu a' ghaoth fhaighinn 'nan cùl, gu cothrom a bhith leò, leis a' ghaoth 's an t-uisge bhith an aghaidh chàich, agus bha an tùs aig na Muilich 's thòisich am blàr garbh aig àite ris an abairear an Earasaid air crìoch Bhaile an Àbaidh, 's chaidh pilleadh thoirt air Clann Dòmhnaill.

Bha gobha ann an Ìle do'm b' ainm MacEachairn, is thug MacGill'Eathain leis aon d'a mhic do'm b' ainm Dòmhnall, is bha Dòmhnall sin le Lachann Mór aig Blàr Tràigh Ghruinneart, agus bha mac eile de'n ghobha do'm b' ainm Niall aig a' bhlàr. Cha robh e ach òg tràth chaidh Dòmhnall a bhràthair do Mhuile, 's chan aithneadh Dòmhnall Niall. Choinnich an dà bhràthair aig lùb de'n abhainn, 's ghleachd iad le tuaghan catha. Mu dheireadh bha ar le Niall gun d' aithnich e Dòmhnall, is thuirt e,

"Fhir dhuibh na ciabhaige ruaidhe,
Bu trom do bhuillean is bu luath iad:
Bhris thu liochdaid mo thuaighe,
'S ged rinn thu sin, bu toigh leam buan thu."

Thuirt Dòmhnall, "Bu toigh leat buan mi?"

"B' eadh."

"Ciod e thuige?"

"Nach tu mac a' ghobha MacEachairn an Ìle?"

"Seadh."

"Ma-tà, is mise Niall, am mac as òige."

An-sin sguir an dà bhràthair de'n ghleachd, shuidh iad 'ghabhail sgeul de chéile, 's ghuil iad, 's cha tug iad buille tuille 's a' chath.

Bha boglach aig cùl Chlann Dòmhnaill, is chaidh móran de na Dòmhnallaich anns a' bhoglach, is thàinig droch sgrios orra, 's b' e Éiginneachan Chlann Dòmhnaill theirte ris an àite sin a-rithist, agus dìreach tràth bha na Dòmhnallaich aig imfhios géilleadh, chuala iad sgal pìoba tighinn chuga. Thuig MacDhòmhnaill gum b' iad fir Innis Eòghain bha tighinn gu 'chobhar, is ghlaoidh e ri a dhaoine, "Bithibh tapaidh, ghillean, is e seo Raghnall Dubh air teachd á Innis Eòghain an Éirinn gus ar cobhar."

Thàinig Raghnall Dubh air ceann fir Innis Eòghain, is b' éiginn do Chlann Ghill'Eathain dol air an ais, is lean na Dòmhnallaich iad.

Bha fiughair ri fir Chinn-Tìre 's Arainn, is chuir MacGill'Eathain fir fo cheannard gu fir Chinn-Tìre 'fhaireadh agus an cumail air an ais. Ràinig iadsan àite bràigh Leire-abas agus stad iad ann an-sin, agus gu iad fhéin a ghléidheadh o chadal, thòisich iad air cluich na geàrr, 's cha do rinn iad faire thréibhdhireach. Bha fir Chinn Tìre dol air an adhart gun orra ach am féile beag is an léintean, is ràinig iad mullach Bhoire Chill, is shuidh iad a chur orra an cuid osan is chunnaic iad na Muilich gu h-ìosal fodhpa, is iad ri cluich na geàrrfhiadh, ach chan fhac na Muilich iadsan, 's lean iad air a' chluich. Tràth chuir fir Chinn Tìre orra an osain, rinn iad cabhag, is ruith iad le leathad far an robh na Muilich agus ràinig iad na Muilich gun fhios dhoibh, agus mharbh siad iad. Chaidh na Muilich adhlac anns an àite sin fhéin, agus b' e Tòrr nam Muileach an t-ainm chaidh thoirt air an àite sin a-rithist.

Bha fir Chinn Tìre a' faotainn sealladh air Tràigh Ghruinneart á far an robh iad, is chunnaic iad gun robh Clann Ghill'Eathain dol air ais, agus chaidh iad gu cur air thoiseach orra, 's thàinig iad air na Muilich am fagus do Chamag na Gobhainn is strì iad ris a' ghrunnd chruaidh a bhuidhinn aig Bruach an Adhraidh. Bha fir Chinn Tìre an tùs agus fir Arainn 'nan déidh a' tighinn gus an Cruadhlach.

Tràth bha fir Arainn dol gu Blàr Ghruinneart, chaidh iad le'm bìrlinnibh gu Port na h-Abhainn, aig beul Loch an Dàla. Thug iad am bìrlinn gu tìr. Bha fear de Chlann Fhearghais ris an abairte "Donnchadh nan Cuaran" chòmhnaidh ann am baile ris an abairte "Baile nan Càrn" air fearann Chlaidh Bhaile, agus an déidh do na h-Arannaich am beagan airgid bh' aca chur am falach, ràinig iad e, 's thuirt iad, "Càit' am bheil Tràigh Ghruinneart?"

Thuirt Donnchadh, "Tha aig ceàrn mu thuath Ìle." Bha e cho sean nach b' urrainn da coiseachd, ach fhuair e each bàn a bh' aige, 's chaidh e leò gus an do leig e fhaicinn dhoibh làrach a' bhlàir, ach cha do phill neach dhiubh tuille dh'fhios nam bàtaichean, is laigh iad (na bàtaichean) an-sin gus an do ghrod iad.

Thàinig air na Muilich gum b' éiginn doibh dol tre àite bog far an robh sùil-chritheach, is bha na casan aca dol fada sìos anns an làthaich is iad a' call an cuaran ann, 's chaidh móran dhiubh a mharbhadh aig an àite sin, agus b' e Éiginneachan Chlann Ghill'Eathain an t-ainm a chaidh thoirt air an àite sin a-rithist.

Tràth chunnaic Lachann Mór an cruaidh-chàs anns an robh a dhaoine, chaidh e fhéin aig tùs a' chath agus gheàrr e bealach le a chlaidheamh throimh Chlann Dòmhnaill, is ghléidh e am bealach fosgailte gus an d'fhuair a dhaoine throimhe. Chaidh iad o sin gu bràigh Bhruach an Adhraidh. Bha fir Chinn Tìre an-sin dlùth roimh Chlann Ghill'Eathain, is bha Clann Ghill'Eathain an droch staid dheth. Chaidh Lachann Mór e fhéin air tùs a shluaigh, 's gheàrr e an-sin a-rithist le a chlaidheamh bealach throimh Chlann Dhòmhnaill is leig e a dhaoine a-mach throimhe.

Bha Dubh Sìth aig an àite sin le a ghunna, is e am falach ann an craoibh dhòmhail chaorainn, agus tràth fhuair Lachann Mór am bealach a gheàrradh throimh Chlann Dòmhnaill, chaidh e throimh a' bhealach gus an robh e aig an taobh a-mach dhiubh. Cho luath is a fhuair Dubh Sìth sealladh air Lachann, ghrad-stiùir e beul dois a ghunna ris, is leig se an urchair air, is bhuail am peilear Lachann.

Tràth chaidh Lachann Mór a leònadh, dh'fhalbh e air adhart is a cheann ag amharc sìos. Bha gille Lachainn leònta le claidheamh, gidheadh bha a shùil air Lachann, agus lean se e, is e tuaiream fichead slat 'na dhéidh. Chaidh Lachann Mór air adhart tuaiream air dà cheud slat is thuit e, agus cha b' urrainn do a ghille dol na b' fhaide, 's leig se e fhéin sìos air a' bhlàr.

Bha fear de na Dòmhnallaich a ghabh beachd air Lachann, is a thug aire gun robh fàinne air a mheur, is lean se e gus am fàinne fhaotainn. Tràth ràinig e far an robh Lachann, bha Lachann marbh. Bheir e air làmh Lachainn gus am fàinne thoirt bhàrr a mheur, ach bha meur Lachainn air at cho mór leis a' chlaidheamh is nach tigeadh am fàinne dheth ann. Chuir an Dòmhnallach làmh Lachainn air car beag fraoich a bha an-sin, 's thog e an claidheamh gus an làmh a gheàrradh bhàrr Lachainn, oir is gum faigheadh e am fàinne thoirt dheth air a shocair a-rithist. Bha gille MhicGhill'Eathain gabhail beachd air, is tràth bha an Dòmhnallach togail a chlaidheamh gus am buille 'thoirt, thug gille MhicGhill'Eathain togail air fhéin; chuir e saighead 'na bhogha; leig se air an Dòmhnallach i, 's mharbh se e.

Tràth thuit Lachann Mór, sgaoil a dhaoine o chéile, 's bha gach fear dhiubh cogadh mar gum biodh gach fear air a làimh fhéin, is theirte Goirtean Blàr MhicGhill'Eathain ris an àite far an deach crìoch air a' bhlàr. Theich na Muilich gu dol gu Poll Nùstaig far an robh na bàtaichean, ach bha na fir-bhàtaichan cumail freiceadain, is tràth thuig iad gun robh Clann Ghill'Eathain air an sgrios, theich iad o'n chladach leis na bàtaichean, agus tràth chunnaic na Muilich gun robh choltas orra gum biodh iad air an sgrios, theich iad a-staigh do Eaglais Chille Naomh, an dùil nach marbhtadh iad anns an Eaglais, ach bha iad air am mealladh. Dhruid na Dòmhnallaich dorsan na h-eaglais is chuir iad sop teine rithe. Bha cùrsa na gaoithe air atharrachadh aig an àm, is shéid gaoth làidir o'n àird an ear-thuath 's cha b' fhada gus an robh toll throimh thugha na h-eaglais.

Bha aon fhear measg nam Muileach do'm bu shloinne MacMhuirich. Bha e làidir luath, 's streap e an àird gu mullach balla na h-eaglais; leum e leathad agus theich e. Ruaig buidheann de na Dòmhnallaich 'na dhéidh. Theich esan gu Caol Naomhaidh; ach bha na bàtaichean air fàgail tìr, 's cha robh dòigh aig MacMhuirich air, ach theich e gus na tràgha 's thug e oidhirp gu snàmh a-mach a dh'ionnsaigh Eilean Naomha. Leig fear de na Dòmhnullaich saighead 'na dhéidh. Bhuail an t-saighead e anns a' mhàs. Cha tug e oidhirp gus an t-saighead thoirt á 'mhàs ach shnàmh e gu clach mhóir ris an abairte a' Bhadag, bha a-mach anns a' mhuir, is bha bad feamainn oirre bhiodh 'ga luasgadh leis an tonn. Sheas MacMhuirich air a' Bhadaig, is thug e an t-saighead á 'mhàs. Bha an tràigh ann aig an àm is dh'fhan MacMhuirich air a' Bhadaig gus an do shaoil an tòir gun robh e bàthaite 's gun d'fhalbh iad, is an-sin shnàmh esan air ais gu tìr. Dh'fhan am fear sin ri bheò an Ìle. Phòs e ann, is bha sliochd aige 's b' iad Clann Mhuirich na Badaig theirte riutha. Bha e 'na ghnàth-fhacal an Ìle, ag ràdh "cho math foighidinn ri fear na saighde."

Chaidh na h-uile neach eile de na Muilich bha anns an eaglais a losgadh.

Tràth shaoil Clann Dòmhnaill gun d'fhuair iad Clann Ghill'Eathain bh' aig a' bhlàr gu léir mharbhadh, bha iad a' sgaoileadh o chéile 's bha gach fear dol do 'dhachaigh fhéin. Bha aig Mac an t-Sagairt Stoiseagh—bràthair Mhic an t-Sagairt Chorsabal—ri dol dhachaigh deich mìle tre mhonadh. Thàinig e gu àite 's chuala e gàire. Chaidh e ceum thar an rathaid gu ruig far an robh an gàire. Bha fear leònta an-sin 'na laighe, 's dh'fharraid Mac an t-Sagairt, "Ciod fàth do ghàire, dhuine?"

Thuirt am fear leònta, "Chan ann o ghuin a thàinig an gàire, 's ann a bha mi a' bruadar gun tàinig fitheach a dh'itheadh mo mhionaich, is gun do rib e 'chasan 'nam chaolan is cha b' urrainn da leum." Is thog Mac an t-Sagairt MacGhill'Eathain. Thug se dachaigh e, agus bha MacGhill'Eathain naoi mìosan an taigh Mhic an t-Sagairt.

Tràth bha Mac an t-Sagairt los dol dachaigh le MacGhill'Eathain, chaidh e do Chorsabal is dh'iarr e Niall, mac a bhràthar, gu dol leis do Mhuile, oir is gum biodh aon earbsach aige leis. Fhuair e Niall leis is thug e dithis de mhic fhéin leis. Chuir e MacGhill'Eathain do Mhuile, ach is ann bha na Muilich ro chaomhnail ris, is thàinig e dhachaigh rithis, is <thill e> 'na dhéidh sin, b' e beatha Chlann an t-Sagairt do Mhuile.

Bha a' bhanaltrum leis an deach Lachann Mór altrum chòmhnaidh anns an Roinn Ìleach. Fhuair i fios gun deach Lachann Mór a mharbhadh aig Tràigh Ghruinneart, is chuir i roimpe gun tìodhlaiceadh i e. Bha gille aice. Theirte "Donnchadh Dubhchasach" ris, do bhrìgh gun robh fionna dubh a' fàs air a chasaibh. Thug i air Donnchadh Dubhchasach an càrn a chur air each a bh' aice, 's chaidh iad gu Tràigh Ghruinneart a thogail corp Lachainn Mhóir, gus a thoirt gu Cille Chomain gu e bhith air a thìodhlacadh ann.

Dh'fhalbh iad 's ràinig iad Tràigh Ghruinneart. Cha robh cobhan air bith aca gu corp Lachainn Mhóir a chur ann no neach gus iad a chuideachadh gus an corp chur air a' chàrn; ach chuir iad fhéin suas e, agus dh'fhalbh iad leis. Bha an aghasdar aicese, is i a' treòrachadh an eich, is bha Donnchadh Dubhchasach a' freasdal do MhacGhill'Eathain a chumail ceart air a' chàrn. Tràth bha iad air an t-slighe, chaidh spàg a' chùirn sìos ann an easgaidh. Thug clab Lachainn crathadh. Rinn Donnchadh gàire.

Phill muime Lachainn far an robh an gille, 's dh'fharraid i dheth, "Ciod fàth do ghàire?"

Thuirt esan, "Tha mar a ta clab Lachainn Mhóir a' crathadh tràth théid spàg a' chùirn thar torrain is anns na h-easgaidh."

Chuir ise a làmh a-staigh fo a h-earasaid. Thug i a-mach biodag agus stob i anns a' ghille i, agus mharbh si e. Chaidh an gille adhlac ann an-sin, is b' e "Càrn Donnchaidh" theirte ris an àite sin a-rithis.

Chaidh a' bhean air a h-adhart gu Cille Chomain, leis an each agus an càrn, a' giùlan corp MhicGhill'Eathain, agus fhuair i an corp a thìodhlacadh a-staigh ann an Eaglais Chille Chomain, is chuir i leac-lighe air uachdar, agus dealbh Lachainn Mhóir MhicGhill'Eathain, e fhéin is a chlaidheamh r'a thaobh geàrrte air an lic. B' ann air a-staigh na h-eaglais bha uaigh Lachainn Mhóir, gus gun deach eaglais ùr a chur suas ann an linn Mhaighstir Alex Cameron, am fagus do'n bhliadhna 1840; chaidh uaigh Lachainn Mhóir fhàgail aig taobh a-mach na h-eaglais. Tha leac-lighe Lachainn ri fhaicinn aig oisean na h-àird an ear-thuath de'n eaglais.

Drochaid Lag nan Cladhairean

Air do neach a bhith gabhail an rathaid o'n Cheann Mhór gu Gleann Cuaich thairis air a' mhonadh ris an goirear an Làirig, chìthear drochaid thar allt ann an lag, beagan mu'n ruigear am mullach. Is e Drochaid Lag nan Cladhairean a theirear ris an drochaid gus an latha an-diugh air son nì a thachair an-sin o chionn iomadh bliadhna.

Aig an àm sin, bha e 'na nì cumanta do dhaoine tapaidh a bhith togail creiche, no mar their sinne aig an latha seo, bhith ri mèirleadh air crodh agus air caoraich. Bha e 'na nì co-measail aig an àm sin is gum bu tric rachadh àrd uaislean a thogail creiche o'n nàimhdean.

Thachair gun tàinig buidheann de dhaoine a-staigh air Gleann Cuaich mu fheasgar air là àraid nuair a bha gach duine 's an dùthaich air falbh, agus thug iad lom sgrìob air gach ceithear-chasach am bràigh a' ghlinne. Cha robh neach a chuireadh stad orra ach seann daoine, mnathan agus clann, agus b' fhaoin an gnìomh dhoibhsan dol an càramh nan creachadairean.

Thug na daoine an Làirig orra leis na bh' aca, ach air dol thar a' mhullaich dhaibh, dh'fhàs an oidhche cho dorcha 's nach bu léir dhaibh ceum de'n t-slighe. Chuir iad rompa uime sin tàmh ann an lag an uillt gus am briseadh an latha, oir bha iad làn chinnteach nach b' eagal do thòir a bhith orra.

Bha seann duine anns a' ghleann d'am b' ainm Iain Mór agus chuir esan roimhe ionnsaigh a thoirt air a' chreach a thilleadh.

Cho luath 's a chaidh a' chreach ás an t-sealladh thar a' mhullaich, thog Iain Mór air ás an déidh, gun neach aige ach sgonn de bhalach a b' ogha dha agus trì no ceithir coin.

Chunnaic e far an robh na daoine leis a' chrodh agus air dha <tighinn gu cnoc>

a bha dlùth dhaibh, ghlaodh e gu h-àrd, “Tha iad an-seo, fhearaibh, tha iad an-seo! Bithibh an sàs annta!”

Rinn am balach glaodh ’ga fhreagairt air an taobh eile, agus an-sin, stuig iad na coin ris an spréidh.

Thug an crodh an rathad a thàinig iad orra, ach shaoil leis na creachadairean gun robh an gleann air éirigh an tòir orra. Ghabh iad ’nan deann leis a’ bhruthach gun stad gus an robh iad air taobh eile a’ Cheann Mhóir.

Air an oidhche sin, bha bròn is mulad an iomadh taigh anns a’ ghleann bhòidheach sin, ach mun do bhris an latha chualas fuaim geumnaich a’ chruidh a’ tighinn suas an sliabh agus Iain Mór air an cùl a’ cur nan con riu.

Uaidhe seo, chaidh Lag nan Cladhairean a thoirt air an àite ’s an robh na creachadairean a’ cur seachad na h-oidhche, agus is e sin is ainm da air an latha an-diugh.

Blàr Chàirinnis

Anns a’ bhliadhna 1601, thug Clann Dòmhnaill Uibhist, agus Clann ’ic Leòid na h-Earadh là fuilteach aig Fèith na Fala, ann an Càirinnis, an Uibhist mu Thuath. Is ann eadar Dòmhnallaich Shléibhte agus Leòdaich Dhùn Bheagain a thòisich an aimhreit a bha ’na màthair-adhbhair air Blàr Chàirinnis. Tha e air aithris gur ann mar seo a thòisich an aimhreit.

Phòs Dòmhnall Gorm Shléibhte nighean ’ic Leòid Dhùn Bheagain agus ciod air bith a bha aige ’na h-aghaidh, tha e coltach nach robh e fhéin is i fhéin glé réidh, agus is e thàinig ás a’ chùis gun tug e litir-dhealachaidh dhi, agus gun do chart e dhachaigh do thaigh a h-athar i.

Thug seo tàmailt mhór do Shir Ruairidh MacLeòid agus d’a chàirdibh gu léir, ach is e a dhorranaich buileach iad, an dòigh anns an deach a cur dhachaigh.

Bha i fhéin air leth shùil, no cam mar a theirear, agus gus a’ chùis a dhèanamh cho tàmailteach is a ghabhadh dèanamh, fhuair Dòmhnall Gorm seann each bàn cam, gille cam, agus cù cam, agus chuir e an gille, is an cù, is an t-each a dh’aon sgrìob a Dhùn Bheagain leatha. Bha a’ Bhaintighearna cham air muin an eich chaim, gille cam a’ falbh ’na cheann, agus cù cam a’ falbh ’nan déidh.

An uair a ràinig a’ chuideachd neònach seo Dùn Bheagain, agus a chaidh am beag sgeul chun a’ mhóir sgéil, cha robh Leòdach ri tràigh anns an Eilean Sgitheanach no anns na h-Earadh, nach robh ann an rùn nan tuagh do Dhòmhnall Gorm is d’a chàirdibh anns gach àite.

Tha adhbhar a bhith a’ creidsinn, gun do dhìoghail iomadh neach fad iomadh bliadhna air a’ ghnìomh mhaslach a bha seo, ged nach eil cunntas againn m’a dhéidhinn.

B’ e Dòmhnall Glas MacLeòid ceann-feadhna nan Leòdach anns na h-Earadh. Bha e, uair de a shaoghal, ’na dhuine ro threun, ach aig an àm seo, bha e air fàs trom lapach, agus cha b’ urrainn da dol a-mach air cheann a chuid ghaisgeach treuna, a thogail creiche no a thoirt blàir.

Ach bha a mhac ’na dhuine òg tapaidh gaisgeil, ann an treun a neirt, agus déidheil air glòir is urram fhaotainn dha fhéin is d’a chinneadh.

Chuala e mu’n tàmailt a thugadh d’a chàirdibh an Dùn Bheagain, agus chan fhaca e dad a b’ iomchaidhe na falbh a dh’Uibhist mu Thuath air cheann dà fhichead fear treun a thogail creiche chum aicheamhail a thoirt, air aon dòigh no dòigh eile, do na Dòmhnallaich. "Mur pàigh thu fhéin e, pàighidh do mhàileid e."

Thog na fir orra, agus dh'falbh iad, cuid anns a' bhìrlinn aig mac Dhòmhnaill Ghlais, agus cuid eile ann am bàtaichean-aisig.

An uair a ràinig iad Uibhist, dh'acraich iad na bàtaichean an Loch nan Ceall, aig bun na Fadhlach a Tuath.

Ghabh iad air aghaidh agus thog iad a' chreach gu furasta an Càirinnis, agus o nach robh ùine gu leòr aca gu dol chun nam bàtaichean leis a' chrodh, is e rud a rinn iad, chruinnich iad iad do Theampall na Trìonaid, gus am biodh iad a' falbh an làr-na-mhàireach. Ghabh iad fhéin seilbh air Taigh a' Chnuic, on a bha e an àite àrd fradharcach, am bràighe a' bhaile.

Bha iad a' cur seachad na h-ùine leis gach fealla-dhà agus toileachas-inntinn a b' urrainn daibh, a' làn chreidsinn gun soirbheachadh gach cùis leò, mar bu mhiann leò.

Ach cha robh e an dàn gum faigheadh iad am miann anns a' chùis seo, oir mun deach a' ghrian fodha air an ath là, bha "caochladh cuir air clò Chaluim."

Bha duine treun ann an Uibhist mu Dheas ris an cainteadh gu cumanta Dòmhnall mac Iain 'ic Sheumais. Bha an duine seo ainmeil ri a linn air son a mhór ghràidh a dh'fhìrinn, a dh'onoir, agus a cheartas. Mas fhìor an sgeul, tha e air aithris gun robh e an còmhnaidh a' strì ri bhith 'cur ás do'n chreachadh, do'n spùilleadh, is do'n làmhachas-làidir a bha 'na chleachdadh cho cumanta anns an àm.

Nuair a thàinig na Leòdaich air tìr an Uibhist mu Thuath, thuig muinntir an àite gu math gu dé bha fainear dhaibh, agus is e a bh' ann, chuir iad fios cabhagach gu mac Iain 'ic Sheumais, mar a bha a' chùis air thuar a bhith. Bha esan mar a bha e riamh cho ealamh ris an fhacal, agus air falbh a bha e le dà fhear dheug de na ceatharnaich bu chalma is bu cholgarra a bha ri'm faotainn an Uibhist mu Dheas.

Air tràigh oidhche, chaidh iad thar Fadhail nan Làrnan is thar Fadhail 'ic an Aoidheir, agus beagan roimh bheul an là, ràinig iad Càirinnis. An uair a ghabh iad beachd air cur a' bhaile, agus a thuig iad gun robh na creachadairean fhathast gun fhalbh, dh'fhalaich iad iad fhéin ann am fèith, am bràighe a' bhaile.

Nuair a thòisich an là air soilleireachadh, mhothaich iad gun robh barrachd cuideachd aig Taigh a' Chnuic is a bu chòir a bhith ann, agus thuig iad có a bha aca.

Thilg mac Iain 'ic Sheumais saighead, agus leòn e fear dhiubh. Leis an ath shaigheid, leag e fear eile.

Ghabh iad an t-eagal, agus thuirt fear dhiubh, "Tha mi gu mór air mo mhealladh, mur ann o làimh Dhòmhnaill 'ic Iain 'ic Sheumais a thàinig na saighdean, agus mas ann, tha eagal mór orm gum bi là dubh againn dhcth."

Cha robh iad fhathast cinnteach có an àird ás an robh na saighdean a' tighinn, ach is e rud a rinn iad, thionndaidh iad an aghaidhean gu ceithir àrdaibh an adhair, agus an uair a thàinig an treas saighead, thuig iad gur ann o'n àird an ear-thuath a bha na saighdean a' tighinn.

Cho luath agus a bha aca, bhrùchd iad a-sìos an cnoc.

An uair a chunnaic mac Iain 'ic Sheumais iad a' cromadh le beàrradh a' chnuic, thuirt e, "Nis, 'illean, ma rinn sibh riamh e, dèanaibh an-diugh e, oir tha mi am barail gu bheil triùir aig gach fear agaibh r'a chur gu làr."

"Ma-thà," ars iadsan, "chan fhad a bhios."

Bha e fhéin is a ghillean cho ealanta air a' bhogha, is gun tug iad tanachadh math air na Leòdaich mun do thàrr iad, ach gann, cromadh le beàrradh a' chnuic.

An uair a dhlùthaich iad ri chéile, 's ann an-sin a bha an cath teth teann:

> Thachair ri chéile na suinn,
> Mar bhruaillein thonn air druim a' chuain,
> Bha beuman beucach dlùth ri chéile;
> Am bàs a' leum thar tréin 's an t-sliabh,
> Mar neul de chlachaibh-meallain garbh,
> 'S gaoth mhór 'na cirb ag éirigh.

De'n dà fhichead fear, cha do thàrr ás ach an dithis. Thuit càch gu léir ach an ceannard—mac Dhòmhnaill Ghlais—anns a' chath.

Theich esan le a bheatha.

Thug mac Iain 'ic Sheumais teann òrdugh gun a mharbhadh air chor sam bith, ach, nam bu chomasach e, a ghlacadh beò.

Chaidh e faisg air dà mhìle, mun tàinig fear de shaighdearan mhic Iain 'ic Sheumais suas ris air tràigh, faisg air a' Bhaile Shear.

Ged a bha an dithis aca air an trom lot roimhe sin, thug iad deannal air iomairt-chlaidheamh.

Cha ghéilleadh mac Dhòmhnaill Ghlais is e beò, ach bha e a' gabhail iomain-chùil, gus mu dheireadh an deachaidh e a-mach air a' mhuir chun na duilleig.

Ged a bha toil aig an fhear eile a ghlacadh beò a-réir òrdugh a mhaighstir, an uair a thòisich an sàile ri dol anns na lotaibh, dh'fhàs e goirid 's an fhoighidinn, agus le aon sàthadh de'n chlaidheamh, chuir e crìoch air anns a' bhad an robh e, agus dh'fhàg e marbh air an oitir e.

Theireas Oitir 'ic Dhòmhnaill Ghlais ris an oitir gus an latha an-diugh.

Thìodhlaiceadh colainnean nan Leòdach far an do thuit iad: air Leathad a' Bhuailte, mar a theirear ris an àite riamh on a thugadh am blàr ann. Chuireadh an cinn ann an uinneagaibh an teampaill, far am bheil cuid diubh, is dòcha, fhathast ri'm faicinn.

Chan eil cunntas againn cia lìon a thuit de na Dòmhnallaich anns a' bhlàr fhuileachdach seo, ach, air a shon sin, faodaidh sinn a bhith cinnteach gun do thuit an àireamh bu mhó dhiubh.

Fhuair Dòmhnall mac Ian 'ic Sheumais e fhéin iomadh lot, ged a chaidh an latha leis. Ach thàinig e gu math dheth 'na dhéidh sin.

Tha e air aithris, ged nach ruig sinn a leas a chreidsinn, gun robh an fhèith a' ruith le fuil, agus uime sin, theirear Fèithe na Fala rithe gus an là an-diugh.

Theagamh gun saoil cuid gun robh e eucomasach do dhà fhear dheug cur ás do dhlùth air dà fhichead fear, ach mar a tha an seanfhacal ag ràdh, "Is fheàrr duine na daoine."

A bharrachd air a sin, an uair a bha na Dòmhnallaich 'gam falach fhéin anns an fhèith, agus càch a' cromadh leis a' bhruthaich, bha an cothrom aca orra, agus mun do thàrr iad sealltainn chuca no uatha, bha àireamh mhath dhiubh air an leònadh. Mar seo, chaill cuid mhór dhiubh am misneach gu buileach.

A thaobh nan Dòmhnallach, tha e air aithris, gun robh iad anabarrach ealanta air a' bhogha, agus, mar an ceudna, gun robh am boghachan cho làidir agus nach b' urrainn do neach sam bith an lùbadh ach iad fhéin.

Tha e furasta a thuigsinn, gun tilgeadh iad saighdean astar glé fhada. Leis na nithibh seo a bhith gu léir 'nam fàbhar, a bharrachd air iad a bhith 'nan daoine ro threun, tha e soilleir, nach bu nì doirbh dhaibh an là a chur.

Nuair a chuala Dòmhnall Gorm mu Bhlàr Chàirinnis, agus mu ghaisge a charaid, bha e ro thoilichte, agus mar chomharradh air a thaingealachd airson a threubhantais, thug e dha Gabhaltas na Cuidrich anns an Eilean Sgitheanach. Gu cinnteach, bha e 'na làn airidh air, agus còrr.

Clann Ghriogair agus Coin Dubha nan Caimbeulach

An uair a thàinig an t-òrdugh rìoghail a-mach gu Clann Ghriogair a sgrios, agus gun aon sean no òg, beag no mór d'an chinne threun mhisneachail sin 'fhàgail beò, cha robh aon d'an nàimhdean fuileachdach a bu déine air an tòir na na Caimbeulaich agus Donnachadh Dubh, Morair Bhealaich. Cha bu leòir leò daoine bhith 'ruagadh nan Griogarach agus 'gam murtadh, ach fhuair iad dà chù a leanadh Griogarach cho dian agus nach robh seòl dol ás aige.

Ghlac na Caimbeulaich bean de Chlann Ghriogair agus thug iad oirre an dà chuilean seo 'thogail air a broilleach. Agus an uair a dh'fhàs na coin, bha iad cho déidheil air na Griogaraich, agus gun togadh iad fàile aoin diubh am-measg ceud fear de chinneach air bith eile.

Mar seo, chaidh móran d'an chinneach bhochd sin a ghlacadh 'nan àitibh-fuirich leis na coin dhubha sin, agus a chur gu bàs, gus mu dheireadh an deachaidh dòigh 'fhaotainn air na coin a mharbhadh. Thachair e mar seo.

Bha duine d'am b'ainm MacEóghainn a' tàmh aig Taobh Loch Tatha aig an robh ban Ghriogarach mar mhnaoi. Bha eagal air gum biodh a bhean air a murtadh leis na coin, agus bha blàths 'na chridhe do Chlann Ghriogair air sgàth a mhnatha.

Chuir e roimhe cur ás do na coin nam b' urrainn da. Thòisich e le bhith ag ràdh nach robh na coin a' glacadh ach neach air bith a thigeadh 'nan rathad, agus gun robh gach uile neach an cunnart uapa.

Air do fhéill a bhith anns a' Cheann Mhór, chaidh MacEóghainn chum na féille, ach mun d'fhàg e a thaigh féin, fhliuch e a làmh agus a dhòrn le fuil a mhnatha.

Chaidh na coin a leigeil am-measg an t-sluaigh a dh'fheuchainn an glacadh iad aon de Chlann Ghriogair anns a' chuideachd. Chuir MacEóghainn e fhéin 'nan rathad an déidh da bhith ag ràdh ris gach neach mun cuairt da gun leanadh na coin air Caimbeulach cho ealamh ri neach eile.

Thog aon de na coin fàile na fola a bha air a làimh, agus ann am priobadh na sùl, bha e an sàs ann. Bha 'fhios aig gach neach nach bu Ghriogarach MacEóghainn. Dh'éirich buaireas am measg an t sluaigh, agus chaidh aon de na coin a spadadh an sin, agus am fear eile latha no dha ás a dhéidh. Mar seo chaidh cur ás do na coin dhubha.

Latha Blàr Shròn a' Chlachain

Mu mheadhan na seachdamh linne deug, nuair a bha an Ridir Raibeart Caimbeul 'na uachdaran air oighreachd Bhraid Albann, thuit e mach gun robh banais mhór bhrèagh aig Caisteal Fhionn Làirig làimh ri Clachan Chill Fhinn.

Bha Ridir Bhealaich a' toirt a nighinn ann am pòsadh do Sheumas Mèinn á Cùl Dara ann an Gleann Lìomhann, curaidh a choisinn mór chliù anns na cogaidhean aig Gustabhus Adolphus.

Nuair a bha cuirm na bainnse aig a h-àirde, thàinig teachdair, is e ruith le cabhaig, a dh'innseadh gun robh buidheann de Dhòmhnallaich na Ceapaich agus Ghlinne Comhann air dol thairis air abhainn Dochart aig Baile Chroisge, ag iomain creiche a thog iad am Braid Albann is an àitean eile.

Bha Caimbeulaich Bhraid Albann air bhreathas gu dol 'nan déidh, ach thuirt am Mèinnearach, a bha glé eòlach air òrdugh catha, gum biodh e cunnartach dol air an tòir suas uchdach Shròn a' Chlachain, a chionn gum biodh am bruthach, grian déidh a' mheadhan-là, agus a' ghaoth a' cumail cothruim ris na Dòmhnallaich, agus an aghaidh nan Caimbeulach. Bha e los gun toireadh iad cuairt rathad Ghleann Lòcha, gum faigheadh iad gu mullach an uchdaich, agus gun tigeadh iad air na Dòmhnallaich o mhullach Shròn a' Chlachain.

Ach bha na h-òganaich a bh' aig a' bhanais làn àrdain, agus theagamh làn fìona, agus comhairle cha ghabhadh iad. An àite sin, 's ann a rinn iad fochaid air, ag ràdh, "Am Mèinnearach bog, am Mèinneirach bog."

"Rachaibh air adhart ma-tà," ars am Mèinnearach, "agus chì sinn có tha bog mun tig deireadh an latha."

Thachair gach nì ceart mar bha sùil aig a' Mhèinnearach a thachaireadh e. Fhuair na Dòmhnallaich a' bhuaidh-làrach, agus chaidh an ruaig a chur air na Caimbeulaich.

'S iomadh euchd gaisgeil a rinn am Mèinnearach anns a' chath fhuileachdach agus mharbhtach seo. A dh'aon bheum le 'chlaidheamh, sgud e an ceann bhàrr Mac Iain Ghlinne Comhann.

Mar fhrith-ainm theireadh iad ris an t-saighdear ainmeil seo, "Crùnair ruadh nan cearc." Bha Mac Iain a' tilgeadh an ainme seo air ás an aodann nuair a thàinig e am fagus da gu còmhraig a dhèanamh ris, agus tha e air aithris nuair a bha 'cheann dol sìos am bruthach, car mu char, gun tuirt e uair is uair, "Cearc, cearc, cearc."

B' e Seumas Mèinn am fear mu dheireadh a chaidh thairis air abhainn Lòcha nuair a bha iad a' tilleadh dh'ionnsaigh a' chaisteil an déidh an ruaig a chur orra.

Air dha sealltainn air ais, thug e an aire do fhear de na Dòmhnallaich a' snàmh 'na dhéidh, 's e gu 'amhaich anns an linne. Chuir e ás da gu grad, agus thilg e corp an duine mhairbh air a dhruim gu bhith 'ga dìonadh o shaighdean a luchd-tòrachd, agus nuair a leig e sìos e aig Caisteal Fhionn Làirig, bha seachd saighdean an sàs ann.

Bha àr nan Caimbeulach cho mór is gun deach ochd deug de'n uaislean adhlacadh air an ath là aig caibeal a' chaisteil.

Bha Aonghus, ceann feadhna na Ceapaich, air a mharbhadh aig Blàr Shròn a' Chlachain, cho math ri Mac Iain Ghlinne Comhann, agus móran eile bharr orra.

Tha e air aithris timcheall Chill Fhinn agus air feadh Bhraid Albann, ged tha e duilich creideas a thoirt da, gun deach am Mèinnearach agus buidheann eile beagan an déidh seo, air tòir nan Dòmhnallach, gun d' rinn iad suas riù, agus gun tug iad a' chreach bhuapa.

Bha aon neach air a leòn 's a' bhlàr seo, a theich gu àirigh Choire Charmaig an Gleann Lòcha, agus bha e air fholach beagan làithean le boireannach a mhuinntir Loch Abar. Ach nuair a fhuair fear-pòsta na mnà seo eòlas air an àite 's an robh e air fholach, chuir e ás da.

Creachadair Loch Éire

Chaidh an dròbhair o'n iar sìos taobh Loch Éire is a thriùir ghillean ag iomain a' chruidh, is iad a' dèanamh air Baile Chraoibh far an robh sùil aig an duine chòir ris a' chrodh a reiceadh air probhait mhath an ath là, oir b' e sin an Fhéill Mhìcheil, <aig> a' mharg a bu mhò a bha ann an Albainn aig an àm sin, is car iomadh bliadhna roimhe is an déidh sin.

Thàinig là mór na féille, is rinn an dròbhair a dhìcheall a chum a chuid cruidh a reiceadh ri Sasannach brèagha a bha ag iarraidh cruidh air son an toirt dhachaigh do Shasann. Mar a bha nàdurra, dh'iarr an dròbhair tuilleadh airgid air a' chrodh na bha dùil aige ri fhaotainn is bha an Sasannach a' tairgseadh beagan nas lugha na bha 'na bheachd a thoirt orra mun cailleadh e iad.

An déidh a bhith deasbaireachd car tacain, chòrd na daoine mu'n phrìs is chaidh am bargan a dhaingneachadh le deoch mhath leanna.

Fhuair an dròbhair airgead is air dha fhéin is a ghillean biadh a ghabhail, stiùir iad ris an iar. Ràinig iad Naomh Faolain, neo mar a theireadh sluagh ris o shean Am Port Mór, is leis gun robh an t-àite sin dà mhìle dheug o Chraoibh, tuigidh sinn nach bu mhiste iad deoch fhaighinn 's an taigh-òsta bheag a bha aig Naomh Faolain. Nuair a dh'fhalbh an dròbhair le dithis de na gillean, dh'fhuirich fear 'nan déidh 's an taigh-òsta oir cha robh e làn shàsaichte.

Ghabh iad an rathad gu socrach gus an d'ràinig iad Cachaileith nan Gàidheal a tha còrr is mìle o Naomh Faolain far an do thachair tubaist dhoibh a chuir droch ghean orra uile. Leum fear fiadhaich colgarra a-mach rompa air an rathad, claidheamh 'na làimh dheis is daga 'na làimh chlì.

Thuirt e riu an guth neo-bhàigheil, "A-mach le bhur sporain gu ealamh neo bidh bhur beatha agam!"

Cha robh dhoibh ach sin a dhèanamh gun dàil. Le cridhe tùrsach trom, dh'fhàg an triùir bochd falamh dha-rìreamh oir ghabh <e an t-airgead uile a bh' aca>. Bha luach a' chruidh dhìth air an dròbhair is bha an dà ghille gun sgillinn dhuais.

Ràinig iad an taigh-òsta a bha aig Ceann Loch Éire sgìth gun mhisneach. Bu mhiann leò an anail a ghabhail 's an taigh-òsta, ach peighinn cha robh aca air son bìdh no dibhe, is bha iad a' gearan ri chéile mar a thachair dhoibh.

An ùine gun bhith ro fhada, thàinig am fear a dh'fhuirich 'nan déidh aig Naomh Faolain a-staigh do'n t-seòmar 's an robh iad. Thug e sùil mun cuairt is thuirt e mu'm biodh e fo ioghnadh, "Ciamar air thalamh nach eil sibh air òrdachadh leann? 'S ann a tha sibh uile mar gum biodh sibh air bhur crochadh! Seo, seo, togaibh oirbh, is faighibh leann a-staigh gu grad, oir tha mi fhéin teth tartmhor."

Fhreagair an dròbhair, "Chan eil bonn-sè ruadh againn. Thug robair bhuainn ar n-airgead gu léir."

"Mo nàire! Mo nàire! Gun aidicheadh sibh leithid de nì! Triùir cheatharanach air an spùilleadh le aon dhuine! Dh'fhalbh bhur cliù gu buileach."

Le sin a ràdh, dh'éigh e air leann dhoibh uile is phàigh e an leann cuideachd.

Dh'fhaighneachd an dròbhair dheth, "Nach do thachair thusa air an robair idir?"

"Ma-tà, thachair," fhreagair an t-òganach, "ach sgillinn cha d'fhuair e uamsa. Ghlaodh an robair gu stràiceil rium, 'Liubhair t' airgead dhomh.' Gun fhacal, tharraing mi a-mach mo sporan air dhòigh is gun do thuit an trom chuid de'n airgead air an rathad. Chrom esan gu umhail gu 'thrusadh ach bhuail mise e gu cruaidh air a chlaigeann le mo bhata 'ga chur 'na phaisean is an fhuil a' ruith gu dlùth á 'cheann, is ás a shròin. Spùill mi e is thug mi leam a chlaidheamh is a dhaga. Is cinnteach mise nach éirich e á siud 'na chabhaig."

Sgaoil an sgeul is chaidh buidheann de dhaoine làidir òga sìos an rathad a dhèanamh greim air. Fhuair iad e far an deachaidh 'fhàgail leis a' ghille. Cheangail iad a làmhan air a chùlaibh air eagal dé dhèanadh e nuair a dhùisgeadh e ás a phaisean. An-sin ghiùlain iad e gu Magh Bhàird far an robh e air dhìteadh gu bàs an ath là leis an Tòiseach ainmeil mu'm bheil an gnàth-fhacal, "Chan ann a h-uile latha bhios mòd aig Mac an Tòisich."

Gun dàil, chaidh an robair a chrochadh air croich àrd Bhaile Chraoibh a bha air a mallachadh leis na seann Ghàidheil nuair a rachadh iad seachad oirre, is gu dearbh, chan ann gun adhbhar.

Murt Ghlinn Comhann

Is gann gun deach aona mhìos seachad, nuair a thàinig Caiptein Caimbeul Ghlinn Lìomhann le freiceadan shaighdairean do Ghleann Comhann. B' e an leisgeul a bh' aca gun tàinig iad a thogail cìs teachd a-staigh agus càin eile.

Nuair a dh'fhoighnich Mac Mhic Iain dhiubh co-dhiù a thàinig iad mar chàirdean no mar nàimhdean, fhreagair an Caimbeulach agus thuirt e gun tàinig iad mar chàirdean agus mar choimhearsnaich, agus thug e 'fhocal nach éireadh cron sam bith d'a fhéin no d'a chinneadh.

Air tàille a' ghealltanais seo, chuir Cloinn Dòmhnaill fàilte is furan orra, agus fad cheithir là deug, fhuair iad aoigheachd gun choimeas o fhir Ghlinn Comhann.

Mu dheireadh thall, thàinig oidhche a' mhì-fhortain chruaidh! An déidh do Mhac Mhic Iain agus do'n Chaiptein Chaimbeul an latha chaitheadh an cuideachd a chéile, dhealaich iad mu sheachd uairean na h-oidhche le mùirn is le meas do chàch a chéile.

Nuair a thug Mac Mhic Iain fainear gun robh am freiceadan a' fàs am meudachadh, bhuail amharas air gun robh foill agus cealgaireachd anns a' chùis. Ach, chan éisteadh 'athair no a bhràthair ri droch amharas sam bith an aghaidh onair Fir Ghlinn Lìomhainn. Chuala Iain agus Alasdair, mic Mhic 'ic Iain, na saighdearean a' dèanamh cagar nach robh an gnothach a' tighinn riu idir, gun robh iad deònach gu leòir seasamh aghaidh ri aghaidh ri fir a' ghlinne, ach gur e nì nàr tàmailteach a bh' ann tighinn orra bho chùl an cinn.

Tha beul-aithris an t-sluaigh ag innseadh dhuinn gun robh a' chùis a chuir fear de na saighdearan cho trom is gun d'iarr e air fear an taighe tighinn ceum a-mach leis, ach a chionn gun robh e air mhionnan nach abaireadh e diog, labhair e mar seo ri cloich mhóir a bha mu choinneamh:

> A chlach ghlas a tha 's a' Ghleann,
> Ge mór do chòir a bhith ann,
> Nam b' fhios duit a-nochd mar thachras,
> 'S cinnteach nach fanadh thu ann.

Thug an Comhannach ás, agus ghabh e dìreach a dh'ionnsaigh Mhic 'ic Iain, agus dh'innis e dha mar a thachair. Dh'iarr Mac Mhic Iain air a chuid ghillean sùil a thoirt a-mach feuch gu dé a chìtheadh iad. Ach mun deach iad ach glé ghoirid, chunnaic agus chuala iad am pailteas.

Mun do thill iad a dh'innseadh do'n athair, chunnaic iad gun robh an taigh air chuartachadh leis na saighdeirean. Chuala iad urchraichean nan gunnachan am-measg glaodh, caoidh agus gal agus bas-bhualadh nam mnathan agus na cloinne.

Bha iad gu tur neo-dheas gu strì ris na saighdeirean a bha uile fo airm. Chaidh na saighdeirean a-staigh do sheòmar Mhic 'ic Iain. Loisg iad air, chaidh an urchair tro 'chlaigeann, agus thuit e marbh an uchd a mhnatha.

Chaidh a-nis an ceòl feadh na fìdhle. Thòisich a' chasgairt. Mun robh e sè uairean 's a' mhadainn, chaidh dà fhichead Comhannach a chur do'n t-Sìorraidheachd.

Chaidh na taighean a chur ri theine. Bha freiceadan làidir anns gach bealach. Cha b' urrainnear do na dìol-déirce thruagha teicheadh taobh sam bith. Bha sneachda trom air a' bhlàr. Cha robh e 'nan comas dol a-mach ri Bealach an Innein, no idir ri Gleann Lic na Muidhe.

Chaidh na bh' aca ris an t-saoghal a thogail. Chaidh an cuid cruidh agus chaorach, agus gach spréidh a bh' aca, a shaodachadh ás a' ghleann. Is e seo is ciall do'n phort:

A mhnathan a' ghlinne seo, ghlinne seo, ghlinne seo,
A mhnathan a' ghlinne seo 's mithich dhuibh éirigh,
Tha an crodh air an togail, tha an crodh air an togail,
Tha an crodh air an togail, is na fir air an reubadh.

Chaidh na saighdeirean a-staigh do gach taigh far nach d'fhàg iad ach banntraichean agus dìlleachdain. Ann an taigh a bha siud, theich giullan beag fo'n leabaidh agus nuair a dh'iarr na saighdeirean air tighinn a-mach, fhreagair e agus thuirt e, "Stad gus an criom mi mo chnàimh."

Is coltach ris gun robh an giullan a' criomadh cnàimh feòla nuair a bhuail na saighdeirean a-staigh. Chunnaic oifigeach bean bhrònach thruagh 'na seasamh am fasgadh creige, agus leanabh air a gàirdean.

Air ball, thug e òrdugh do dh'fhear d'a chuid dhaoine falbh agus cur ás do'n phàiste mas e leanabh-gille bh' ann. Is e leanabh-gille a bh' ann da-rìreabh ach bha an saighdear bàigheil blàth-chridheach, agus cha robh 'chridhe aige dochair a dhèanamh air an leanabh.

Thill e thun a chomanndair, agus dh'innis e mar a bha a' chùis. Fhuair e òrdugh e dhol air ais agus an leanabh a mhurt, agus mar bharantas gun do choimhlion e a dhleasnas, bha e ri a chlaidheamh a nochdadh do'n oifigeach smeurta le fuil an leanaibh.

Ach mo thruaighe! Bha an t-òrdugh cruaidh, agus bu chruaidh chridheach am fear a thug e. Ach cha robh comas air.

Dh'fhalbh an saighdear le cridhe trom, ach nuair a bha e faisg air bean a' mhì-fhortain agus a' chruaidh-fhortain, thug e an aire gun robh cuilean beag a' cur furan air, is e 'na sheasamh aig casan na mnatha.

"Seo mo chothrom!" ars an saighdear ris fhéin.

Thug e a chlaidheamh ás a thruaill, agus spàrr e tro'n chù e. Agus le glòir, mar gum b'eadh, agus le miad-mhór, thug e a chlaidheamh smeurta le fuil a dh'ionnsaigh a' chaiptein, a bha làn-thoilichte gun deachaidh 'òrdugh a choimhlionadh.

Móran bhliadhnaichean an déidh seo, chunnacas fìor sheann duine a' gabhail an rathaid ann an Strath na h-Àpainn. 'S e beul na h-oidhche bh' ann. Bha frasan sneachd agus glìb a' spùtadh a-nuas thar monaidhean Ghlinn a' Ghèarrloch. Cha robh an seann duine ach fann. Bha e 'na choigreach 'na dhùthaich fhéin.

Thàinig an oidhche. 'S i oidhche bhreun dhorcha fhuar a bh' ann. Cha robh an rathad ach leth-oireach ach chunnaic an seann duine solas fada bhuaidh ach ged a bha, cha b' fhada 'ga ruighinn e. B' e seo taigh Dhail na Tràighe.

Mu dheireadh, ràinig e taigh na h-aoigheachd, agus fhuair e fàilte a chuir blàths air cochall a chridhe.

Ach mun deach e a-staigh, sheas e air an stairsneach, agus bheannaich e an taigh a-réir an t-seann chleachdaidh Ghàidhealaich:

Beannaichear an taigh 's na bheil ann,
Eadar fhiodh, is chlach is chrann,
Móran bìdh, pailteas aodaich
Is slàinte dhaoine do na bheil ann.

An déidh dha suidhe sìos, agus greim bìdh a ghabhail, thòisich a' chracaireachd agus an còmhradh. Thug an seann duine cunntas air a chaithe-beatha. Bha e 's an arm-dhearg agus ged a bha, bha e an-diugh gun dachaigh gun charaid ris an t-saoghal. Thuig fear an taighe gum b' e seo fear de mhurtairean Ghlinn Comhann, agus bha e am beachd cur ás da.

Ach sheòl an seann duine nach bu Chaimbeulach e, agus nach do dhòirt e boinne fala anns a' ghleann. Dh'innis e mar a chaomhainn e beatha an leanaibh air gualann na mnatha mhì-fhortanaich thruaighe, ged a fhuair e òrdugh a chur gu bàs.

Dh'atharraich fear an taighe a bheachd, an àite a chorc a chur ann, 's ann a leum e suas, chuir e làmh mu mhuineal an t-seann duine agus phòg e e. Dh'innis e dha gum b' esan an leanabh, agus gum bu tric a dh'innis a mhàthair dha an sgeul ceudna.

Fhuair an seann duine dachaigh bhlàth an oidhche ud, agus gach latha is oidhche fhad 's a bha e beò.

Na Sìdhichean ann an Siorramachd Rois

Bha ann an earann de Ros o chionn ghoirid duine diadhaidh àraidh d'am b' ainm Iain. Thachair da gun robh làir shearraich aige agus air dhi bhith anns a' mhonadh, agus an t-àm d'am bu chòir searrach a bhith aice fagus do làimh, chaidh e an àird do'n mhonadh glé mhoch air Là na Sàbaid a dh'fhaicinn an robh an searrach aice, agus mur robh, bha e a' dol a dhèanamh tàmh 'ga caithris.

Air dha bhith 'ga sireadh greis, fhuair e i ach cha robh an searrach aice. Air dha am Bìoball a thoirt leis, rinn e suidhe ri taobh na làire agus thòisich e air a leughadh. Am feadh a bha e a' leughadh, chuala e fuaim mór mun cuairt da, agus ann an tiota, bha daoine móra liatha 'nan seasamh aig a chasan.

"Ciod e an leabhar a th' agad an-sin 'ga leughadh?" ars aon diubh ris.

"Tha," ars Iain, "am Bìoball."

"Am bheil thu a' faicinn geallaidh sam bith do mo leithid-sa ann?" ars an duine.

"Có e do leithid-sa?" ars Iain.

"Is mise," ars esan, "aon de na h-aingle a thuit a-nuas bho'n chathair."

"O," ars Iain, "chan eil. Chan eil mise a' faicinn geallaidh sam bith air son do'n leithid sin ann."

Nuair a chuala e nach robh gealladh sam bith d'a leithid-san anns a' Bhìoball, thug e ràn mór ás, agus dh'fhalbh e a' sgreadail agus a' sgreuchail a dh'innseadh an sgeòil bhrònaich do chàch.

Na Sìdhichean ann an Raithneach

Bha mac tuathanaich an Raithneach a thuit ann an euslaint, agus a bhiodh a' dol do'n mhonadh, mochthrath agus tràth-feasgair, feuch am faigheadh e na b' fheàrr.

An uair a thàinig an samhradh, agus a chaidh an crodh chum na h-àirighe, dh'fhalbh e 'nan déidh, agus dh'fhuirich e 'nan cois gus an do phill iad dhachaigh chum an t-sratha an toiseach an fhogharaidh.

Air latha ceòthar ciùin dh'fhalbh e 'gan trusadh dh'ionnsaigh na buaile-bleoghainn, ach chaidh e air iomrall 's a' cheò, agus bha e ùine mhath 'gan sireadh mun tàinig e orra. Fhuair e iad mu dheireadh ag ionaltradh ann an coire mór brèagh le feur gorm brìghmhor suas gu ruig an sùilean. Bha an là ceòbanach blàth agus feur a' brùch-dadh a-nìos gu bras ás an talamh agus, a thaobh gun robh e sgìth leis an teas, agus le siubhal a' mhonaidh, shuidh e sìos air tolman uaine a ghabhail analach.

Cha robh e ach goirid an-sin gus an cuala e guth, a' tighinn o bhun gach bileag fheòir aig a chasan, agus ag ràdh, "Cuid dhomhsa dheth, cuid dhomhsa dheth."

Dh'éist e an-sin tacain, agus a-nis bha an guth ceudna a' tighinn o bhun gach bileag fheòir a bh' anns a' choire. Sheall e feuch am faiceadh e có uaidh a thàinig na guthannan ach cha robh duine, beag no mór, ri fhaicinn. Dh'éist e a-rithist, agus an uair a chuala e a' ghàir cheudna an treas uair, thuig e gum b' ann o na sìdhichean a thàinig e. Agus ghlaodh e cho àrd riutha fhéin, "Agus cuid dhomhsa dheth cuideachd."

Air ball sguir a' ghàir, agus an-sin dh'iomain e an crodh chum na buaile.

Bha na banaraichean 'gam feitheamh, agus ioghnadh orra gu dé a ghléidh iad cho fada. Thòisich iad air am bleoghainn ach mun d'fhuair iad an leth seachad, cha robh soitheach air a' bhuaile nach robh a' cur thairis le bainne.

Cha b' urrainn iad a thuigsinn ciamar a dh'fhàs am bainne cho pailt ann an ùine cho goirid. Mu dheireadh, thòisich iad air an t-sìde a mholadh agus a ràdh gum b' i a b' adhbhar do'n phailteas.

Dh'éist mac an tuathanaich gu foighidneach ris gach nì a chuala e, ach thuirt e ris fhéin nach robh am bainne cho pailt anns na h-uile baile 's a bha air a' bhaile acasan an latha sin, agus nach biodh e cho pailt an siud cuideachd, nan do leig esan leis na sìdhi-chean, an uair a bha iad 'ga tharraing 'gan ionnsaigh anns a' choire.

An Tuathanach agus na Sìbhrich

Air do thuathanach àraidh aig an robh gabhail-fearainn anns an eilean seo anns na làithean a tha seachad, a bhith aon latha an toiseach an Earraich anns an achadh a' leantainn nan each anns a' chrann-treabhaidh, bhuail mar bu tric an t-acras e.

Ars esan ris fhéin, "Nan robh agam ach greim arain, chumadh e suas mi gu àm an tràth-nòin."

Air dha teachd gu ceann-iomaire an achaidh, mhothaich e fàile taitneach a chuir barrachd geurachaidh air a chàil: fàile bonnaich air ùr dheasachadh.

Ars esan, "Bu mhath leam crioman de'n bhonnach sin itheadh," agus lean e air aghaidh aig cùl nan each anns a' chrann gus an do thill e a-rithist gu ceann an iomaire. Agus dé a chunnaic e ach bonnach air ùr dheasachadh 'na laighe air an làr f'a chomhair.

Chuir seo ioghnadh air, ach thog e is dh'ith e am bonnach, agus bonnach a bu mhìlse, cha d'ith e a-riamh.

"Gu dearbh," ars esan, "Bu mhath leam bolla de'n mhin on d'rinneadh am bonnach sin fhaotainn."

Thug e car eile le na h-eich, agus air dha teachd a-rithist gus an àite cheudna, faicear bolla mine 'na shuidhe air an làr. Dh'fhuasgail e na h-eich ás a' chrann, agus thug e am bolla mine dhachaigh, agus a leithid de mhin cha d'ith e riamh: bha i cho milis blasta.

Thòisich e air breithneachadh mu'n chùis, agus thàinig e gus a' chòmh-dhùnaidh gum b'e seo obair nan sìbhreach, agus gum b' e a dhleastanas an caoimhneas a dhìoladh.

Nuair a thàinig a mhin fhéin ás a' mhuileann, dh'fhàg e bolla dhi aig ceann an iomaire far an d'fhuair e roimhe seo bonnach agus min nan sìbhreach agus thug iadsan leò min an tuathanaich.

Ùine ghoirid an déidh seo, thachair na sìbhrich air anns an achadh agus bha an caoimhneas air tionndadh gu feirg, a chionn ghlac iad e, agus ghabh iad air le buailteanan gu math agus gu ro mhath.

Dh'fheòraich iad deth, "Car-son a thug thu dhuinn min de'n t-seòrsa ud?"

"Thug mi dhuibh," ars an tuathanach, "min cho math 's a bha agam."

"Ach," ars iadsan, "a' mhin a thug sinne dhut, b' ann de'n ghràinne-mullaich a rinneadh i."

"Ma tha sin mar sin," ars esan, "bheir mise dhuibh min cho math ris a' mhin a thug sibhse dhomhsa."

Leis a' ghealladh seo, leig iad an tuathanch mu sgaoil, agus dachaigh ghabh e cho luath 's a bheireadh a chasan e, agus bhuail e an gràinne-mullaich de'n arbhar, chuir e do'n mhuileann e, agus dh'fhàg e bolla de'n mhin far am faigheadh na sìbhrich i.

Bho sin gus an do shiubhail e, bha e fhéin agus na sìbhrich 'nan deagh chàirdean.

Glaistig Ghlinn Dùror

Bha glaistig an Gleann Dùror ris an abradh iad a' Mhaighdean. Bu bhoireannach saoghalta a bha innte an toiseach. Bho cheann dà no trì cheud bliadhna, bha i 'na banaraich eadar Gleann Dùror agus Gleann a' Chaolais, agus tha a h-ainm agus a sloinneadh, agus eadhan am baile 's an d'àraicheadh i, fhathast air chuimhne.

Thugadh air falbh i ás a laighe-shiùbhladh leis na sìdhichean, agus cha do thill i tuilleadh. Ach a-réir beul-aithris, thionndaidheadh i 'na ban shìdhe no 'na glaistig, a ghabh fasgadh ann an easaibh agus ann an còsaibh nan creag eadar an dà ghleann. Bha i gu sònraichte a' tathaich Eas nam Mèirleach air taobh deas Beinn Bheithir agus bu tric a chunnacas an-sin i le luchd gabhail an rathaid.

Is coltach gun do lean rithe 'na glaistig an spéis a bha aice roimhe do chrodh agus do gach seòrsa spréidhe. Gu minic bha i r'a faicinn am meadhan a' chruidh mar gum bitheadh i 'gan cunntas, agus ro fhaidhrichean, agus aig àm atharrachadh tuath, mar gum biodh i a' cur air leth a' chuid de'n stochd a bha falbh, no a' gabhail seilbhe anns a' chuid a bha air tighinn. Ma bha aon de'n tuath a b' fheàrr leatha na càch, bha i ro chùramach m'a spréidh-san agus aig àm dol air imrich, chuireadh i gach bacadh eadar e agus an togail bhàrr an fhearainn.

A-réir beul-aithris, thachair seo an uair mu dheireadh o cheann deich bliadhna fichead. Co-dhiùbh, o sin gu seo chan fhacas is cha chualas a' ghlaistig. Theagamh gun do ruaigeadh ás a' ghleann i le sgreadail fhideag nam bàtaichean smùide a' dol sìos is suas an Linne Sheilich, no le urchairean luchd-buidhinn cloiche na creige éiteige aig bun Eas nan Con.

Co-dhiùbh, dh'fhalbh i, agus chan eil duine 'ga h-ionndrainn.

Is iomadh sgeul a bha air innseadh m'a timcheall, agus is iomadh meadar math bainne a chaitheadh oirre le banaraichean air àirighean a' ghlinne. Oir an oidhche a dh'fhàgadh iad am meadar làn bainne aice, gheibheadh iad gach nì ceart an dara mhàireach. Ach an oidhche nach fàgadh, bhiodh na laoigh air an leigeil a-mach ás a' chrò, agus an crodh air an deoghal air an ath mhadainn.

Tàillear Ruadh Raithneach

Bha an Tàillear Ruadh a chòmhnaidh an Raithneach. Coltach ris a' chòrr d'a sheòrsa, bhiodh e a' dol o thaigh gu taigh a dhèanamh aodaich de'n chlò a bhiodh mnathan grunndail a' dèanamh d'am fir agus d'am mic anns na h-àmaibh a chaidh seachad.

Uaireigin, is e a' tarraing dlùth do thaigh far an robh obair beagan làithean aige ri dhèanamh, thàinig am feasgar air, agus chunnaic e, ann an doillearachd an anmoich, aon coltach ri leanabh fìor bheag, a' ruith air thoiseach air, agus a' gléidheadh ás an t-sealladh air chùl gach pris agus gach cnuic ri taobh an rathaid.

Chruadhaich e a cheum an dùil gum beireadh e air an duineachan iongantach a bha roimhe, ach an àite a bhith a' buidhinn, b' ann a bha e a' call leis gach ceum a bheireadh e. Cho luath 's a thug e seo fa-near, thòisich e air ruith le a uile neart, ach a dh'aindeoin a bhoicinn, cha b' urrainn e an t-astar eatorra a ghiorrachadh.

Mu dheireadh, chaill e a fhoighidinn cho buileach is gun do thilg e an siosar mór air an duineachan sgiobalta a bha an toiseach air, agus bhuail e anns na h-easgaidean e. Thuit an sìbhreach, oir b' e sin a bha ann, air 'aghaidh, agus mun d'fhuair e éirigh, bha e an gàirdeanaibh an tàilleir, agus an siosar tarsainn air a bhroilleach.

"Innis domhsa càite am bheil thu a' dol, mo ghille maith," ars an Tàillear.

"Tha mi air mo rathad o'n t-Sìdhean Mhór gus an taigh air thoiseach ort, a dh'fhaotainn tacain de bhainne-cìche bean an taighe," fhreagair an gàrlaoch crìon.

B' e seo a' cheart taigh gus an robh an Tàillear a' dol.

"Agus gu dé nì thu ri leanabh na mnatha fhéin," ars e an-sin.

"U! Cuiridh mi a-mach e do mo mhuinntir air uinneig-chùil an taighe agus bheir iadsan leò e do'n àite againne," fhreagair am fear eile.

"Agus an cuir iad dachaigh e an uair a gheibh thusa do leòr de bhainne-cìche a mhàthar?"

"U! Cha chuir, cha chuir tuilleadh."

"Nì sin an gnothach," ars an Tàillear, agus leig e ás a phrìosanach.

Cho luath is a fhuair e comas a choise, shìn e ás a dh'ionnsaigh an taighe, agus bha e a-staigh mun d'ràinig an Tàillear. Bha an taigh aige dha fhéin, oir bha fear an taighe agus a bhean anns a' bhàthaich a' leigeil a' chruidh, agus gun duine a-staigh ach an leanabh anns a' chreathall. Thog e an leanabh 'na ghàirdeanaibh, agus shìn e a-mach e air an uinneig-chùil, mar shaoil e, do na sìbhrich eile. Ach bha an Tàillear rompa, agus ghabh e gu sàmhach an leanabh 'na ghàirdeanaibh, agus dh'fhalbh e leis gu taigh peathar dha a bha goirid ás, agus dh'fhàg e air a cùram e.

An uair a thill e, fhuair e a' bhean air thoiseach air, agus an tàcharan anns a' chreathall, an impis sgàinidh a' caoineadh. Thog a' bhean e, thug i dha deoch, agus an-sin chuir i air ais e anns a' chreathall. Cha robh e fada an-sin an uair a thòisich e air glaodhaich is air caoineadh a-rithis. Thog i e, agus thug i dha deoch eile. Ach a-réir coltais, chan fhoghnadh nì leis ach a bhith air 'fhàgail an còmhnaidh air a' bhroilleach.

Chaidh a' chluich seo air a h-aghaidh fad beagan làithean eile. Ach air do fhoighidinn an Tàilleir ruith a-mach, leum e mu dheireadh bhàrr a bhùird-obair, thug e a-staigh làn cléibh de mhòine, agus chuir e teine mór air an teallach.

An uair a bha an teine an teas a ghabhalach, leum e a-null do'n chreathall, thog e leis an tàcharan, agus mum b' urrainn duine a bha a-staigh dol 's an eadraiginn, thilg e an teis-meadhan na lasrach e.

Ach leum an slaightear crìon a-mach tro'n luidhear, agus o mhullach an taighe, ghlaodh e gu caithreamach ris a' mhnaoi, "Fhuair mi siud de shùgh do chléibh, ge b' oil leat."

Agus thug e an rathad air.

A' Bhean a Ghoid na Sìdhichean

Bho chionn fada bha buidheann shìdhichean a' còmhnaidh ann an Cnoc 'ic Eóghainn an Druim a' Ghineir. Bha iad fhéin agus tuathanach àraidh do'm b' ainm MacMhurchaidh anabarrach càirdeil mu chéile. Bhiodh esan a' dol gu tric air chéilidh leò, ach bha e daonnan a' dèanamh brath-ghabhail gun sàthadh e sgian, no snàthad mhór, no crioman iarainn de'n t-seòrsa sin, am bràigh an dorais aca a chum an rathaid a bhith réidh dha gu teachd a-mach.

Oidhche de na h-oidhchean a chaidh e a choimhead orra, fhuair e iad uile cruinn air mullach a' chnocain mu theinn ag ullachadh airson turais éiginn. Spìon gach aon diubh geothastan, agus air dhaibh facail dhìomhair aithris, chaidh iad casan-gobhlach air a' gheothastan, agus an àird gabhar iad anns an adhar cho aotrom ri iteig.

Rinn MacMhurchaidh an nì ceudna: spìon esan geothastan, chaidh e casan-gobhlach air, agus ag aithris nam briathran-sìdhe, suas gabhar e ás an déidh cho luath 's cho aotrom ri h-aon diubh fhéin. Stiùir iad an cùrsa nunn thar Maol Chinn-Tìre, an rathad a bu ghiorra gu Éirinn.

Ann an ùine ghoirid, fhuair MacMhurchaidh e fhéin ann an cidsin tuathanaich an Éirinn far an robh bean an taighe 'na laighe ri uchd a' bhàis, agus gach sean chailleach 's an àite a' frithealadh dhi.

Ann am priobadh na sùla, spiol na sìdhichean a' bhean bhochd air falbh, agus dh'fhàg iad 'na h-àite ploc fiodha an cruth na mnatha. An-sin thog iad orra thun an dachaigh air a' cheart dòigh anns an d'fhàg iad, is MacMhurchaidh agus bean an tuathanaich 'nan cuideachd.

Nuair a ràinig iad an cnocan sìdhe an Druim a' Ghineir, thug iad a' bhean do MacMhurchaidh air son gun deachaidh e leotha do dh'Éirinn, is dh'fhan i leis mar a bhean phòsta.

Seachd bliadhna an déidh seo, air feasgar blàth samhraidh, thàinig déirceach bochd Éireannach an rathad agus air dha bhith sgìth, shuidh e air a' chloich-chnotaidh ri taobh doras MhicMhurchaidh.

Bha bean an taighe a' bleoghann nam bó agus gach uair a rachadh i seachad eadar a' bhàthaich is an taigh-bainne, theireadh an déirceach, "Ma-tà, mur biodh gun do chuir mi mo bhean le mo dhà làimh fhéin anns a' chiste-mhairbh, mhionnaichinn gum bu tusa i."

B' e deireadh an sgeòil gun d'fhalbh a' bhean leis an déirceach Éireannach, a fear-pòsta dligheach.

Siùnnsair MhicCruimein

An uair a bha òganach an fhuilt dhuinn de fhine nam fear-fonn fiùghail a' cluich air pìob mhór nan dos an grunnd Sloc nam Pìobairean, bhuail ruisg a shùl le iongantas agus leum a chuisle le aoibhneas ri faicinn rìbhinn nam buadh a bu mhaisiche na rìbhinn sam bith a bha beò. Fo cheithir ranna ruadha an domhain, cha d'fhuaras comhalt do'n mhaighdinn. Bha siùnnsair airgid 'na làimh agus shìn i siud do MhacCruimein.

Thuirt i ris gun tugadh an siùnnar dha buaidh air fir-chiùil na Cruinne gu léir. Ach an déidh là is bliadhna gum feumadh e falbh do dh'Uaimh an Òir.

Ghlac an t-òganach am feadan airgid agus chaidh a chur gu luath fo gheasaibh. Cha dealaicheadh e ris ged a gheibheadh e beartas an t-saoghail gu léir. Air dha cluich air inneal nam pung binn, chualas ceòl nach cualas a leithid. Thàinig an uiseag is an smeòrach a dh'éisteachd is dh'fhuirich iad gu léir 'nan tost. Thàinig na féidh bho bheinn a' cheò a dh'éisteachd na caismeachd bhinn. Thàinig an dòbhran donn gu bruaich nan allt agus ròn nan tonn gu fonn a dh'fhairchluais. Dh'fhàs an t-euslan slàn agus dh'fhàs brònach sona. Bha linn an àigh air teachd.

Mhair an sòlas fad là is bliadhna. Ach thàinig an uair is thàinig a' mhionaid. Air madainn shona shamhraidh, thog an t-òg air gu bhith triall. Chuir e cùl ri 'chàirdean is dh'fhàg e dachaigh nam beò. Chuir e 'aghaidh air Uaimh an Òir agus sheinn e port air nach eil sgeul ach na briathran:

Cha tig mise, cha ruig mise
Cha tig mise á Uamh an Òir;
Bidh na minn bheaga
'Nan gabhair chreagach
Is a' chlann laga nam fir-àir;
Bidh na mic uchda
'Nam fir aca
Mun tig mise á Uamh an Òir.

Iain Dubh Mór agus an Uruisg

Ann an cearn de Chinn-Tìre tha allt a' ruith troimh ghlaicean ris an abrar Allt na Béist, agus mas fhìor e, thugadh an t-ainm seo air an allt a chionn is gun robh, a-réir seanchais, anns an linntean a dh'fhalbh, uruisg uamhasach, no uile-bhéist de'n t-seòrsa sin, a' tuinneachadh am-measg chòsan an uillt.

Bha an uamh-bhéist seo a' cur oillt agus uamhais air a' choimhearsnachd uile, agus cha robh neach a rachadh fagus do'n àite far an robh an uruisg a' dèanadh còmhnaidh. Chluinnteadh air uairean raoiceil agus nuallan ha h-uile-bhéist fada air astar, a' cur eagal an cridhe air sean is òg, agus rachadh iad mìltean air chuairt seach dol thar an allt dlùth do'n àite sin.

Ach bha aon duine anns a' choimhearsnachd a rinn suas 'inntinn—thigeadh mar dh'fhaodadh, buaidh no bàs—gun tugadh e dùbhlan do'n uile-bhéist, agus, nan soirbhicheadh leis, gum biodh an t-àite cuidhte de'n uamhas seo. B' e sin Iain Dubh Mór, duine treun sgairteil gaisgeil.

B' iomadh comhairle a fhuair Iain gun gnothach a bhith aige ris an nì uamhasach sin, gum b' fheàrr leigeil le cùisean mar a bha na a bheatha 'chur an cunnart, ach thug e cluas bhodhar do gach comhairle.

'S e bh' ann air feasgar samhraidh rinn e làn uidheamachaidh gu cath a chur ris an uruisg, agus thog e air gu àite-tuinneachaidh na béist. Nuair a bha Iain a' dlùthachadh air an àite sin, chuala an uruisg faram nan cas, agus thugar ràn aiste a sgoltadh na creagan, agus a chuir crith air Iain, gaisgeil mar bha e.

Ràinig e oir an uillt, agus thug e dùbhlan do'n bhéist tighinn a-mach ás na frògan.

Ràn oillteil fhuair e mar fhreagairt. Ceum no dhà thug e air adhart gu meadhan an uillt, agus seasar air cloich leathainn a bha an-sin. A-mach gabhar an uruisg 'ga choinneachadh is coltas fiadhaich air a gnùis. Co-dhiùbh, b' e duine no beathach no an dà chuid, cha robh Iain cinnteach, ach ged a b' e an Donas fhéin a bh' ann, cha rachadh e aon cheum air ais. Chuir e e fhéin ann an òrdugh catha le 'chlaidheamh 'na làimh.

"Buail mi," ars an uruisg.

"Cha bhuail, ach buail thusa mise," ars Iain.

"Cha bhuail," ars an uruisg, "ach buail thusa mise."

"Cha bhuail," fhreagair Iain, "ach ma bhuaileas thusa mise, buailidh mise thusa."

Mar seo chum iad air ré ùine fhada, gun aon diubh 'toirt a' cheud bhuille. Ach mu dheireadh thall, thug an uruisg ionnsaigh air Iain. Ma thug, sheas Iain a ghrunnd gu duineil, agus thug e seachad tuilleadh mór na bha e a' faotainn, a' slachdadh is a' sàthadh le 'uile neart. Chuir iad an cath gu cruaidh sgaiteach, gus an robh iad ar-aon cho sgìth 's gun do stad iad de'n chòmhraig a tharraing an analach. Sheas Iain mar a bha e deas gus a' chath ath-thòiseachadh, ach a-réir coltais, fhuair an uile-bheist tuilleadh na chòrd rithe.

Tacan beag agus labhair i mar seo. "Tha mi 'faicinn," ars ise, "agus tha dearbhadh agam 'nam cholainn gur duine gaisgeil thu, agus gun d'fhuair do ghaisgeachd buaidh tharam. Cha do shaoil mi gun robh aon neach 's an sgìre seo, no an sgìre eile, aig robh de dhànadas tighinn 'am aghaidh no dùbhlan a thoirt dhomh mar rinn thusa. Cha toir mise tuilleadh còmhraig dhuit, ach airson do threubhantais bheir mi dhuit do roghainn de dhà nì, agus a-réir do roghainn, bidh e dhuit."

"Cluinneam an dà nì sin," ars Iain.

"Co-dhiù 'ghabhas thu," ars an uruisg, "ealain gun rath, no rath gun ealain?"

Gun móran beachdachaidh a dhèanadh mu'n chùis, fhreagair Iain, "Gabhaidh mi ealain gun rath."

"Mar sin biodh e," ars an uruisg, "á seo a-mach cha chuir mise tuilleadh dragha air neach beò, agus chan fhaicear is cha chluinnear mi an-seo no an àite sam bith eile gu bràth."

Am priobadh na sùla, bha an uruisg ás an t-sealladh, agus ghabh Iain a rathad dachaigh.

Dh'innis e mar thachair, agus ged a b' e duine fìrinneach Iain, bha móran de na coimhearsnaich a bha 'cur teagaimh 's a' chùis, gus an do dhearbh iad dhaibh fhéin gun robh iad da-rìreabh cuidhte de'n chùis-eagail a chuir dragh orra fad iomadh bliadhna, agus gum b' e Iain Dubh Mór an gaisgeach curanta a thug am fuasgladh seo dhaibh.

An déidh mar thachair, thòisich Iain air 'obair làitheil mar bu ghnàth leis, agus bha mór-ioghnadh air fhéin is air a choimhearsnachd uile cho math, cho sgiobalta, 's cho ealanta 's a chuireadh e obair tro 'làmhan. Bha gach obair, gach ceàird, gach dreuchd a ghabhadh Iain os làimh air an coimhlionadh cho ealamh, cho math, 's cho iomlan, 's gun deachaidh cliù is tapadh a ghnìomharan air fad is air fàrsaingeachd na tìre. Bha lìonmhorachd obaire de gach seòrsa a' tighinn dha làimh na h-uile latha.

Ach ged a bha saothair Iain 'na mhór bhuannachd do'n dùthaich mun cuairt, a dh'aindeoin na dhèanadh e, cha robh soirbheachadh sam bith a' leantainn a shaothrach dha fhéin no d'a theaghlach. Ged a thigeadh duais a shaothrach dha làimh, cha leanadh e ris. Bha Iain cho bochd aig deireadh na seachdain is a bha e aig a toiseach.

Ainmeil is mar bha e airson ealantas a làimhe, cha robh rath 'ga leantainn, agus thuig e nuair a bha e tuilleadh is anmoch gun d'rinn e an droch roghainn dha fhéin nuair a roghnaich e ealain gun rath.

An Leannan Crodhanach

Bha cailin òg ann aon uair aig an robh gille dreachail mar leannan. Bhiodh e gu tric a' dol 'ga faicinn an uaigneas, ach chan innseadh e 'ainm, no far an robh e chòmhnaidh. Gach uair a rachadh e choimhead uirre, gheibheadh e i daonnan ri snìomh. Bha e ro dheònach gun ruitheadh i air falbh leis, agus a sìor ghuidhe uirre i dhol leis ach dhiùlt i sin a dhèanadh.

Uair de na h-uairean a chaidh e 'ga faicinn, bha i air tì tòiseachadh air sac mór rolag olainn a shnìomh. Thairig e dhi gun snìomhadh esan an sac rolaig nan gealladh i dha a dhol leis. Bha i sgìth de'n obair, agus thug i gealladh dha gun rachadh i leis air chùmhnant gum biodh i saor o'n ghealladh nam faigheadh i a-mach 'ainm mum biodh an sac rolaig snìomhte.

'S e bh' ann gun do thog e an sac air a dhruim is ghabh e an rathad. Air oidhche àraidh 'na dhéidh sin, air dhi a bhith dol gu taigh caraid, agus a' dol thairis air allt domhain ann an àite uaigneach, chuala i fuaim cuibhle-shnìomhaich agus duanag òrain ag éirigh á ìochdair an uillt. Chuir seo iongantas air a' chailin agus theann i dlùth do'n àite ás an tàinig an fhuaim.

Dé chunnaic is a chuala i ach sean duine crìon crìopach dubh-neulach 'na shuidhe aig cuibhil mhóir a' snìomh gu dian, agus a' seinn gu h-aighearach:

'S beag fhios a th' aig mo leannan-sa
Gur "Crodhanach" is ainm dhomh.

Thuig a' chailin a-nis an seòrsa leannain a bh' aice, agus gum b' ann am frògan an uillt a bha 'àite-còmhnaidh.

Nuair a chuir e crìoch air an obair, chaidh e a-rithist a dh'fhaicinn na cailin, agus a dh'iarraidh duais a shaothrach. Cho luath 's a chunnaic i e, dh'aithris i na briathran a chuala i:

'S beag fhios a th' aig mo leannan-sa
Gur "Crodhanach" is ainm dhomh.

Cha luaithe chuala "Crodhanach" na facail sin na ás an t-sealladh gabhar e 'na shradan dearga suas an luidhear, agus tuilleadh dragh cha do chuir e air a' chailin.

Cù Dubh Mhic a' Phì

Chaidh Mac 'ic Ailein Àrasaig, Tighearna Mhùideairt, a shealgaireachd feadh a chuid frìthe fhéin, is e òg, is e gun phòsadh. Chunnaic e làn damh féidh m'a choinne cho brèagha 's a chunnaic e riamh. Chuir e 'ghunna r'a shùil, is leum e 'na bhoireannach cho brèagha 's a chunnaic e riamh air fad. Thug e a-nuas an gunna bho shùil, is bha e 'na làn damh féidh mar a bha e roimhe. Na h-uile uair a chuireadh e 'ghunna r'a shùil, bhiodh e 'na bhoireannach, is na h-uile uair a bheireadh e ri làr i, bhiodh e 'na làn damh féidh.

Chuir e an-seo an gunna r'a shùil, agus dh'fhalbh e gus an robh e ri broilleach. Thug e an leum sin ás, is rug e oirre eadar a dhà làimh.

"Cha bhi thu air do dhealachadh uam idir," ars esan. "Cha phòs mi gin ach thu."

"Na dèan sin, a Mhic 'ic Ailein," ars ise. "Chan eil turas sam bith agad rium. Cha fhreagair mi ort. Cha bhi latha am feast, fhad is a bhios mise agad, nach fheum thu mart a mharbhadh dhomh."

"Gheibh thu sin," ars Tighearna Mhùideairt, "ged iarradh tu dithis 's an latha."

Ach thòisich a' bhuaile aig Mac 'ic Ailein air fàs tana. Thòisich e an-seo air a cur air falbh, is cha b' urrainn da. Chaidh e an-seo thun seann duine bha air a' bhaile, a bha 'na fhear-comhairle aige. Thuirt e ris gum biodh e briste 's nach robh fhios aige dé an seòl a ghabhadh e air a cur air falbh. Thuirt an seann duine còir ris, mur an cuireadh Mac a' Phì Cholbhasa air falbh i, nach robh e beò a chuireadh air falbh idir i.

Anns a' mhionaid sin fhéin, chaidh litir a chur gu Mac a' Phì. Fhreagair Mac a' Phì an litir, is thàinig e gu Àrasaig.

"Dé seo an turas a th' agad riumsa," ars Mac a' Phì, "a Mhic 'ic Ailein?" Chuir Mac 'ic Ailein an céill da mar a thàinig am boireannach ud air is nach b' urrainn da a cur air falbh.

"Falbh thusa," arsa Mac a Phì, "agus marbh mart di an-diugh mar a b' àbhaist, cuir a dìnnear thuice do'n t-seòmar mar a b' àbhaist, is thoir dhomhsa mo dhìnnear an taobh eile an t-seòmair."

Rinn Mac 'ic Ailein mar a dh'iarr e. Thòisich i air a dìnnear, is thòisich Mac a' Phì air a dhìnnear fhéin. Nuair a bha Mac a' Phì ullamh d'a dhìnnear, sheall e a-null oirre-se.

"Dé do naidheachd, a Shìdheanach?" ars esan.

"Dé sin duitse, a Bhrian Brugh?" ars ise.

"Chunnaic mis' thus,' a Shìdheanach," ars esan,
"is tu a' gabhail coinne ris na Fiantaichean,
is tu a' falbh le Diarmad Ó Dhuibhne,
's tu a' falbh leis o phill gu pill."
"Chunnaic mis' thusa," ars ise,
"a Bhrian Brugh,
is tu a' marcachd air seann each dubh,
leannan na mnà seanga sìdh,
is tu 'ga sìor-ruith o bhrugh gu brugh."

"Coin is gillean ris a' bhiast," ars Mac a' Phì. "Is fhada m' eòlas oirre."

Ghlaodh iad a h-uile cù is duine a bha an Àrasaig, is chuireadh ás a déidhinn iad. Theich i air falbh a-mach rubha Àrasaig, is chan fhac iad an t-ath-shealladh di.

Chaidh Mac a' Phì dhachaigh gu Colbhasa aige fhéin an-seo. Chaidh e là de na làithean a shealgaireachd, is thàinig an oidhche air mun tàinig e dhachaigh. Chunnaic e solas, is rinn e dìreach air an t-solas. Chunnaic e móran dhaoine 'nan suidhe a-staigh an-sin, is seann duine liath còmhla riutha 'nam measg.

Labhair an seann duine is thuirt e, "Mhic a' Phì, thig air t' aghaidh."

Ghabh Mac a' Phì air 'aghaidh suas, is dé a thàinig 'na rathad ach galla cho brèagha 's a chunnaic e riamh, is cuileanan òga aice. Chunnaic e cuilean aice, a bha dubh 's an dath, nach fhaca e cuilean riamh a bha cho dubh no cho brèagha ris.

"Bidh an cù-sa agam fhìn," ars Mac a' Phì ris an duine.

"Cha bhi," ars an duine. "Gheibh thu do rogha cù de na bheil aice, ach chan fhaigh thu am fear sin."

"Cha ghabh mi aon de na bheil aice," ars Mac a' Phì, "ach am fear-sa."

"Bhon a tha thu a' cur romhad a thoirt leat," ars an duine, "cha dèan e ach feum an aon latha dhuit, is nì e sin gu math dhuit. Thig air a leithid seo dh'oidhche is gheibh thu e."

Ràinig Mac a' Phì an t-àite air an oidhche air an do gheall e tighinn. Thug iad dha an cù, "Is thoir an aire dha gu math," thuirt an seann duine. "Cha dèan e feum dhuit am feasd ach an t-aon latha."

Thòisich an cù dubh air fàs 'na chuilean brèagha, nach fhaca duine riamh cù a bha cho mór no cho brèagha ris. Nuair a bhiodh Mac a' Phì a' dol a shealgaireachd, ghlaodhadh e an cù dubh, is ruigeadh an cù dubh an doras, is thilleadh e an-sin is laigheadh e far an robh e roimhe. Bhiodh na daoine uaisle 'bhiodh a' tighinn gu taigh Mhic a' Phì ag iarraidh air an cù a mharbhadh, nach b' fhiach dha a bheathachadh. Theireadh Mac a' Phì riu iad leigeadh leis, nach tàinig latha a' choin duibh fathast.

Thàinig an-seo móran dhaoine uaisle a-nall á Ìle a thadhal air Mac a' Phì, is a dh'iarraidh air dol a-null a Dhiùra a shealgaireachd. Bha Diùra 's an àm sin 'na fhàsach, gun duine a' gabhail còmhnaidh ann, is gun àite air an t-saoghal coltach ris air son fhiadh agus earbachan. Bha àite an-sin far am bu ghnàths le daoine uaisle a rachadh a shealgaireachd ann fuireach, ris an abradh iad an Uamh Mhór.

Chuir iad bàta air dòigh gu dol thar a' chaol a-null an latha sin. Dh'éirich Mac a' Phì gu falbh, agus sia deug de dhaoine uaisle òga còmhla ris. Ghairm a h-uile fear riamh an cù dubh, is ràinig e an doras, is thill e, is laigh e far an robh e roimhe.

"Cuir an gunna ris," ars na daoine uaisle òga.

"Cha chuir," ars esan. "Tha là a' choin duibh gun tighinn fhathast."

Ghabh iad gu cladach, is shéid a' ghaoth, is cha d'fhuair iad thairis an latha sin.

Rinn iad deas a-màireach air son falbh. Ghairmeadh an cù dubh, is ràinig e an doras, is thill e far an robh e roimhe.

"Marbh e," ars na daoine uaisle, "is na bith 'ga bheathachadh nas fhaide."

"Cha marbh mi," ars Mac a' Phì. "Thig là a' choin duibh fhathast."

Ach dh'fhartlaich orra dol fairis an latha seo, aig cho doirbh is a bha an t-sìde, is thill iad.

"Tha fiosachd aig a' chù dhubh," ars na daoine uaisle.

"Tha fios aige gun tig a latha fhéin fhathast," ars Mac a' Phì.

Air an treas latha, bha latha brèagha ann. Ghabh iad gu port, is cha tuirt iad diog ris a' chù dhubh an latha seo. Chuir iad a-mach am bàta gu falbh. Sheall aon de na daoine uaisle, is thuirt e gun robh an cù dubh a' tighinn, is nach fhaca e a leithid de chreutair riamh, leis a' cholg a bha air a' tighinn. Leum e, is b' e an ceud chreutair a bha a-staigh 's a' bhàta.

"Tha là a' choin duibh a' dlùthachadh oirnn," ars Mac a' Phì. Thug iad leò biadh is eudach laighe, is ghabh iad air tìr ann an Diùra. Chuir iad seachad an oidhche sin 's an Uaimh Mhóir. Agus an làrna-mhàireach, chaidh iad a shealg nam fiadh. Beul uidhe ri anmoch, thàinig iad dhachaigh. Chuir iad àirde air an t-suipeir. Bha teine brèagha aca 's an uaimh agus solas. Bha toll mór air fìor mhullach na h-uamha, a thiocadh duine a-mach is a-staigh air.

Nuair a ghabh iad an suipeir, rinn na daoine uaisle òga sìneadh 's na leapannan.

Dh'éirich Mac a' Phì is bhuail e air garadh chùl-chas a dhèanamh ris an teine 'na sheasamh. Thuirt a h-uile fear de na daoine òga gum b' fheàrr leis gun robh a leannan fhéin aige an-siud a-nochd, is nam biodh, gum biodh e gu math dheth.

"Ma-tà," ars Mac a' Phì, "b' fheàrr leam fhìn mo bhean a bhith 'na taigh fhéin. Tha e gu leòr leam fhìn a bhith an-seo a-nochd."

Thug Mac a' Phi sùil uaidhe, is chunnaic e sia deug de bhoireannaich a' tighinn a-staigh air doras na h-uamha. Chaidh an solas ás, is cha robh aca de sholas ach na bha an teine a' dèanamh.

Ghabh na boireannaich a-null far an robh na daoine uaisle 'nan leapannan. Cha robh Mac a' Phì a' léirsinn leus leis cho dorcha 's a dh'fhàs an uamh. Cha robh e a' cluinntinn guth aig duine thall.

Dh'éirich na boireannaich 'nan seasamh, is sheall té dhiubh air Mac a' Phì. Sheas i mu 'choinne mar gum biodh i a' dol a thoirt ionnsaigh air. Dh'éirich an cù dubh is chuir e an colg sin air fhéin. Thug e leum ás thuca. Ghabh iadsan an doras. Leum an cù dubh ás an déidh gu beul na h-uamha.

Nuair a dh'fhalbh iad, thill an cù dubh a-nuas is laigh e aig cois Mhic a' Phì. Beagan 'na dhéidh sin, chuala Mac a' Phì tartar os a chionn ann am mullach na h-uamha, gun robh dùil aige gum biodh an uamh mu 'cheann. Sheall e os a chionn, is chunnaic e làmh duine a' tighinn a-nuas ás an toll, mar gum biodh i a' dol a bhreith air fhéin, is 'ga thoirt a-mach tro'n toll, tro mhullach na h-uamha.

Thug an cù dubh an leum sin ás, agus eadar a' ghualainn agus an uilinn rug e air an làimh agus laigh e oirre an-siud.

Thòisich a' chluicheachd aig an làimh agus aig a' chù dhubh. Mun do leig an cù dubh ás a ghreim, chagainn e an làmh gus an do thuit i air an ùrlar. Dh'fhalbh an rud a bha am mullach na h-uamha, is bha dùil aig Mac a' Phì gum biodh an uamh mu 'cheann. A-mach a ghabh an cù dubh ás déidh an rud a bha a-muigh. Cha b' e seo uair a b' fheàrr a bha Mac a' Phì 'ga fhaireachdainn fhéin, is an cù dubh 'ga fhàgail.

Nuair a bha an là air soilleireachadh, dé a bha an cù dubh ach an déidh tighinn. Laigh e làimh ri Mac a' Phì. An ceann beagan mhionaidean, bha e marbh.

Nuair a thàinig soilleireachd an latha, sheall Mac a' Phì, is cha robh duine de na bha còmhla ris 's an uaimh aige. Thug e leis an làmh, is ghabh e gu cladach a dh'ionnsaigh a' bhàta. Ghabh e a-steach innte. Chaidh e gu ruig Colbhasa, gun chù gun duine.

Thug e leis suas an làmh, los gum faiceadh daoine na fhuair e dh'uamhas an oidhche a bha e 's an uaimh. Chan fhaca duine 'bha an Ìle no an Colbhasa a leithid de làimh riamh idir, is cha robh iad a' smaointeach gun robh a leithid ann. Cha robh ach bàta a chur gu Diùra, is na cuirp a bha 's an uaimh a thoirt dachaigh.

Sin crìoch là a' choin duibh.

Cailleach an Lagain

'S i Cailleach an Lagain a' bhana-bhuidseach mu dheireadh air an d'fhuair mi iomradh 's an dùthaich, agus air son sìdhichean, chan eil duine am Bàideanach a chunnaic a h-aon diubh riamh. Ma-thà, cha chuala mise mu dhéidhinn.

Theagamh gum bheil feadhainn de'r luchd-leughaidh nach cuala an sgeula mu bhean an Lagain, agus air an adhbhar sin, their mi focal no dhà mu'n uilebhiast. Ma tha gach sgeula fìor, is i a chuir ás an rathad Iain Garbh mac GilleChaluim Ràrsaidh. Ach air an latha 'rinn i sin, fhuair ise acaid is galar a bàis. Air dhi pilleadh, an déidh Iain Garbh a bhàthadh, thug i am monadh oirre agus a-steach gun deach i do bhothan anns an robh fear de 'cuid nàbaidhean a' gabhail tàimh.

Bhiodh an duine seo gu math tric a' sealg agus nam biodh stoirm ann, mar a thachair gun robh air an là ud, bu chleachdach leis 'anail a leigeil. Agus ma dh'fhaoidte, an oidhche 'chur seachad anns a' bhothan a dh'ainmich mi.

Air an là seo, bha e a-staigh 's an deagh ghealbhan air a bheulaibh, agus e 'ga thiormachadh is 'ga gharadh fhéin. Sùil dha'n thug e air an doras, ciod e chunnaic e ach cat peallach odhar agus gur gann a bha e a' leantainn a chéile leis a' bhochdainn. Bha dà chù aig an t-sealgair, agus leum iad air a' bhéist cho luath 's a thàinig e gus an doras.

Cha bu luaithe 'leum na coin air na thug e ràn ás, agus aig an àm cheudna, dh'iarr e air an t-sealgair tròcair a dhèanamh air. Ghabh an sealgair mór ioghnadh air do'n chat labhairt ris. Agus a chum is gum faiceadh e ciod an seòrsa beathaich a bh' aige, chaisg e na coin. Is an uair a chaisg, chan fhac' e ach an cat mar a bha e an toiseach.

"Thig gus an teine is dèan do gharadh," deir an sealgair.

"Cha tig," ars an cat, "oir tha eagal orm gun geàrr do chuid chon mi."

Thug an cat an-seo ròineag fhada do'n t-sealgair, ag iarraidh air aig an àm cheudna na coin a cheangal leatha ris a' mhaide-cheangail.

Chuir an sealgair an ròineag mu'n mhaide-cheangail, agus leig e air ris a' chat gun do chuir e air na coin i mar an ceudna. An-seo, thàinig an cat thun an teine agus cha bu luaithe 'thàinig na shìn e air fàs mór.

Thug an sealgair an aire do seo, agus ars esan, "Droch shiubhal ort, a bhiast leibide-ach, is tu tha 'fàs mór."

Agus ann am prioba na sùla, bha an cat cho mór ri mialchu agus an ath shealladh, chruth-atharraich a' bhiast i fhéin, is có bh' aige ach té de 'bhana-nàbaidhean ris an canta gu coitchionn "Bean an Lagain," agus air an robh e cho eòlach is a bha an liagh air a' phoit.

"A shealgair nam beann," deir ise, "thàinig crìoch do làithean-sa. 'S fhada b' fhuathach leat mi fhéin is mo sheòrs,' ach a-nise gheibh sinn buaidh."

Leum i air, is rinn i greim air a sgòrnan ach cha bu luaithe leum na leum na coin oirre-se.

"Teannaich is tachd, a ròineag!" ars ise, 's i an dùil gun robh an ròineag mu amhaic-hean nan con, is cha bu luaithe 'thuirt, na gheàrr an ròineag am maide-ceangail.

Bha na coin an sàs innte, 'ga caobadh is 'ga reubadh, ach mu dheireadh fhuair i uapa, 's am prioba na sùla, dh'fhalbh i air iteig an cruth fithich.

Gu sgeula goirid a dhèanamh dhuibh, fhuair i bàs an oidhche sin. Thachair do dhithis choisichean a bhith aig a' cheart àm a' tighinn seach am Monadh Liath eadar Srath Éire 's Bàideanach is ciod a chunnaic iad ach boireannach 'na ruith 's 'na teann-ruith a' tighinn 'nan coinneamh, agus chaidh i seachad orra gun aon fhocal a ràdh. Cha deach iad fad air an aghaidh an uair a choinnich dà chù dhubh iad 'nan teann-ruith air lorg a' bhoireannaich. Goirid an déidh seo, choinnich duine dubh iad, a' marcachd air each dubh. Stad am marcaiche dubh agus dh'fheòraich e am faca iad am boireannach is na coin 'na déidh.

Thuirt gum fac.'

"Saoil sibh am beir iad oirre mun ruig i an cladh?"

Thuirt na fir nach biodh iad fada 'na déidh co-dhiù. Is an-sin dh'fhalbh am marcaiche. Cha b' fhada gus gun d'rug e orra tighinn air ais agus am boireannach seachad air a bheulaibh air an dìollaid, an dara cù an slaoda ri 'sliasaid air taobh clì an eich, agus an cù eile an slaoda ri 'cloich air a thaobh deas.

"Rug thu oirre."

"Rug," ars am marcaiche, "dìreach aig doras a' chlaidh."

Thàinig na fir do Bhàideanach agus dh'innis iad mar thachair doibh air an t-slighe. Is bu mhuladach e oir chan eil teagamh nach e spiorad Cailleach an Lagain a chunnaic iad a' ruith thun a' chlaidh, oir b' àite seunta e, agus am Fear-Millidh air a tòir.

MacLeòid Dhùn Bheagain is na Bana-Bhuidsichean

An uair a bha buidseachd 's an tìr, agus a bha an t-uasal is an t-ìosal a' toirt géill do gheasaibh, is e an t-olc a bhatar a' cur ás leth nam bana-bhuidsichean. Ach mas fìor an aithris, bha cuid dhiubh a dhèanadh gnìomh càirdeil.

Thachair té dhe gach seòrsa ri MacLeòid Dhùn Bheagain, ceann-cinnidh nan Leòdach, aig àm Blàr Inbhir Lòchaidh. An là dh'fhàg MacLeòid an dùn le 'chuid dhaoine, thàinig muinntir na dùthcha a-mach a dh'fhaicinn nan saighdearan air an t-slighe chon a' chogaidh, agus a leigeil slàn le na fearaibh.

Bha boireannach àraidh 'na suidhe air an tobhta, a cùlaibh ris an tughadh is i snìomh le cuigeal. Nuair a bha MacLeòid a' dol seachad oirre, ghlaoidh i, "Mo dhùrachd dhuit, a MhicLeòid!"

"Do dhùrachd dhuit fhéin," fhreagair esan, agus aig an aon àm, thilg e bonn airgid air an rathad. Leis a' chabhaig a rinn ise air son greimeachadh air an airgead, thuit i leis an tobhta is chaidh bior na cuigeil tro chlàr a h-aodainn. Thionndaidh cumhachd an airgid a mì-rùn 'na h-aghaidh fhéin.

Air latha Inbhir Lòchaidh, thug MacLeòid an aire gun robh feannag a' sgiathalaich os a chionn fhad is a bha an cath a' dol air adhart.

Thuit móran de na Leòdaich, ach thill MacLeòid gu sàbhailte do'n Dùn.

Beagan ùine an déidh sin, thòisich mnathan na dùthcha a' gearain gun robh am bainne a' call an toraidh. Bha àireamh neo-àbhaisteach de'n chrodh a' bàsachadh is a' dol leis na creagan. Thuit amharas air boireannach àraidh agus chaidh a toirt gu mòd air beulaibh MhicLeòid. Thug esan a-mach binn a crochaidh.

"Nam bu chuimhneach leatsa, a MhicLeòid," thuirt ise, "nuair a bha mise 'nam fheannaig dhuibh a' cumail uait nam peilearan aig Blàr Inbhir Lòchaidh, cha dèanadh tu sin."

"Is fìor sin, a bhean. Leigibh ás i," arsa MacLeòid.

Eóghann a' Chinn Bhig

Bha uaireigin tighearna air Loch Buidhe ann am Muile ris an abairteadh Iain Beàrnach MacGill'Eathain agus bha mac aige do'm b' ainm Eóghann. B' e Eóghann a' Chinn Bhig a theirteadh ris.

Tràth dh'fhàs Eóghann a' Chinn Bhig suas gu bhith 'na dhuine, phòs e nighean duine uasail de Chlann Dùghaill a mhuinntir Lathurna. Bha bean Eóghann a' Chinn Bhig 'na sgrubair gàbhaidh, agus ro dhroch nàdarrach. B' e a' Chòrr Dhubh NicDhùghaill an t-ainm a bha aig muinntir Mhuile oirre.

Cha robh a' Chòrr Dhubh NicDhùghaill ro thoileach luchd-tadhail a bhith a' dol a chur dragh oirre, agus cha bu toigh leatha aoigheachd a thoirt do neach air bith.

Fhuair i a thoirt air Eóghann a' Chinn Bhig, e a thogail taighe dhi ann an lochan do'n ainm Loch Sguabain, agus is e clacharan a bha eadar Eilean Loch Sguabain agus tìr a chum is nach biodh feadhainn a' dol bitheanta rathad an taighe.

Tràth bha Eóghann a' Chinn Bhig agus a bhean ré tamaill a chòmhnaidh ann an Eilean Loch Sguabain, thòisich ise ri farmad a ghabhail ri bhith a' faicinn a h-athar-chéile a chòmhnaidh ann an caisteal rìomhach, agus i fhéin a chòmhnaidh ann an taigh suarach ann an Eilean Loch Sguabain. Agus cha tugadh i fois do Eóghann a' Chinn Bhig a dh'oidhche no a latha, ach ag ràdh ris, "Thar leam gum faodadh tu tuilleadh fearainn na tha agad 'fhaotainn bho t' athair, agus thar leam gum bheil t' athair glé fhada a chòmhnaidh anns a' chaisteal. Thar leam gum faodadh e an caisteal a thoirt dhuitse a-nis, agus dh'fhaodadh taigh bu shuaraiche gnothach a dhèanamh dhasan a-nis. Is tusa an t-oighre co-dhiù. Is ann ort a thig gach fearann is caisteal agus gach nì a tha ann aig a' cheann mu dheireadh. Agus mar is luaithe a gheibh thu tuilleadh fearainn agus an caisteal, 's ann is fheàrr."

Cha do leig i fois no clos le Eóghann a' Chinn Bhig a latha no a dh'oidhche gus an deach e a dh'ionnsaigh 'athar a dh'iarraidh tuilleadh fearainn agus a' chaisteil uaidh.

Thuirt 'athair ris, "Gléidhidh mise mi fhéin an caisteal, agus na tha agam de dh'fhearann fhad is beò mi, agus 'na dhéidh sin, gheibh thusa iad, ach gléidhidh mise na tha agam, fhad is beò mi."

Chaidh Eóghann a' Chinn Bhig dhachaigh, agus cha bu luaithe a ràinig e dhachaigh, na thòisich a bhean air, a chionn a bhith cho faoin is gun géilleadh e do dhuine aosmhor mar a bha 'athair. Chaidh Eóghann a' Chinn Bhig air ais a dhà no trì a dh'uairean a dh'ionnsaigh 'athar, a dh'agart tuilleadh fearainn agus a' chaisteil uaidh.

Ach cha ghéilleadh 'athair gu nì air bith a thoirt do Eóghann a' Chinn Bhig ach na bha aige roimhe. Aon de na h-uairean chaidh Iain Beàrnach a-mach còmhla ri a mhac Eóghann a' Chinn Bhig, agus tràth bha iad aig àite do'n ainm Iomaire nam Marcaiche, chuir iad a-mach air a chéile gu ro dhona, agus bhuail Eóghann buille air 'athair anns a' bheul, agus leag se e, agus chuir e dà fhiacail ás. Agus thog sin connspaid agus droch nàdur eadar Eóghann a' Chinn Bhig agus Iain Beàrnach 'athair.

Dh'fhalbh Iain Beàrnach, agus ràinig e MacGill'Eathain Dhubhairt, agus chasaid e ris mar a rinn a mhac air.

Thionail MacGill'Eathain Dhubhairt a dhaoine, agus chaidh e a thoirt a-mach dìolaidh o Eóghann a' Chinn Bhig air son mar a bhuail e 'athair. Thionail Eóghann a' Chinn Bhig daoine, agus chuir e fhéin is MacGill'Eathain Dhubhairt blàr aig Dàil a' Bhroinein aig Cùl a' Ghàra Mhóir. Chaidh an latha an aghaidh Eóghann a' Chinn Bhig, agus chaidh an ruaig air a dhaoine. Cha robh a' Chòrra Dhubh NicDhùghaill toilichte le sin. Fhuair i daoine bho a h-athair á Lathurna, agus chan fhoghnadh leatha ach gun rachadh latha eile blàir a chur. Shuidhich iad latha gus am blàr a chur aig Ceann a' Chnocain an Gleann Forsa.

Latha no dhà roimh latha a' bhlàir, chaidh Eóghann a shealg do Bheinn an t-Sealbh. Thàinig ceò air a' bheinn, agus cha d'fhuair e sitheann no sealg a dhèanamh ach chaidh e air seacharan leis a' cheò air feadh na beinne.

Aig ciaradh an fheasgair, thàinig e gu sruthan a bha dearg le fuil. Chaidh e an àird ris a' mhonadh ri taobh an t-sruthain, a shealltuinn cia dé a b' adhbhar do'n fhuil a bhith anns an allt. Iar dha dol an àird gu glaic a bha an-sin, chunnaic e ban-sìdh, agus dùn de léintean fala aice, agus i 'gan nigheadh ann an linn a bha anns an allt. Bha cìochan leobhar oirre, agus bha iad togte an àird thar a guallainn.

Thàinig Eóghann a' Chinn Bhig air a cùlaibh gun fhios di. Bheir e air a cìche, agus chuir e 'na bheul i agus dheoghail e agus thuirt e, "Muimeachas agam ort. Tha mi a' leigeadh mar fhianais ort fhéin gun do dheoghail mi do chìoch."

Thuirt ise, "A ta eagal orm nach dèan sin móran maith dhuit. Chan eil agad ach ro dhroch bhean aig an taigh. Nam biodh bean mhaith agadsa aig an taigh, dh'fhaodadh e bhith gun dèanainn-se maith dhuit. Ach tha do bhean cho dona is gum bheil eagal orm nach urrainn mise móran maith a dhèanamh dhuit."

"Cia dé a ta thu a' dèanamh ann an-seo?"

"Tha mi a' nigheadh nan léintean fola aig an fheadhainn a thuiteas là Blàir Chinn a' Chnocain an Gleann Forsa, agus tha mi an dùil gum bheil do léine-sa agam ann an-seo, còmhla ri càch."

"Am bheil mise gu tuiteam anns a' bhlàir?"

Thuirt a' bhean-sìdh, "Ma bheir do bhean-sa dhuit ìm, gun thu fhéin 'ga iarraidh, an latha a bhios tu a' dol a dh'ionnsaigh a' bhlàir, thig thu dhachaigh beò ás. Ach mur toir i dhuit ìm gun thu fhéin 'ga iarraidh, cha tig thu dhachaigh beò ás a' bhlàir."

Tràth thàinig latha a' bhlàir, bha bean Eóghann a' Chinn Bhig 'ga ghreasad gu e a dhol a dh'ionnsaigh a' bhlàir. Chaidh Eóghann agus chruinnich e a dhaoine do a h-ionnsaigh, a chum is gun tugadh i biadh dhaibh mum falbhadh iad. Chuir ise air am beulaibh aran eòrna, agus meug bàn. Agus chuir i air beulaibh Eóghann a' Chinn Bhig e fhéin aran eòrna 's uighean loisgte. Shuidh Eóghann a' Chinn Bhig ré tamaill mu choinneamh a' bhidhe gun a bhith 'ga itheadh. Mu dheireadh, thilg e a bhròg air an àite far an robh an t-ìm an tasgaidh ach cha do ghabh ise suim.

Thuirt esan, "Cha toir bròg no bruidhinn atharrachadh air droch bhean," agus e ag éirigh, agus a' cur air a bhròige.

Thuirt ise, "Dèan suidhe, agus ith mum falbh thu."

"Chan ith. Cha bhi ri a ràdh gun deach aran-eòrna, 's uighean loisgte, agus meug bàn a thoirt a-mach air mo thaobh-sa an-diugh," agus dh'fhalbh e gun nì air bith itheadh. Agus cha d'ith na daoine a bha leis nì air bith nas mò.

Dh'fhalbh iad a dh'ionnsaigh a' chatha, agus choinnich iad ri an nàimhdean aig àite ris an abrar Ceann a' Chnocain ann an Gleann Forsa.

Bha MacGill'Eathain Dhubhairt ann air cheann a dhaoine, agus e ro thìtheach air Eóghann a' Chinn Bhig fhaotainn a mharbhadh.

Chaidh an cath a chur, agus b' ann an aghaidh Eóghann a' Chinn Bhig a chaidh an latha. Chaidh an ruaig a chur air a dhaoine. Bha Eóghann a' Chinn Bhig e fhéin air muin eich, agus chaidh a chas a gheàrradh bhàrr an eich aig Eóghann a' Chinn Bhig, agus beireachd air fhéin 'na phrìosanach, ach chuir MacGill'Eathain Dhubhairt an ceann dheth.

Mac 'ic Ailein agus Luideag an Uillt

O chionn fad an t-saoghail, bha Mac 'ic Ailein a' còmhnaidh ann an daingneach lochain air an robh Dùn Buidhe, ann an Dùn Gainmheacha, Beinn na Faoghla. Bha cabhsair chlachan eadar an cladach agus an dùn, agus 's ann oirre a bhiodh daoine a' triall a-null agus a-nall. Air meadhan a' chlachain seo, bha leac air a caramh air alt is gun dèanadh i fuaim mhór bùirich, ach cas a chur oirre, agus gheibheadh mar seo, muinntir an dùin brath air teachd caraid no nàmhaid. Bha a leithid seo de lic air cabhsair h-uile dùn no daingneach lochain. Is i "an leac-brathaidh" no "a' chlach-fhaireachaidh" a bhiodh aca air an lic.

Bha fear de ghillean móra Mhic 'ic Ailein a' dol dhachaigh turas, uair anmoch de'n oidhche, agus ri linn da gabhail thairis air a' chloich-fhaireachaidh, có air a chuir e clisgeadh ach air a' bhean-nighe, agus i a' nigheadh léine air a làn-dìchill ri taobh a' chlachain.

"Có dha a tha thu a' nigheadh na léine sin?" ars an gille mór.

"Do Mhac 'ic Ailein," ars Luideag an Uillt. "Tha a mhanadh a-mach air, cha téid a bheò a-null air an staran seo am feast tuilleadh."

Ràinig an gille mór taobh leapaidh Mhic 'ic Ailein cho luath 's a bha 'na chasan, a dh'innseadh fàisneachd na Luideige, agus, ma dh'innis, is ann an-siud a bha a' chabhag is am fire-faire, 's an ùpraid. An uair a chaidh am beag-sgeul gus a' mhór-sgeul, chunnacas gum b' e a b' fheàrr dhaibh an imrich a thogail gun feitheamh mionaid. Chuireadh a' choit air dòigh, agus dh'fhàg Mac 'ic Ailein an dùn, e fhéin is a theaghlach is a dhaoine, laithreach bonn.

Thog Mac 'ic Ailein an-sin Caisteal Bhuiridh air creig bhig ann am meadhan lochain air taobh an iar Beinn na Faoghla, ach tha an lochan sin a-nis air a lìonadh le siaban. Tha barrachd is sia ceud bliadhna uaidh sin a-nis.

A' Bhean-Ghlùine agus Bànrigh nan Sìbhreach

Bho chionn fada roimhe seo, bha sean chailleach a' còmhnaidh ann am Baile Mhìcheil a bhiodh ri banachas-ghlùin. Air latha àraidh 's i a' buain le h-aon de na coimhearsnaich, dé thàinig trast uirre ach losgann mór grannda 's i trom le losgainn òga.

"Tha mi a' guidhe 's ag aslachadh ort," ars a' chailleach, is i a' cur an losgainn a thaobh le bàrr a' chorrain ghobhlaich, "nach dealaich thu ri do luchd gus am bi mo dhà làimh-se timcheall ort."

Cha robh tuilleadh air aig an àm, ach oidhche no dhà an déidh sin, có thàinig thun an dorais aice ach gille air muin eich 'na dheannaibh, agus e a' glaodhaich uirre i dh'éirigh gu luath luath, a dhèanadh cuideachaidh is cobhair air mnaoi a bha 's a' ghlaodhaich. Ghreas i uirre, is chaidh i air muin an eich aig cùlaibh a' ghille, ach an àite crùm an rathaid a ghleidheadh, 's ann a ghabh e a-muigh 's a-mach rathad cùil Àird-Bheinn.

"Càite fo chromadh nan speur," ars a' chailleach, "am bheil an aire dhuit dol, no cia fhada tha romhad?"

"'S e luaths do theangaidh," ars an gille, "a ghluais do chasan a-nochd. Chuir thu Bànrigh nan Sìbhreach beaga fo gheasaibh 's i an riochd losgainn, is chan fhaigh i fòir no fuasgladh gus am bi do dhà làimh timcheall uirre, ach air an anam a tha 'nad chorp, feuch nach gabh thu biadh no deoch no tuarastal, air neo bidh thu mar tha mise, fo shileadh nan lòchran, gun chomas tillidh gu taigh no teaghlach."

Ràinig iad uamh Àird-Bheinn, agus chaidh iad a-steach do sheòmar cho brèagh, 's nach fhaicte a leithid 's an domhan. Bha Bànrigh nan Sìbhreach air leabaidh, is móran de na sìbhrich bheaga a' feitheamh 's a' freastal uirre.

Rinn a' chailleach gach nì a bha feumail, is cha robh fada gus an do rugadh mac mór meamnach.

Nuair a bha an leanabh glan sgeadaichte, thug iad sàbh do'n bhean-ghlùine a dhungadh a shùilean, chum is gum faigheadh e Sealladh an Dà Shaoghail. Ach thuit gun do thachais a' chailleach a mala 's an sàbh air a meuran, is cha luaithe a thachais na fhuair i Sealladh an Dà Shaoghail 'na leth-shùil. Agus a-nis an seòmar a chìtheadh i cho brèagh leis an darna sùil, chìtheadh i leis an t-sùil eile e 'na tholl dorcha làn neadach an damhan-allaidh.

On a bha a h-uile nì deas, cha robh ach biadh is deoch a chur air a beulaibh, ach dhiùlt i a-muigh 's a-mach e. B' éiginn leotha an-sin gun gabhadh i pàigheadh airson a saothrach, agus thairig iad dhi làn an dùirn de'n òr ach an t-òr a bha cho buidhe bòidheach do'n darna sùil, cha robh air ach coslas innearach do'n t-sùil eile, agus cha ghabhadh i dubh no dath dheth.

On a chunnaic na sìbhrich nach robh math dhaibh a bhith rithe, chuir iad i air druim an eich. Agus an-sin dh'aithnich i an gille gum b' e mac coimhearsnaich a bh' ann a ghoideadh le na sìbhrich, agus dùil aig a mhuinntir gun do shiubhail e.

Ràinig a' chailleach a bothan fhéin mu ghoir a' choilich, is cha luaithe a ghlaodh e na chaidh an gille 's an t-each ás an t-sealladh, agus chan fhaca i iad gu bràth tuilleadh.

Clann MhicGlaisein ann an Lios Mór

A-réir beul-aithris, bha Sealladh an Dà Shaoghail aig Cloinn MhicGlaisein Chreaganaich an Lios Mór. Fhuair aon aca an comas seo air an dòigh a leanas.

An uair a bha a phàrantan a' dol leis air son baistidh do dh'Eaglais na Sgìreachd, shuidh iad fad beagan mhionaid a ghabhail foise air cnoc, làimh ri Allt Aogain, àite aig an robh ainm a bhi 'na ionad-tathaich sònraichte aig na sìdhichean. Am feadh a bha iad a' cur seachad an sgìos, leig iad sìos làimh riu an leanabh, paisgte ann am breacan, agus e 'na shuain chadail.

Agus an uair a dh'fhalbh iad a-rithis, dhì-chuimhnich an té, ris an d'earbadh e, a thoirt leatha. Cho luath is a chaidh a ionndrainn, phill iad air an ais, agus fhuair iad e 'na shuain chadail far an d'fhàgadh e.

Cha robh atharrachadh air bith ri fhaicinn 'na choltas; gidheadh, bha na sìdhichean maille ris, agus dh'fhàg iad aige Sealladh an Dà Shaoghail.

Ruith an comas a fhuair e an-sin sìos uaidhsan dh'ionnsaigh a shliochd ré iomad gineil. Tha aon diubh a bha ann an toiseach an linn seo fathast air chuimhne mar thaibhsear comharraichte.

Seo aon de mhóran sgeòil a bha aon uair air an innseadh m'a thimcheall.

Bha bràthair-céile aige a chaill a cheud bhean 'na laighe-shiùbhladh, agus a dhiùlt fad ùine 'na dhéidh sin comhfhurtachd a ghabhail. Air feasgar-eigin, is e a' pilleadh dhachaigh an cuideachd MhicGlaisein, agus a' caoidh na bha uaidh, thuirt MacGlaisein ris: "Cha ruig thu leas a bhith a' caoidh mar sin air son do mhnatha. Ma thoilicheas tu, bheir mise air a h-ais dhuit i gun mhóran dàlach."

Ach ghrìos fear a' bhròin air gun sin a dhèanamh.

"Ma-tà," ars MacGlaisein, "sin i, a' leum romhainn o chnocan gu cnocan 'na h-eun glas. Agus mur leig thu leamsa a toirt air a h-ais dhuit mun tig crìoch na bliadhna, chan fhaic thu tuilleadh i. Oir tha i leis na sìdhichean, agus tha iadsan a' dol air imrich an ùine ghoirid, agus aon uair is gum falbh iad, chan urrainn mise a toirt air a h-ais gu bràth."

Sguir a' bhantrach a chaoidh air son a mhnatha agus mun tàinig crìoch air a' bhliadhna, phòs e té eile.

Air oidhche na bainnse, thuirt MacGlaisein, is e a bhith an làthair, r'a chompanach, "Seall thar mo ghualainn, agus chì thu a' cheud bhean a' seasamh eadar an dara té agus a fear."

Ach dhiùlt a chompanach an cuireadh.

Am Fiosaiche ann am Fàrr

Tha duine beò fathast an sgìr' Dhiùrinis aig am beil fiosaidheachd. Chunnaic agus chuala e iomadh nì ioghantach: solasan, cistean-laigh,' tìodhlacan, grogadaich, agus éigheachd muinntir air am bàthag.

Bha e fhéin agus nàbaidh tighinn dhachaigh glé anmoch aon oidhch.' Ghabh iad rothad goirid, agus thàinig iad seachad a taobh bàghach beag. Air dhaibh bhith dul seachad air seo, thug an duine ialt mhór, mar gum biog eallach trom air a thilgeil air dhruim.

Dh'fhaighnich a chompanach dheth ge dé bha cur air.

Fhreagar es, "A dhuine, nach fac' thu an g-corp sin ag éireadh air mo dhruim?"

Ruith an duine eile air falbh ag éigheachd, "Cha d-téid mis' gu bràth tuille maille riuts' an déidh an oidhche tuitim!"

Ùine bheag an déidh seo, cha séathach 'chall air a' chladach, agus cha' na làmhan uile a bhàthag. Thàinig aon do na corpan air tìr anns a' bhàghach seo, agus chum ás gu feigheag iad e gu àit' gus an deidheag a' chist' laigh a dhèanaig, cha' an g-corp a thogail air druim an duine seo, dìreach anns an àit' far an d'foireach e corp tighinn air a mhuin roimhe.

Nuair cha' an g-corp 'thogail air a dhruim, thug an duine an ionn' sèors' ialt agus a thug e roimhe. Chuimhnich a nàbaidh, 'bha ann an sin, an nì a thachair nuair a bha iad tighinn dachaigh anmoch.

Bruadar nam Marbh ann an Srath Theimheil

Tha an saoghal air fàs cho glic a-nis nach faigh neach ach gann éisteachd ma dh'innseas e mu thaibhsean, uruisgean, no bruadairean. Nuair a bha mo sheanair a' siubhal na tìre, b' iongantach na chitheadh agus na chluinneadh e. Cha bhiodh e a-mach oidhche dhorcha gun solas fhaicinn a' dol do'n chladh no nam biodh e a' dol dlùth do'n chladh, chluinneadh e fàs-fhuaim aig an ùir a' tuiteam air a' chist' a dh'innseadh ciod an oisinn anns an rachadh a' cheud uaigh 'fhosgladh.

'Na laighe air an leabaidh, chluinneadh e sgeuchail agus raoiceil a' dol seachad air an rathad mhór agus bhiodh fhios aige gun robh fear d'a choimhsearnsaich gu bhith air a ghiùlan seachad ann am beagan ùine.

Cha tigeadh coigreach chum an dorais nach robh fhios aige air greis mun tigeadh e, leis a' choileach. Cha bhiodh sgeul ùr a thigeadh d'a ionnsaigh nach abradh e gum b' e sin brìgh a' bhruadair a bh' aige. Cha robh nì riamh a thachair da nach do bhruadair e mu dhéidhinn air tùs ach bha an tubaist air nach robh e 'faicinn brìgh nam bruadar gus an tigeadh iad gu crìche. Dh'fhalbh na taibhsean agus na bruadaran agus cha chluinnear iomradh orra ach an seann sgeulachdan.

Bha gille òg an Srath Theimheil agus air dha ionnsaigh a thoirt air dol tro'n abhainn, chaidh a sguabadh air falbh agus chaidh a bhàthadh. Chruinnicheadh na bha 'dhaoine anns a' choimhearsnachd agus chaidh iad a shireadh a chuirp <feadh> na h-aibhne. Fad seachdain, bha càirdean agus luchd-eòlais gu dian leis gach innleachd 'ga iarraidh ach cha d'fhuaras e.

Chaidh a-nis sgur de bhith 'ga iarraidh agus bha 'mhàthair bhrònach ag ràdh nam faigheadh i corp a mic gum biodh i làn strìochta do'n chall a thàinig oirre.

Beagan oidhchean an déidh seo, bha 'bhean 'na cadal agus ar leatha gun tàinig a mac gu bruaich a leapach. Bha neul a' bhàis air 'aghaidh agus bha e air chrith le fuachd.

"O mhàthair mo ghaoil," thuirt e. "Tha mise fuar fuar, 'am shìneadh an-siud agus nach eil caraid a thogas mo cheann."

"Mo leanabh, càit' am bheil do chorp, no an téid t' fhaotainn fhathast?" fhreagair a mhàthair.

"Siribh air mo shon agus gheibh sibh mi. Théid m' fhaotainn agus chan fhaigh duine no gille mi agus tha sinn de'n aon chinneadh."

Ged a dhùisg a' bhean, cha chreideadh i gum bu bhruadar faoin a bh' ann agus chuir i ìmpidh air na daoine éirigh aon uair eile.

Bha cuid am barail gum b' e cù a dh'fheumadh an corp 'fhaotainn ach bha e anns a' bhruadar gum biodh an neach a gheibheadh e de'n aon sloinneadh no cinneadh. 'Nam measg-san a chaidh a-mach, bha troich no luspardan agus air dha sùil a thoirt fo bhruaich, chunnaic e an corp. B' e seo an neach nach robh 'na dhuine no 'na ghille agus bha e de'n aon sloinneadh ris a' ghille a chaidh a chall.

Chapter Notes

Introduction

1. MacInnes, *Dùthchas nan Gàidheal*, 467.
2. Grant, *Essays on the Superstitions*, 27–29.
3. Hillers, "Storytelling and the International Folktale," 155–57.
4. Jackson, "The Folktale in Gaelic Scotland," 133, 125.
5. Bruford and Macdonald, *Scottish Traditional Tales*, 9–10; Douglas, "Narrative in Traveller Scotland."
6. Campbell, *Popular Tales*, vol. 1, 175.
7. For a substantial collection of Gaelic tradition and literature from the Lennox and Menteith, see Newton, *Bho Chluaidh gu Calasraid*.
8. Campbell. *Popular Tales*, vol. 1, lviii.
9. For an overview of Scottish Gaelic literary tradition, see Newton, *Warriors of the Word*, 80–121.
10. Most recently edited in Ó Baoill, *Mairi nighean Alasdair Ruaidh*, 44. Previous editors and translators of this poem do not seem to have paid much attention to the term *eachdraidh* in this verse. It means most specifically "history" in the modern sense, but it was the main term used for what contemporary scholars call now in English the "medieval Gaelic romance tale." See Bruford, *Gaelic Folk-tales*, 8.
11. Shaw, "Storytellers in Scotland," 35.
12. *Ibid.*
13. Campbell, *Popular Tales*, vol. 1, xiv.
14. Black, *An Lasair*, xiii–xiv.
15. Sinclair, "Na Seann Sgeulachdan," with some minor emendations to the translation.
16. Thomson, *Foirm na n-Urrnuidheadh*, 179.
17. Allardyce, *Scotland and Scotsmen*, vol. 2, 408–09, 414–15.
18. Campbell, *Popular Tales*, vol. 1, xv.
19. *Ibid.*, xxix–xxxi.
20. *The Scottish American Journal* December 14, 1887. This article was signed with the initials "S.J." which suggests that it was written by the editor of the newspaper, whose same initials appear on other editorial content during that time.
21. Smith, "The Seven Unwritten Rules."
22. MacKay, "Gruagach an Eilein Uaine," 182.
23. Campbell, *The Fians*, xi–xii.
24. McGowan, *Journey to the Hebrides*, 101
25. Shaw, "The Collectors," 348–49.
26. For biographical details about Dewar and his fieldwork, see Black, "The Dewar Project."
27. Watson, "The Collecting of Highland Legends," 115.
28. MacDonald, "Narrative Collection and Scholarship," 18; Cheape, "'Tha Feum Air Cabhaig.'"
29. Jackson, "The Folktale in Gaelic Scotland," 135.
30. His original article was translated into English in 1965. See Olrik, "Epic Laws."
31. Quoted in Linda Dégh, "Folk Narrative," 60. However, Alan Bruford, "Gaelic Folk-Tales," i–ii defines "motif" more strictly as a structural element abstracted from the details that are used to embody it.
32. My scheme is somewhat similar to that of John F. Campbell in *Popular Tales*, vol. 1, xxxii on.
33. See discussion in Newton, *Warriors of the Word*, 166–68 and *Everyday Life of the Clans*, 36–43.

Chapter One

1. Dégh, "Folk Narrative," 62–67.
2. Bruford, *Gaelic Folk Tales*, 23, 34–35, 213; Bruford and MacDonald, *Scottish Traditional Tales*, 16–17.
3. Campbell, "On Current British Mythology," 331–32.
4. Campbell, *Popular Tales*, vol. 1, xviii–xix.
5. My translation of Campbell, *Popular Tales*, vol. 2, 130–33.
6. Iwase, "The Feigned Illness Motif," 153.
7. Fraser, "A Study of Scottish Gaelic Versions," 65.
8. MacInnes, *Dùthchas nan Gàidheal*, 284–85, 314.
9. My revised translation from *The Celtic Magazine* 13 (1888): 212–18.
10. The word in the original Gaelic text is *gruagach* "long-haired one." Long hair was a marker of noble status for men in medieval Gaelic society.
11. My revised translation from MacInnes, *Folk and Hero Tales*, 94–125.
12. Koehler, "Bàillidh Lunnainn."
13. My translation of MacKay, "Cànain nan Eun."

14. Nilsen, "P. J. Nicholson."

15. Shaw, "Scottish Gaelic Traditions of the Cliar Sheanchain."

16. *Ibid.* 146–48.

17. Hillers, "The Abbot of Druimenaig."

18. For the meaning of *dìleann* as "earth's crust," see MacDonald, *Gaelic Words and Expressions*, 99.

19. My translation of MacNeacail, "Seanachan Mór."

20. Bruford, *Gaelic Folk Tales*, 68, 160–02.

Chapter Two

1. Kane, *Wisdom of the Mythtellers*, 33.

2. Carmichael, *Deirdre*, 137–38. My thanks to Ruairidh MacIlleathain for highlighting the significance of this quote.

3. Newton, *Warriors of the Word*, 227–31.

4. My translation of Grant, *Aig Tigh na Beinne*, 130–31, 132.

5. For the version from John MacDonald and discussion of it, see Wiseman, "Brae Lochaber," 109–114. For the version from Ireland and an insightful analysis, see Ó Crualaoich, *The Book of the Cailleach*, 101–04, 235–36.

6. Menzies, *Òran na Comhachaig*, 24–27.

7. Ó Crualaoich, *The Book of the Cailleach*, 103. The original Gaelic text of this tale uses the word *breac*, which can mean either "salmon" or "trout." I have chosen the former meaning.

8. My translation of Macpherson. "Iolair Loch-Treig," with reference to Parker, *Na Daoine Sidhe*, 34–39.

9. Shaw, "A Gaelic Eschatological Folktale."

10. My translation of the "Achadh nan Gàidheal" column in the 16 Feb 1928 issue of *The Casket*.

11. My translation of MacDhomhnaill, *An Ceathramh Leabhar Leughaidh*, 219–20.

12. There is a useful summary on the Nature Scotland website at https://www.nature.scot/landscapes-and-habitats/habitat-types/coast-and-seas/coastal-habitats/machair. Accessed 21 November 2021.

13. My translation of MacRury, "An Teine Mor," 160–61.

14. Campbell, *Clan Traditions*, 120.

15. My translation of MacFhionghuin, *Leabhraichean Leughaidh*, 17–19. A very similar version is given in English translation in Forsyth, *In the Shadow of Cairngorm*, 36. It is told in a mixture of Gaelic and English in Campbell, *Popular Tales of the West Highlands*, vol. 1, 277.

16. My translation of the manuscript in the John F. Campbell archives of the National Library of Scotland, folio 420, page 85.

17. Adapted from Campbell, *Clan Traditions*, 119.

18. My translation from MacLeod, *Celtic Annual 1912*, 22.

19. Campbell, *More West Highland Tales*, vol. 2, 364–65; Campbell, *Records of Argyll*, 304–05.

20. My translation of *Mac-Talla* 7.7 (9 September 1898): 56.

Chapter Three

1. Flahive, *The Fenian Cycle*, 7–8.

2. Campbell, *Popular Tales*, vol. 1, xiii.

3. Campbell, *The Fians*, 3.

4. On the connection of this storyteller to the literary tradition, see Shaw, "Scottish Gaelic Traditions," 154, 156.

5. My translation of Carmichael, "Toirioc na Taine," 25–27.

6. See discussion in Campbell, *Leabhar na Féinne*, 9–15.

7. My adaptation of Campbell, *Leabhar na Féinne*, 10. I have corrected all personal and place names to modern forms.

8. Bruford, "Oral and Literary Fenian Tales," 47–48.

9. My translation of *The Celtic Review* 2 (1906): 263–72.

10. See Campbell's comments in *Leabhar na Féinne*, xxvi, 37.

11. My translation of Campbell, *Leabhar na Féinne*, 37–38.

12. Campbell, *The Fians*, 165.

13. My translation of Dòmhnallach, "Sgeulachd Gharaidh." The same text was printed previously in the first volume of *Guth na Bliadhna* and attributed there to "A. MacD." Ronald Black has included it in the list of the works of Father Allan MacDonald.

14. Bruford, *Gaelic Folk-Tales*, 8, 115–16.

15. Campbell, *More West Highland Tales*, vol. 1, 275–76.

16. My revised translation of Campbell, "Fionn's Enchantement."

17. My revised translation of Campbell, *Popular Tales of the West Highlands*, vol. 3, 78–80.

18. My revised translation of MacDonald, "Bàs Bhrain agus Dhiarmaid."

Chapter Four

1. Dégh, "Folk Narrative," 72–77; MacInnes, "Gaelic Hero-Tales."

2. Campbell, *Popular Tales*, vol. 1, xlii.

3. Campbell, "Current British Mythology," 334–35.

4. I have not included accounts of the Jacobite movement from the 1680s to 1740s in this chapter but mostly events that precede that era. An entire other volume of songs and stories from Gaelic oral tradition about the Jacobite Risings could be compiled.

5. MacInnes, *Dùthchas nan Gàidheal*, 49–50.

6. *Ibid.*, 57–58, 63.

7. MacGregor,"The Genealogical Histories."

8. Newton, *Warriors of the Word*, 300.

9. Grant and Cheape, *Periods in Highland History*, 138.

10. Newton, *Warriors of the Word*, 157–63.

11. My revised edition and translation of Carmichael, "The Barons," 358–59. See also Campbell, *Records of Argyll*, 321–22, 326.

12. Markus, "How to Arrange Your Corpses."

13. My translation of MacDonald, "Calum-Cille agus Dobhran a Bhràthair." This tale is a variant of ML 7060 "The Disputed Site for a Church" in Christiansen's migratory legend scheme.

14. My translation of Carmichael, "Naoimh Chinntaile."

15. My translation of Henderson, *The Norse Influence*, 327–30.

16. For the latter, see *The Celtic Magazine* 11 (1888): 566–67.

17. Ó hÓgáin, "The Mystical Island," 252–54.

18. Ní Fhloinn, "Tadhg, Donncha and Some of Their Relations," 241.

19. My revised translation of Mackenzie, *The Book of Arran*, vol. 2, 284–88. This legend includes plots F 14 and F 75 in Donald Archie MacDonald's migratory legend classification scheme.

20. Wiseman, "'A Noxious Pack,'" 100–101.

21. My revised edition of Grant, *Legends of the Braes O' Mar*, 16–17.

22. My translation of Mackay, "Sgeulachdan Ghlinn-Urchudainn," 76–79, with reference to Mackay, *Urquhart and Glenmoriston*, 99–104. This legend includes plots F 94 and F 100 in Donald Archie MacDonald's migratory legend classification scheme.

23. Campbell, *Popular Tales*, vol. 1, lviii.

24. My revised translation of MacKay, "Sgeul air Calum Garbh Mac Eòghainn," with reference to MacKechnie, *The Dewar Manuscripts*, 92–98.

25. Bruford and MacDonald, *Scottish Traditional Tales*, 482.

26. My translation of MacDhùghaill, "Fionnladh Dubh Mac Rath."

27. MacInnes, *Dùthchas nan Gàidheal*, 177.

28. Menzies, *Òran na Comhachaig*, 32–40.

29. See, for example, Campbell, *Popular Tales*, vol. 2, 102–09.

30. My translation of Diarmad, "Donull Mac Fhionnlaidh," with reference to Wiseman, "Chasing the Deer," 315, and Black, "The Little Man of the Highlands." The meaning of *Mac an Riochd* is explained in *The Celtic Monthly* 13 (1905): 129.

31. For the word *seanghal*, see Campbell, *More West Highland Tales*, vol. 2, 114–15.

32. My translation of Dewar, *Ms. vii, Ian Deoir: earran 1. Blar Traigh Ghruinneaird*, 1–19.

33. My translation of *The Highlander* 22 September 1877.

34. Ó Baoill and Bateman, *Gàir nan Clàrsach*, 50.

35. My translation of *An Gàidheal* 5 (1876): 309–11, with reference to MacKay, "Blàr Chàirinis."

36. Gillies, *In Famed Breadalbane*, 139.

37. My translation of Campbell, "Seann Sgeulachdan," 75–76.

38. Macdiarmid included an English account very similar to this text in his paper "Folklore of Breadalbane," 147–48.

39. Gillies, *In Famed Breadalbane*, 147–48.

40. MacKechnie, *The Dewar Manuscripts*, 242–44. There is yet another version of the event in Robertson and Dilworth, *Tales from Highland Perthshire*, 312–15.

41. My translation of Diarmad, "Latha Blar Shron-Chlachain." I have removed the author's quotes of two poems.

42. Grant and Cheape, *Periods in Highland History*, 152–53, 158.

43. My translation of MacDhiarmaid, "An Creachadair."

44. I heard the major elements of this tale myself from the late Archie Kennedy of Glencoe and the late John MacInnes.

45. Ó Baoill and Bateman, *Gàir nan Clàrsach*, 190–99; Newton, *Warriors of the Word*, 152, 154–56; Campbell, *The Lairds of Glenlyon*, 275–77.

46. My translation of Mhic Eóghain, "Gleann Comhann."

Chapter Five

1. I classify the tales in this chapter based on the migratory legend index (A-Z) in MacDonald, "Migratory Legends of the Supernatural in Scotland," which sometimes also provides a corresponding index into Reidar Christiansen's migratory legend classification scheme (ML).

2. MacInnes, *Dùthchas nan Gàidheal*, 459.

3. The best guidebook to the Gaelic menagerie is Black, *The Gaelic Otherworld*. For the *each-uisge*, see also Black, "An t-Each-Uisge."

4. The most useful discussions of Gaelic cosmology and belief systems can be found in Newton, *Warriors of the Word*, 202–242; MacInnes, *Dùthchas nan Gàidheal*, 425–500; Black, *The Gaelic Otherworld*; Bateman and Purser, *Window to the West*, 836–942.

5. Newton, *Warriors of the Word*, 221.

6. Armstrong, *A Short History of Myth*, 4–5.

7. Bateman and Purser, *Window to the West*, 851.

8. Newton, "'Bha Mi 'sa' Chnoc.'"

9. See the extended discussion in the Introduction to Black, *The Gaelic Otherworld*.

10. Armstrong, *A Short History of Myth*, 10–11.

11. Carey, "The Three Things Required of a Poet," 47, 50, 52.

12. See Black, *The Gaelic Otherworld*, xxv.

13. My revised edition of the Gaelic verses and emendations of the translation from Carmichael, *Carmina Gadelica*, vol. 2, 352–53. A variant of F 1.B.

14. My translation of *The Highlander* 13 Apr 1881. A variant of F 1.A and ML 5050.

15. My revised translation of MacDougall and Calder, *Folk Tales and Fairy Lore*, 128–30.

16. My revised translation of MacKenzie, *The Book of Arran*, vol. 2, 264–65. A variant of F 111.

17. For others, see Carmichael, *Ortha nan Gàidheal*, vol. 5, 306–19 and Gillies, "Alexander Carmichael and Clann Mhuirich."

18. Adapted from Carmichael, "Highland Mythology," 68–69. This article has the appearance of having been a collaboration between Alexander and Elizabeth. The tale was drawn in to illustrate the word *frìde* (and its derivatives), but comparison with the original Gaelic text, discussed in Gillies, "Alexander Carmichael and Clann Mhuirich," 24, shows the fairies are the only beings originally mentioned in the text. I have therefore emended the text to more accurately represent a translation of Carmichael's fieldwork, but I have not reproduced the fieldnotes examined by Gillies. A variant of F 89.

19. My revised translation of MacDougall and Calder, *Folk Tales and Fairy Lore*, 266–68.

20. See Black, *The Gaelic Otherworld*, 82–104 and Black's corresponding endnotes.

21. My adaptation of Forsyth, *In the Shadow of Cairngorm*, 52–53.

22. *The People's Journal* 14 August 1886.

23. My revised translation of MacDougall, *Folk Tales*, 142–47. A variant of F 63 and ML 5085.

24. My revised translation of MacKenzie, *The Book of Arran*, vol. 2, 259–60. A variant of F 53.A and ML 6050.

25. Anon, "Fairy Tales," 158–59. A variant of F 11 and F 101.

26. My translation of Ros, "Ceòl-Mór agus Clann Mhic Cruimein," 45–46. A variant of F 15 and F 101.

27. Campbell, *Popular Tales of the West Highlands*, vol. 2, 85–86.

28. My translation of Donnrua, "Iain Dubh Mor." A variant of F 100.

29. My revised translation of MacKenzie, *The Book of Arran*, vol 2, 282–83.

30. My adaptation of Anon, "Fairy Tales," 166–68. A variant of F 58.A.

31. Campbell, *The Fians*, 174.

32. Black, *Gaelic Otherworld*, 334, 633.

33. Cameron, "The Macfies," 207–11.

34. Note that I have emended *sianach* ("spell-caster") in the original text to *sìdheanach* ("fairy"). There is very little evidence of the use of the term *sianach / seunach* in Gaelic and she is not shown casting spells in the tale. Furthermore, *sìdheanach* is a better poetic match for *Fiantaichean* in the next line.

35. Scowcroft, "The Irish Analogues to Beowulf."

36. Bruford and MacDonald, *Scottish Traditional Tales*, 470.

37. My revised translation of Campbell, "MacPhee's Black Dog," 265–69. A variant of F 112.

38. For discussion of the death of Iain Garve, see Black, *The Gaelic Otherworld*, 184–85; Carmichael, *Ortha nan Gàidheal*, vol. 5, 300–04. For discussion of other variants of this tale, see Campbell, *More West Highland Tales*, vol. 2, 313–15, 378–83.

39. Campbell, *More West Highland Tales*, vol. 2, 314.

40. My translation of Cuairtear an Cinn a' Ghiuthsaich, "Cailleach an Lagan." A variant of W 3 and W 19.

41. My adaptation of Grant, *Legends of the Braes o' Mar*, 47–48. A variant of W 40.A.

42. My translation of A.M., "Buidseachd."

43. Black, *The Gaelic Otherworld*, 501.

44. *Ibid.*, 235.

45. Goiridh Dòmhnallach of Kingsville, Cape Breton, personal communication.

46. Newton, *Warriors of the Word*, 154–57.

47. MacKillop, *Dictionary of Celtic Mythology*, 109; Black, *The Gaelic Otherworld*, 132.

48. Black, *The Gaelic Otherworld*, 139.

49. *Ibid.*

50. Lysaght, "Aspects of the Earth-Goddess."

51. Black, *The Gaelic Otherworld*, 22–23; Newton, *Warriors of the Word*, 137- 161, 293.

52. My revised translation of Sìthiche, "A' Bhe-an-Nighe," 212–15. A variant of F 130.A.

53. My revised translation of *ibid.*, 348–49. A variant of F 130.A.

54. My revised translation of MacKenzie, *The Book of Arran*, vol. 2, 261–62. A variant of F 27 and ML 5070.

55. MacInnes, *Dùthchas nan Gàidheal*, 449.

56. My revised translation of MacDougall, *Folk Tales and Fairy Lore*, 182–84.

57. My revised translation of Craigie, "Some Highland Folklore,"376.

58. My translation of *The Highlander* 18 May 1878.

Epilogue

1. For some discussion of these issues, see Shaw, "Gaelic Cultural Maintenance"; Newton, *Warriors of the Word*, 28–43, 65–79, 119–21; Stiùbhart, "Uses of Historical Traditions."

2. Campbell, "The Moving Picture," 103.

3. Davis, *The Wayfinders*, 198.

4. Nicolson, *A Collection of Gaelic Proverbs*, 278.

5. McIntosh, *Soil and Soul*, 71, 121, 120.

6. McFadyen and Sandilands, "On 'Cultural Darning and Mending,'" 160.

Bibliography

Allardyce, Alexander, ed. *Scotland and Scotsmen in the Eighteenth Century*, 2 vols. Edinburgh and London: W. Blackwood and Sons, 1888.

A.M. "Buidseachd." *An Gàidheal* 39.12 (1944): 140.

Anon. "Fairy Tales." *The Celtic Review* 5 (1908–09): 155–71.

Armstrong, Karen. *A Short History of Myth*. Edinburgh: Canongate Books, 2005.

Bateman, Meg, and John Purser. *Window to the West: Culture and Environment in the Scottish Gàidhealtachd*. Sleat: Clò Ostaig, 2020.

Black, Ronald, ed. "The Dewar Project." In *Rannsachadh na Gàidhlig* 10, edited by Wilson McLeod, Anja Gunderloch and Rob Dunbar, 73–86. Aberdeen: Aberdeen University Press, 2021.

______. *The Gaelic Otherworld*. Edinburgh: Birlinn, 2005.

______. *An Lasair: Anthology of 18th Century Scottish Gaelic Verse*. Edinburgh: Birlinn, 2001.

______. "The Little Man of the Highlands." *West Highland Free Press* 19 April 2002.

______. "An t-Each-Uisge." *Scottish Studies* 37 (2014): 125–33.

Bruford, Alan. *Gaelic Folk-Tales and Mediæval Romances*. Dublin: The Folklore of Ireland Society, 1969.

______. "Oral and Literary Fenian Tales." *Bealoideas* 54–55 (1986–1987): 25–56.

Bruford, Alan, and Donald A. MacDonald, eds. *Scottish Traditional Tales*. Edinburgh: Birlinn, 2003.

Cameron, Alastair. "The Macfies in Legend and Romance." *Transactions of the Gaelic Society of Inverness* 38 (1962): 206–16.

Campbell, Angus Peter. "The Moving Picture." In *As An Fhearann / from the land*, edited by Malcolm MacLean and Christopher Carrell, 99–103. Edinburgh: Mainstream Publishing, 1986.

Campbell, Archibald, ed. *Craignish Tales*, Waifs and Strays of Celtic Tradition 1. London: David Nutt, 1889.

______, ed. *Records of Argyll: Legends, Traditions, and Recollections of Argyllshire Highlanders*. Edinburgh: William Blackwood and Sons, 1885.

Campbell, Duncan. *The Lairds of Glenlyon*. Perth: S. Cowan and Co, 1886.

______. "Seann Sgeulachdan mu Bhraid-Albann" *An Gàidheal* 3 (1874): 75–77.

Campbell, John F. "Fionn's Enchantment: A Popular Tale of the Highlands of Scotland." *Revue Celtique* 1 (1872): 193–202.

______. ed. *Leabhar na Féinne*. London: Spottiswoode and Co., 1872.

______. *More West Highland Tales*, 2 vols. Edinburgh: Birlinn Ltd., 1994 [1940, 1960].

______. "On Current British Mythology and Oral Traditions." *The Journal of the Ethnological Society of London* 2 (1870): 325–40.

______, ed. *Popular Tales of the West Highlands*, 4 vols. Edinburgh: Edmonston and Douglas, 1860–62.

Campbell, John G. *Clan Traditions and Popular Tales of the West Highlands and Islands*, Waifs and Strays of Celtic Tradition 5. London: David Nutt, 1895.

______. *The Fians; or, Stories, Poems & Traditions of Fionn and His Warrior Band*, Waifs and Strays of Celtic Tradition 4 (London: David Nutt, 1891).

______. "MacPhee's Black Dog." *Scottish Celtic Review* 4 (1885): 262–73.

Carey, John. "The Three Things Required of a Poet." *Ériu* 48 (1997): 41–58.

Carmichael, Alexander. "The Barons of Bachuill." *The Celtic Review* 5 (1909): 356–75.

______. ed. *Deirdre and the Lay of the Children of Uisne*. Edinburgh: Norman MacLeod, 1905.

______. "Naoimh Chinntàile." *The Celtic Review* 4 (1908): 371–72.

______. ed. *Ortha nan Gàidheal / Carmina Gadelica*, 6 vols. Edinburgh: Scottish Gaelic Texts Society, 1900–71.

______. "Toirioc na Taine." *Transactions of the Gaelic Society of Inverness* 2 (1873): 25–42.

Carmichael, Elizabeth. "Highland Mythology." *The Celtic Review* 5 (1908): 48–70.

Cheape, Hugh. "'Tha Feum Air Cabhaig': The Initiative of the Folklore Institute of Scotland." *Scottish Studies* 37 (2014): 53–62.

Cuairtear an Cinn a' Ghiuthsaich. "Cailleach an Lagan." *An Deò-Gréine* 11.11 (1916): 170–71.

Davis, Wade. *The Wayfinders: Why Ancient Wisdom Matters in the Modern World*. Toronto: House of Anansi Press, 2009.

Dégh, Linda. "Folk Narrative." In *Folklore and Folklife*, edited by Richard Dorsan, 53–83. Chicago: University Of Chicago Press, 1982.

Dewar, John. *The Dewar Manuscripts, Volume*

One, ed. John MacKechnie. Glasgow: William MacLellan, 1964.

______. Ms. vii, Ian Deoir: earran 1. Blar Traigh Ghruinneaird. 1950.

Diarmad. "Donull Mac Fhionnlaidh agus Oran na Comhachaig." *An Gàidheal* 5 (1876): 328–34.

______. "Latha Blar Shròn-Chlachain." *An Deò-Ghréine* 16 (1921): 84.

[Dòmhnallach, Gilleasbuig.] "Sgeulachd Gharaidh." *An Sgeulaiche* 1 (1909): 298–301.

Donnrua. "Iain Dubh Mor agus an Uruisg no Ealdhin gun Rath." *An Deò-Gréine* 5.5 (1910): 70–71.

Douglas, Sheila. "Narrative in Traveller Scotland." In *Oral Literature and Performance Culture*, edited by John Beech, et al, 49–57. Edinburgh: John Donald, 2007.

Evans-Wentz, W.Y. *The Fairy Faith in Celtic Countries*. London: H. Froude, 1911.

Flahive, Joseph. *The Fenian Cycle in Irish and Scots-Gaelic Literature*. Cork: Cork Studies in Celtic Literatures, 2017.

Forsyth, William. *In the Shadow of Cairngorm*. Inverness: The Northern Counties Publishing Company, 1900.

Fraser, Joy. "A Study of Scottish Gaelic Versions of 'Snow White.'" *Scottish Studies* 34 (2006): 60–76.

Gilleaspuig mac Dhòmhnaill mac Eóghain. "Gleann Comhann." *An Sgeulaiche* 1 (1909): 420–27.

Gillies, William. "Alexander Carmichael and Clann Mhuirich." *Scottish Gaelic Studies* 20 (2000): 1–66.

Gillies, William. *In Famed Breadalbane*. Perth: Munro Press, Ltd., 1938.

Grant, Anne. *Essays on the Superstitions of the Highlanders of Scotland*. London: Longman, Hurst, Rees, Orme and Brown, 1811.

Grant, I.F., and Hugh Cheape. *Periods in Highland History*. New York: Barnes & Noble Books, 2000.

Grant, Katherine Whyte. *Aig Tigh na Beinne*. Glasgow: Alex McLaren & Son, 1911.

Henderson, George. *The Norse Influence on Celtic Scotland*. Glasgow: James Maclehose and Sons, 1910.

Hillers, Barbara. "The Abbot of Druimenaig: Genderbending in Gaelic Tradition." *Proceedings of the Harvard Celtic Colloquium* 15 (1995): 175–197.

______. "Storytelling and the International Folktale in Scotland." In *Oral Literature and Performance Culture*, Scottish Life and Society 10, edited by John Beech, et al, 153–70. Edinburgh: John Donald, 2007.

Iwase, Hisami. "A Study of the Feigned-Illness Motif in the Gaelic Snow-White." *Scottish Gaelic Studies* 22 (2006): 143–60.

Jackson, Kenneth. "The Folktale in Gaelic Scotland." *Proceedings of the Scottish Anthropological and Folklore Society* 4 (1952): 123–40.

Kane, Sean. *Wisdom of the Mythtellers*. Peterborough: Broadview Press, 1994.

Koehler, Axel. "Bàillidh Lunnainn agus Seachd Saoidh na Ròimhe." *Scottish Gaelic Studies* 26 (2010): 7–22.

Lysaght, Patricia. "Aspects of the Earth-Goddess in the Traditions of the Banshee in Ireland." In *The Concept of the Goddess*, edited by Sandra Billington and Miranda Green, 152–65. London: Routledge, 1996.

MacDhiarmaid, Seumas. "An Creachadair air a Chreachadh." *The People's Journal* 24 June 1922.

MacDhomhnaill, Iain, ed. *An Ceathramh Leabhar Leughaidh*. Glasgow: Blackie and Son, 1923.

MacDhùghaill, Eachann. "Fionnladh Dubh Mac Rath." *The Celtic Annual* 5 (1916): 60.

Macdiarmad, John. "Folklore of Breadalbane." *Transactions of the Gaelic Society of Inverness 26* (1905): 136–56.

MacDonald, Allan. "Calum-Cille agus Dobhran a Bhràthair." *The Celtic Review* 5 (1909): 107–09.

______. *Gaelic Words and Expressions from South Uist and Eriskay*, ed. John L. Campbell. Dublin: Dublin Institute for Advanced Studies, 1991.

MacDonald, Donald. "Bàs Bhrain agus Dhiarmaid." *The Celtic Review* 6 (1910): 131–35.

MacDonald, Donald Archie. "Migratory Legends of the Supernatural in Scotland: A General Survey." *Béaloideas* 62/63 (1994/1995): 29–78.

MacDonald, Fiona. "Narrative Collection and Scholarship." In *Oral Literature and Performance Culture*, Scottish Life and Society 10, edited by John Beech, et al., 9–27. Edinburgh: John Donald, 2007.

MacDougall, James. *Folk Tales and Fairy Lore*, ed. George Calder. Edinburgh: John Grant, 1910.

MacFhionghuin, Lachlann, ed. *Leabhraichean Leughaidh: Leabhar 1*. Glasgow: Blackie and Son, [1943 ?].

MacGregor, Martin. "The Genealogical Histories of Gaelic Scotland." In *The Spoken Word: Oral Culture in Britain, 1500–1850*, edited by Adam Fox and Daniel Woolf, 196–239. Manchester: Manchester University Press, 2002.

MacInnes, Duncan. *Folk and Hero Tales*. London: David Nutt, 1890.

MacInnes, John. *Dùthchas nan Gàidheal: Selected Essays of John MacInnes*, ed. Michael Newton Edinburgh: Birlinn, 2006.

______. "The Gaelic Hero-Tales." In *Oral Literature and Performance Culture*, Scottish Life and Society 10, edited by John Beech, et al, 64–81. Edinburgh: John Donald, 2007.

MacKay, J.G. "Blar Chairinis." *An Deò-Ghréine* 16 (1921): 67–72.

______. "Cànan nan Eun." *Scottish Gaelic Studies* 3 (1929–31): 160–87.

______. ed. *Gille a' Bhuidseir / The Wizard's Gillie and Other Tales*. Glasgow: MacLaren, 1946.

______. "Gruagach an Eilein Uaine." *Scottish Gaelic Studies* 1 (1926): 156–87.

______. "Sgeul air Calum Garbh Mac Eòghainn." *An Deò-Gréine* 13 (1917): 88–91.

Mackay, William. "Sgeulachdan Ghlinn-

Urchudainn." *Transactions of the Gaelic Society of Inverness* 2 (1873): 74–80.
______. *Urquhart and Glenmoriston: Olden Times in a Highland Parish*. Inverness: Northern Counties Newspapers, 1893.
MacKechnie, John, ed. *The Dewar Manuscripts: Volume One*. Glasgow: William MacLellan, 1964.
MacKenzie, William. *The Book of Arran*, 2 vols. Glasgow: Hugh Hopkins, 1914.
MacKillop, James. *Dictionary of Celtic Mythology*. Oxford: Oxford University Press, 1998.
MacLean, Calum. *The Highlands*. Inverness: Club Leabhar, 1975.
MacLeod, Malcolm, ed. *Celtic Annual 1912*. Dundee: Dundee Highland Society. 1911.
MacNeacail, Pàdruig. "Seanchan Mór an Éirinn's Gobha nan Sgeul an Albainn." *The Celtic Digest* 1.6 (Dec 1938): 31–33.
Macpherson, Donald C. "Iolair Loch-Treig." *An Gàidheal* 1 (1872): 285–86.
MacRury, John. "An Teine Mor (Will o' the Wisp)." *Transactions of the Gaelic Society of Inverness* 19 (1895): 158–71.
Markus, Gilbert. "How to Arrange Your Corpses." Iona's Namescape blog https://iona-placenames.glasgow.ac.uk/how-to-arrange-your-corpses/. Accessed 2021 September 28
McFadyen, Mairi, and Raghnaid Sandilands. "On 'Cultural Darning and Mending': Creative Responses to Ceist an Fhearainn / The Land Question in the Gàidhealtachd." *Scottish Affairs* 30.2 (2021): 157–77.
McIntosh, Alastair. *Soil and Soul: People Versus Corporate Power*. London: Aurum Press, 2001.
Menzies, Pat, ed. *Òran na Comhachaig*. Edinburgh: The Scottish Gaelic Texts Society, 2012.
Newton, Michael. "'Bha mi 's a' chnoc': Creativity in Scottish Gaelic Tradition." *Proceedings of the 1999 Harvard Celtic Colloquium* 18–19 (2006): 312–39.
______. ed. *Bho Chluaidh gu Calasraid / From the Clyde to Callander*. Glasgow: The Grimsay Press, 2010 (2nd ed.).
______. *The Everyday Life of the Clans of the Scottish Highlands*. Ingram / Saorsa Media, 2020.
______. *Warriors of the Word: The World of the Scottish Highlanders*. Edinburgh: Birlinn, 2019 (2nd edition).
Nicolson, Alexander, ed. *A Collection of Gaelic Proverbs and Familiar Phrases*. Edinburgh: Birlinn, 1996.
Ní Fhloinn, Bairbre. "Tadhg, Donncha and Some of Their Relations: Seals in Irish Oral Tradition." In *Islanders and Water-Dwellers*, edited by Patricia Lysaght, Séamas Ó Catháin and Dáithí Ó hÓgáin, 223–45. Blackrock: DBA Publications, 1999.
Nilsen, Kenneth. "P.J. Nicholson and 'Achadh nan Gàidheal.'" In *Bile ós Chrannaibh: A Festschrift for William Gillies*, edited by Wilson McLeod, et al, 315–28. Ceann Drochaid: Clann Tuirc, 2010.
Ó Baoill, Colm, ed. *Màiri nighean Alasdair Ruaidh: Song-Maker of Skye and Berneray*. Glasgow: Scottish Gaelic Texts Society, 2014.
Ó Baoill, Colm, and Meg Bateman, eds. *Gàir nan Clàrsach: An Anthology of 17th Century Gaelic Poetry*. Edinburgh: Birlinn, 1994.
Ó Crualaoich, Gearóid. *The Book of the Cailleach: Stories of the Wise-Woman Healer*. Cork: Cork University Press, 2003.
Ó hÓgáin, Dáithí. "The Mystical Island in Irish Folklore." In *Islanders and Water-Dwellers*, edited by Patricia Lysaght, Séamas Ó Catháin and Dáithí Ó hÓgáin, 247–60. Blackrock: DBA Publications, 1999.
Olrik, Axel. "Epic Laws of Folk Narrative." In *The Study of Folklore*, edited by Alan Dundes, 129–41. Englewood Cliffs, NJ: Prentice-Hall, 1965.
Parker, Winifred. *Na Daoine Sìdhe / Gaelic Fairy Tales*. Glasgow: Sinclair, 1908.
Robertson, Sylvia, and Tony Dilworth, eds. *Tales from Highland Perthshire*. Edinburgh: Scottish Gaelic Texts Society, 2009.
Ros, Niall. "Ceòl-Mór agus Clann Mhic Cruimein." *The Celtic Monthly* 18 (1910): 26–28, 45–47, 65–67.
Scowcroft, Mark. "The Irish Analogues to Beowulf." *Speculum* 74 (1999): 22–64.
Shaw, John. "The Collectors: John Francis Campbell and Alexander Carmichael." In *The Edinburgh History of Scottish Literature*, vol. 2, edited by Susan Manning, 347–52. Edinburgh: University of Edinburgh Press, 2007.
______. "Gaelic Cultural Maintenance and the Contribution of Ethnography." *Scotia* 27 (2003): 34–48.
______. "A Gaelic Eschatological Folktale, Celtic Cosmology and Dumézil's 'Three Realms.'" *The Journal of Indo-European Studies* 35.3 -4 (2007): 249–73.
______. "Scottish Gaelic Traditions of the Cliar Sheanchain." In *Celtic Languages and Celtic Peoples: Proceedings of the Second North American Congress of Celtic Studies*, edited by C. Byrne, Margaret Harry and P. Ó Siadhail, 141–58. Halifax: St Mary's University, 1992.
______. "Storytellers in Scotland: Context and Function." In *Oral Literature and Performance Culture*, Scottish Life and Society 10, edited by John Beech, et al, 28–41. Edinburgh: John Donald, 2007.
Sinclair, Alasdair MacIlleEathain. "Na Seann Sgeulachdan," ed. Shay MacMullin and trans. Seumas Watson. An Rubha 16.2 (2019): 12–13.
Sithiche. "A' Bhean-Nighe." *Guth na Bliadhna* 9 (1912): 195–221, 333–66.
Smith, K.D. "The Seven Unwritten Rules of the Ceilidh House." *The West Highland Free Press* 5 April 1991.
Stiùbhart, Dòmhnall Uilleam. "Uses of Historical Traditions in Scottish Gaelic." In *Oral Literature and Performance Culture*, Scottish Life and Society 10, edited by John Beech, et al, 124–52. Edinburgh: John Donald, 2007.

Thomson, R.L., ed. *Foirm na n-Urrnuidheadh.* Edinburgh: Scottish Gaelic Texts Society, 1970.

Watson, Rev. William. "The Collecting of Highland Legends and the Necessity for Collecting Them Now." *Transactions of the Gaelic Society of Inverness* 6 (1878): 102–19.

Wiseman, Andrew. "Brae Lochaber: Gaelic Oral Tradition and the Repertoire of John MacDonald, Highbridge." Unpublished masters thesis. University of Glasgow, 1996.

______. "Chasing the Deer: Hunting Iconography, Literature and Tradition of the Scottish Highlands." Unpublished doctoral dissertation. University of Edinburgh, 2007.

______. "'A Noxious Pack': Historical, Literary and Folklore Traditions of the Wolf (Canis Lupus) in the Scottish Highlands." *Scottish Gaelic Studies* 25 (2009): 95–142.

Index

Index

www.ingramcontent.com/pod-product-compliance
Lightning Source LLC
Chambersburg PA
CBHW081332090726
47907CB00011B/2451

* 9 7 8 1 4 7 6 6 9 0 0 2 5 *